ABOUT MEREDITH APPLEYARD

Meredith Appleyard lives in the Clare Valley wine-growing region of South Australia. As a registered nurse/midwife she practised in a wide range of country health settings, including the Royal Flying Doctor Service. She has done agency nursing in London and volunteer work in Vietnam. When a friend challenged Meredith to do what she'd always wanted to do—write a novel—she saved up, took time off work, sat down at the computer and wrote her first novel. Realising after the first rejection letter she needed to learn more about the craft of writing, she attended workshops, joined a writers' group and successfully completed an Advanced Diploma of Arts in Professional Writing with the Adelaide Centre for Arts. Meredith lives with her husband and border collie Lily, and when she's not writing she's reading! *Home at Last* is her fourth novel.

meredithappleyard.com.au

Home At Last

Meredith Appleyard

First Published 2019
First Australian Paperback Edition 2019
ISBN 9781489254573

Published by
Mira
An imprint of Harlequin Enterprises (Australia) Pty Limited (ABN 47 001 180 918), a subsidiary of
HarperCollins Publishers Australia Pty Limited (ABN 36 009 913 517)
Level 13, 201 Elizabeth St
SYDNEY NSW 2000
AUSTRALIA

A catalogue record for this book is available from the National Library of Australia
www.librariesaustralia.nla.gov.au

Printed and bound in Australia by McPherson's Printing Group

'When I was at home, I was in a better place.'
William Shakespeare (from *As You Like It*)

1

It was spring. Warm, lemon blossom–scented breeze wafted in through the window, lifting the lace curtain. Three fat, lumbering blowflies bumped aimlessly against the glass. The kitchen clock ticked.

A blood-curdling scream rent the air. Anna jumped, knocking over her cup. Milky dregs puddled on the tabletop. She surged to her feet, grabbing for the dishcloth on the sink.

An ashen-faced man appeared in the doorway. He looked rough, unshaven, with dark circles under his eyes. They'd met briefly when the station hand had ferried them in from the airstrip. The husband. Brad, Brett—she couldn't remember which. His Adam's apple bobbed as he swallowed.

'Nick, the nurse, says can you come ...?' he croaked, and then his hand flew to his lips. He grunted and disappeared as suddenly as he'd appeared. Moments later a door slammed somewhere followed by muffled retching.

From the front of the house another shriek, this one ending in a sob. Anna flinched. More retching came from the direction of the toilet. Louder this time. She lobbed the soggy dishcloth into the sink and, although it was way outside her job description, she took off in the direction of the scream.

As a Royal Flying Doctor Service pilot, her job was to fly the aircraft and keep everyone safe while they were on board. If flying conditions weren't optimum, it was her call whether they flew or stayed on the ground.

For everyone's sake it was best if the pilot didn't know anything about the condition of the patient. Then any flight decisions the pilot made wouldn't be influenced by a rapidly deteriorating trauma victim or a critically ill child.

But working in a small team in a remote location made it nearly impossible not to know something about the patient. Anna got that and Nick Harrison, the flight nurse, would know the rules too. He would only ask for her help if he genuinely needed it.

She found them in a bedroom at the front of the house, where an overhead fan was stirring the fetid air. A young woman, her eyes squeezed shut in a blotchy tear-stained face, lay on a single bed covered with a plastic sheet. Blood congealed against her bare buttocks.

Nick, dark head bent, was focused intently on what was happening between the woman's splayed legs. He looked up as Anna entered the room. Their eyes met and she saw relief in the grey-green depths.

'Anna,' he said to her, 'this is Rachel. Her baby has come early. Brett had to leave suddenly. I'm sorry, but could you—'

Anna's throat constricted. Instinctively, she moved towards Rachel, reaching for her hand. Rachel's grip was vice-like.

Sweat plastered wispy blonde hair to her forehead. A plastic bag of IV fluid dangled from a hatstand beside the bed and Anna traced the transparent tubing to Rachel's arm.

Anna held on to Rachel's hand, looking everywhere but at what Nick was doing further down the bed.

The room's walls were painted a soft yellow with a colourful mural of farmyard animals at eye level. With a jolt Anna realised this room was the nursery. She squeezed Rachel's hand. Rachel's eyes remained shut and tears coursed down her cheeks faster than the fluid running into her vein.

Nick stood up. Rachel opened her eyes, dropped Anna's hand and wordlessly reached for the small, ominously still bundle cradled in Nick's large hands. Her tears didn't stop as she hugged her baby and pressed a trembling kiss to its cool forehead.

'Anna, thanks, and can you please find Brett, see if he's good to come back,' Nick said calmly, although his expression was strained. There was blood all over his gloved hands.

'Sure,' she said, and sped from the room, wanting desperately to cover her ears and block out the sound of Rachel's keening.

Anna found Brett in the shade on the front verandah. His eyes were red-rimmed; a large, calloused hand trembled as he stroked the head of a black-and-tan dog, its muzzle grey with age.

'Brett, Rachel needs you.' Anna's voice was clogged with unexpected tears. He paused, gave the dog one final pat and stood up. 'I'm so sorry,' she said, overwhelmed by the need to say something.

He nodded, sucked in a shaky breath and trudged inside.

The dog smiled, tongue hanging out, but his brown eyes were sad. His tail thumped half-heartedly. Anna understood how the old boy felt.

Walking to the edge of the wide verandah, she glanced at her watch, squinting in the mid-afternoon brightness. She needed to clear her head, block out the sights, sounds and smell of that tiny bedroom. She contemplated the scene in front of her.

A narrow strip of patchy lawn and several straggly lavender bushes bordered the cracked cement path leading to the homestead. In the distance there was an assortment of shabby sheds, a water tank and a rusting tractor. A willy-willy swirled dust and debris in its path. In a nearby gum tree a flock of corellas wailed mournfully.

The ute with the stretcher from the aircraft on the back was parked under the gum tree. Anna wondered where the station hand who'd driven them in from the airstrip had disappeared to. Would he reappear when it came time to take them back to the aircraft?

Returning home to the Broken Hill base after a routine patient transfer to Adelaide, their flight had been diverted to Elder Creek station. The station property was in South Australia, closer to Adelaide than Broken Hill. Anna guessed that as soon as Nick was satisfied the patient was stable, they'd be flying Rachel back the way they'd come. In that case she'd have to amend the flight plan.

If Brett travelled with his wife, they'd need to refuel in Adelaide. She went inside to wash her hands and rustle up another cup of tea. She crossed her fingers, hoping Nick wouldn't need her again in that front bedroom.

'Right for taxi?' Anna's lips brushed the microphone. They were homeward bound again, their distraught patient dispatched to the Women's and Children's Hospital in the capable hands of ambulance paramedics. The sun was low in the sky.

'Cabin secure,' came Nick's tired reply.

Waiting for instructions from air traffic control, Anna watched as a Jetstar Airbus took to the skies. Eventually it was their turn to taxi into position for take-off. With the familiar surge of adrenaline, Anna pulled back on the control and they were on their way.

When they'd reached the top of their climb, no sooner had she let her shoulders loosen than Nick's voice crackled through the intercom.

'You know, I've been racking my brains and I've finally worked it out,' he said. 'Broken Hill High School, early noughties.'

Even with a voice thickened by fatigue and distorted by the King Air's tinny intercom, Anna couldn't miss the smugness in his tone. Her fingers flexed on the control.

'You were in the same year as me?' he said, enough uncertainty in his voice to make it a question.

Anna rolled her lips together. She had no intention of helping him out. Then with more confidence he added, 'Your old man, Max Kelly, was the principal. He replaced Gary Fielding when he left—very suddenly, I might add.'

With a sinking feeling Anna realised he didn't need help; he'd worked it out all by himself.

Nick laughed. She repositioned her headset, backed off the volume. 'They reckoned it was us Year Twelve boys who finally pushed the poor bastard over the edge.'

'Really?'

'It wasn't us ... I swear. Gary Fielding was sleeping with the Year Ten history teacher. She looked a bit like Cameron Diaz. His wife found out and their marriage was history.'

'You don't say,' Anna murmured, aiming for disinterest, but powerless to prevent the memories flooding back.

She remembered her horror the day her dad had come home from school and said they were moving to Broken Hill, the heated conversations between her parents when they thought she wasn't listening. Tina, Anna's mother, was comfortable in suburbia, and objected vehemently to yet another uprooting. In her eyes a transfer to Broken Hill was tantamount to banishment, regardless of her husband's promotion.

Max Kelly, a perpetual assistant principal, had embraced the windfall. Anna had been easily mollified with the promise of flying lessons. By then her older sister Teresa was married with a young family of her own. She'd barely raised an eyebrow.

'So,' Nick said, his voice propelling Anna back to the present, 'what did you do when school finished? From memory, Max Kelly stayed on as principal for the next five years or so, but I don't remember seeing you around.'

'He stayed for six years, actually. Then Mum threatened to go back to the city, any city, without him if necessary. And haven't you got a good memory.'

'What I had was a younger brother who was always in trouble. So, where'd you go?'

'Away,' she said. It had been a turbulent time in her life. Her stay in the rural city had been short and shattering and something she didn't like to dwell on.

'Yeah, we all go away, but many of us bounce right back.'

'Mmm,' Anna murmured.

Returning to Broken Hill in March for work had been one of life's little ironies. This time Anna had chosen to come, telling herself it was a stepping stone in her career and she'd stay as long as it took to get where she really wanted to be. Anna wasn't sure yet where that would be, only certain that it'd to be closer to Adelaide, where she'd come from.

'Why'd *you* come back?' she said.

She waited, heard the hiss of indrawn breath. He said, 'Not a day goes by that I don't ponder that very question.'

Nick didn't say anything more and Anna was happy to leave the memories in the past. She glanced over her shoulder back into the cabin. He was staring pensively out the tiny round window, his large, capable hands resting on solid thighs. He looked exhausted.

It was after her days off the previous week that Neville Abrahams, the senior flight nurse, had introduced her to Nick Harrison, relieving flight nurse. He'd started at the beginning of November and although he was new to the current team, he wasn't new to Broken Hill or the RFDS, if the grapevine was to be believed.

When they'd been introduced, there had been something *vaguely* familiar about him. But then his eyes were memorable—not green or grey, rather somewhere in between, and framed by thick, dark lashes lush enough to make a girl jealous. Any hint of femininity was lost in the distinct masculinity of his other features.

Ten seconds was all the time she'd squandered trying to place him. Now she knew. Who'd have thought it'd been that fateful year at Broken Hill High School.

Nick didn't initiate any further conversation and forty minutes later, the sun a whisper away from kissing the horizon, they began their descent. Anna shifted her focus from the unwanted memories to the instrument panels and air traffic control. The refueller would be waiting when they landed. The onboard oxygen needed recharging. She emptied her mind of everything and concentrated on the job at hand.

Post-flight tasks and paperwork dealt with, Anna was in the staff carpark, unlocking her red, ten-year-old Holden Commodore when Nick caught up with her.

'Buy you a drink?' he said.

'No, thanks. Long day, and I have stuff to do.' Buy cat food, put on a load of washing, really urgent stuff.

'That's a shame. I wanted to say thanks for what you did today with Rachel Carmichael. You were terrific, stepping in when Brett lost his lunch. I know asking you to do it was above and beyond.'

'I didn't do much, only held her hand.'

'Don't underestimate hand-holding, Anna. In my experience, sometimes that's all anyone can do.'

'Sure,' she said.

He tipped his head to the side. 'And you're all right with it? It was a bit in-your-face. A lot to take in.'

'You're right. It was a lot to take in.' Anna tossed her leather satchel onto the back seat and shut the door. 'But I wasn't in there very long, and I have been in a labour ward before. A proper one, that is.' But not one where the baby was premature and stillborn. She didn't say it out loud but the words were there any way.

'Have you?' he said, with obvious curiosity.

She hesitated, uncomfortable with the direction the conversation was going. 'My sister has two children, and her partner wasn't the most supportive of men,' she said briskly, wrenching open the driver's side door. Divorcing him was one of the smartest things her sister had ever done.

'Ah, so you're an auntie.'

'I am. They've grown up and live away from home.'

'You sure you don't want to go for a drink? Coffee? Talk some more?'

Anna shook her head. Nick folded his arms. It was almost dark and she could feel more than see him staring at her.

'What?' she said, fisting one hand on her hip.

'You wanna know why I remember you from high school?'

'Not really.'

'I'll tell you anyway … I thought you were hot,' he said and leaned closer. 'Your hair was longer, not as curly. I used to watch you play hockey.'

His smile was a flash of white in the gloom. He was attractive; she was attracted. As far as she knew he was unattached. She'd been single forever. It could have been simple, but it wasn't. She said, 'No-one knows I lived here when I was a teenager. If they remember a high school principal called Max Kelly, they haven't made the connection.'

He raised his eyebrows and pushed his hands into his pockets. 'Well, your secret's safe with me,' he said. 'And if you ever change your mind about that drink, you know where to find me.'

Anna watched him cross the carpark and climb into a late-model 4WD dual cab. She'd noticed it earlier, a shiny new addition to the staff carpark. It was a metallic grey-green colour, not unlike his eyes. With a roll of her eyes she dropped into the sagging driver's seat of her Commodore.

Anna didn't remember Nick from school. She tried not to remember anyone. Not hard to do, because at school, when her contemporaries realised she was the principal's daughter, they avoided her like the plague. Anyway, that year she'd been preoccupied with her first flying lessons, and her first flight instructor …

The car interior was warm, bordering on uncomfortable. Anna opened the windows and by the time she reversed out of the park Nick Harrison's vehicle had disappeared.

It was several kilometres from the aerodrome and Royal Flying Doctor Service base into town. Low scrub gave way to the city limits. Street lights twinkled. Traffic was sparse, the roads wide. The evening commute was over, but the Coles supermarket, open until late, was a hub of activity.

Anna joined the people hurrying up and down the supermarket aisles picking up last minute supplies for late dinners or lunch the next day. She grabbed the cat food and a frozen dinner, filed through the self-serve lane and was home ten minutes later.

Home was a circa 1970s double-fronted brick-veneer on the northern outskirts of the city. The floor plan was simple: three bedrooms and a bathroom on one side, separated by a wide passageway, with the sitting room, kitchen-dining and laundry on the other side. An archway provided access to the dining area through the sitting room.

Anna shared with Beth Samuels, a midwife from the hospital. Beth was as blonde as Anna was dark. Size-wise they'd never be able to swap clothes or shoes, and Beth's bubbly personality was the perfect foil for Anna's quiet reserve. Anna's rent helped Beth pay the mortgage. They were both shift workers and it was an arrangement that worked well.

The cat, an ageing Siamese called Albert, belonged to Beth, but it was Anna who remembered to feed him.

When she let herself in, the house was silent. Beth was on afternoon shift. Anna turned on lights, opened windows and flicked on the overhead fan in the sitting room. It was November; the nights could be pleasantly cool but daytime temperatures were pushing well into the mid-30s.

In the laundry the over-sized cat flap rattled and Albert sashayed into the kitchen, yowling.

'All right, all right,' Anna muttered, unpacking the shopping bag. Spooning food into his bowl, she screwed up her nose. 'Don't know how you can eat this stuff, mate.' His tail flicked. She put the bowl down on his placemat. He sniffed it and snuffled up several mouthfuls. Licking his chops, he wandered off.

'And thank you too,' she called after him.

It wasn't until later when Anna was in the shower, lathering shampoo into her hair, that it struck her: maybe Nick Harrison had needed to debrief about the day. He'd had an awful time.

Delivering a stillborn baby, and all that blood; dealing with the distressed mother and the monosyllabic father. And then the flight back to Adelaide with the traumatised mother and her deceased baby.

She rinsed off and hopped out of the shower. After a cursory towelling dry, she pulled on faded denim cutoffs and a T-shirt over her still-damp body.

'Move, Albert,' she said, toeing him in the rear to shift him out of the doorway.

When she located her staff phone list, the call went directly to Nick's voicemail.

Resisting the impulse to hang up, she left a message. 'Nick, hi, it's Anna. I'm sorry about earlier. You'd had the day from hell ... If you need to talk ...' Then she felt ridiculous, muttered, 'Oh, never mind,' and stabbed at the phone with her finger to disconnect.

Of course he'd have friends to debrief with: other flight nurses, people who'd understand better than she did what he'd been through. He was probably doing that right now and that's why his phone was off.

She nuked the frozen pasta dinner. It was tasteless, a little less so after a liberal lacing of butter and parmesan cheese.

Afterwards, propped against the cupboard, she ate raspberry-ripple ice cream straight from the carton. Albert watched through slitted eyes, tail slashing from side to side.

Anna was flicking through an aviation magazine, the television a low murmur in the background, when the doorbell pealed. She rubbed her eyes, stretched and padded barefoot to the front door. At this time of night it'd most likely be Scott, Beth's boyfriend. If he was in town he'd probably had a few beers and couldn't find his key. Anna flicked on the front light and reached for the door handle, a gentle rebuke on the tip of her tongue.

2

The door opened and Anna stood there, backlit by light from the hallway. Judging by the look on her face it wasn't him she'd been expecting. Nick waved a bottle of wine in his hand, holding on to his smile. 'I know it's late, but—'

'How did you know where I lived?'

He raised his free hand in a defensive gesture. 'Beth is a mate. I've known her for years. You know how she gossips.'

'She's still at work.'

'I know she is. I came to see you, to take you up on your offer.'

Her expression wasn't exactly welcoming. His forced cheerfulness flagged. He felt sad, wrung out and lonely. Broken Hill might have been his home once, but that had been years ago.

'You were right, Anna,' he said, sighing. 'It was a bitch of a shift. But it's late. I should have called first.'

'I thought you'd be debriefing over a few beers with your colleagues.'

'Nah, they're all tucked up in their cosy little lives.'

Anna pushed open the screen door and stood back to let him pass.

'Thanks,' he said, making for the kitchen. Anna followed through the sitting room and on into the kitchen.

'You seem to know your way around.'

'Yeah, Beth had a physio living here, way back when she first bought the place. We, that is the physio and I, spent a fair amount of time together. She, er, gave a great massage.' Nick put the wine on the bench and started opening cupboard doors looking for glasses.

'No wine for me, thanks,' Anna said. 'But you go right ahead.'

'But I brought it for you, to thank you. I took a punt on you liking dry white.'

'Thanks, but no thanks.'

He regarded her for a long moment and she met his appraisal head-on. She wasn't going to change her mind. He returned the wine glasses to the shelf.

'Would you have preferred beer?'

'I'm on roster in the morning so it wouldn't have mattered what you brought. Do you want tea? Coffee? Water?'

'Water is good.'

Anna opened the fridge, filled two glasses with cold water and handed one to him.

'What happened to the physio?' she said.

He followed her around the breakfast bar to the dining table, noticing the way her denim shorts hugged her backside. He pulled out a chair and sat down facing her.

'Nicole? She decided she hated the place and moved back to Mildura.'

'Shame. Bet you were disappointed.'

Nick lifted the glass to his lips, taking a slow sip. At the time he had been disappointed, but he'd moved on quickly.

'So, I remember you saying you'd been in a labour ward before,' he said, changing the subject because he didn't want to discuss the women in his past life. 'But have you ever experienced anything like you did today?'

'No, but because of my gender I've occasionally been asked to do things that the flight nurses wouldn't ask of the male pilots.'

'And being a bloke, a lot of people don't expect me to be the flight nurse. More often than not they think I'm the pilot or the doctor.'

'Yeah,' Anna said, and he felt a rush of warmth when her lips tipped up in a smile. 'Funny how in an age of such political correctness, gender stereotyping is alive and well. I've noticed it's more pronounced in the country.'

'Could be. I've never really thought about it.'

Anna picked up her glass, wiping away the condensation ring on the tabletop with the side of her hand. 'How do you reckon Rachel's getting on?' she said. 'I'm no expert but she looked a bit fragile. Beats me why her husband didn't go with her. She could have done with the support.'

'I don't know why he wouldn't go. I tried to change his mind but he was adamant. And to answer your first question, Rachel struck me as the type of person who, with support, will slowly work her way through this and get on. My instinct tells me he's the one to watch.'

'What do you think happened to make her go into labour so early?'

Nick considered the question. It was one he'd asked himself a time or two. 'Hard to say,' he said. 'I'll leave that up to the doctors to decide. But—'

Anna lifted her eyes, meeting his. 'But what?'

'I don't know for sure,' he said, frowning. 'There was something else going on. When we first arrived at the homestead and I was assessing Rachel, she was quite open with me, but then Brett came into the bedroom and she clammed right up. From then on her answers to my questions about when she last felt the baby kick, when her waters broke, when the contractions started, were very vague.'

Anna went to the fridge for the water, refilling Nick's glass and then her own.

'Thanks,' he said and leaned both his elbows on the table. 'How did Brett seem to you?'

'Anxious, upset, not much to say. Like a lot of men. I heard him throwing up in the toilet … When I went to get him, after you'd handed Rachel the baby, his eyes were all red, as if he'd been crying.'

Nick dropped his head onto his hands. 'It was a girl. Rachel called her Matilda. I tried to resuscitate her,' he said, slowly massaging his temples, trying to forget the tiny, lifeless body. 'I was wasting my time and we both knew it, but I had to try.'

'You don't think he hurt Rachel, do you?'

'Who, Brett? What makes you say that?'

'I don't know. Nothing in particular, but same as you, things felt a bit off to me.'

He shook his head. 'Between you and me, she had some recent bruising on her left hip and buttock. When I asked her about it, she got all vague again, said she'd been clumsy. My best guess? In the last couple of days she'd had a fall of some kind … Where? How? I've no idea, but maybe it's what started it all.'

'Maybe she fell off a horse.'

Nick's mouth turned down. 'Nah. Why would she even have been on a horse in the first place? She was going on thirty weeks pregnant. She wouldn't put herself at such risk.'

'She's a station manager's wife. They're expected to do things. And there was a stack of photos on the fridge of her on a horse, camp drafting and stuff. Looked like she was pretty skilled at it.'

'Yeah, but that doesn't mean she'd been on a horse recently.'

'Only a thought. Maybe she'll tell the doctors at the Women's and Children's Hospital.'

Anna sat back, lacing her fingers together behind her head. She rocked back on the chair and stretched. 'Not that it's any of my business.'

'You were there so of course it's your business. Though I've documented everything, and then some, it's probably best if we keep our speculations to ourselves,' he said.

'I won't say anything,' Anna said. She dropped her arms and sat forward in the chair.

'Tomorrow I'll give Brett a follow-up call. He might have changed his mind and driven to Adelaide to be with Rachel. In my opinion it's where he should be.' He finished off the water, contemplating the empty glass. Anna was startled when he pushed himself to his feet.

'It's later than it was. I'd better get going, unless there's anything else you want to talk about?'

She shook her head. 'And you're okay?' she said, tilting her head to look up at him.

'I'll be fine,' he said, and hoped he would be after a solid night's sleep.

'Anything I can do?'

Nick gazed down at her, her brown eyes wide and guileless. 'It wasn't my first stillbirth,' he said, 'but it was a new experience to have no back-up, to feel so helpless. On top of being powerless to change the outcome.'

'I thought you were awesome. From what I observed, and a layman's perspective of course, no-one could have done any more, or any better.'

'Maybe,' he said, shrugging. 'It's the downside of this type of health care. In a hospital help is never far away. It brought home again how there's only so much one person can do when you're miles and hours from getting any help. My only consolation is that the duty doctor said he wouldn't have been able to do anything more than I did. And even if they'd sent another plane with a doctor, the outcome wouldn't have changed. At least we were in the vicinity and they could divert us. We got there quicker than if we'd been coming from Broken Hill.'

'Some consolation I suppose,' Anna said and stood up.

'Some,' he said, suddenly feeling awkward. If it had been Beth, or any of his other female colleagues, after an experience like this he would have hugged them. With Anna, he wasn't so sure.

'Here, take the wine with you,' she said, brushing past him to grab the bottle from the bench.

'Keep it. I brought it to thank you. If you don't drink it I'm sure Beth will see it doesn't go to waste.'

'You're right,' she said, her throaty laugh sending tingles down his spine. 'She will enjoy it.'

Nick blinked, realising he was staring at her mouth, a tsunami of lust suddenly surging through him. Ripping his gaze away from her, he forced himself to move in the direction of the front door.

At seventeen she'd been hot. Attractive, self-possessed and just like now, totally oblivious to the effect she'd had on him. When the senior flight nurse had introduced them, he'd recognised her instantly. She hadn't a clue who he was.

Now, a lifetime later, she was a knockout. The years had added a luscious ripeness to her, along with a quiet maturity.

'Good night,' he said, letting himself out.

'Night,' she said, stepping out onto the verandah behind him. 'Thanks for dropping by. Sorry I was bit rude earlier, but I thought you were someone else.'

A man, he'd bet. Envy twisted like a corkscrew. In the shadows her expression was unreadable.

With an ache in his groin Nick trudged across to his 4WD, promising himself that this time around, Anna would never, ever, forget him.

Nick's mate Danny was sprawled on the couch in his one-bedroom flat watching sport on Foxtel. They'd been friends since preschool. Empty beer cans and chip packets littered the coffee table and floor.

All Nick wanted to do now was sleep. But Danny's sofa doubled as Nick's bed so sleep wouldn't be happening until Danny stumbled off to his own bed. Nick was half tempted to retrace his steps and drive out to the base, sleep there.

It had been fortuitous for Nick that Danny's girlfriend had walked out shortly before Nick had arrived in Broken Hill. But on nights like this Nick wished his sleeping arrangements were different.

'Mate, grab a beer. Plenty in the fridge,' Danny slurred. 'It's not clogged up with yoghurt and rabbit food and all that other shit … Not anymore.'

Nick counted six cans strewn about. His mate was at the maudlin stage of tonight's inebriation. Resigned, Nick went to the fridge. He was about to get the story all over again: why Brooke had left, what a bitch she had been anyway, and how her leaving was the best thing ever. Then there'd be the boozy tears, Danny hoping she'd come back, that he'd do anything if only she would.

With foresight born of experience, Nick did a quick scan for Danny's mobile phone. It was on the sofa beside him. As Nick sat down he nudged it along so it slid between the cushions. It'd save him the tussle later when Danny tried to make the usual drunken late-night call to his ex-girlfriend. These calls never ended well.

It was midnight before Nick spread out his sleeping bag on the sofa bed. After four consecutive twelve-hour day shifts, tomorrow he'd move on to night shifts—three nights of them—followed by three days off. At least no-one would question him sleeping in the quarters at the base while he was on nights. After all, that's what the accommodation was meant for.

He stretched out, swiped at mosquitos and tried to ignore the rumbling snores coming from the bedroom.

Couch-surfing at his age was beyond ridiculous, particularly in Broken Hill, a place he'd left imagining he'd only ever return for visits. If he dwelled on the chain of events that'd led him back to where he was now, he'd want to punch something.

Instead he wrapped the pillow around his head and vowed that come pay day he would find somewhere better to live. Until then he'd be grateful to Danny for his generosity and hope Brooke didn't decide to move back in, at least for a few more weeks.

3

Normally, Anna didn't wait up for Beth to come home, but that night she did. Beth would be wired after her afternoon shift and up for a chat.

In the wake of Nick's visit, Anna had been rehashing the day's events. And then there was the way Nick had looked at her and how that look had had her pulse jumping and her skin feeling too tight. Anna glanced at the clock and flicked on the electric kettle. Headlights swept into the drive and minutes later, the sound of a key in the front door.

'Anna,' Beth said, dumping her bag onto one of the dining chairs. 'You waited up. I heard what a dreadful day you'd had.'

'You did?' Anna took a step back. 'I thought all this medical stuff was supposed to be confidential.'

'It is. Totally.'

'How'd you hear about it?'

'I was at the desk when the RFDS duty doc rang looking for the obstetrician. The duty doc asked me for my input. That poor girl!' She went to the fridge, doing a thorough inventory of the contents before taking out leftover cheesecake. 'I'm starving. You want some?'

'No, thanks, I've already cleaned my teeth.'

'I probably don't need any either,' Beth said, returning the Tupperware container to the fridge.

They made tea and carried it through into the sitting room. Beth toed off her shoes and plonked down beside Anna.

'My feet stink, sorry.'

Anna shifted sideways on the sofa. 'They do, but I'll cope. Busy shift?'

'Three women in labour. You go days with nothing and then three at once and the other midwife goes home sick. Said she had potato salad for lunch and it tasted a bit weird.' Beth paused, shook her head. 'Why would you keep eating if it tasted weird?'

'Sorry, can't help you there.'

Beth tucked up her feet, wriggled around until she was comfortable. 'They replaced her with an enrolled nurse. Management is so stingy with staff I was lucky they replaced her at all. That place is starting to suck, big time. I'm glad to be off tomorrow.'

'Is Scott around?'

'I don't think so,' Beth said with a deep sigh. 'Last I heard he was trucking cattle to Queensland. I'm seriously thinking of giving him the flick. I can't have a relationship with someone I hardly ever see … and then when I do see him, all he wants is sex, a few beers and sleep. Not always in that order.'

'I thought you guys were getting engaged.'

Beth snorted. 'The only reason I know he's away is because I ran into his sister yesterday at the supermarket.'

'Haven't you been together for ages?'

'Yep, we have. But lately there's been a lot less of the being-together bit.'

'Did something happen? I mean, you don't have to tell me—'

'Nothing to tell. He says I'm always at work, weekends and nights. I say if he gave me a bit more notice I could plan ahead.

He doesn't get how nursing rosters work, no matter how often I explain it,' she said, resting her head back and closing her eyes. 'Maybe we're bored with each other. I'm thinking about taking a leaf out of your book, and avoiding men altogether.'

'What do you mean? I don't avoid men.'

Beth opened one eye. 'Convince me. You've lived here what, eight months? You haven't dated or anything.'

'So?'

Beth shifted so she was looking directly at Anna. 'You have everything going for you ... You're taller than me, you're single, you're gorgeous but you live like a nun. You've either got your nose stuck in one of those flying magazines, you're ensconced in your bedroom doing God-only-knows-what, or you're at the swimming pool.'

'I like to swim,' Anna said, surprised that Beth, always so caught up in her own life, had noticed what she did. She nudged Beth with her elbow. 'And how do you know I'm not having hot phone sex when I'm *ensconced* in my room every night?'

'Unless—' Beth said, contemplating Anna until Anna started to squirm.

'Unless what?'

'Unless you're not single at all.' Beth's eyes twinkled. 'I know, you have a hunky boyfriend stashed in Adelaide. You don't want us to meet in case he falls for me.'

Anna threw her hands in the air. 'Sprung! How did you know? Actually,' she said, dropping her voice conspiratorially, 'I have a husband *and* a boyfriend.'

'Yeah sure, girlfriend, and the blokes are beating down my door as well.' Reaching across, Beth patted Anna on the forearm. 'It's okay, I know your love life is none of my business—and if you are having phone sex every night, I'm green with envy.'

They sat in silence for several minutes. Anna finished her tea, wondering what Beth would say if she told her the truth: that she'd never had a husband or a boyfriend.

And then Beth said, 'But you can tell me everything if you want to. I promise not to tell anyone else.' She paused, her eyes going wide and then her face scrunching into a frown. 'You're not gay, are you? Not that it would bother me,' she quickly qualified, straightening up, subtly widening the gap between them on the sofa.

'Relax, Beth. I'm not gay.' Anna's laugh was laced with irony. 'Funny how regularly that question comes up when you're a woman in a male-dominated occupation.'

'Amelia Earhart was a woman,' Beth said.

'Well, there you go.' Anna pushed herself up from the sofa and held out her hand for Beth's cup.

'I still think you should date. I dare you to go out with the next bloke who asks you.'

'Not going to happen. I'm here to work, not start a relationship.'

'You know you can do both.'

'And that's working well for you?'

'Yeah, point taken.' Beth yawned and her jaw cracked. 'Bedtime, I reckon. And I'm not getting up before ten.'

'I'll tiptoe around when I go to the swimming pool at six.'

Beth groaned. 'You are one crazy woman, getting up that early by choice.'

Anna shrugged. The early morning, the promise of a new day, the smell of chlorine, then the silky slide of water. It worked for her. 'The bathroom's all yours,' she said.

'Okay. Thanks.'

Albert materialised in the doorway, purring. Beth scooped him up, burying her face in his fur. ''Night,' she said, her voice muffled against the cat's coat. She wandered off towards her bedroom, yawning again while she hugged Albert. A moment later she was back, minus the cat.

'You know Anna, if you do need to debrief about what happened on the flight today, please say so. I imagine it was awful. Nick would have been glad you were there. And I do know when to keep my mouth shut.'

Beth disappeared again, and minutes later Anna heard the unmistakable groan of the water pipes that meant she had turned on the shower.

Carrying their empty cups through to the kitchen, Anna stacked them in the dishwasher and refilled the electric kettle for the morning. The neighbour's dog yapped. It rarely stopped. It was a pint-sized bitzer, incongruously named Hercules.

Staring blankly through the kitchen window, Anna was caught unawares by the thick clog of tears in the back of her throat. The day had been long, unsettling and upsetting.

Pushing the palm of one hand firmly into her abdomen, she slowly inhaled then exhaled. She closed her eyes and counted through each breath until the feeling subsided.

For a moment she'd been back in the Carmichaels' nursery where hopes and dreams had been so cruelly ripped away. Now the loss and inconsolable grief they had to deal with. Remorse and self-reproach would follow. What woman wouldn't flog herself for answers as to why it had happened. If she could have done things differently. Rachel would be no different and Anna felt for her.

Nick's reminiscing on the flight home had resurrected memories Anna would rather have left buried. And tonight at home, she'd been joking with Beth about phantom boyfriends and phone sex, avoiding the truth about who she'd left behind in Adelaide.

What a superficial life she'd created for herself here in Broken Hill. It wasn't consciously planned that way, and if questioned

Anna would have said she didn't keep secrets, she just didn't share information about her life indiscriminately. But the more she got to know Beth, the more she liked her openness and humour and the more her own reticence about life away from Broken Hill bothered her.

Only today she'd asked Nick not to say anything about her being in Broken Hill when she was a teenager. In doing so an innocuous fact had been turned into a secret. And did anyone except her really care what she had been doing back then?

The dog continued yapping and a light flicked on next door. The barking stopped. Anna loosened her grip on the edge of the sink, killed the kitchen light and went to bed. Tomorrow would be a new day.

4

The sun had been up for an hour and the sky was endlessly blue. Driving with the window down, Anna felt a hint of the heat to come. Thirty-five degrees was the forecast high.

Nearing the RFDS base, she whizzed past a dirty, white Commodore sedan parked in the scrub about ten metres from the side of the road. It wasn't the first time she'd noticed it because it was the same model as her own car. Unremarkable, except that it'd been parked in the same place every morning, and was never there in the afternoons.

'Probably someone living in their car,' Beth had said when she'd mentioned it to her. 'Every town has its homeless.'

Anna hadn't shared that she'd once briefly lived in her car, and it had scared the living crap out of her. If it hadn't been for Teresa's generosity, she would have had no other choice but to go on living in her car until she'd found a job. Perhaps that's why someone sleeping in a car in isolated scrub on the outskirts of town disturbed her so.

Turning onto Airport Road, Anna forgot about the battered old Commodore, shifting her thoughts to the day ahead. She was flying a routine clinic run. They'd visit two small communities and the health centre in the oil and gas fields. Anticipation effervesced in her. Nothing beat a day's flying in perfect weather. And flying patients and health professionals around was heaps more rewarding than moving freight and fly-in-fly-out workers from one place to another had been.

Pulling into the last parking space that'd have afternoon shade, she grabbed her gear and locked the car.

Six days had passed since the flight to Elder Creek station; the memory was as vivid as if it'd been only six hours.

She was itching to ask Nick for news about Rachel and Brett. Had Rachel returned to Elder Creek and how was she? What about the funeral for Matilda? Had Nick been in contact with Brett?

Patient matters weren't Anna's domain. Inadvertently overhearing any news was unlikely in the pilots' room. Nick was the only person she could ask, and he'd been on night shift. Now he had three days off. Anna hadn't run into him since he'd come by Beth's all those days ago.

Knowing he was rostered off made detouring through the nursing and medical area in the hope of bumping into him pointless. Instead she wove her way through admin past the deserted reception desk and empty offices, and unlocked the door to the pilots' room. She flicked on the lights.

The room was smallish but functional: a desk with a computer terminal, and shelves crammed with various manuals and guides. Maps and charts covered every available space on the dove-grey walls. Nondescript brown carpet tiles did nothing to lift the utilitarian decor.

Logging onto the computer, Anna filed the day's flight plan and confirmed the airstrips she'd be using were good to go. The weather forecast hadn't changed.

The aircraft was parked outside the hangar, the battery cart waiting alongside it. Anna waved to the engineer, carried out the routine pre-flight checks and made her final walk around.

'Come on folks, big day ahead,' Anna said, hurrying the last of the passengers towards the aircraft. It was almost eight. They had about ten hours in front of them and she was itching to get off the ground. She double-checked the wing lockers after the dentist and her assistant had stowed their gear.

There were seven passengers on board today—two doctors, a medical student, a practice nurse, a mental health worker, and the dentist and dental therapist. After they'd settled into their seats, Anna climbed in. She hoisted up the steps, and closed and locked the door.

Scooting through to the cockpit she scanned the cabin on her way, confirming equipment and personal items were secured. Satisfied, she climbed into her seat, stowing her gear before shrugging into her seatbelt and slipping on her headset. Completing the pre-start checklist she gave the waiting engineer the thumbs up. She was ready to start the engines.

On start-up the seatbelt sign illuminated and Anna glanced over her shoulder. All passengers were belted in.

Moments later the familiar buzz had her lips twitching as she conversed with air traffic control and taxied towards the runway. It never changed. She couldn't imagine doing anything else.

Flying solo for the first time had been the greatest high of Anna's life. The freedom, the being-in-control. And nothing beat the feeling of accelerating down the runway, that kick of adrenaline, a g-force in itself, then the heady sensation the moment the wheels left the runway and the horizon disappeared. She'd been captivated aged ten after a scenic tour on the Gold Coast and the joy had never, ever faded.

Anna's touchdown for the first drop off was textbook. Heat mirages distorted the surface of the narrow bitumen strip. When she opened the aircraft door a blast of hot air greeted them. And a cloud of flies.

Giving the Aussie salute, five of the passengers disembarked. She helped them unload their gear. Two dust-covered 4WDs waited by the airstrip to ferry the team into the small outback town where they'd hold their clinics.

They were in the air shortly afterwards, en route to the next stop, a small settlement on the Cooper Creek. She loved this approach: the unmistakable tree-lined banks of the meandering water course, and the Strzelecki Track snaking in from the south.

Aircraft unloaded and secured, she and the remaining passengers piled into the 4WD standing by to take them the short distance to the clinic.

A handful of motley patients were waiting when they pulled up, perched on plastic chairs in the shade outside the weathered demountable building that housed the clinic.

'Thanks for the lift,' the RFDS doctor said to the driver, hitching his pack over his shoulder. Grinning at the medical student he said, 'Showtime!'

'I'll be in the tearoom,' Anna said, making her way to the closet-sized space.

There was milk in the fridge, biscuits in the tin and a thoughtful person had turned on the air conditioners. Anna drank coffee, did her paperwork and half-heartedly flicked through a days-old edition of the *Advertiser.*

'We still have five patients to see,' the medical student said when she came in to the tearoom, just as Anna reached the last page of the newspaper.

Anna stood up and stretched. 'Won't give us much time for lunch,' she said. They always ate at the camp mess in the oil and gas fields. The food was good and plentiful. And there was the legendary soft serve ice cream machine. Anna could never resist.

'I'm going for a walk. If you need me I'll be down by the creek.'

Dropping tea bags into two mugs the medical student's mouth gaped. 'You're not seriously going to walk outside in this heat, and with all those flies?'

'I am,' she said. 'I'll be back here within the hour.'

Should have bought a hat, Anna thought, wandering along the bitumen road. Two lone 4WD utes baked in front of the iconic single-storey hotel. A red dog was tied up in the shade, panting, ears twitching, a container of water a tongue's length away.

The picnic tables were deserted. The grey nomads were off exploring cooler climes closer to the coast.

It was vaguely humid nearer the creek. The perennial ribbon of water drifted between sandy banks and native vegetation. With sweat already trickling down her back, Anna reneged on her original destination—the causeway across the Cooper Creek—instead following a well-trodden narrow path and settling for a shady spot near the water.

On the opposite bank a ring of muddy scum metres up a gum tree's trunk provided a high-water mark. Today the water was low, the flow sluggish and silent. The flies didn't give up.

Wiggling her bottom into a comfortable position on the sandy verge, Anna lay back. Resting one hand on her forehead she squinted up through the rustling foliage to the blue sky above. Filling her lungs with the hot, eucalyptus-scented air, she closed her eyes, willing her mind to go blank.

But it didn't, it wouldn't. Isabelle was never far from her thoughts.

Anna missed her daughter, and worried about her. Izzy was fifteen, and living 500 kilometres away, fending for herself.

Anna's eyes crinkled at the corners. When she'd said that to Teresa, her sister's jaw had dropped before she'd fired back, 'Fending for herself? At one of Adelaide's best private schools, and me looking out for her on the weekends? You have got to be joking!'

Teresa had a point but it still hadn't been easy for Anna to up and leave her daughter to pursue the job in Broken Hill. No matter how excited she'd been about the prospect of being a Royal Flying Doctor Service pilot.

Bottom line was, if the regional airline hadn't made her redundant she wouldn't be here now. She'd still be moving freight and fly-in-fly-out workers.

Being a single mum holding down a full-time job, Anna hadn't been paying attention to the airline's problems. Or the machinations of the other *male* pilots when the word went around that someone would be losing their job. Curiously, Anna, the only female pilot, had been the one to go.

She'd consoled herself by saying the job was boring; however, regular money going into her bank each month had taken the edge off the boredom. Anna had known she'd have put up with the job until Izzy finished school, then her plan had been to apply for positions she wanted, not settle for the one she needed.

As fate would have it redundancy meant a job she wanted came along sooner than planned. And because unemployment wasn't an option, she had little time for soul-searching before applying and weighing up the pros and cons of being an 'away' parent.

Anna had applied for the position, crossing her fingers and toes. New challenges, new horizons. It was as if she was stepping out on her own.

'Why can't I come with you?' had been Izzy's indignant reaction when Anna told her about the job.

'Because you'll be better off staying put at school. I don't know how long I'll be there. I'm hoping the experience will lead to a job with the RFDS closer to home,' Anna had replied, ignoring her daughter's mutinous expression.

Eventually, Izzy came around. She'd found the idea of her mum being a pilot for the flying doctors pretty cool.

From the moment she'd discovered she was pregnant, at not much older than her daughter was now, Anna's life hadn't been her own. She'd taken the responsibility of single parenthood with a tenacity that had belied her years. But that didn't mean she hadn't dreamed of other things.

When after a second interview they'd offered her the position, she'd been over the moon. In a flurry of activity Anna and Izzy had packed up their home, a unit they'd rented for the past five years. Anna had left Izzy in the care of a private school and her only aunt, Teresa, and taken off, dizzy with the sudden freedom.

That didn't mean that anxiety, and sometimes guilt for abandoning her teenage daughter, weren't only ever a thought away. It didn't matter how many times Teresa said, 'Don't worry! Having a teenager around will be like old times. It's lonely rattling around in this huge house on my own,' Anna still worried.

She wriggled into a more comfortable position, letting the chorus of cicadas soothe her. In the distance a vehicle rumbled past on the road. Anna felt in her pocket for her phone, knowing full well there wouldn't be a signal out here. Anyway, it was a school day and Izzy would be in class. But as her fingers curled around the device she felt tangibly closer to her daughter, all those hundreds of kilometres away.

Three take-offs and landings later, Anna deposited the passengers back where they'd started ten hours earlier. Behind her aviator sunglasses, Anna's eyes were gritty with fatigue. Her shirt was creased, trousers smudged with dirt and her boots dusty. The others looked as tired, trudging across the tarmac to the hangar, weighed down by the accoutrements of their chosen professions. There wasn't any chattering at this time of the day.

The RFDS doctor, Tim Carpenter, hung back to walk with Anna. He was around her age—early to mid-thirties—tall, lean, and with carrot-red hair and a freckled complexion that was at odds with the harsh outback sun. He was brash and opinionated but she liked him. The flight nurses respected him.

'We're having farewell drinks for Lisa tonight. My place. Come along,' he said. 'Won't be a late night.'

'Lisa, the medical student? She's only been here a few weeks … I only met her today,' she said.

Tim wiggled his eyebrows. 'Any excuse for a few drinks.'

They walked into the hangar and Anna stopped, took off her sunglasses. She was above average height but Tim was taller. 'You haven't asked me to one of your little soirées for a while.'

'I gave up asking you because you always said no.'

'Well, there you have it,' she said, turning towards the pilots' room. Tim latched onto her shoulder. She glanced at his hand and then up at him. His hand fell to his side.

'Why do you always say no, Anna?' he asked softly.

He was right, she did always say no, to every social invitation, and in the beginning there'd been a lot of them. The flight nurses and the doctors were a very social mob. As were the pilots. But as an absentee single parent, Anna couldn't justify to herself having fun *as well as* a job she enjoyed. She was there to work. And when a pilot vacancy came up at the Adelaide RFDS base, she'd be out of there. It was futile to make friends when her own farewell drinks could be the next ones she attended.

'I have things to do,' she said when she realised Tim was waiting for an answer.

With a niggle of irritation she remembered using the very same excuse with Nick Harrison only days before.

Tim flipped off his trademark navy blue bucket hat and raked long fingers through sweat-matted hair. 'Whatever,' he said, nonchalant.

Unsettled and annoyed because of it, she watched him lope off, disappearing into the admin offices. Next time someone asked her somewhere, she thought, she should consider saying yes. That's if there was a next time.

She slogged her way to the pilots' room, and finished her shift by filling out her log book with the day's hours and flight details. The place was deserted.

The moment she cleared the building she hooked out her mobile phone and hit Izzy's number. She needed to hear her daughter's voice, reinforce what her priorities were.

'Mum,' Izzy said, on what felt like the hundredth ring. 'What's up?'

'Nothing's up. I miss you. I wanted to make sure you're okay.'

'Why wouldn't I be? What's Aunt Teresa been saying?'

'She hasn't said anything. We haven't talked today. Is there something she should have said?'

'No!' Isabelle said, her vehemence tripping Anna's alarm bells.

Anna unlocked the car and threw her bag inside. 'Talk to me, Izzy,' she said and slid behind the wheel. All Anna heard was her daughter's breathing.

'Izzy,' she prompted.

'I have a date. Sort off.'

'What do you mean, sort of?'

'There'll be a group of us. We're going to see a movie.'

'Where did you meet him? How old is he?'

'Mum—'

'You're only fifteen, Izzy. Has Teresa met him?'

'I'm almost sixteen!'

'How old is he?'

'He's nineteen and yes she has met him. He helps in her garden and cleans the pool.'

Anna started the car and slid down a window. 'You cannot go out with him, Isabelle. He's too old for you.'

'Mum! He only turned nineteen a few months ago, and his dad *owns* the landscaping and gardening business.'

'I don't care if his father owns ten landscaping businesses, you are not going out with a nineteen-year-old until you're nineteen yourself.'

'That is so not fair, Mum. Clara's last boyfriend was nineteen.'

Anna closed her eyes, fanning herself with a discarded takeaway menu. The cabin was like an oven. So much for parking in the shade. She closed the window and turned on the air conditioner. This wasn't the conversation with her daughter that she'd needed.

Up until now Izzy's lack of interest in boys had been a welcome bonus. She'd appeared content with her gaggle of girlfriends. Anna expected that to change sometime, and apparently it had.

'Where are you now?'

'At Aunt Tee's.'

'It's Tuesday night. You're only meant to be away from school on weekends.'

'Student-free day tomorrow, so any students who could go home were allowed to.'

Anna felt her blood pressure rise a notch. 'Is Teresa there?' she said, and before Izzy could answer she snapped, 'Put her on.'

She heard whispering and then her sister said in her usual no-nonsense tone, 'Annalise, Damien is a lovely young man. I've known his father for ages. I've watched the boy grow up.'

'Isabelle is fifteen.'

'There are four other kids going. Damien is the oldest. He likes Izzy, she likes him. What is the problem?'

'She is *too* young, Teresa.'

'I was dating Ryan when I was Izzy's age.'

'And look how well that turned out.' Anna regretted the words the second they were out. Before she had a chance to retract, Teresa shot back, 'Well, at least Damien's not married with children.'

Teresa's words winded Anna more effectively than a punch to the stomach would have. The silence between them grew.

'I'm sorry,' they both said in unison.

'Look,' Anna said. 'It's probably better if we discuss this later. I'm on my way home. It's been a long, hot day.'

'Okay,' Teresa said. 'We'll talk later.' They disconnected.

Anna dropped her phone onto her lap and her head into her hands, wishing she hadn't made the call.

5

Nick tapped on the Commodore's window and Anna took her hands away from her face, blinking rapidly. Her eyes were red-rimmed. He motioned for her to open the window.

'What's wrong?' he said.

'Nothing, thanks. Only tired.'

Nick studied her face. 'I don't believe you.'

She drew in a lungful of air and sat up straighter, slipping on her sunglasses. 'Can't help that.'

'Anna—'

The air conditioner's compressor cut in. 'Look, I really need to get moving before this car overheats.'

He nodded, straightened up and stepped away from the car. She reversed out of the park and accelerated off. Nick stood with his hands on his hips, staring after her. It was over a week since he'd seen her. He swore, locked his ute and walked across to the hangar. She could be pricklier than a three-day growth.

It was after six and the huge hangar doors were open but the offices were deserted. He'd chosen this time of day for that reason.

As much as he didn't mind his colleagues he didn't feel in the mood for idle conversation. Two days trying to sort out his mother hadn't put him in the best of moods.

He checked the roster, read the communications book and scanned the staff notice board. Pathetic really, driving all the way out to the base on his day off to check his roster, which he knew wouldn't have changed.

Who was he kidding? He'd hoped to see Anna. And the less time he spent at Danny's place, the better. His mate was either pissed, on the way to getting pissed or hung over from the previous night's binge.

That morning when Danny had crawled out of bed long after he should have been at work, Nick had said, 'You'll lose your job if you don't cut back on the booze, mate.'

'Eff off, *mate*,' had been Danny's sullen response.

Running out of reasons to be at the base on his day off, Nick drove back into town. Without conscious thought he bypassed the turnoff to Danny's.

Anna's dusty red Commodore was parked in the driveway behind Beth's gleaming, black Ford ute. He pulled into the kerb and walked up the driveway, giving the alloy wheels and low-profile tyres on Beth's vehicle an admiring glance.

It was almost dark, light glowing around the edges of the front bedroom's curtains. Anna's bedroom. Instinct advised against ringing the front doorbell and coming face to face with Anna. He let himself through the carport and into the backyard, and made for the back door.

When he passed the kitchen window, Beth was working at the sink, her head bent. He rapped on the window, setting off the neighbour's dog. Beth jumped, looked up, her eyes wide. He hitched a thumb towards the door. She nodded.

'Jesus, Nick, what are you doing creeping around backyards?' She unlocked the screen door and let him in. He followed her through the laundry and into the kitchen.

'I thought Anna would answer the front door.'

'Right,' Beth said, raising one eyebrow while wiping her hands on a tea towel.

There was a wok on the stovetop, piles of meticulously chopped vegetables and a bowl of green prawns sitting on the counter.

'She's here?' Nick's eyes darted to the open passage door.

'Of course she's here. She lives here. Didn't you see her car?'

Nick nodded, wondering why he'd come. He rubbed his fingers across his lips. 'I, um, ran into her out at the base. She looked upset. I thought I'd see if she was okay.'

'But you didn't want her to answer the door.'

Nick looked everywhere but at Beth. 'I don't want her to think I'm prying. I get the feeling she's a very private person. '

Beth jabbed him in the bicep. 'What, that old Nick charm not doing its job this time?'

'You've got me there,' he said. He liked Beth, he really did. They went back a long way, had done their midwifery training together. There wasn't much they didn't know about each other's earlier lives, but sometimes—

Beth flicked him with the tea towel. 'Loosen up, Nick. I haven't seen her yet. She came home, went to her room. Respecting the other person's privacy is what makes sharing a house work. I heard the shower a while ago.'

Nick let his shoulders relax. 'What's for dinner?'

'*We're* having stir-fried prawns with ginger, garlic and chilli. I don't know what you're having.' Steam billowed out when she lifted the lid on the rice cooker. 'You still staying with that loser, Danny?'

'For the time being.'

'My guess is all you'll be having there is a liquid dinner, unless you cook or pick up takeaway.'

'His girlfriend left him. He's grieving.'

Beth dropped the rice spoon onto the bench top. 'I love how you can say that and keep a straight face.'

Nick propped himself against a cupboard and folded his arms. 'Tell me, how's Scott?'

Beth threw him a caustic glance. 'How would I know? I never see him.'

'What, the old Beth charm not working so well, hmm?'

Beth's jaw firmed and her bottom lip jutted. 'Touché,' she said.

Nick sighed. 'I'm sorry. I didn't come here to snipe at you.' He pushed himself upright. 'I'll go.'

Beth echoed his sigh. 'Why did you come?'

'I told you why. Anna seemed upset—'

'I don't mean now, I mean why are you back in Broken Hill? And because you haven't told me voluntarily, I'll ask. Where's your wife?'

Beth lit the gas ring under the wok. They both stared at the wok until heat shimmered off its surface.

'Well?' Beth splashed in oil, following it with the ginger, garlic and chilli. Nick's eyes watered from the fumes.

'We've been separated for eight months. House is on the market. Neither of us can afford to buy the other one out.'

'What happened?'

Beth had her back to him as she flicked the prawns and then the vegetables into the sizzling wok. What had happened? Nick wasn't sure. One minute they were in love, married, happy, and then they weren't.

'Lauren said she was bored. I came home one day after pulling a double shift and my gear was on the front verandah. She'd changed the locks.'

'Shit, that's harsh.'

'She didn't have to tell me twice.'

'What'd you do?'

'Couch-surfed until my mates started to hide when they saw me coming.'

Beth flipped the vegetables and prawns around the wok and Nick's mouth began to water.

'We'd used her savings to pay the deposit on the house, and my money was, and still is, being funnelled into the mortgage. The house is on the market now. It's in a good location, although it needs work.'

'That's a shame. You've always wanted your own home,' Beth said, turning to face him.

'You didn't like her.'

'I didn't know her. I only met her that once in Sydney, when I came down for the wedding.'

'Yeah, and you got shit-faced at the reception and told me I'd be back in Broken Hill before I knew it, that the marriage wouldn't last because the only person she was in love with was herself.'

'Did I say that? I don't remember. Must have been pissed.' Beth turned back to the stove to deal with the food.

'Funnily enough you were right, on both accounts.'

'Nevertheless, breakups aren't easy, for either person.'

'Don't be too sorry. Really, it was inevitable. Although I'd be lying if I didn't admit I was devastated when I found myself locked out of my own home.'

Blindsided by Lauren's looks and slick city style, at first Nick hadn't been able to believe she was interested in him, the boy from Broken Hill. Turned out she hadn't been, not for long anyway.

He shoved the old hurts aside. Ruminating on them was a waste of time. It was how it was.

'So, in answer to your original question, I was homeless and wholly fed up with my life in Sydney, and when I heard from an RFDS mate there was relief work here, I applied. It's only for a few months while someone's on long service leave, but it gives me a chance to regroup while I work out what I want to do next.'

'I bet Marlene's pleased.'

'Not that I'd know. If you recall, I rarely please my mother. She liked Lauren, God knows why.'

'Probably because Lauren was the woman you'd chosen to share your life with. Does she know you two have split?'

'Nope.'

Beth eyed him with curiosity but when he didn't elaborate, she thrust a recycled takeaway container crammed with prawn stir-fry and rice into his hands. 'There's your dinner,' she said. 'If you go now it'll still be hot when you get home. I'm in a bit of a rush … Antenatal classes tonight and I'm doing a session. I'll tell Anna you called in.'

'You spoil me,' Nick said dryly, accepting Beth's offering without burning his fingers.

'It's a one-off, mate, because for a moment there I felt sorry for you.' She reached up on tiptoes to peck him on the cheek. 'As cliché as it might sound Nick, you deserve better than Lauren.'

'Aw,' Nick said, 'and there's me thinking you didn't care.'

'I do care,' Beth said, practically pushing him out of the back door.

The meal was a bonus, but he would have preferred to have seen Anna.

Nick drove across town to Danny's. By the time he arrived out the front the cab reeked of garlic and ginger prawns. His stomach rumbled.

'Bugger it,' he muttered, and scrounged around in the glove compartment for a plastic fork. If he took the food inside he'd feel obliged to share it with Danny. He opened the window, stayed put and ate.

It was delicious. Beth was a damned fine cook. A pity he'd never thought of her in any other way than as a friend. There'd never been the slightest hint that she'd felt any different about him. Nick wondered if Anna liked to cook.

Lauren didn't cook. She didn't vacuum, mop floors, clean toilets, pay the bills or do the grocery shopping. Nick had done their laundry from day one. He quickly cut off that train of thought. The food was good, and he didn't want to give himself indigestion.

When he'd finished he dumped the empty container in a malodorous wheelie bin propped against the wall. He stared down the driveway at the breezeblock units. Even the darkness couldn't hide their shabbiness. Any wonder Brooke had walked out on Danny. Beth was right—his mate was a loser.

People in glass houses, Nick thought, the gravel crunching underfoot. He was thirty-five, the same as Danny. Nick's wife had thrown him out and for whatever reason the end result was the same: Nick was back in Broken Hill, had temporary employment and was couch-surfing.

He knocked on the door and let himself in. 'Honey, I'm home,' he called.

6

The following morning Anna walked the two blocks to the swimming pool as the sun winked its way over the horizon. The night had been cool and she shivered as she stripped down to her one-piece bathing suit.

There were several swimmers already slicing through the water. Luckily, her usual lane in the 50-metre pool was vacant. She methodically worked her way through a stretching routine before plunging into the water, cold enough to make her gasp.

After the first two laps she found her groove, driving through the water, enjoying the silky feel of it, the rhythm of each breath. Twenty laps in the pool and she felt invigorated, the angst of the previous evening put back into perspective.

Last night after dinner, Anna had FaceTimed Teresa and Izzy. Her sister had apologised again for her earlier waspish comment.

'It's okay,' Anna replied. 'We both said things we didn't mean.'

In the end Anna accepted that she had to trust her daughter to make the right choices. This was no easy call for Anna. She knew firsthand how teenage hormones and rebelliousness could lead to disastrous choices.

Feeling pleasantly pumped after her workout, Anna went home and found Beth sitting at the dining room table reading the newspaper and drinking coffee.

'You're up early.'

'I start at eight.' Beth yawned and rubbed her puffy eyes. 'Why didn't you stop me having that glass of wine when I came home after antenatal classes?'

Anna chugged down a glass of water, wiped her mouth with the back of her hand before refilling the glass. 'You looked like you were enjoying it.'

Beth groaned. 'I was.'

'I'll go have a shower, wash off the chlorine, and then the bathroom's yours.' Anna paused in the doorway. 'Did you ever hear how Rachel Carmichael got on?'

Beth looked up from the newspaper.

'You remember, the woman from Elder Creek who had the stillbirth.'

'Yeah, I remember. I haven't heard a thing, which is unusual. She might not have gone back home to the station yet.'

'I know it isn't any of my business but it would be good to know that she's okay.'

'You could ask Nick.'

Anna scratched her head. She had been going to ask Nick, but after yesterday evening … She'd seen the concern, and something else, in his expression when he'd tapped on her car window.

And then her bewildering urge to tell him what had been wrong. And cry on his shoulder, if he'd let her. The experience had shaken her and she'd decided the best thing for her would be to keep a safe, professional distance from him.

Beth was still watching her. The cat flap rattled. Albert strolled into the kitchen.

'I'll see what I can find out,' Beth said, and Anna breathed a grateful sigh that Beth's attention had shifted to the cat.

'Thanks,' she said, hightailing it to the bathroom.

It was in the wee hours of Friday morning when Anna saw Nick again. She was in a deep, dreamless sleep when her mobile phone jangled her awake. Heart pounding she sprang up, reached for the phone and swung her feet to the floor. It was 1.46 am.

'Anna Kelly,' she said, wide awake now.

'Nick Harrison, Anna. Priority one.' He named a small outback town less than an hour's flying time from the base.

'Got that. See you soon.'

They disconnected and Anna switched on the bedroom light, rubbing her eyes. Priority one meant forty-five minutes from call-out to aircraft doors closing and the crew ready for taxi. A doctor accompanied the flight nurse on a P1. All the information the pilot was ever given was where they were going and the priority of the call.

Taking a moment she scrolled through the weather forecast. She'd checked it before she went to bed. A south-westerly change preceded by a band of thunderstorms was heading their way, but not expected until mid-morning. She'd keep a close watch on it.

Anna dressed and went out to the kitchen. Careful not to wake Beth, she switched on the electric kettle and went to the bathroom while it boiled.

Her travel mug was ready by the kettle. She topped it up and pocketed a protein bar, locking the front door on her way out. The two am news burst onto the car radio as she was reversing out of the driveway.

Lights blazed at the base and the aircraft was standing in front of the hangar. In the pilots' room Anna filed her flight plan and checked NOTAMs—notices to airmen. She collected the info she might need to refer to inflight and headed out to the aircraft.

After stowing the bungs and prop stays in the wing locker she made a final fuel check. Then a last minute trip to the bathroom, and finally back to the staff room to refill her travel mug with coffee.

Nick had pushed a trolley loaded with gear out to the aircraft.

'I thought you were on day shift,' she said, handing up equipment as he secured it in the cabin.

'I was. Someone's off sick.'

The doctor appeared, pretty and blonde, her high-vis vest ridiculously big on her tiny frame. Anna had seen her around the base but hadn't flown with her before.

The doctor extended her hand, the one not awkwardly clutching her travel mug and headset. 'Hi, I'm Serena Morris.'

'Anna Kelly.' She shook the doctor's tiny hand, feeling Amazonian beside her.

Anna glanced at the time. Nick encouraged Serena towards the aircraft steps. Two minutes and their forty-five minutes were up.

The flight went smoothly, the sky a blanket of stars. A road-weary station wagon with a bleary-eyed driver was waiting at the airstrip to transport them to the nursing outpost. Their chauffeur was Clarry—his wife, Ruth, was the registered nurse. He'd been hauled out of bed, and was grumpy as a result.

The outpost clinic's rooms were tiny, the walls were thin, and voices carried. That's why, an hour and a half later, Anna deduced that things for Nick, Serena and their patient weren't going as smoothly as the flight had.

Anna yawned, flicking through a months-old *House and Garden* magazine. More coffee, or not? She counted the cups so far … No more coffee. She'd need to sleep later.

She stood up, stretching the stiffness out of her back, walking around the room and peering out the window over the sink.

The night was fading. Dawn was approaching and the sky lightening to a deep suede blue. A door banged shut, a muffled cry and then Nick appeared in the doorway. Smudges of fatigue shadowed his eyes and his dark hair stood on end, like he'd recently dragged his fingers through it.

'Would you mind putting the kettle on?' he said. 'We're packing up shortly.' He scrubbed at his face with both hands. 'The patient didn't make it. Poor old bugger. He arrested twice and we couldn't get him back the second time.'

'I'm sorry. You're having a tough time.' Anna filled the electric kettle and turned it on.

'Yeah, I am. They say death comes in threes. I wonder who'll be next?'

There was a Tupperware container on the shelf and Nick lifted the lid and helped himself. He crunched into a biscuit. 'Ruth's Anzac biscuits are the best in the civilised world.'

He offered the container to Anna. She shook her head. Serena came into the tiny tearoom. It was beginning to get crowded.

'Ruth is with the patient's wife and daughter. Of course in a community this size, she knows everyone. I said we'd make tea,' Serena said, and promptly dropped into one of the chairs, leaned her head back against the wall and closed her eyes.

Anna glanced at Nick. He lifted his eyebrows before moving to the kitchen cupboard and taking out several mugs. Anna touched his arm. 'I don't mind doing it,' she said, 'if you want to keep packing up. We need to get moving as soon as we can. There's a weather front on its way and if we dawdle it could make the trip home bumpy.'

'Right. Did you get that, Serena?'

She nodded without opening her eyes.

Anna lined up the ceramic mugs on a wooden tray, dropped in the teabags. Nick handed her the long-life milk from the fridge.

'Thanks,' he said, and smiled.

The carton of milk almost slipped through her fingers. A smile like that should come with a NOTAM.

'I'll go and get on with packing up,' he said, leaving her in the tearoom with Serena.

Anna made the tea, loading the tray with milk, sugar and biscuits. Serena opened her eyes, stood up and held out her hands.

'Thanks, awfully sweet of you,' she said, and swept out of the room with the refreshments.

'You're welcome,' Anna muttered under her breath.

On the return flight they were treated to a spectacular light show in the south-west; thunderstorms ahead of the forecast change. By the time Anna made her final approach, the wind had picked up and the windsock was at right angles to its supporting pole. She touched down only to have a sudden gust lift them off the ground again. The aircraft bounced several times before it finally settled onto the runway.

'Sorry about that folks,' she said when they'd taxied to the apron. She shut down and collected her gear. The refueller would be along, and the engineers would start work shortly and tow the aircraft into the hangar out of the weather.

'Home without a minute to spare,' Anna said with a grin when she climbed between the seats into the cabin.

Nick had already opened the door. In the sharp early morning sunshine Serena could be seen hurrying across the tarmac towards the emergency entrance, clutching her flapping high-vis vest.

'She looks to be in a hurry.'

'Went a tad green when it started getting bumpy. The old white-knuckle syndrome each time we touched down.' It was Nick's turn to grin.

Anna rolled her eyes. 'We're here in one piece, aren't we?'

'Never doubted you,' he said.

Anna's cheeks warmed at the unsolicited praise. She knew she was a good pilot. She worked at it. But rarely did she receive compliments from the crew.

Surprisingly, Serena returned with the trolley and made a cursory attempt at helping unload the gear before rushing off again.

Although the engineers started their day soon, given the wind Anna decided to replace the prop stays and bungs and chock the front wheel of the aircraft. She locked the aircraft when they'd finished unloading.

'Buy you breakfast?' Nick said. They were crossing the tarmac towards the emergency entrance, Nick pushing the laden trolley.

'Thanks, but I'm going for a swim—followed by sleep.'

The electronic doors opened and Anna followed him inside. The place was deserted, too early for the day staff.

'We can go for a swim first. Fine by me.'

'Nick—'

'Anna,' he mimicked. 'I'll keep asking until you say yes. You might as well get it over and done with. It won't take me long to restock and finish the paperwork. I'll meet you at the aquatic centre. If I'm not there when you arrive, start without me. And then I'm buying you breakfast.'

'Nick, there's no point—'

'You have to eat, don't you?' he said, cutting her off. 'And I like to swim. Let's start with that, see where it takes us.'

She closed her eyes, shook her head slowly. 'I don't date,' she said, hating the way her cheeks flamed.

'Who said this was a date? It's two colleagues going for a swim and a meal after a difficult call-out.'

Anna opened her eyes to find him watching her intently. She swallowed. He was right. It had been difficult for him. 'I can do that,' she said, barely recognising her own voice.

A door closed noisily somewhere in the building. Serena reappeared, hair combed and minus the high-vis vest.

'You're still here,' she said, looking Anna up and down. She turned to Nick, who had started unloading the trolley.

'I thought we could go for breakfast,' she said. 'That place near the hospital is open early.'

Nick's gaze flicked to Anna and back to Serena. 'Sorry mate,' he said, 'but I already have plans.'

Anna opened her mouth to invite Serena to join them, then she remembered Serena's high-and-mighty attitude from earlier.

'I'll see you later, Nick,' she said instead, walking off. Let Dr Morris make what she liked out of that.

7

'She pouted! When you said you had plans already, she pouted.' Anna laughed and the low, husky sound did something to Nick's insides.

Towelling her hair dry after their swim, Anna's hand stilled. She stared at Nick, mouth open.

'What?' he said, pulling his T-shirt down over a wet torso.

'You and the doc … There's not something going on between the two of you, is there?'

Nick lifted an eyebrow. Not before hell froze over. Serena Morris was a facsimile of Lauren.

'Not that it's any of my business if there is,' Anna blurted, vigorously rubbing her hair with the towel.

Nick wrapped his fingers around her wrist, and then gently eased down the hand holding the towel. Her skin was cool.

'Anna,' he said, her chocolate-brown eyes wide. 'There is nothing going on between Serena Morris and me. Never has been, never will be, as much as she likes to pretend otherwise. Got that?' Unable to resist, he swiped his thumb across the tender skin of her wrist.

'Got it,' she said. He let go of her hand and stepped back. Snatching up her T-shirt, she clutched it to her chest, but not before he'd glimpsed her body's reaction to his touch. Interesting.

'And don't pretend there're barriers where there aren't, Anna,' he said. 'Now, breakfast. I thought I'd cook for us at your place. I know my way around Beth's kitchen.'

'So I gather. Where do you live?' Anna tugged on her T-shirt and stepped into washed-out denim cutoffs.

'I'm staying with a mate temporarily.'

Anna shoved her wet towel into a hessian carryall. 'I heard on the grapevine you're relieving a flight nurse on leave. How'd you manage that? I mean, how'd you hear about it? They said you were living in Sydney. Didn't you have a job there?'

Nick threw his towel over his shoulder and they walked towards the pool entrance. By this time of the morning all the lanes were full, two swimmers in some.

'Ah, the good old grapevine. Yes, I've been living and working in Sydney. I used to live and work here and I keep in touch. I've relieved for the RFDS before—here and in Alice Springs.' He threw Anna a quick sideways glance. 'So what else have the gossips been telling you?'

He felt sick at the thought that Beth might have told her about Lauren. There was something proper about Anna and he was certain she wouldn't want anything to do with him outside their professional relationship if she knew he was married. Never mind that they'd been separated for months.

'Nothing more, but then I'm not a great one for gossip,' she said, oblivious to the way his facial expression relaxed.

Nick veered towards the carpark. When Anna didn't follow he stopped and turned back.

'I'm on foot,' she said. 'I'll see you there.'

He opened his mouth, wanting to protest. But then changed his mind and nodded, striding across to his 4WD.

Bag slung over a shoulder, Anna appeared lost in thought when he passed her on the drive back to Beth's.

Happily, there was no sign of Beth's ute, so Nick pulled into the driveway behind Anna's car. While he waited for her he perused her early model Holden. Single, and on a pilot's salary, he wondered idly why she drove such an old clunker.

'Lusting after my vintage car, I see,' she said, walking down the driveway towards him. Her expression was amused. It wasn't the car he lusted after.

'Your back passenger tyre could do with some air,' he said. 'You might have a puncture and a slow leak.'

She angled forward and peered at it. 'You could be right,' she said. 'Damn. I'll get onto it later.'

'After breakfast I can change the tyre if you like, drop it off and they can repair it while you sleep.'

He grabbed the bag of groceries off the front seat of his 4WD. He'd stopped at Coles on the way to the pool.

'I do know how to change a tyre.'

'I'm sure you do. I was offering to help,' he said, following her across the verandah.

'Thanks, Nick, but I can see to it.'

He held the screen door wide while she unlocked the main door. 'You don't like anyone helping you, do you?'

'I'm not used to it,' she said.

Nick plonked the bag of groceries on the kitchen counter. 'You'd get used to it if you let yourself.'

She unpacked her swimming bag. 'And then what do I do when there's no-one around to help, like there usually isn't ...?' She draped the wet towel over her arm. 'I'll go and hang this on the clothesline.'

He wanted to ask who had let her down so badly in the past that she could no longer rely on others. But he didn't. Maybe when they knew each other better.

'I didn't know what you'd have so I picked up a few things,' he said when she returned from the clothesline.

He was unpacking the groceries, and pulled out a cellophane bag of kale. Anna picked up the greens and raised her eyebrows.

'It's good for you,' he said, searching for a frying pan. 'I assumed you'd have bread to make toast.'

'We do. I'll make the toast but after I rinse off the chlorine. Makes me itch. Do you want a shower?'

Nick spun around, frying pan in hand. 'Are you offering to wash my back?'

'Tacky,' she said.

'It was a bit.'

While she showered Nick threw together a breakfast of bacon and scrambled eggs with braised mushrooms and tomatoes. He wilted the kale in the pan before serving. Anna came back, smelling like heaven.

'Mmm,' she said, 'something smells good enough to eat.'

'You're right about that,' he said, and if she got the double meaning, she didn't let on.

She dropped bread into the toaster. He couldn't take his eyes off of her. He wanted to forget breakfast and bury his face in the fragrance of her neck. He wanted to massage the tenseness out of her shoulders. He wanted to kiss her until they had to come up for air. He just wanted.

The toast popped up and he startled, realising he'd been staring. She was oblivious. She lifted out the toast and dropped in two more slices.

'Do you want tomato sauce?' she said, going to the fridge.

'Not for me, thanks,' he said, clearing his throat before carrying their plates to the table.

'I am starving, and this looks delicious.'

'I'm a man of many talents. Say the word and I'll demonstrate more of them, until you beg me to stop—' He winced when he clocked the expression on her face. 'Too tacky?'

'Too corny.'

'I'll have to try harder.'

She rolled her eyes.

They ate in silence. When they'd finished Nick pushed his plate to the side and wiped his mouth on a paper serviette. He leaned back and said, 'Now tell me Annalise Kelly, what have you been up to since that last year of high school ...?'

'Annalise?'

'You'd be surprised what I remember.'

'My mother and sister are the only people who call me Annalise.'

He tilted his head to the side. 'It's a beautiful name. It suits you.'

'When I was a kid I hated it. I used to get called Woggo.'

'With a last name like Kelly?'

'Yep. My grandmother on Mum's side was called Annalise. I wanted a name like Rebecca or Melissa. Something normal.'

'What's normal? Kids will bastardise any name. They called me Nickel Arse, until I was bigger than they were.'

'You're right. Kids will always tease.'

'Yes, but you're not answering my question, Anna.'

'Why do you want to know what I've been doing since high school?'

Nick snorted. 'Why do you think? I want to get to know you. That's what friends do, they get to know each other.'

'Nick,' Anna said, her tone uncompromising. 'I'm here to work and get as much experience as I can. When an RFDS vacancy comes up closer to home, I'm out of here. Could be two weeks, could be two months.'

'Could be two years.'

She raised her eyebrows.

'I know that's unlikely but wouldn't it be a bit lonely if you hadn't made any friends, or hadn't had a social life along the way?'

She leaned back in the chair and sighed. 'Why is everyone suddenly interested in my social life? I'm here because of the job. Unlike you, I have no ties to this place, and no desire to develop any—'

'Ah, so there was more gossip.'

Anna shifted in her chair. 'Look, someone said your mother still lives here, and your brother—'

'Someone has been chatty—'

She held up her hand. 'Nick, as you said, people gossip. While I don't seek it out I'm no deafer to it than you are.' Chair scraping on the vinyl flooring, she stood up, smothering a yawn. 'Please, we're both tired. Go home, get some sleep. I'll clean up, and thank you for breakfast. I probably wouldn't have eaten.'

'That's my point,' he said, not moving. 'I want to know about you directly from you, not from the workplace grapevine.'

Stacking their empty plates on the table, Anna paused. A frown dragged her eyebrows together and crescents of fatigue bruised the translucent skin beneath her eyes. He pushed himself to his feet.

'You're right, we're tired. But we will continue this conversation another time.'

'Whatever,' she said, taking the dirty crockery to the sink. She returned the leftover groceries to the shopping bag while he watched.

'Here,' she said, sliding the bag towards him.

He ignored it and stepped into her personal space. She backed away, bumping up against the pantry cupboard.

'We are not done here, Annalise Kelly, whatever you might think, or not think.' His voice was low, and he was taken aback by the depths of his own certainty. He didn't touch her except to whisper the tip of his index finger down her cheek. Satisfaction shot through him when she shivered. She wasn't as immune to him as she liked to pretend.

'I'll see you later,' she said, shifting sideways, distancing herself from him.

'You will. As soon as tonight, if we fly.'

She nodded but gave nothing away.

Nick left. He drove to Danny's place, relieved to find his mate had gone to work today, because he was too tired to make the trip out to the base.

Stripping off he stood under a tepid shower until his head ached and his skin started to wrinkle. Closing the blinds and making the room as dark as possible, he stretched out on top of his sleeping bag on the sofa bed. Nick was tired but wired. And frustrated. No matter what direction he forced his thoughts, they always drifted back to Anna.

8

Anna's determination to pretend she wasn't attracted to Nick wasn't enough: sleep wouldn't come. The way the tip of his finger had skimmed down her cheek. It was a careless caress that had shivered right through her.

Squeezing her eyes shut, shoving her fist in her mouth, catching the whimper before it escaped her throat. It felt like a lifetime since a man had looked at her the way Nick did.

'Can't happen,' she mouthed against her knuckles. 'My life is complicated enough as it is.'

With no hope of sleep and desperate to take her mind off Nick, Anna picked up her phone from the bedside cupboard and began scrolling through her hugely neglected social media sites.

When that didn't put her to sleep she moved on to Izzy's social media sites, vacillating between feeling like a trespasser and a righteous parent. How else was she to know what her daughter was up to? Her daughter didn't tell her.

And that's how she stumbled on the photo of Isabelle up close and personal with Damien, all nineteen-years' worth of lean muscle and sun-bleached blond hair.

Anna bolted up in bed, her heart pounding and her body flashing hot and then cold, all thoughts of Nick evaporating. She rapidly flicked to another of Izzy's sites only to find the identical photo, posted the day before. *After* Anna had vetoed Izzy going anywhere with him, regardless of what Teresa thought of him.

She leapt off the bed to pace around the semi-darkened bedroom. The blockout curtains didn't block out all the daylight.

Guilt gnawed at her. If she'd been there with Izzy, this wouldn't be happening. What sort of a parent was she? Here she was, getting all hot and bothered about a man and what might be, when she should be with her daughter, guaranteeing she didn't make the same mistakes Anna had.

Two more night shifts and then Anna had three days off. She'd fly to Adelaide and talk to Izzy face-to-face. Reason with her. Lay down the law if she had to. Obviously, her daughter couldn't be trusted.

Before she could think it through any further she hit Teresa's number. It was late morning on a weekday. Her sister was an HR consultant and worked from home.

'I saw them,' Anna accused the moment Teresa picked up.

'Who?'

'Izzy, with that nineteen-year-old *man*. Damien. On Facebook.'

'Oh, that. I warned Izzy this is how you'd react.'

'What's that supposed to mean?'

'Anna, I took that photo days ago when Damien was here cleaning the swimming pool. She cropped out his dad in the background. I was there all the time.'

'Oh,' Anna said and flopped back onto the bed. 'I must have sounded a bit over-the-top.'

'No, you sounded like the parent of a teenage daughter. I know you're anxious, but give her some space. A girl's entitled to her first crush without her mother breathing down her neck.'

'You sound as if you're on her side.' Anna would never forget her own first crush. If only her mother had been breathing down her neck, Anna might have made different choices.

'I'm on both your sides,' Teresa said. 'She's a good kid, Anna. You've done a brilliant job, and now you have to trust her.'

'I saw the photo and I thought—' She sighed heavily into the phone. 'Best I don't tell you what I thought.'

'Worry is what parents do.'

'Should I come home? I have days off coming up. I can book a seat on the first flight out of here. It would be good to see you both.'

'Anna, I'm flying to Sydney on Monday, an unexpected business trip, and Izzy has exams most of the week.'

'Oh, yeah, I'd forgotten about exams,' Anna said, feeling on the outer, redundant as a parent.

'You'd end up spending a chunk of money, only to see Izzy when she's focused on school, and me not at all.'

'You're right. I overreacted. And it is expensive. But I miss her and I'm so far away if she needs me.' Anna rubbed her gritty eyes. 'I'd better go. I spent most of the night flying. Now I'm trying to sleep because I'm on again tonight.'

'Anna, you have to stop second-guessing your decision to be where you are. It's pointless. You made the decision, *we* made the decision, for all the right reasons. You've been away for months, and it's working at this end. Isabelle is coping amazingly well.'

'I know, I know. But I'm so far away, and she's so young and vulnerable.'

They said goodbye and Anna disconnected feeling marginally better than when she'd made the phone call. Her sister was always so level-headed. But had she been as pragmatic when her own daughter, Miranda, had been fifteen? No, was the short answer.

Eleven years separated Anna and Teresa, and they hadn't been close as children. They'd made up for it as adults. When Anna lobbed on Teresa's doorstep announcing she was pregnant and keeping the baby, her sister, with two children of her own, had taken her in with open arms.

A pity her parents hadn't been as understanding or forgiving. Tina Kelly had hated Broken Hill, spending as little time there as possible, leaving her teenage daughter to navigate adolescence on her own. Anna saw her father more at school than she did at home. But he'd willingly forked out the money for flying lessons; it was a pricey way of mitigating his own guilt for ignoring his daughter and leaving her to fend for herself.

When Anna had made the decision to continue with the pregnancy, they'd completely withdrawn their support. To this day Anna's relationship with them remained strained.

Her parents had eventually divorced. When Anna told them she was going to work in Broken Hill, and Izzy would be staying in Adelaide, her mother had left her speechless when she'd accused Anna of selfishly putting her career first. Max Kelly hadn't commented.

Nevertheless, her parents' relationship with Isabelle was strong. They'd never blamed their granddaughter for the sins of her mother. But they'd never forgiven their daughter for those same sins.

In moments of self-doubt, like earlier when she saw the photo of Izzy with Damien, Anna dreaded that her mother's accusations were true—that she had effectively abandoned Izzy to pursue her career. But like Teresa had said, constantly second-guessing the decision was pointless.

In another month school would be over for the year and there'd be more decisions to make. Izzy wanted to come to Broken Hill for the holidays. Anna had mixed feelings about the idea and was guiltily avoiding addressing her own reluctance to have her two lives converge.

Exhausted, mentally and physically, she pulled the sheet up under her chin and willed herself to sleep.

That night, much to Anna's bemusement, Beth came home after a session at the pub and declared, 'We're having a dinner party tomorrow night. Haven't had one in forever.'

Feet up on the sofa, Anna's jaw cracked when she yawned. Four hours of light sleep was all she'd managed. 'I didn't think anyone had dinner parties anymore.'

'That's why it is such a good idea.' Beth disappeared into the kitchen, returning a few minutes later with an armful of cookbooks. 'Shove over,' she said, sitting down beside Anna, the books sliding out of her arms onto the carpet.

'Now, let's plan the menu for our dinner party.' Grinning with anticipation she reached for a dog-eared *Women's Weekly Dinner Party Cookbook*.

'*Our* dinner party?'

'Yep, *our* dinner party,' Beth said, handing Anna the cookbook and reaching for another.

Anna reluctantly took it. 'You know I'm rostered on tonight and tomorrow night. The chances of us going flying on a Saturday night are pretty high.'

Beth looked up. 'And?'

'Only saying,' Anna said.

'Most of the people I know are shift workers. Try finding a time when no-one's working or on call.'

Anna opened the book in her lap, absently flicking through it. 'Wow! Beef in red wine … Braised leek salad … Where on earth did you get these books, Beth?'

'They came with the house,' she said. 'My great-aunt liked to cook.'

'Oh,' Anna said, dropping the book back onto the pile. Why anyone would want to spend hours skewering ice cream balls with toothpicks and then dipping them in chocolate was beyond her.

Television remote in hand she began surfing the channels. 'Nothing worth watching,' she said, flicking off the television. 'So tell me who *we've* invited to our dinner party. Isn't tomorrow night short notice?'

'Nah, I've already asked them. How many dining chairs are there? Eight?'

'Yep, but you still haven't told me who's coming.'

Balancing Stephanie Alexander's *The Cook's Companion* on her knee, Beth reached for her mobile phone. 'It doesn't matter who's coming, you need to meet more people, have some fun.'

'I have fun all the time,' Anna said, sounding as indignant as she felt.

'When?'

'Every time I climb into the cockpit.'

Beth clicked her tongue. 'I mean fun that involves other people, or at least one other person.'

'Beth, I—'

'Stop right there. I can't un-invite people. I don't know why I didn't think of doing this months ago, when you first moved in.'

Anna stared at her housemate, who was basically her landlord. It had taken three months of searching while living in the hospital's staff accommodation to find this place. There was no way she wanted to move. In her mind, her next move would be back to Adelaide.

'Beth, I like you, and I like living here, but I don't remember anything in our agreement about you organising a social life for me. And please, do not try any matchmaking!'

Beth scratched her head, one-handedly scrolling through her phone contacts. The cookbook slipped sideways on her lap. 'No point asking Scott—' she muttered, catching the book before it landed on the floor.

Anna threw her hands in the air. 'Have you heard a word that I've said?'

'He hasn't been in touch, but then neither have I, and I know he's back because I saw his ute. We haven't had sex for two months. What other eligible men do I know?' Scowling, she kept scrolling. 'All married, or boring. I need to get out of this place if I want to meet more men.'

With a groan Anna flopped back on the sofa and closed her eyes, praying that tomorrow night she'd have to fly to a far-flung location.

A few minutes later Beth put her phone to one side and rubbed her hands together. 'It's a done deal. Six guests, ready, willing and able. Four of them are men, all of whom I'd have sex with if they'd have me.'

'Go girl,' Anna said, tongue-in-cheek.

'I wish. Unfortunately, two are married, and I know at least one of the other two would prefer to sleep with you.'

'Yeah, right,' Anna said. Picking up her empty cup she took it through to the kitchen.

'Seriously,' Beth said when she returned, 'I think men find you being a pilot very, very sexy. I would if I was a bloke.'

'Jeez, Beth, what am I supposed to do with that information?'

'Ignore it. The guests will be here for pre-dinner drinks at six tomorrow night.'

'Who *have* you invited?'

With a self-satisfied smirk Beth said, 'I'll let it be a surprise.'

9

Nick was getting to the good bits in a dream involving Anna and chocolate topping when his phone vibrated its way off the bedside cupboard and crashed onto the floor. Three hours earlier he'd collapsed onto the narrow single bed at the base. His colleague was still out sick and he'd agreed to pick up her two remaining night shifts. Knowing that if he flew it would be with Anna had made the decision a no-brainer.

And as the senior flight nurse said, it'd be easier to find someone else willing to replace Nick on day shift.

The flight nurses worked a fixed rotating roster of four day shifts, three night shifts, followed by three days off. The pilots' roster was a five-week rotation and Nick knew the opportunity to work with Anna three nights in a row wouldn't present again during his three-month contract.

It took a moment for Nick to orientate to his surroundings before scrambling for his phone. Awake or asleep, Anna was on his mind—and other parts of his anatomy.

Picking up the phone he saw the duty doctor's name on the screen.

'Shit,' he grumbled. He'd slept poorly at Danny's during the day and his body craved more sleep.

A sick three-year-old with a fever that hadn't responded to the mother's ministrations, the duty doctor relayed. The child had a history of chest infections and febrile convulsions.

Of all the disciplines, Nick was most wary of paediatrics. All you had to do was turn your back and a toddler or baby's condition could deteriorate alarmingly. And the little bodies and miniature equipment felt awkward in his man-sized hands.

Buttoning up his shirt, a thought stopped him cold.

'Nah,' he said out loud, shaking his head to dislodge the premonition. No way this would be death number three. He didn't believe in that superstitious crap anyway.

He tucked in the shirt, slipped on his high-vis vest and bent to lace up his boots. Rubbing a hand over his chin, he regretted not shaving earlier, before falling into bed. Now there wasn't time. He'd wasted precious minutes thinking about Anna.

The moment he'd disconnected from the duty doctor he'd phoned the on-call pilot: Anna. She'd answered on the second ring, voice husky with sleep. Remembering his dream he'd almost groaned out loud.

Twenty minutes later she was striding across the hangar towards him. God, but she was gorgeous.

'How'd you sleep?' he said.

'So-so. Never enough.' She lifted one of two takeaway coffees out of a cardboard tray, handing it to him. 'Large, with an extra shot. Like you ordered.'

'Thanks.' He took a grateful sip. 'I'll get you the money.'

'My shout. After all, you provided breakfast.'

Their eyes met. The tension from that morning hadn't dissipated. She started backing away.

'I need to file my flight plan, check the weather forecast. The airstrip—' She spun around and was quickly swallowed up by the gloom of the hangar.

Fifty-three minutes after the duty doctor's call they were lined up on the runway. The child's temperature had come down a notch and the doctor had downgraded the flight to a P2, urgent but not life-threatening, and no doctor required. He'd stay tucked up in his bed.

Their destination was a small community thirty minutes flying time away, which meant Anna would be occupied the entire flight and there'd be no time for chat.

While they were in the air Nick flicked through the patient's file—relatively long for someone so young. That done, he gazed out the aircraft window. Being up here at night surrounded by nothing but stars he always felt as if he was suspended in space. Disconnected from everything.

Since his life in Sydney had disintegrated, he'd been searching for another place to belong. What he'd told Beth was true: he didn't know what had gone wrong between him and Lauren. Except that it'd probably been all wrong from the beginning.

After his initial ambivalence towards Broken Hill, he was discovering that being back in his hometown was strangely comforting. Everything was familiar. Which was ironic because it was those same familiar things that had smothered him and driven him to find a new life in Sydney in the first place.

The pitch of the twin engines changed; they'd begun their descent.

The local ambulance was waiting at the airstrip with the three-year-old patient and mother on board. As soon as the propellers came to a standstill, Nick opened the door. Fresh, dew-scented air rushed in.

He climbed into the back of the ambulance, quickly assessing the patient and taking handover from the community's registered nurse. The little boy was flushed, his breathing rapid. He didn't open his eyes when Nick laid the back of his hand on the child's brow, and then repositioned the oxygen mask.

'Meet Toby. His temp's down to thirty-nine point five,' the RN said. 'Oxygen sats are on the low side of normal.' She handed over the paperwork. 'Sorry to get you out in the middle of the night, but you never know with kids.'

'No worries. I wasn't doing anything other than sleeping,' Nick said, and winked.

Together they loaded the patient and the passenger. Nick took his time settling them both, doing a full set of observations.

Alison, the child's mother, sank into a spare seat and buckled up the seatbelt.

They were ready to taxi twenty-five minutes after they'd landed. It was three am. Nick stifled a yawn.

The sky was clear, a billion stars, with no remnants of the weather front that had passed through the day before.

'It's okay, mate,' Nick said in a soothing voice, when halfway through the flight Toby started fretting. He pulled at the oxygen mask and the monitor leads. He looked feverish, eyes glassy, his dark curls matted to his forehead. His temperature had risen a fraction.

Then Toby started to cry, a high-pitched squeal, tears mixing with the snot pouring out of his nose. He slapped and clawed at Nick's hand when he moved to wipe his nose and put the oxygen mask back in place. Without the supplemental oxygen, the child's saturations dropped alarmingly.

Alison opened her eyes, craning as far forward as the seatbelt would allow.

'Is he all right?'

'A bit restless,' Nick said, wishing his tiny patient had an IV access. He looked up and caught Anna glancing over her shoulder into the cabin. She mouthed, 'Is everything okay?' and he nodded.

Alison released her seatbelt and moved closer, crooning to her son.

'We've started our descent and it's probably playing havoc with his ears,' Nick said, hoping that's all it was. 'You'd better buckle up again.' Alison kissed her son's cheek and moved back to her seat.

He took the child's vital signs again, grateful his temperature was static. Thousands of metres above the ground, a convulsing patient was the last thing any flight nurse needed.

Nick glanced at his watch. The return flight seemed a whole lot longer than the flight out had been. When they touched down with a bump, relief loosened Nick's shoulder muscles.

Taxiing towards the hangar his relief deepened when he spotted the waiting ambulance. But he didn't relax completely until the patient had been transferred, and the ambulance's tail-lights were flickering down the road.

Standing beside Anna, watching until the vehicle disappeared, Nick shook his head and said, 'Kids make me nervous. I'm certainly not cut out to be a parent.' He scrubbed his face with both hands.

'Probably different when it's your own.'

Nick raised his eyebrows, shoved his hands into his pockets and said, 'So they say, but I'm in no hurry to find out if it's true. I'll go get the trolley for the gear. And the oxygen is low.'

By the time they'd unloaded the equipment, and he'd restocked and put everything away, it was after four in the morning. Anna had recharged the onboard oxygen from the portable cylinders in the hangar.

'I have a couple of things to finish and then I'm off home,' she said. 'I'll see you, but hopefully not until after tomorrow night. Flying three nights in a row wouldn't be fair.'

'You're right about that,' he said. 'I'm camping here so I'll lock up. Drive carefully.'

It was when he was turning off the lights that he remembered Beth's dinner invitation. He glanced at the time. Only thirteen and a half hours away. Bloody hell. Why had he said he'd go?

Because Anna would be there, that's why. And she'd obviously forgotten about it, or she didn't know he'd been invited.

10

The overhead fan groaned, barely moving the air. The bedroom was warm and stuffy when Anna woke at ten-thirty on Saturday morning. There was an air conditioner in the window but it rattled and spewed out lukewarm air.

She listened, wondering what had woken her. The house was otherwise silent. Her mouth was dry and her limbs sluggish. She closed her eyes, hoping she'd drop off again, knowing she wouldn't.

Beth was out, a note on the kitchen counter saying she'd gone to the supermarket. Anna went to the fridge looking for something to eat. She could do with one of Nick's cooked breakfasts right about now. A bowl of cereal topped with tinned peaches would have to suffice.

Anna was standing in the kitchen shovelling in cornflakes when Beth returned laden with shopping bags.

'Bloody hell, it's hot out there already! It's not summer until next month, for goodness sake,' she said, her round face beetroot-red, her strawberry-blonde hair limp with perspiration. 'You went flying then.'

'The conditions were perfect.'

Beth gave her head a small shake. 'Weird. Someone who actually likes going to work.'

'Yeah, well—' Anna rinsed her cereal bowl and put it in the dishwasher. 'What are we having for dinner?' She began poking around in one of the grocery bags.

Beth swatted her hand out of the way. 'Go do the vacuuming. They'll be here before we know it.'

'And there I was planning to sleep away the afternoon.'

Beth shooed her out of the kitchen.

When the guests arrived at six, they weren't a total surprise. Anna had met speech pathologist Barb Boscoe before. Her husband, Laurie, was short and stocky with a shaved head that probably glowed in the dark. He came across as a bit of a smart-arse.

Carol Petrucci was a midwife at the hospital, and her husband Mario ran his own courier business. Anna liked Carol; she and Mario had three children—two boys, eight and ten, and a girl around Izzy's age. They lived nearby and Carol sometimes dropped by to drink wine and bitch about work with Beth.

The only surprises were Tim Carpenter and Serena Morris.

'What are you doing here?' Serena blurted when she saw Anna.

'I live here.'

Serena gave Anna the once-over. 'I didn't know that,' she said, obviously miffed that she was out of the loop.

Tim barrelled in with an esky of drinks and Anna withdrew to the kitchen, pulling out her phone to check she hadn't missed the call-out she was counting on. Izzy and Teresa's faces beamed back at her from the home screen. There were no missed calls. Disappointed, she jammed it back into her pocket.

'You're meant to be mingling with the guests,' Beth said, manically chopping something at the sink.

'They're mingling okay on their own. I didn't know you knew Serena Morris.'

'I've met her before, but I don't know her. Tim rang before and asked if he could bring her. What could I say? We'll need to find another chair, set another place.'

'Why? We have eight chairs and eight guests.'

Beth threw Anna an exasperated look. 'Nick's coming. I invited him. I didn't invite her. There's another chair in my bedroom.'

Anna glared at Beth's back. That explained why Serena had finagled an invitation to dinner. 'I have a better idea. I'll go out to the base. I'm on call anyway and there's plenty to do out there. I can pick up a pizza on the w—'

Beth spun around, knife in hand. 'No, you don't. This is *our* dinner party. Nine will fit at the table. I don't mind perching on the corner. I'll be up and down anyway.'

Anna raised her hands, her attention focused on the knife. 'Okay, okay, you can put down the knife,' she said. 'I'll get the chair, and set another place.'

Beth nodded and turned back to her task.

'One more thing,' Anna said, pausing in the kitchen doorway.

'And what would that be?'

'Why would you want to sleep with Laurie Boscoe?'

Beth threw back her head, her laugh coming right from her belly.

Anna was manoeuvring the chair through Beth's bedroom door when Nick arrived. He let himself in the front door and Anna felt a punch of attraction from down the length of the passageway. Why fight it? In jeans and a sage-green shirt he was the best-looking man there. The best-looking man she'd ever seen.

'Hello,' she said the moment he noticed her standing there.

'Hello. Do you want a hand with that?'

She shook her head but he came and took the chair from her anyway, handing her a bottle of wine.

'Where do you want it?'

Anna's eyes widened and heat flashed up her neck.

Nick grinned. 'The chair, Anna, where do you want the chair?'

'Oh, the chair. In the dining room, thanks. There's an extra person.'

Anna followed him into the empty kitchen and through to the dining area. The others were in the sitting room. Anna set another place. They shoved the chairs along so they'd all fit.

Laughter and chatter came from the room next door. Nick stiffened. 'Please don't tell me Beth invited Serena.'

'She didn't. Tim did.'

'Seriously? It's bad enough having to work with her again, let—'

'You've worked with her before?'

'Briefly, in Sydney, and believe me, that was enough.'

Beth bounced in from the sitting room brandishing an empty wine bottle. 'We need more bubbly. Nick, you're here!'

Anna watched as Nick leaned in and gave Beth a peck on the cheek. She totally got why Beth would want to sleep with Nick.

Observing the easy familiarity between them as she went to the fridge for more bubbly, she wondered if they ever had.

With a soft drink in hand and proffering the bubbly, Anna did her best to mingle with the guests but was relieved when Beth announced dinner was ready.

'No, we haven't, not ever,' Nick whispered, close to Anna's ear, his breath tickling her skin.

The diners, fully sated on fillet steak, were straggling out of the dining room and into the sitting room. Nick was behind Anna, bringing up the rear.

The hairs on her arms stood up. She angled her head sideways. If she moved a millimetre, they'd be touching. He was close enough for her to glimpse the kaleidoscope of colours that made up the iris of his eyes. Eyes that changed with his every mood. Now, they were more green than grey, sparkling with amusement.

'I've been watching you and I know you've been wondering. Don't deny it,' he added when she opened her mouth to respond. He smiled, and although she hadn't touched a drop of alcohol, her head spun like she was tipsy.

'Beth and I have only ever been friends, without benefits.'

Anna cleared her throat. 'I'm sure she wouldn't be averse to it happening, all the same.'

Nick raised his eyebrows. 'Not going there,' he said, 'and besides, I fear our Tim has been bitten by the Beth bug.'

'You're kidding?'

'I'm not.'

'But he brought Serena.'

'They're only colleagues. He hasn't taken his eyes off of Beth.'

'I didn't realise until tonight that they even knew each other.'

'The world of doctors and nurses is small, especially single ones in a place like Broken Hill,' he said. 'They drink at the same pub. And you would have known that if you'd ever come along.'

Anna ignored the jab. Beth appeared, swaying as she stood at in the archway between the sitting room and the dining area.

'You blokes still out here. Shall I make coffee?' she said and propped herself against the arch.

Anna wiggled past Nick. 'I'll get the coffee. You did the food, Beth, and it was fabulous. Go and join your guests.'

'*Our* guests.'

Anna rolled her eyes.

'There's cheese, and chocolates,' Beth slurred, and waved towards the kitchen.

'We'll do it,' said Nick. 'You go and sit down, before you fall down.'

'Might have had a few wines, but I'm fine,' she said, standing up straighter before wobbling back into the sitting room. Anna looked at Nick. He shook his head and started clearing the table.

'Never could hold her grog,' he said.

'I'll put the kettle on.'

'So, who drew the short straw to clean up?'

'Beth did the food. The least I can do is clean up.' Hands on hips she surveyed the mess, debating whether to leave it until the morning.

'Do it now,' Nick said, reading her mind. 'I'll help.' He rolled up his sleeves and started scraping plates.

An hour later, coffee had been had and order restored to the kitchen. Carol and Mario were walking home, and Barb and Laurie were waiting out the front for their taxi. There was no sign of Serena, and Tim was snoring on the sofa, his head on Beth's lap.

'Told you,' Nick said, seeing the stunned look on Anna's face.

'She's practically engaged to Scott. They've been having their problems, but—'

'Scott's history, trust me,' Nick said. 'Let's go out the back and drink our tea. We wouldn't want to wake the lovebirds.'

Anna frowned. 'Where's Serena?'

'Talking to Barb and Laurie. But who cares?'

Wordlessly, she followed him out to the back verandah. The night was balmy. The air felt fresh after the sweltering kitchen.

Beth's house was on the edge of town. The view from the backyard was red sand and saltbush in the daylight, the sky a mantle of stars at night.

Not wanting to attract the bugs, they didn't turn on the verandah light. Nick sat down on Beth's creaky old swing seat, patting the space beside him. Anna sat down as far from him as the seat would allow, which wasn't far. The seat rocked as he shifted, moving so their thighs brushed. There was nowhere for her to go, except a different seat.

'I'm not going to jump you, Anna,' he said, sounding almost exasperated.

'I know that, and it's not as if I don't like you,' she said, paused and gave a shaky laugh. 'God, I sound like a fifteen-year-old, not the thirty-four-year old mo—' She stopped herself, feeling Nick's speculative gaze in the darkness. 'I mean, it's not as if we aren't grown-up.' She expelled a tight breath. 'Why don't I shut up?'

'Believe me, Anna, the way I feel about you is totally grown-up. And I do remember how I felt about you when you weren't much older than fifteen. But back then you didn't even know I existed.'

'Who sounds like a teenager now?'

Nick made a low sound that could have been agreement. Anna sipped her tea. She could feel heat radiating off him. Lust and longing swamped her. It had been aeons but she hadn't forgotten the power of these feelings and sensations.

'Nick,' she said quietly. 'You have it so wrong. I might not have noticed you at high school because I was kind of preoccupied that year … But believe me, I'd have to be blind, deaf and dumb not to notice you this time round.'

In the shadowy light from the kitchen she cradled the empty mug in her hands, willing him to say something, anything. Shifting his foot, pushing down and setting the seat swinging, he remained silent. The gentle movement pressed his thigh against hers. She didn't pull away.

Anna closed her eyes and let herself drift; let herself imagine how it would be to have Nick's whole body pressed firmly against her, not only his thigh.

11

'Nick?'

Simultaneously the screen door screeched open and the verandah flooded with fluorescent white light. The neighbour's dog barked. Albert shot across the cement and inside through the cat flap.

Nick's heart took a nosedive. Anna shielded her eyes and shrank back in the seat. He looked over his shoulder and sure enough Serena was standing in the doorway.

'There you are,' she said.

'Yep, here I am,' he muttered. Now Anna's expression was guarded, her shoulders set.

Serena sashayed across to a canvas deckchair and sat down.

'Oooh, don't you two look comfy.'

'Did you want something, Serena?' Nick said.

'A lift home, if you don't mind,' she said and snickered, her eyes darting to Anna. 'Tim's otherwise engaged, the sly dog.'

'Why didn't you go in the taxi with Barb and Laurie?'

'Duh, you *know* I live in the opposite direction to them.'

'You go then, Nick, take Serena home.'

Anna went to stand up the same time he did, stumbling when the seat unexpectedly swung out from under her. He reached out to steady her, his hand lingering on her lower back.

'Oh, yeah … I've been meaning to ask…' Serena said, and the way she said it had an icy curl of dread forming in Nick's stomach.

Anna's attention shifted to Serena. The curl of dread tightened into a knot. He knew what was coming and was powerless to stop it.

'How's your *wife,* Nick?' Eyes round as saucers, Serena shifted her attention to Anna.

'You know Nick's married—' Serena said. 'Oh, I can see by the look on your face that you didn't.'

'We're separated,' Nick growled, but it didn't stop the colour draining from Anna's face. Her shock and discomfort were palpable.

'I don't suppose Nick told you that we'd worked together before, either,' Serena said, her head tipped to the side, a mocking expression on her face.

Anna cleared her throat. 'Actually, he did tell me that,' she said.

'Really?'

'You've made your point, Serena,' Nick said, cutting her off. 'Go and get your things and I'll take you home.' All this said without shifting his gaze from Anna's face. She wouldn't look at him.

'Will do,' Serena said, getting to her feet and bouncing off inside.

Anna's arms were folded across her midriff, her empty cup dangled from her fingers.

'Anna, Lauren and I have been separated for eight months,' he said in a tone tinged with desperation.

She responded with a stiff nod.

'I was going to tell you,' he said, taking a step towards her. She moved back and it was as if she'd slapped him.

'You'd better go,' she said to a point somewhere over his left shoulder.

'Anna, please—'

'She'll be waiting.'

'She can wait!'

Anna looked everywhere but at him. 'All right,' he said, 'I'll go now but we haven't finished with this.'

'Yes, we have,' she said, the finality of the words making him flinch. He scooped up his empty cup and made for the door.

'Nick,' she said.

He stopped, his heart leapt into his throat. He whirled around to face her. 'Yes?'

'Thanks for helping me clean up after dinner,' she said politely. His hopes went as flat as day-old beer.

'You're welcome.' And then there was nothing left for him to do but leave.

Serena was lurking in the sitting room, madly thumbing away on her mobile phone. 'Are you ready?' she said when he appeared in the doorway. He could barely bring himself to look at her.

'Nick, don't be angry,' she said, following him out to his ute.

He didn't speak until they were belted in and he was pulling out from the kerb. 'You're a bitch, Serena. You know that, don't you.'

'That's not very nice,' she said, wide-eyed in the low light of the cabin.

'Believe me, I could be a lot less nice.'

She drew herself up in the seat, flicked her hair over her shoulder. 'I only told her so she wouldn't find out from some old gossip.'

'Spare me the bullshit,' he said, indicating to turn onto William Street.

'Humph,' she said, pretending to ignore him. They travelled in silence for several minutes. When he turned into her street she broke the silence.

'You know, I was shocked when you showed up at the RFDS. I thought you and ... What was her name?'

'Lauren.'

'Oh yeah, Lauren. Anyhow, I thought you were happily married and settled in Sydney.'

Nick slowed and came to a stop in front of the RFDS-owned house Serena shared with another doctor.

'Goodnight, Serena,' he said.

When she unclipped her seatbelt but didn't get out, he tapped his fingers impatiently on the steering wheel.

'I'm sorry things didn't work out for you and Lauren,' she said.

Nick's mouth tightened. 'My private life is none of your concern, and I don't want your sympathy, or anything else.'

'I was only trying to be friendly!'

He glared at her across the console. 'No, you weren't, you were prying.'

'Well, if you do ever change your mind and want to talk, Nick.' She laid a hand on his arm. Repelled, he shook it off.

'In your dreams, Serena,' he said, thankful when she cracked open the door. This conversation had gone on way longer than it should have. Trust her? Not on any level. Working with her was becoming a total pain.

The second she was clear of the vehicle he shoved it into gear and took off. The drive to the base took less time than it should have. He parked in the staff carpark. There were no other vehicles. Locking up, he swiped his security pass to get in to the hangar and made his way to the now-familiar sleeping quarters.

There was nothing homely about the small room. His duffel bag squatted forlornly on the brown carpet tiles. Nick sat on the edge of the bed, mobile phone in his hand. He wanted to talk to Anna; he needed to talk to Anna. His thumb hovered over her number.

He swore, flung the phone onto the narrow bedside cupboard. She wouldn't want to hear anything he had to say.

Unless they got to fly, and then they'd have to communicate.

With that thought reassuring him, he stripped down to his jocks and slid between the cool sheets.

12

Early Sunday morning the swimming pool was deserted. Anna loitered by the entrance until the pool attendant opened up. She was the first swimmer to slice through the glassy surface of the water and despite having slept poorly, she pushed herself through the usual twenty laps. Regardless, the exercise did little to slow her whirling thoughts.

Nick was married. *Married!* He'd insisted he was separated but in Anna's eyes that didn't make him single, just some vague place in between.

He said they'd been apart eight months. Was he hoping they'd get back together? Was his wife? Was this a trial separation?

Nick had wanted to explain but she'd cut him off. It was as if her brain had shut down when Serena had strung together the words wife and married and Nick.

How naive of her to think a man as attractive, kind and caring as Nick would be single and available, and as attracted to her as she was to him.

After he'd left to take Serena home, Anna had gone directly to bed, only to toss and turn. When she couldn't sleep, she'd started thinking, remembering. And in the wee hours where everything loomed larger than life, she'd picked at that one memory like a scab, until it bled …

Anton Leclerc had been a handsome, wiry Frenchman not much taller than Anna, but over twice her age. A charmer and a user, the only commitment he'd ever made was to flying. He took risks, in the air and on the ground.

He'd been Anna's first flight instructor. The one her father had paid to give her flying lessons in her final year of high school.

After the first time Anton had taken her flying, she'd been hooked. With hindsight and the wisdom of adulthood, Anna readily admitted that she'd been as obsessed with Anton Leclerc as she had been with flying.

In the air he'd taught her, encouraged her, told her she was a natural. On the ground he'd made her laugh, complimented her on her attractiveness and quick intelligence. She'd trusted him, had innocently thought her feelings were reciprocated. In a hotel carpark on the back seat of his LandCruiser he'd abused that trust.

When she'd told him she loved him he'd laughed, said she'd get over it.

Weeks later when she'd informed him she was pregnant, he'd stared right through her, ignored her quiet pleading and turned back to the beer waiting on the bar.

Several days after that, a thin woman was waiting for Anna outside the school gates.

'I'm Michelle Leclerc,' she said, 'Anton's wife, for all it's worth.' She lifted her chin towards a familiar 4WD parked on the opposite kerb. 'They're our boys.'

Two teenagers stared moodily from the dusty LandCruiser. Their resemblance to Anton wiped out any doubts about paternity. Anna remembered wanting to be sick.

Early in their acquaintance Anton had smirked when she'd asked him if he was married or had a girlfriend. 'What do you think?' he'd said provocatively, and she'd been too young and inexperienced to know she was being played.

'How old are you?' Michelle had asked.

'I'll be eighteen in a couple of weeks.'

Michelle looked sad. 'I was eighteen too,' she said. 'I'm sorry, and it's not your fault. But don't expect anything from him. We're leaving town. If you are pregnant and you are as smart as he says you are, you'll get rid of it and forget Anton Leclerc ever happened. If I had my time over, that's what I'd do.'

Michelle turned and walked away. Her worn features had been twisted with weariness and were forever etched in Anna's memory.

Anna had thought herself in love once. Last night, sitting beside Nick, she'd wondered if she could fall in love again. She liked him, was attracted to him in a powerful, impossible-to-ignore kind of way.

But in a breathtaking twist of fate, she'd discovered he was married, claiming he was separated, and he hadn't voluntarily shared any of it with her. Talk about déjà vu.

Somewhere around four am, Anna finally drifted into a restless, shallow sleep, her cheeks wet with tears.

Now, hours later, she heaved herself out of the swimming pool. Pulling off her goggles and slicking the water from her hair, she walked to where she'd dropped her towel. It had occurred to her, at about lap fifteen, that she should probably thank Serena. And as unlikely as it was that her intentions had been altruistic, she'd saved Anna from another broken heart.

Given her pathetic track record with men, she could see herself falling head over heels in love with Nick, and him deciding to go back to his wife.

Tiptoeing into the house forty-five minutes later, past a silver Subaru she thought was Tim's, Anna showered as quickly and quietly as possible. Dressed in shorts and a T-shirt, she pushed her feet into sandals and grabbed her car keys. Running into Tim would be embarrassing. Although, chances were they were sleeping soundly after some satisfying sex.

Fuelled by a flurry of frustration and envy, Anna was tempted to bang on Beth's bedroom door as she walked past.

A nearby cafe was open and she stopped for a takeaway double-shot cappuccino and a toasted cheese sandwich. By seven-forty she was driving past the golf course turn off on her way to the base, the sandwich eaten and coffee almost gone.

'What?' she said to herself, when she spotted the familiar white Commodore parked in its usual place, barely screened by the scrub. Striped towels covered the windows. But it wasn't the decor that had her hitting the brakes. Pulled in close behind the Commodore was a 4WD dual cab that looked remarkably like Nick's.

Surely *he* wasn't sleeping in his car? No, he'd said he was staying at a mate's place when he wasn't sleeping at the base. After a half-second debate with herself she did a U-turn and crawled back along the road with her window down.

Anna could hear raised voices. A car door closed with a thud. When she was level with the 4WD, Nick appeared. He was wearing the same clothes he'd had on the night before, and he looked angry. When he noticed her, his expression turned stony.

Damn. Now that he'd caught her being a stickybeak, she was committed. She pulled onto the verge, climbed out and scrambled the ten metres through the scrub to where he was standing.

'Nick? I thought it was your ute. Is everything all right?'

'Getting better by the moment,' he said, his jaw tight, nothing welcoming about his demeanour. She swallowed, already regretting that U-turn.

A woman emerged backside first from the passenger side of the Commodore. She was older; at least mid-sixties, Anna estimated, her hair a greyish-brown cloud about her head. A floral brunch coat sagged above her knees. Her feet were bare.

Anna stared and the woman stared right back. Like a choreographed move they both turned towards Nick at the same time.

'Who the hell is she?' the woman said.

Anna frowned and scratched her head. Why hadn't she kept driving?

'Anna Kelly, meet my mother, Marlene Harrison, formerly of Buck Street, Broken Hill and now residing in her car, in the scrub on the outskirts of this fair city.'

'Nice to meet you, Mrs Harrison,' Anna said, holding out her hand. Her gaze shifted from Nick to his mother and then back again. 'I sure can see the family resemblance.'

Nick's eyes were as grey and turbulent as a stormy sea. He stood there, arms folded, posture rigid. Shaking Anna's hand, Marlene laughed, the sound dry and raspy, typical of a smoker.

'You a friend of Nick's then?'

'We work together.'

'Anna's a pilot, Mum. She works at the base.'

'Oh, you fly those planes. You must be clever, like my Nick here,' she said, nudging her son with an elbow. 'Got his brains from his dad because he sure as hell didn't get them from me.'

Anna shuffled her feet. Beam me up, Scotty, she thought.

'I'd ask you in for a cuppa, but as you can see … ' She left the sentence hanging.

From where she stood Anna could feel Nick's anger and embarrassment. Marlene reached for the cigarette tucked behind her ear and pulled a lighter out of the pocket of her brunch coat. The tobacco smoke made Anna's nose twitch.

'I'll, um, get going,' she said, hitching a thumb over her shoulder in the direction of her vehicle. 'I'm on my way to the base.'

'I thought you had a day off.'

'I do, but Tim stayed over and, you know, I didn't want to hang around, cramp their style.'

Nick nodded, his expression softening slightly. 'I told you they'd get together.'

'Yeah, you did,' she said and found herself smiling at him. He caught her unawares by smiling back, and then she had that tingly thing happening again.

Reminding herself that he had a wife somewhere was as good as dousing herself with a bucket of cold water.

'I'll see you,' she said. 'Bye, Mrs Harrison.'

'See ya, love, and you must call me Marlene. Any friend of Nick's is a friend of mine.'

'Okay. I'll be seeing you, Marlene.'

Backtracking through the scrub to her car she heard Marlene say, 'She seems nice. Attractive. And *tall*.'

'Mum, everyone is taller than you,' came Nick's monotone reply.

Anna smiled.

The article about wind shear in *Aviator* was more than Anna's sleep-deprived brain could handle. She tossed the magazine onto the desk and looked at her watch. Eleven o'clock. Ten minutes since she'd looked last. Was it still too early to go home and intrude in the love nest? Probably. She picked up her empty coffee mug. Put it down again. Another coffee would make it three before lunchtime.

Anna surfed the internet for the next half hour, investigating pilot vacancies at RFDS bases and other aeromedical services. Engrossed in what she was doing, and with her back to the door of the pilots' room, she had no idea how long Nick had been standing there until he cleared his throat. She swivelled around in the chair.

'She lost her job, lost the house, now all she does is drink, smoke, and play the pokies. I found her a flat last time I was home, but she didn't pay the rent and the landlord chucked her out. A friend of Mum's contacted me, said Mum was living rough in her car and I needed to come home and sort things out. I came home but I'm not having much luck sorting things out.'

'Oh, I see.'

'In case you were wondering.'

'No, I wasn't.'

Liar, said his expression.

'What happened to your dad?'

'He died when I was twenty. Mum didn't cope then, and she doesn't cope any better now.'

'She didn't look too bad,' Anna said.

Nick shrugged.

'Well, you can choose your friends but you can't choose you relatives. Isn't that how the old saying goes?'

'Something like that.' He leaned a shoulder against the doorframe and folded his arms. 'Seeing as you've met my mother, I might as well tell you about my brother.'

Anna waited.

'I have no idea where he is. Mum hasn't heard from him in months, thinks he's probably in jail. He most likely is. I'm past caring. I've bailed him out of trouble more times than I want to remember. He's another relative I didn't choose.'

'Your mother is proud of you, that much is obvious.'

Nick's expression was bleak. 'Yeah, my success always meant the family had a cash cow. Until Lauren came along and then the cash dried up for them.'

'I'm sure they didn't think about you like that.'

'Yeah, they did.'

'I'm sorry about that, Nick. If it's any consolation, my mother never has a kind word to say to or about me, and I'm a perpetual disappointment to my father.'

'I would have thought Max Kelly would have been proud of his daughter. Becoming a commercial pilot is no mean feat.'

'There are other ways to disappoint,' she said, her voice flat. 'If it wasn't for my older sister and—' She paused, pressed her lips together. She'd almost said, *my daughter.* Nick might be ready to share his family secrets but she wasn't ready to share hers given what she'd learned last night.

'And?'

'And, I wouldn't survive without her.'

'You're lucky to have her.' Nick frowned, taking in the pile of journals on the desk. 'Why are you still here?'

'Do you reckon it'd be okay to go back to Beth's? Not too soon?'

'You live there, too. Your rent's up to date I take it?'

'Of course it is, but it's her house. I thought if I got home about two … That would give them plenty of time to have a late breakfast or an early lunch … ' She trailed off when Nick's eyes crinkled at the corners. 'It's something I need to clear up with her, you know, in case she expects me to make myself scarce when she has someone stay over.'

'Didn't Scott ever stay over?'

'Occasionally, but he usually showed up late and went early. I rarely ever ran into him.'

'What do you reckon she'd do if you had someone stay over?'

Anna snorted, breaking eye contact. 'Yeah, like that's ever going to happen,' she muttered, spinning the chair around to face the computer screen, picking up where she'd left off.

'Do you want to go to the pub for lunch?'

Anna jumped. She'd thought Nick would leave. She glanced over her shoulder at him.

'Although, I probably look a bit rough,' he said and rasped a hand across his unshaven jaw.

Heat flashed through Anna as she imagined the feel of that stubble rasping against her skin. Her fingers curled into her palms.

'Lunch?' he prompted.

She worked hard to swallow. 'No, I don't think so,' she croaked.

'It's only food, Anna.'

'You're married, Nick.'

He threw his hands in the air. 'We're separated! We have been for eight months.'

An angry silence pulsed between them.

'I'm hungry,' she said, capitulating. 'Tell me which hotel and I'll meet you there.'

He named one. Her heart gave a little kick. She was having lunch with Nick Harrison. Stupid girl.

'We'll talk some more,' he said.

'All right.'

After he'd left, Anna shut down the computer and picked up her wallet and car keys. She flicked off the lights and locked the door, not once asking herself if she was doing the right thing; she knew she wasn't.

She enjoyed conversations with Nick. Regardless, they could talk themselves hoarse and it wouldn't make their situation any less complex. And she hadn't even shared her complications with him.

13

Half an hour later Anna had all but given up on Nick. She'd arrived at the hotel first, found a table and bought a drink. Then she'd fiddled with the menu, read it three times, sipped her drink, glancing at the dining room door every few seconds.

Disappointment ate away at her appetite and she was toying with skipping lunch and going home, when he walked in. He'd changed his shirt, his dark hair was damp, his face clean-shaven. Anna's despondency evaporated. All her appetites returned.

Nick slid into the chair opposite. 'Sorry, but I felt like crap. When I'm on call I never sleep well. And then Mum—' He stopped, his lips thinning. 'I thought you would have given up on me and gone home.'

'I almost did. Do you want to order?'

She handed him the menu, giving herself an excuse to lean in closer and inhale a lungful of whatever cologne he was wearing.

He gave the laminated menu a cursory glance. 'I know what I'm having,' he said.

They went up and ordered their food and Nick asked the barman for a light beer. 'Do you want another drink?' She shook her head.

He stretched out his long legs beside the table when they sat down.

'Mum was impressed,' he said.

'By what?'

'You.'

Anna scowled, pulled at her bottom lip. 'I was only there a few minutes.'

Nick took a deep swallow of his beer and wiped his mouth with the back of his hand. 'She prides herself on being a good judge of character.'

'What will she do?'

'No idea. Rents are prohibitive, and currently I don't have the money to help her out. Funny thing is, she's happy living in her car. She says, get this, the minimalist lifestyle suits her.'

'Ha! That's cute.'

Nick's expression sobered. 'Cute is not a word I'd ever associate with my mother. Quirky. Cantankerous. Sometimes almost cruel ... But never, ever is she cute.'

'But you love her.'

'Of course I love her, she's my mother.'

'Couldn't she get some kind of assisted housing? Surely there's something available.'

'I'm exploring all the options,' Nick said, looking relieved when a waiter appeared at their table with the food.

Anna's mouth watered. 'This looks good,' she said, squeezing lemon onto her fish and chips.

'You know all that saturated fat isn't good for you. When fish is deep-fried it loses any nutritional value.'

She eyed his hamburger with its side serve of chips. He grinned, wrangling the burger. They ate quickly, Anna finishing first.

'Last night was the first Saturday night in ages that I haven't flown,' she said, wiping her fingers on the paper napkin.

'There was a maybe at three am, but the doc talked them through it. They were driving into the hospital this morning instead.'

'And the doctor woke you to tell you? That's a bit mean.' She screwed up the napkin and dropped it onto her empty plate.

'Not really. Sometimes it's helpful to run a decision past another person. If you weren't sure you'd ask one of your colleagues for their opinion, wouldn't you?'

'Sure I would, but I'd do my damnedest not to have to at three in the morning.'

'Sometimes that's when you need a second opinion the most.' He finished his burger and drained his beer. 'Can I get you anything?' he said, standing up with his empty glass.

'I'll have another lemonade, thanks,' she said, rummaging in her wallet. 'My turn to buy.' She held out a twenty-dollar note.

'It's okay, Anna, I can buy you a drink,' he said.

When he came back she picked up where they'd left off. 'You know, you're right. I was thinking back to the times I haven't been 100 per cent sure about something and wanted a second opinion, and it's usually been on one of those middle-of-the-night calls.'

'Two heads are better than one.'

'Yeah,' she said, leaning towards him, her elbows on the table. 'Now tell me what you really think about Beth with Tim?'

Nick wiggled his eyebrows up and down. 'Match made in heaven.'

'How so?'

'They both love to party.'

'And that's a solid foundation on which to build a relationship?'

'Anna, I don't think that kind of relationship is what they have in mind.'

Anna used the straw to poke at the ice in her drink. 'Yeah, I get that, but what about Scott? I thought she wanted to marry him.'

'You're really bothered about Scott, aren't you? You've met him?'

'I have. He seems okay to me.'

Nick threw her an incredulous look and said, 'Scott Broadbent is a tosser. Him and Beth have been on and off so many times. In my opinion? She's better off without him.'

Anna sat back.

'I can almost see you thinking,' he said. 'I reckon you over-think things, Anna.'

'Mmm, maybe. I'm probably naive when it comes to relationships. I thought Beth was with Scott. I knew things had been a bit lumpy lately, but now she's hopped into bed with Tim.'

'You're not naive, Anna. You have a different moral compass than she does. These days people don't seem to commit to relationships for the long haul. The minute the going gets rough, they bail.'

'Is that what happened to you, Nick?'

He took a long swallow of his beer, like he was giving himself time to phrase an answer.

'We bought a house. I was working my backside off to pay the mortgage. She said that I wasn't fun anymore and she was bored.' He curled his lip. 'It's hard to be fun when you're working double shifts. All you want to do in your spare time is sleep.'

'So she bailed.'

'That about sums it up.'

'Do you still love her?' The question popped out of her mouth and Anna slapped her forehead with the heel of her hand. 'Oh jeez, Nick, I'm sorry. That is so none of my business.'

He looked amused more than anything. 'No, Anna, for the record, I don't love her anymore. I don't know if what I felt for her ever was love. I was the boy from the bush, and she bedazzled me. And then she locked me out of the house. After I got over my anger and dented pride, all I felt was relief.'

'What about your house? If you don't mind me asking.'

'I don't mind you asking. It's on the market. She'll get her share of whatever equity's left after we pay out the bank loan. And yes, she's living there, and yes, I'm still paying for it.'

'That doesn't seem fair.' Anna swirled the ice in her glass.

'Life often isn't fair, and I'm sure you've already worked that out for yourself. But don't worry on my behalf. It is better to have the house occupied than empty and her rent will come out of her share of the equity. No way I'm walking away with nothing.'

'Good for you, and yeah, I'd kind of worked out that life isn't always fair.'

Nick drained his beer glass, put it down firmly. 'So there you have it. I'm broke, not quite single, have a mother who lives in her car, and a brother—' He lifted his hands and let them drop onto his thighs. 'God knows where he is and what he's doing, but more than likely it's not legal. What about you?'

Anna swallowed some ice, felt it slide right down to her stomach. 'Me?' she said, and it came out like a squeak.

A cacophony of noise followed by the clanking of coins came from the poker machine room next door. Someone shouted, 'Yes, yes, yes! You little beauty!' and Nick appeared to cringe. Anna wanted to go in and personally congratulate the winner for saving her from answering the question.

'Oh, look,' Nick said and gestured towards the door between the front bar and where they were sitting. Anna craned around him in time to see Tim and Beth walk in, both carrying drinks.

Beth gave a hoot when she spotted them, making a beeline for their table, dropping her backside onto one of the empty chairs.

'I wondered where you two were,' she said, taking them both in.

Anna's face heated when she realised her housemate thought she and Nick had spent the night together.

'I crashed out at the hangar,' Nick said.

'I went swimming and then went out to the base to catch up on a few things. I ran into Nick out there.' Anna hated that she sounded defensive.

'Oh,' Beth said, deflating.

Tim sat down. His eyes were as red as his hair. He sucked on a designer beer like a man who'd spent days in the desert.

'Great dinner party, thanks Beth,' Nick said. 'Much like the old days.'

'Wasn't it.' She smirked, and threw Tim a sideways glance. Now his face matched his hair and his eyes.

Nick got to his feet. 'I'm out of here.'

'What's the rush?' Beth said, her hand on his arm. 'Stay, have another drink. You're not on roster now.'

'Sorry, mate, I gotta go. See you, Anna. Tim, I'll catch you.'

'You will,' Tim mumbled.

Five minutes after Nick's departure, feeling like a spare wheel, Anna scooped up her wallet and car keys. Beth was here, the house was empty, and the idea of an hour or two on her own was too good to resist. First she'd FaceTime Izzy, then she'd have a nap.

'I'm going to go home myself,' she said. Neither Tim or Beth tried to stop her, and with a relieved sigh she took off.

'Mum!'

'Izzy!' When her daughter's image, a reflection of her own younger self, burst onto the computer screen twenty minutes later, happy hormones flooded through Anna. The world made sense again. 'How are you, sweet pea? How was your weekend?'

'Wicked! I went to Clara's yesterday and her dad took us to their farm at Strathalbyn. He's teaching us to drive the tractor.'

'Is he. What about Clara's mum? Was she there too?'

''Course she was. She made scones. We had a barbecue lunch. Clara's *tiresome* little brother came. He is such a mummy's boy.'

'Shouldn't you be studying for your exams?'

'Mum, I have literally been cramming. Aunt Tee is having a shower and then she's dropping me off at school and I'll be back at it. Then she's going out to dinner with a friend.'

'Is she? Who's the friend?'

'Dunno. What have you been doing? Flying much? Anything gory? Have you met any hunky pilots yet? Do you think I should get my hair cut?'

'I haven't flown since early Saturday morning. We picked up a sick child. It wasn't at all gory.' It felt like ages ago, when it'd only been a day and a half. So much had happened in the hours since.

Izzy was tugging at the ends of her glossy dark shoulder-length hair.

'And no, Isabelle, I haven't met any new pilots, hunky or otherwise, and I don't think you should get your hair cut. It suits you the way it is.'

'But I want it to be curly like yours. If it was shorter it probably would be.'

'It wouldn't. Remember when you were younger and you had it shorter? It was as straight as.' The same as your father's.

'Yeah, you're right. Maybe I'll get it streaked or something. What are you doing tomorrow?'

'Good try, Izzy, but there'll be no streaks. And I have days off now, I'm back on Wednesday.'

'When are you coming home again, Mum? I want to learn to drive and Aunt Tee won't teach me.'

'Of course she won't. You're fifteen. She has a BMW.'

'I'll be sixteen before you know it, Mum, and Clara's dad's teaching her.'

'She's already sixteen, and they have paddocks where she can't do any damage. I'll be home on my next weekend off, at the end of the month. We'll discuss it then.'

Teresa's face appeared behind Izzy's. 'That's what I told her,' she said.

Izzy twisted around to her aunt. 'Wow! You look amazing. Must be a special friend. Mum, will you look at Aunt Tee?!' Izzy leaned away from the camera so Anna could see more of her sister.

'Nice. New outfit? Iz, did she shave her legs? It would be an *extra* special friend if she shaved her legs.'

'Both of you, shut up. Isabelle, we need to get going. Go grab your gear. Annalise, I'll deal with you later.'

'Bye, Mum,' Izzy yelled and blew Anna a kiss.

'Love you, have a good week, and behave yourself. Text me.'

'Always do!'

Izzy disappeared from the screen.

'So, who's the friend?' Anna said. 'You never said anything about having a hot date.'

Bright spots of colour stained Teresa's cheeks. 'I don't have to tell you everything.'

'No, you don't. Well, you look gorgeous, Teresa. Have a fabulous time.'

'I will. And while we're on the subject, you should be out having some fun yourself.'

'I went to a dinner party Saturday night.'

Teresa's eye widened with disbelief. 'Did you have a good time?'

'Fantastic,' Anna said, drawing the word out, syllable by syllable.

'Now I know you're fibbing.'

'I am not fibbing. Beth had a dinner party and I went.'

'Doesn't really count. You need to start dating or you'll become a dried-up old hag.'

'Charming! You know I tried dating once, and what a non-event that was. Anyway, all the good ones are taken. And who wants a woman who has a teenage daughter.'

'Anna, Izzy is nearly all grown up. In no time she'll be making her own way in the world. You're still young enough to have more kids if you want to.'

'Bye, Teresa. Have a good time.'

Teresa made a face. 'I want you to be happy, Anna.'

'I am happy.'

'There's happy, and there's *happy*.'

'You'd better go or you'll be late. We can talk about my love life, or lack thereof, some other time.'

'Okay. Bye, sweetie.' Teresa kissed the tips of her fingers and pressed them to the spot Anna's face would be at her end. Then the screen went blank.

Anna rubbed her eyes. More kids. Did she want that? Perhaps. She remembered Nick saying he was in no hurry to become a parent. Had his wife wanted kids, and was that one of the reasons their marriage had broken down?

She sighed. Logging off and shifting the laptop onto the bed beside her, she shimmied her backside down the bed until she was lying down.

Outside, the shadows were lengthening. The weekend was nearly done, and what a disconcerting time the last few days had been.

Swimming and breakfasting with Nick, Beth's dinner party and its aftermath, meeting Marlene Harrison, and a lunch at the pub with Nick. You could almost say she had a social life.

A key sounded in the front door. The blind on the back of the door rattled against the glass as the door opened.

'It's me,' Beth called at the top of her voice. Seconds later she pulled up in Anna's open bedroom doorway grinning from ear to ear.

'What a weekend, girlfriend! Did I get laid, better than your average carpet, or what? That Tim—'

'Stop!' Anna covered her ears. 'I have to work with the man.'

'He's sweet.'

'Sweet?'

'Yeah, he's sweet. He made coffee, brought me breakfast. And, he's good in bed. He does this thing—'

Anna leapt off the bed. 'Enough already,' she said, flinging the bedroom door shut.

Beth's laughter pealed from down the passage. Anna counted to ten and opened the door again. She could hear Beth chattering to Albert. She padded down to the kitchen.

'Are you seeing him again?'

'Maybe.' Beth bent down and scooped up the cat. Anna could hear him purr from where she was standing. 'And don't say, what about Scott?'

'Okay, I won't.' Anna went to the fridge for cold water.

Beth sighed, long and deep. 'Scott and I have been over for the last year at least. Probably longer if I'm honest. It was easier to keep seeing him. You know, sex every now and then with someone familiar.'

No, Anna didn't know, but she wasn't about to share that little gem with Beth.

She hadn't had the time or the inclination between the baby, one or two jobs, and flying lessons when there was time. And then it had been all about getting up as many flying hours as she could.

The times she had dated, the men were unmemorable, the sex even more so and Anna stuck with being a celibate single parent.

And here she was, thirty-four, with little relationship experience, sexual or otherwise. But she had a gorgeous daughter.

Though Anna would be a liar if she said she'd never fantasised about what her life might have been, but for those minutes of unprotected sex on the back seat of a 4WD.

'Earth to Anna,' Beth said, peering at her with a concerned expression on her face.

'Sorry.' Anna gave her head a sharp shake.

'You were miles away. Anything you want to share?'

She shook her head. 'What?' she said, when Beth kept studying her.

'Nothing. But I'm here if you ever do want to talk,' Beth said, and Anna nodded.

14

Sunrise at 10,000 metres never failed to move Nick. The night was dark, the moon had long since set. Pre-dawn lightened the sky, followed by the gold-brushed pastels of dawn. And then the first rays of sunlight streaked across the land and sky. A new day, a pristine palette.

Nick rubbed his eyes. Both of his patients were sleeping, one on the stretcher and the other in a seat, giving him a few minutes respite to take in the view.

Shortly they would begin their descent into Broken Hill and the last of his six night shifts would be over. Perpetual tiredness was something that went with the job. Any wonder shift workers had a shorter lifespan.

They landed and he assisted the two grateful patients into the back of the waiting ambulance. Routine patient transfers between Broken Hill and Adelaide were generally completed earlier in the night. But they'd been diverted to retrieve a man with chest pain from the oil and gas fields. By the time Nick unloaded, restocked and put away the equipment, he'd have been at it for almost thirteen hours.

'For God's sake, Nick, you look dead on your feet. I can finish up here,' Neville Abrahams, the senior flight nurse said, and practically pushed him out the door of the storeroom.

'Okay, okay,' he said, backing out of the room. 'I'll catch a few hours' sleep here first, before I go home.'

Home. The couch at his mate's was hardly what you'd call home. The irony of it was that his current situation wasn't much better than his mother's.

Brain fuzzy with exhaustion he stripped and collapsed onto the narrow bed, his feet hanging off the end. Never again would he volunteer to pick up extra nights. After setting the alarm to wake him in three hours, he covered himself with the sheet and fell into a deep sleep.

Anna's car was in the carpark when he left the base at noon. He'd looked at the rosters and knew she was on a day shift. She'd gone flying while he slept.

It was Wednesday and Nick hadn't seen her since lunch at the hotel on Sunday afternoon. He needed to see her. He missed her, and there was unfinished business between them.

Nick felt as if he was being frustrated at every turn: Serena shooting off her mouth on Saturday night, and then Beth and Tim showing up at the pub on Sunday right after he'd bared his soul to Anna in the hope she'd open up to him.

He threw his duffel onto the backseat of the dual cab. Three hours of sleep, a shower and a double dose of caffeine had taken the edge of his tiredness but not his frustration. Right now he needed food and then he'd be fortified and ready for the appointment with the social worker and his mother.

For the time being he would push Anna to the back of his mind.

Nick hoped his confidence in the social worker's ability to resolve the issue of his mother's homelessness wasn't misplaced. The woman had sounded optimistic when he'd spoken to her and made the appointment. Marlene had promised to meet him there.

Thoughts focused on where he'd eat, he nearly missed his mother's car parked in its usual spot in the scrub.

'What now?' he muttered, braking hard.

Generally, by this time of the day his mother would be somewhere around town, either doing her washing at the laundromat, having a shower at a caravan park or drinking coffee at McDonalds. It was a bit early for her to be ensconced in the gaming room of one of the hotels.

The tyres screeched as he pulled over and steered the vehicle into the scrub. Nick stopped the ute and climbed out, scanning the nearby vegetation. Even in the shade the car's interior would be like an oven. He circled the silent vehicle—the windows were each down a few inches but covered with the usual towels, the back window blocked by piles of clothes. He felt his heart thumping in his chest, and it was nothing to do with the caffeine he'd ingested.

He tried one of the door handles. Locked. By now his heart was lodged in his throat.

Rattling the door handle he rapped heavily on the front passenger's side window. 'Mum!' he shouted through the gap in the window. When there was no response he kept rapping and shouting.

Nick ripped his phone out, his thumb hovering above the first of three zeros when a towel curtain lifted. His relief was palpable, and with it came a pulse of anger.

'Unlock the damn door.'

With clumsy fingers she complied and he wrenched open the door to a blast of hot, sour and sickly air.

'What time is it?' She wheezed between each word, squinting in the bright light. Her hair looked like a bird's nest, her nightie rank with sweat.

'Midday. You sound terrible. Where are your puffers?'

'Ran out,' she said, coughing.

He reached for her hand, sliding his fingers along her wrist. The skin beneath his fingertips was clammy, her heart racing as she doggedly dragged air in and out of ravaged lungs. The light sleeping bag she slept in was a crumpled mess. He reached for her brunch coat, draped across the steering wheel. 'Here, put this on and I'll take you to the hospital.'

Without protest, a testament to how sick she was, Nick carried her to his ute, buckled her in and drove her to the A&E.

Marlene was admitted with a chest infection and acute exacerbation of emphysema. The doctor in A&E took arterial blood gases and inserted an IV line, giving a loading dose of antibiotics. The RN did baseline observations, an ECG and hooked Marlene up to a nebuliser.

They'd missed their appointment with the social worker. While he waited in A&E he called to fill her in and reschedule for a week's time. The social worker was sympathetic.

Nick hung around for a couple of hours until his mum was settled into a hospital bed in the medical ward. The room was the one closest to the nurses' station. Nick felt powerless at the sight of her hunched on the edge of the bed, labouring over each breath.

'Mum, I'll bring in more clothes and stuff later, and see to your car,' he said.

She nodded without opening her eyes.

Back in his ute in the hospital carpark, Nick sat and stared listlessly out the window. Completely drained, he barely had the energy to decide what to do next. Finding food, and more coffee, was his first priority, he decided.

Locking the car again, he slogged across to the cafe on the opposite side of the road, mindlessly ordering a bacon and egg sandwich with a side of potato wedges and a double-shot flat white. So what if the saturated fat killed him.

Halfway through the sandwich, Nick dropped it onto the plate, wiped his hands and fumbled his phone out of his pocket. He searched through his contacts until he came to his brother's last-known number. Before he could change his mind he hit call.

Believe it or not the number was still connected. It rang through to message bank.

'Mum's in hospital. Ring me back,' Nick said, and disconnected with more pressure than necessary.

He finished the remains of the sandwich. Dunking the wedges in sweet chilli sauce, he ate them too—not because he was enjoying them but because he needed the fuel. And he couldn't afford to waste food.

His brother called back when Nick was walking to his ute. The caffeine and carbohydrates had begun to penetrate his fatigue when he heard Lachlan's breezy, 'Bro, how's it going?'

'Mum's crook again. I took her to A&E and they've admitted her.'

'You're back in the Hill? How long since?'

'Nearly a month, and you'd know that if you ever returned my calls.'

'What do you think I'm doing now? And what about Mum ringing me for a change?'

Nick leaned on the side of the ute, closed his eyes and pushed the heel of his hand into one eye and then the other. This is how it always was between them; each managed to push the other's buttons.

'She lives in her car, Lachlan. She doesn't have a phone. And the only slot she ever puts money in is a poker machine.'

'What happened to the flat?'

'She didn't pay her phone or electricity bills, so they cut them off; she didn't pay the rent, so the landlord threw her out.'

'No shit?'

'Yeah, no shit.'

'What are you gonna do?' Lachlan said after a prolonged pause.

Gripping the phone until his knuckles went white, Nick said through gritted teeth, 'What am *I* going to do? Don't you mean, what are *we* going to do? She's your mother as well as mine.'

'Shit, man, I'm in Darwin. I can't drop everything. And I'm not exactly rolling in it. You wouldn't be able to ring me back though, would ya? I'm on a prepaid.'

Yeah, Nick knew what he meant. Lachlan was always broke. At least he wasn't in jail. They disconnected and Nick rang him back.

'If you want me to come home, you or Mum will have to send me some dollars,' he said the second he picked up.

'I doubt Mum has any dollars to send you, and guess what? Neither do I.'

'Bullshit! What happened to your job?' Lachlan sounded stunned and Nick couldn't hold back a smirk.

'I quit. My wife will soon be my ex-wife, and the house in Sydney is on the market.'

'Jesus, Nick! Have you turned into some kind of shit magnet, or what?'

'Or what. And you need to get in touch with Mum. Call her at the hospital. She's really sick this time.'

'Yeah, no worries ... I can do that,' Lachlan said.

Nick confirmed he'd let Lachlan know if Marlene's condition deteriorated, and then he terminated the conversation with a curt 'Ring her tonight.'

Lachlan had been fourteen when their father had died. Nick had been in Sydney working two menial jobs to put himself through a nursing degree at university.

In the aftermath of his father's sudden death, Nick had deferred uni for a year and returned to Broken Hill to try to keep his mother and brother out of trouble. And he'd worked two jobs there, too, because Lachlan was still at school and his mother could barely hold down one job.

Work, it was all he'd ever done, and look where it'd gotten him. Lachlan had always been a bludger, and look where that had gotten *him*—no cares, no responsibilities and seeing Australia.

Nick's jaw began to ache from gritting his teeth. He swore, rammed the ute into gear and drove out to where his mother's car was parked. He needed to do something with the vehicle before night fell.

15

'If that dog next door barks and wakes me up tonight, I'll strangle the little bastard,' Tim said, yawning. He walked alongside Anna as they crossed the tarmac to the hangar.

'You'll have to get in line behind Beth and Albert. The cat loathes the dog.'

'I'm with the cat.'

Tim had stayed over with Beth every night since the dinner party. Anna liked Tim but wasn't sure that that stretched to sharing her home with him. And Beth's house wasn't large, the walls thin.

'You know what, Anna?' Tim said, slinging an arm across her shoulders as they reached the emergency entrance. 'You don't have to disappear into your room because I'm there.'

They paused on the threshold, waiting while the electronic doors opened. The practice nurse had been ahead of them, pushing the trolley stacked with the drug and immunisation boxes, the bush clinic and emergency bags, and other miscellaneous equipment. The clinic runs were long days.

Anna flicked Tim a sideways glance. She *had* been spending more time in her room. She'd sat in the library with her laptop yesterday afternoon because Tim had been at Beth's.

'I didn't think you'd want me cramping your style.'

Tim pulled her against him in a one-armed hug as they walked through the double doors together. 'You aren't. I'm a big boy. Ask Beth,' he said, and winked.

Anna elbowed him in the side and he dropped his arm.

'Truthfully,' he said, 'it's more about me not cramping your style. You live there. If you feel uncomfortable with our displays of affection or—'

'Seriously?' she said.

'Thought I'd put it out there,' Tim said.

Anna returned the aircraft keys to the lock box. The refueller and the engineers were already doing what they needed to do with the aircraft.

Tim dumped his bag onto the desk and stripped off his high-vis vest, throwing it over the closest chair. 'What shall I pick up for dinner?' he said. 'I promised Beth I'd cook.'

'You choose,' Anna said. 'I'll see you later.'

Tim lifted his arm in half a wave, his attention already elsewhere. Anna made her way to the pilots' room to finish off before she went home.

Kyle Peterson, the chief pilot, was coming out of the room, keys in hand, ready to lock the door. When he saw Anna he pocketed the keys and pushed the door wide.

'How'd you go?' he said.

'Pretty good, considering we were late taking off—one of the landing lights was faulty and had to be fixed. And a bit of dust blew up this arvo … Nothing serious.'

Kyle grunted. His communication style was to the point and always work-related, without humour. And although she suspected he hadn't worked with many, or any, female pilots, to date he'd always been fair and consistent in his dealings with her.

'Kyle, do you want to go for a drink?' she blurted. She'd been chewing over what Tim had said about her saying no to social invitations. Surely talking shop with her boss over a beer could be classed as socialising.

Kyle's broad, ruddy features flinched. Anna couldn't tell if he was intrigued, or horrified. She wished the floor would open up and swallow her. Kyle cleared his throat.

'I mean, I thought you might want to have a quick drink ... To debrief. On your way home to your wife and children ...'

He stared at her and nodded slowly, as if to say, *Yeah, I knew that's what you meant.*

'Look, forget I suggested it, okay?' She sidled past him into the pilots' room. 'Good night, Kyle,' she said, shutting the door firmly.

Anna leaned against the door and counted to ten. She took a peek through the narrow pane of glass. He'd gone. Thank God.

Her mobile phone vibrated in her pocket. She whisked it out but didn't recognise the caller ID.

'Hello?'

'Anna?'

'Who is this?'

'It's Nick. You sound kind of weird.'

She scanned the caller ID again then pressed the phone back to her ear. 'I didn't recognise the number—'

'I'm on a mate's phone.'

'—and a few minutes ago I asked Kyle out for a quick drink on the way home and I thought he might have changed his mind and was ringing me back.'

'You what?'

'Well, everyone's telling me I have no social life, so I asked Kyle—'

'Kyle Peterson, your *colleague* Kyle Peterson?'

'Yes, and why are you laughing?'

'I'm not laughing … What did he say?'

'Nothing. He was too shocked. I think he thought I was making a pass at him, and here I was trying to be sociable. You are laughing!'

'Not laughing, just smiling. I would love to have seen his face. Are you still at the base?'

'I am. Why?'

'I need a favour. Could you please pick me up? I'll tell you all about it when you get here.' He rattled off directions to a place out past the golf course.

'Okay. I'll be about fifteen minutes.'

'Sweet. I'll be waiting on the side of the road.'

Nick was pacing up and down on the side of the dirt road, his hands shoved into his pockets. Even in the low light of evening Anna could see he was coiled tighter than a spring. There were no lights on in the tumbledown house and associated sheds behind him.

'Thanks,' he said, sliding into the passenger seat and dragging the seat belt over his shoulder.

'Where to?'

'Danny's place, if you don't mind. Back out onto the main drag and I'll direct you from there.'

Nick leaned back in the seat and closed his eyes. 'Mum's in hospital with a chest infection and flare-up of her emphysema. I found her in a bad way yesterday lunchtime and took her to A&E.'

'Oh, no! Will she be all right?'

'She'll recover soon enough. This isn't the first time, and it won't be the last, but each time her recovery isn't as complete as the time before. She won't give up the smokes and they're killing her.'

'So what are you doing out here?'

'I dropped off her car at Snake's place. He's letting me store it in one of his sheds.'

'Snake?'

'Another mate. Can't remember his real name.' Nick scratched his head. 'Not sure if I've ever known.'

'How's Marlene now?'

'Marginally better, but not that good, because she hasn't started demanding cigarettes yet.'

'Is there anything I can do?'

He shook his head. His directions were succinct and ten minutes later she pulled up on the street beside a depressing block of units.

'Thanks for the lift,' he said, unbuckling his seat belt. Opening the door he paused, one foot in and one foot out of the car. Anna heard him sigh.

'I won't ask you in because Danny'll most likely be on his fourth or fifth beer by now, and he's not a happy drunk.'

A black cat slunk across the road. Impaled by the beam of the headlights it stopped and stared, before flicking its tail and disappearing into the night.

'Do you want to go for a drink?' she said.

Anna saw a flash of white when Nick grinned. 'Aw, I dunno,' he drawled, some of his tension easing. 'Knowing you're only asking me because Kyle knocked you back makes me feel kind of second-best.'

Anna flicked him on the arm. 'I only asked him because I don't like drinking on my own and I didn't want to go home yet.'

'Tim's there?'

'He's practically moved in. It's Beth's house and I want to give them space.'

'Have you eaten?'

Anna shook her head.

'Tell you what, I've spent the day cleaning and detailing Mum's car so I'm not exactly dressed to go out, but we could grab some takeaway.'

'Are you sure? All those kilojoules and saturated fats?'

'Bring it on,' he growled. He swung his foot back in, closed the car door and refastened his seatbelt.

Anna put the car in gear and drove off feeling lighter and happier than she had in days.

They parked at one of the town's lookouts and carried their paper-wrapped food to a picnic table. The place was deserted, and the solitary streetlight was just bright enough for them to see what they were eating.

'Do you always have a hamburger with the lot?' she said as Nick unwrapped his package.

'I do. I tell myself I'm getting at least one of the five serves of vegetables I'm supposed to eat every day. And it's not deep-fried.'

Anna contemplated her meal. 'Mine's all deep-fried. Do you want some chips? There's more than I can eat.'

Nick pushed his paper wrapping over and she loaded it with chips.

'At least I don't drink that sugary shit,' she said, eyeing Nick's can of Coke.

He opened the drink and took a long pull. 'You're right. It's sugary shit.'

'It must have been hard,' Anna said a while later, wiping her mouth on a tissue.

'What must have been hard?' Nick said, picking at the last of the chips.

'Having to give up your house, and then come here and camp on someone's sofa.'

'It was unbelievably hard. The place was your typical "renovator's dream" and even though the bank owned more of it than we did, I had plans for it.' Nick screwed up the paper and put it in the bag with Anna's. 'And it's weird not having a permanent address. Everything you do, people want to know where you live. I've ended up renting a post-office box while I'm here, so at least I can give an address.'

'What does your mum do about an address?'

'Her friend Rhonda lets Mum use her address, bless her heart. Mum collects mail every couple of weeks.' Nick drained the Coke and crunched up the can. 'Rhonda's older than Mum and she isn't that well and her family are pushing her to go into care.'

'You know, the importance of an address isn't something you'd ordinarily give much thought.'

'Of course you wouldn't. Why would you?'

'You'd be surprised, Nick.'

He leaned towards her, reaching across the cement-topped table, capturing one of her hands in both of his. 'So surprise me, Anna.'

Anna swallowed, hard. He would be more than surprised if she told him she'd lived in her car for a while, and that she had a fifteen-year-old daughter.

'You're married, Nick,' she said, trying to pull her hand out of his warm, strong grip. He wouldn't let go.

'We're separated, Anna.'

'Yeah, but what if you decide you want your wife and your address back? That you don't want to settle for a mate's couch and a post-office box?'

Nick's mouth hardened and he let go of her hand. Anna flexed her fingers, immediately missing the contact. He stood up and grabbed their bag of rubbish. If she could see his eyes now, Anna knew they'd be a thundery grey.

'It's been a long day,' he said, and traipsed across to the rubbish bin.

Anna picked up her unfinished bottle of water and swung away from the picnic table. Nick was standing by the bin, looking out at the city lights below them.

Anna wanted to walk over and stand beside him, link her fingers with his. Tell him about Izzy. Tell him how attracted she was to him, and that yes, she would like to be his friend and see where it took them. But she didn't.

'Maybe Marlene could use your post-office box,' she said when he was back in earshot. 'You know, if her friend Rhonda goes into care.'

'Yeah, maybe,' Nick said with little conviction.

They drove back to Danny's place and Nick didn't hang about. 'Thanks. Be seeing you,' was all he said.

With a sharp sense of loss Anna watched him walk away. Moments later a door slammed on the end unit, and the front light went out.

16

Anna was overwhelmed with relief when she arrived home to an empty house. Tim's car was parked on the street but Beth's ute was gone.

Checking her phone she discovered Beth had sent a text: they were going to the pub to eat, and come along if she felt like it.

Standing in the blissfully quiet kitchen, pondering whether to make tea or settle for a glass of milk, Anna started when manic barking erupted next door. Within seconds the cat flap clattered and Albert shot in, ears flat, tail slashing from side to side.

'What's up, mate? That Hercules giving you trouble again?'

Albert regrouped, strolling over, arching against her leg.

'Don't worry, I'm here, and there's that big ol' fence between you and him,' Anna soothed, bending down to swipe her hand along the cat's satiny back. She filled his dry food bowl and topped up the water.

The salt on the fish and chips had given her a killer thirst. Nick was right, she needed to make healthier food choices.

To stop herself thinking about Nick and the confusion that came with it, Anna booted up her laptop to FaceTime Izzy. More and more it felt like the two lives she was straddling were rapidly diverging. Talking to her daughter would be a reality check. She needed to remind herself she was a parent first and foremost.

Izzy didn't answer, or respond to Anna's text message. After a minute's hesitation, Anna trawled through her daughter's social media sites. Lots of chatter about exam week, and thankfully no more photos of Damien. Along with relief came remorse. Prying into Izzy's world always made Anna feel a bit sick in the stomach. She *was* trying to trust her.

Aware she wouldn't have the house to herself much longer, Anna rushed through a shower, irritated to find Tim's shaving gear and toiletries crammed into her side of the bathroom cabinet. His track pants had been draped over the edge of the bath. To make room for his, her towel had been scrunched up at the end of the rail. It was damp and musty from her shower that morning.

Annoyed, she hung her towel in her bedroom. But if she didn't want to start looking for somewhere else to live she'd have to suck it up. And see who lasted the longest—her or Tim.

Anna didn't cross paths with her housemate until after a swim the following morning. It was Friday. Anna was rostered on a day shift and there was no requirement to be at the base unless called out to fly, or if there were pilot checks or training to do.

Last time she'd looked there hadn't been any booked hospital transfers. But that could have changed overnight.

'Where's Tim?' she asked Beth.

Beth was still in her nightie. She had serious bed hair and eyes puffy from sleep. 'He went home to his place,' she said, yawning while she filled the electric kettle. 'What happened to you last night? I thought you'd meet us at the pub.'

'We got back later than usual from the clinic run. I had a few things to do out at the base and then decided on an early night.'

Beth regarded Anna thoughtfully. 'An early night, huh?'

'Yes! I was tired.' Telltale heat crept into Anna's cheeks. Damn it. To avoid looking at Beth, she fossicked in the cupboards for a bowl and the box of breakfast cereal, and then remembered there wasn't any milk.

'You don't have to explain to me, girl. Nick is *hot*.'

'What's he got to do with anything?'

Beth spooned coffee grounds into a single-serve plunger while she waited for the kettle to boil. 'He's gorgeous. If you had any brains at all you'd go out with him.'

'He's a colleague and he's married.'

'Colleague?' Beth snorted. 'Trust me, that marriage is history.' Beth cast Anna a calculating look. 'There's nothing stopping you.'

'Not going to happen,' Anna said, trying not to sound as if she needed to convince herself first.

Beth's gaze shifted to the box of cereal Anna was returning to the pantry. 'There's milk,' she said. 'I bought it last night. You know that cereal has practically no nutritional value, and it's full of sugar and salt.'

'Oh for goodness sake, not you picking on what I eat as well,' Anna said, and filled the bowl to the brim.

'Who else's been picking on what you eat?'

Anna ignored the question. Beth made herself wholegrain toast, filled a mug with coffee and then said, 'I'm going back to bed.'

Anna was rinsing her cereal bowl when a call from Glenda, the flight nurse on duty, came through. They had a P2 to a station property east of Broken Hill. Ninety minutes max until taxi for take-off.

'I've never flown into Daisy Hill station before. Have you?' Glenda said.

'No, I don't think I have. I'll check it out. See you at the base.'

She gulped down her coffee, and then bolted for the bathroom.

That morning, Anna needed every one of those ninety minutes to prepare. Her car didn't start the first time, giving her a scare. She'd had the leaking tyre repaired but there was no spare money to fix the car if something went seriously wrong.

The internet was down at the base, so her flight plan had to be phoned through to air services, and she used her mobile to pull up NOTAMS.

And the flight nurse discovered that the stretcher loader wouldn't work and the oxygen tanks hadn't been recharged. They really pushed it to be in the air on time.

As luck would have it, the day didn't improve. Anna was on the base leg of her approach into Daisy Hill when she zeroed in on several cattle meandering along the dirt strip.

She pulled up the aircraft and went around while the station manager cleared the strip.

When they landed the wind was whipping up the dust. Anna took an extra few minutes to secure the aircraft. By then Glenda was really grumpy.

Their patient was the station manager's mother, holidaying with her son and daughter-in-law. Anna gathered from what she overheard that the unfortunate woman had fallen, and the signs and symptoms strongly indicated a fractured left hip.

'Muggins me,' the patient said. 'Slipping in that damned shower the day I'm going home.'

She was a large, solid woman, with short, spiky grey hair. Although she tried to help them every way she could, even after Glenda had given her pain relief, moving her onto the vacuum mattress and the stretcher was difficult.

By the time they'd strapped her on she was as white as a sheet, and sweat was glistening on her forehead.

Glenda whispered to Anna, 'I hope that engineer fixed the stretcher loader properly.'

'I'm sure he did,' Anna said. 'And if not there're plenty of strong blokes here who can help us lift.'

Glenda didn't look convinced as she went about hoisting the last of her gear onto the back of the 4WD ute alongside the patient.

The ride out to the airstrip on the station ute tray would have been slow, bumpy and uncomfortable for the patient. Anna didn't envy Glenda either, crouched beside her in the heat and the flies.

Two lean, rust-coloured cattle dogs kept up with them the whole way, loping along beside the vehicle.

'This ute goes nowhere without 'em,' the station manager said. 'If they can't ride on it or in it, they follow it.'

The stretcher loader didn't fail and they were airborne thirty-five minutes later, redirected to Dubbo Base Hospital. They rarely flew into Dubbo and Anna had filed a revised flight plan while she waited for Glenda to stabilise the patient at the homestead.

Daisy Hill station was roughly halfway between Broken Hill and Dubbo. But if they flew the patient to Broken Hill they'd be flying her on to Adelaide later. There was an orthopaedic surgeon in Dubbo, and none in Broken Hill.

Dubbo was a busy regional airport with daily services to Sydney, Brisbane and Melbourne. Such a contrast to the single dirt strip at Daisy Hill, Anna thought, waiting for clearance from traffic control to begin their descent.

At the airport, while Glenda handed over the patient to the ambulance crew and the aircraft was refuelled, Anna filed their return flight plan. When she powered up her personal mobile phone, she was dismayed to discover four missed calls—all from Teresa.

The first two calls had been before they'd even taken off from Broken Hill. Caught up with the pre-flight dramas, checking her personal phone hadn't entered her head. Anna silently berated herself. Teresa would only call during the day if it was urgent.

Izzy. Something must have happened to Izzy. Palms clammy, she hit Teresa's number, beyond frustrated when it went to voicemail. Izzy's number did the same.

Her insides in a knot, Anna kept trying until they were ready to taxi. Before she switched off her mobile phone she sent both Teresa and Izzy a text message saying where she was and her ETA in Broken Hill.

The aircraft seemed to stand still. The hour-and-a-half return to Broken Hill was the longest flight she'd ever experienced. When her attention wasn't focused on getting them safely up in the air and then back down again, Anna was conjuring up worst-case scenarios. One minute she was castigating herself for not being there for Izzy, and the next she was telling herself to get a grip, that speculating was futile.

It might not be about Izzy. It could be nothing.

'Are you okay?' Glenda said after they'd landed and were unloading the equipment.

Anna dug her phone out of her pocket for the umpteenth time since landing: still nothing from Teresa or Izzy. 'I had a heap of missed calls from home. Now no-one's returning my calls.' She slid the phone back into her pocket. 'I worry,' she said.

'I'd worry too. You go. I can finish here.'

'Thanks, but we're almost done.'

Walking to the pilots' room twenty minutes later Anna was relieved to see that Teresa had finally messaged.

I'll ring u in 10.

Anna was perched on the edge of the chair filling in her logbook when Kyle Peterson walked in. He looked cheerful. A squeamish feeling settled on top of the anxiety already in situ. She'd hoped not to see Kyle until they'd both forgotten her impulsive invitation to meet for a drink.

'How'd you go?'

'It's a long haul to Dubbo and back.'

Kyle sat down, the chair creaking in protest. He regarded her for several long seconds. Oh, no, she thought, he was going to take her up on her offer.

Her relief was profound when all he said was, 'That it is,' and nodded his head slowly.

Anna's phone vibrated against her thigh and she threw up a heartfelt prayer of thanks. Digging the phone out she glanced at the screen, expecting it to be Teresa. It was.

'Sorry Kyle, but I need to take this.'

'Go,' he said with a flick of his wrist. And was that amusement on his face? Surely not.

The moment she was out of earshot she took the call. 'What's up?'

'It's Izzy,' Teresa said, confirming Anna's worst fears. 'She's been rushed to hospital.'

Anna's heart felt like it stopped, right before it began to race.

17

'Is she all right? What happened? How bad is it?' Anna shoved open the back door of the hangar. The late afternoon heat hit her like a physical force. Blood pounding in her head, she strode across the carpark towards her car.

'Anna? Are you still there?'

'Yes, of course I'm still here. Is she okay? Please tell me what happened.' She unlocked the car, threw her satchel across onto the passenger's seat and fell into the driver's seat. Her hands were trembling.

'She's had an emergency appendicectomy,' Teresa said, her voice thick with fatigue.

Anna pushed her head against the backrest and closed her eyes, loosening the grip she had on the phone. It was unbelievably hot in the car, even with the door open, and the steering wheel burned her fingertips. 'Go on.'

'Apparently, she'd had abdominal pain for a couple of days, and thought it was her period coming. Then early this morning, the school nurse rang saying she'd been vomiting and had a temperature.'

'Why didn't you go get her, take her to the doctor?'

'They have a GP they call in. I went to the school as soon as they rang me.'

'Why didn't they ring *me?*' Angry tears burned her eyes.

'Anna, I'm the emergency contact for the school, remember? We agreed to that, given you're there and I'm here.'

Yes, they'd had that discussion and it was their decision, but that didn't lessen the helplessness she felt not being there when her daughter needed her.

'The doctor diagnosed acute appendicitis, and then everything happened so fast … They called the ambulance and she was in hospital and being prepped for surgery. As soon as I knew what was happening, I rang you. When you didn't answer, I called your housemate—'

'You rang Beth?'

'You weren't answering! What was I supposed to do? I told her it was urgent. I'd looked at your roster and knew you were on day duty. You could have been anywhere. I thought Beth might have a clue. She rang the base and they said you were flying.'

'Where's Izzy now? Can I speak to her?' Anna would think about Beth later.

'Yes, she's right here—groggy, but she wants to say hello.'

Anna held her breath.

'Mum?'

'Izzy—' Anna hiccoughed, choking back a sob.

'Mum, please don't cry. I'm okay. A bit sore, but I'm okay. I have a drip, and I'm only allowed to suck ice until tonight.'

'I'm sorry I wasn't there for you, Izzy. Will you please forgive me?'

'Jeez, Mum, you were out there saving lives. Aunt Tee was here, and Zoe, the school nurse, was fantastic,' Izzy said, her words beginning to slur.

'I love you, sweetie. You just rest and get better. Put your Aunt Tee back on.'

'She's fine now, pretty sleepy,' Teresa said. 'And if you need to come home and see for yourself, I can pick you up at the airport, anytime.'

Anna blew out a pent-up breath. 'I'll drive. I'll go home, pack a bag. If I leave soon I can be there before midnight—'

'Are you crazy? You've worked all day. And what about the kangaroos?'

'They'll have to find someone to cover me tomorrow. Then I'm off for two days and I'll drive back Monday,' Anna said, as if Teresa hadn't spoken. The idea of a six-hour drive was daunting. The car needed a service and Teresa was right about kangaroos, but—

'Anna, stop and listen. Be sensible—fly down in the morning. If it's about the money, I can lend you the fare.'

'It's not about the money,' she said, sharper than she intended.

Anna pressed her fingertips firmly against her lips, forcing back another surge of tears. 'I didn't mean to sound ungrateful. You've always been so generous.'

'I know you're not ungrateful, Anna. I know what it's like to be a mother and feel totally helpless. But you know I love Izzy and I look out for her as if she was mine.'

After making arrangements for the following morning, they said goodbye and disconnected. Anna sat for a moment collecting her thoughts and composing the conversation that she'd have to have with Kyle. Although she could walk back into the hangar and speak to him face-to-face, a phone call was far more appealing.

'I'm sorry,' she said after she'd explained that she needed to take a day of urgent personal leave. 'I'll be back for work on Tuesday.'

Kyle could hardly refuse. Anna hadn't had a day's leave since she'd started, usually being the one who filled in for others.

She started the car, turning the air conditioning to high while she booked her return flight. On the drive to Beth's she rehearsed what she'd tell her.

Beth wasn't home. When she came in much later, Anna was perched cross-legged on her bed balancing her laptop. She'd been going through her expenses. After paying off the debt for her flight training, she'd been saving for the deposit on a house. The balance was steadily growing, but nowhere near as quickly as house prices. Private schools were expensive. But thank God she'd hung on to their private health insurance, even though it cost a small fortune.

'Did your sister catch up with you?' Beth said from the bedroom doorway.

Anna looked up from the screen. 'Yeah, she did. Thanks.'

Beth put down the bag of groceries and waited expectantly. Anna closed the computer and put it to one side, swinging her legs off the bed.

'I have to make a quick trip to Adelaide tomorrow. I'll be back late Monday afternoon.'

Beth raised her eyebrows, obviously waiting for more information. Anna sat on the edge of the bed and for a heartbeat she was tempted to spill everything to her housemate. Sharing with someone else would be cathartic. But the urge to confide passed. She would deal with this.

'Some family stuff I need to sort out,' she said.

'I see.' Beth didn't push for more information. 'Do you need a ride to the airport in the morning?'

'No, thanks. I'll leave my car in the RFDS staff carpark. It'll be secure there.'

'Okay. You've obviously thought it all through.' Beth nodded, picking up the bag of groceries. 'What shall we have for dinner?'

Anna trailed Beth through to the kitchen, food the last thing on her mind. 'Is Tim coming over?'

'No.'

Anna frowned. 'Trouble in paradise?'

'No! He's working. And I needed a couple of uninterrupted nights of sleep.'

Anna held up her hands. 'Please, that's enough information.'

'You are such a prude.'

Anna's hands dropped to her sides. 'Do you think so?'

Unpacking the groceries, Beth paused. 'You are a bit,' she said. 'But not in a priggish way. More an innocent or naive sort of a way.'

'Right. Should I be offended or something?'

'Anna,' Beth said, pausing at her task. 'Have you ever had a significant long-term relationship?'

Anna stiffened. 'How is that any of your business?'

Beth huffed with exasperation. 'It probably isn't. You've never mentioned anyone special and most healthy, well-adjusted people our age have relationship experience and/or baggage.'

Anna crossed her arms, tightly. Beth's inquisition on top of everything else that had happened that day was too much.

'Help me out here,' Anna said, around the clog of tears burning her throat. 'Do I poke my nose into your business? No, I don't, so why are you so interested in mine?'

Beth sighed and threw her hands in the air. 'Because I like you, I admire and respect you. You've made a success of a career in a predominantly male profession. But sometimes I could shake you. Like now. I can see that you're hurting, and something's not right. I want to help and you won't tell me anything.'

Like a wrecking ball Beth's words broke the dam wall and Anna's tears let go. Beth reached around to the box of tissues on the breakfast bar and handed her a wad. Anna could have hugged Beth for not trying to hug her.

She blew her nose and said, 'I have a daughter, Isabelle—she's fifteen. She's at boarding school in Adelaide.'

Beth's jaw dropped.

Anna rolled her lips together in an attempt to hold back more tears. Now she'd started unloading there was more that needed to be said.

'She was sick in the night and this morning she had an emergency appendicectomy. When my sister couldn't get me, she rang you. Right now I feel like a complete failure as a mother, because I should be there, not here.'

'How is she now?'

'Sore. I spoke briefly to the surgeon earlier and he said the appendix didn't rupture and that she'll recover quickly.'

'And, if you don't mind me asking, where was her father through all this?' Beth said with her usual forthrightness.

'He's not in the picture.'

'What, not now or not ever?'

Trust Beth to cut straight to the heart of things. Anna reached for more tissues. 'Not ever,' she said.

'Bloody hell, Anna.' Beth sank back against the cupboard. 'That came totally out of left field.'

Anna blotted her eyes. 'I miss Izzy like you wouldn't believe.'

'I'm trying to get my head around you having a teenage daughter. I was convinced you had a bloke, and the long-distance relationship stuff wasn't working.'

'No, nothing at all like that.'

'Phew! A daughter. This calls for a glass of wine,' Beth said, and being closest to the fridge Anna reached in and passed her the open bottle of riesling. 'Sure you don't want one?'

Anna shook her head. Beth filled a wineglass to the brim. 'Well, come and sit down. You know I'll help out any way I can. You only need to ask. And of course I have more questions.'

'Mmm, thanks, I thought you would. Doesn't mean I'll answer them.'

'You must have been pretty young,' Beth said when they were settled, on opposite sides of the dining table.

'I was seventeen when I got pregnant, but I'd turned eighteen when I had Izzy. I was young, but not as young as some.'

'You didn't ever think of a termination?'

'Nope, although my parents, especially Mum, were keen for that. In the end, Teresa turned out to be all I could have ever wanted in an older sister. She had her own children, a difficult marriage, and then I landed on her doorstep pregnant and straight out of school.'

'Has your daughter ever asked about her dad?'

Anna leaned back, lifted her arms above her head and stretched. She felt as if she'd been run over by a truck. With a sigh she dropped her elbows to the table, resting her chin in her hands.

'Yes, she has asked. And I've never lied to her. She knows he didn't want to play a part in her life. Early on I made the decision that I'd tell her everything when she's old enough. What she does with the information will be up to her, but I've had no contact with him since, and haven't a clue, or a care where he is.'

The cat flap clunked and Albert strutted in. When he didn't receive the attention he was after, he wandered over to his dry food and hunkered down.

'One more question, and then I'll leave you alone,' Beth said. Her wineglass was empty and she was picking at the label on the bottle, slowly shredding it. 'Why didn't you tell me you had a daughter at boarding school when you first moved in? She could have come and stayed. Can I tell Tim?'

'That's two questions.'

'Ha ha,' Beth said.

'Truthfully? I wasn't looking to make friends. I was only looking for a place to be when I wasn't at work, but you have this way about you, Beth. You're an unstoppable force.'

'Yep, I've been told that before, and not always as nicely.'

'As for your second question? Do you mind if I think about that? Regardless of today's so-called enlightened society, people are quick to judge.'

Beth pushed back her chair and stood up. She scooped up the wineglass and the near-empty bottle. 'Anna, people know you for the competent, professional person you are, but I won't tell Tim if you're not ready for me to.'

Anna felt as if unwittingly, a load had been lifted off her shoulders. True, a load she'd put there herself. But no matter what her housemate said, there was no need to share her other life with all and sundry. Especially since she hadn't even told Nick.

18

Teresa was waiting for Anna in the Adelaide airport arrivals. The sisters hugged, quick and fierce.

'I can't wait to see Izzy. Is she really okay?'

'Yes, she is. I thought you'd want to go straight to the hospital.'

Anna nodded. With no wait for luggage, they were on the road in minutes.

Settling into the leather upholstery, Anna leaned her head back and closed her eyes. 'Thanks,' she said.

'For what?'

'For everything.'

'You look tired,' Teresa said, giving her sister a brief sideways appraisal.

'Not much sleep. I told Beth about Izzy. She was gobsmacked, convinced I was having hot phone sex in my room when really I'd be FaceTiming you and Izzy.'

Teresa looked incredulous. Changing lanes without indicating, a horn blared and she glanced in the rear-view mirror. 'Up yours too, mate,' she said.

Used to her sister's driving, Anna didn't so much as crack open an eyelid.

'You know, while I was lying awake at two am I got to thinking how much you've done for Izzy and me. Right from when I lobbed on your doorstep, you've always been there for me, no questions asked.'

'You're my sister. You were in trouble. I have always loved you, and I love Izzy.'

Opening her eyes, Anna sat up straighter and watched the mid-morning traffic. For Teresa, everything was black or white. And so it had been for Anna until recently. In her job and her life her purpose had been clear and simple: be a good mother and a safe and reliable pilot.

The move to Broken Hill, leaving Izzy behind, sharing a house with Beth, meeting Nick—and suddenly her life's purpose wasn't as clear or as simple.

'Enough about me,' Anna said. 'Tell me what you've been doing.' She studied Teresa's profile as she concentrated on the traffic. 'Somehow you look different. I know, you've had your hair streaked. And you've lost weight.'

'I have, nearly five kilos.'

'Wow. It wouldn't be anything to do with that *friend* you had dinner with the weekend before last, would it?'

'No, Anna, it wouldn't. My hair is going grey and my GP told me if I didn't lose a few kilos I'd need to go on blood pressure medication.'

'Is your blood pressure okay now?'

'Yes,' Teresa said, curtly.

Got it, Anna thought. There's more to this friend business, but big sister isn't ready to share.

They found a park and then walked along the tree-lined footpath to the private hospital.

'You go on,' Teresa said when they reached the main entrance. 'I need to make calls, and then I'll follow you up.'

'All right. And thanks,' Anna said, knowing Teresa was giving her time to be on her own with Izzy.

A nurse directed Anna to a private room, the door wide open. Izzy was propped up in bed, eyes closed, earbuds in her ears. Pausing on the threshold, Anna experienced a suffocating surge of emotions. Love. Relief. Regret. Her daughter was whole and beautiful, and she wasn't a little girl anymore. Izzy's eyes opened.

'Mum!' she cried, plucking the earbuds out of her ears.

Anna flew across the room, dropping her shoulder bag and folding her arms around her daughter. She drew in Izzy's familiar smell: strawberry-scented shampoo and the body moisturiser she loved, overlaid with the unfamiliar smell of antiseptic and surgical dressings.

Anna wiggled her bottom onto the edge of the bed, fingers linked with Izzy's. 'When did they take out the drip?'

'This morning, after I had some apple juice.'

'Do you feel hungry?'

'Not really but the nurse said I could have something light for lunch. Where's Aunt Tee?'

'Making phone calls. Is there anything you want me to do? Have you had a wash, or a shower?' Anna began rummaging through the bedside cupboard drawers. 'Do you need more T-shirts and knickers?'

'Mum, please don't fuss. Because my appendix didn't rupture, the doctor said I can probably go home tomorrow. If I don't have a temperature or anything.'

Anna's hands stilled and she stared at Izzy. Since when did she fuss?

Teresa tapped on the door and came in carrying a cardboard tray with two coffees. 'I got you a soft drink, Izzy.' She put a bottle of lemonade on the bedside cupboard. 'And a strong latte for you.' She handed one of the cups to Anna and frowned. 'Did I interrupt something?'

'Mum was fussing, as per usual.'

'I don't fuss,' Anna replied firmly, closing the drawer.

'Mothers fuss, it's our job,' Teresa said.

Anna raised her eyebrows. Tina had never fussed. She'd barely shown any interest in either of her daughters.

Unbidden, an image of Marlene Harrison popped into Anna's head. Had Marlene fussed over her sons? Anna imagined that in her own way she would have.

Izzy dozed. Anna and Teresa conversed quietly over their coffee.

When they'd finished their drinks, Teresa said she had work to do. 'I'll be back later. Ring me if you need anything.'

Mother and daughter wiled away the time chatting and dozing. They shared Izzy's lunch. Mid-afternoon, Anna went for another coffee and lemonade.

On her return, walking towards her daughter's room, Anna was astonished to hear a deep masculine voice followed by what was unmistakably Izzy's giggling. Her heart bumped into a higher gear. She stepped into the doorway.

A young man with a mop of sun-bleached hair was sprawled in the chair beside the bed. Izzy, eyes wide, was hanging on his every word.

Damien. Anna recognised him from the photo online. He wore faded board shorts and a T-shirt; and he was way more attractive, and dangerous, in 3D.

'Hi, I'm back,' she said with forced brightness, coming into the room.

Damien looked her way and she was struck by a pair of piercingly blue eyes. Izzy looked guilty, but only for a moment.

'Mum, this is Damien! Isn't it wicked that he came to visit? Aunt Tee told him I was in hospital.'

He stood up. He was tall, broad-shouldered. He had thongs on his feet. It would be rude not to shake his outstretched hand. She put the drinks on the overway table and took the proffered hand.

'Nice to meet you, Mrs Kelly,' he said, and she cringed. Mrs Kelly was her mother.

'It's Anna, please,' she said, shaking his hand. His grip was warm, firm. He grinned and with mounting dread she understood exactly why Izzy had a crush on him.

'Anna it is then, and you look more like Izzy's sister than her mother.'

Anna's instant impulse was to preen at the compliment, and then slap him, scream at him to keep away from her beautiful, innocent daughter.

'That's kind of you,' she said stiffly. 'But I'm *definitely* her mother.'

Although the smile didn't budge from his lips, it seemed to dim in his eyes. He offered her his chair. Peevishly, she declined. He sat down again.

'She looks great, doesn't she, considering she only had her appendix out yesterday,' he said, beaming at Izzy.

Izzy giggled, her brown eyes wide and adoring. 'Damien's been down the coast surfing,' she said.

'Oh,' Anna acknowledged over the rim of her coffee cup.

'Yeah,' he said, leaning forward in the chair and clearing his throat. 'I work with my dad. We have a landscaping business. First days off in ages. The weather's perfect, so I hit the beach.'

'I've *always* wanted to learn how to surf,' Izzy said.

'Really? First I've heard of it.'

'Mum,' she hissed, glaring at her mother.

Anna turned and tossed the empty cup into the bin. The coffee had been lukewarm.

Damien pushed himself to his feet. 'I'd better get moving,' he said. 'See ya, kiddo.' He gave Izzy a playful punch on the arm. 'And you better get well so you can help me clean your Aunt Tee's swimming pool.'

He turned to Anna. She folded her arms. 'Bye, Damien,' she said.

'Catch ya,' he answered, but obviously thought better of hitting her with another of his audacious grins.

When he'd gone Izzy folded her arms, stuck out her bottom lip and said, 'Well, thanks for nothing, Mum. I doubt he'll be visiting me again any time soon.'

'Like I said to you on the phone, he's too old for you.'

Izzy rolled her eyes, carefully easing herself down in the bed. 'We're friends,' she said. 'What's wrong with that?' Closing her eyes she pretended to be asleep.

Anna blew out a frustrated breath, fully aware her view was a jaundiced one when it came to men and what they were after. And now Izzy looked upset as well as tired and sore.

Anna hadn't forgotten what it was like to be a teenager. Perching on the edge of the bed, she smoothed the hair back from her daughter's forehead.

'Sweetie, you'll have to trust me on this one. You're only fifteen.'

Without opening her eyes Izzy moved her head in an attempt to shake off her mother's hand. Anna took the hint and moved away. Izzy continued to feign sleep, and after about ten minutes she slept for real.

Anna couldn't take her eyes off her daughter, relaxed and peaceful in sleep. She yearned to reach out and touch her, hold her;

forever protect her from the world. Smiling at the fancifulness of that notion, she dug out her mobile phone.

There was a text from Beth. *How's it going in the big smoke? How's Izzy? Are you okay? Nick was looking for you.*

She messaged back: *Izzy home tomorrow if all's well.*

Seconds later her phone pinged again.

Told Nick you had a family emergency. Marlene still in hospital.

Ok. Thanks. See you late Monday arvo.

Later in the car on the way back to Teresa's place, when she couldn't hold it in any longer, Anna said, 'Damien came to visit Izzy.'

'Ah,' Teresa said, 'that explains why Izzy was giving you the silent treatment.'

'Why'd you tell him Izzy was unwell?'

'Me? I didn't tell him. More likely Clara did. But Damien did message me to ask if it was okay to visit Izzy.'

They travelled in silence, Anna fighting her resentment. Damien should have messaged her, she was Izzy's mother.

'How old was Miranda when she went on the Pill?' Anna blurted when they were almost home. She'd been thinking about it since she'd walked up the hospital corridor and heard Damien's honeyed baritone.

'What?' Teresa's head swung sideways. 'You're not serious?'

'I am,' Anna said, her voice firming with resolve. 'He is a man, she's still a girl. And if she insists on going behind my back—'

Teresa indicated and turned into the driveway. The garage door whirred open and when they were parked she turned to Anna.

'Don't underestimate your daughter. She is one smart little cookie.'

With the air conditioning off, the car quickly became hot and stuffy. Anna pushed open the door.

'I don't care how smart she is. He's too old for her. I would never forgive myself if she made the same mistakes I did.'

'Anna, the circumstances are so different.'

'Granted, some of the circumstances might be different. But don't forget I have firsthand experience of what a teenage girl will do when an older, more sophisticated male sets his sights on her, and she thinks she's in love.'

Teresa sighed. 'I don't know the right answer, Anna. All I know is that Miranda didn't go on the Pill. I offered, she refused. She said there was no way she was sleeping around, and when she found the right person, there'd be time then to make a decision. At the time I was blown away by her maturity. I felt guilty for even suggesting it.'

Tears welled in Anna's eyes. 'It's that trust issue again, isn't it?'

'Yep,' Teresa said. She reached over and gave Anna's arm a pat. 'Don't over-think it, Anna. They never stop surprising you. Now let's go inside before we melt. I've put clean sheets on your bed.'

Anna sniffed. Fingers crossed Teresa was right. She followed her sister inside.

19

Nick watched Anna walk into the terminal towing a cabin-sized suitcase, her expression set. He nudged Beth, standing beside him. She looked up from her phone and waved. Anna's eyes widened. Weaving around several other passengers she headed in their direction.

'Welcome back,' said Nick.

'Thanks, I think.' Anna's brow puckered and she moved her attention to Beth. 'What's with the welcoming party anyway? I've only been gone three days.'

'We missed you,' said Beth.

'Like I believe that.'

'We did!'

Passengers milled about waiting for their luggage. Beth moved off in the direction of the exit. 'Come on, Tim's meeting us at the pub,' she threw back over her shoulder.

Anna grabbed Nick's arm. 'Why are you really here?' she hissed. 'What am I missing?'

He reached for her overnight bag. She tightened her grip on the handle.

'Trust me, it wasn't my idea,' he hissed back.

Well, that wasn't a lie. Meeting Anna and going to the pub for a meal hadn't been his idea. None of what they had to tell her had been his idea. So why *was* he here? Because although the news they were going to drop on her hadn't been his idea, it was a brilliant idea. Now all he had to do was convince Anna.

'My car's in the RFDS secure park,' Anna said when they were back outside in the heat.

'We'll drop you off,' Beth said.

'I can walk. It's not far. It'll be good to stretch my legs. And I might give the pub a miss, thanks. I'm sorry to bail. It's been a long day and I'm beat.'

'I'll walk with you,' Nick said and reached again for her overnight bag. She swung it into her other hand, away from him.

'I can manage,' she said through gritted teeth.

'See you at the pub. I'll order your usual,' Beth said, seemingly oblivious to the tussle going on between Nick and Anna. She waved and kept walking towards her car.

Nick's jaw tightened. The smart thing would be to follow Beth, let Anna go home on her own. Anna took off. And what did he do? Fall into step beside her.

'Go with Beth,' she said.

'I have a sneaking suspicion we won't see you at the pub if I do.'

'And that's a problem, because?'

'Because it is,' he said, helpless to stop irritation creeping into his voice.

She increased her pace and so did he. 'Why do I get the feeling I'm being railroaded?' she said, eyes fixed on the footpath.

Nick blew out a sharp breath. 'You know how Beth is. Sometimes it's easier to do what she says.'

Anna glanced his way briefly without slowing her pace. 'Never figured you as a yes-man Nick.'

He jammed his hands into his pockets, clamped down on an angry retort. 'So,' he said instead, 'did you sort out the family emergency in Adelaide?'

'For now,' she said. 'How is your mum?'

'Still in hospital. Slowly improving. I'm trying to find respite care for her. You know, somewhere she can stay and recuperate after they discharge her from hospital.'

'What does she think of that?'

'Reckons she'll be all right in her car. Not going to happen, I tell her, and then she sulks.'

'Yeah, I can imagine.'

Was that amusement in her voice? If it was it hadn't made it to her lips when he had a quick peek.

They walked the remaining distance in silence. Underfoot, the day's heat radiated upwards. Anna's Commodore was parked under the long shadow of a straggly tree. When he opened the passenger-side door, the hot air almost took his breath away.

'This warm in Adelaide?'

'Not quite.'

They hit the road and Nick directed her to the hotel they'd lunched at the day after Beth's dinner party. The carpark was chock-a-block, Beth's shiny ute was parked next to Tim's Subaru. Anna pulled up behind their vehicles.

'Okay if I drop you off here? Doesn't look like there are any parks, anyway. I'm exhausted, and I have a full-on clinic run tomorrow.'

How could he argue with that? She was in the driver's seat. He reached for the catch on his seatbelt just as a car several parks along reversed out.

'Look, there,' he said. She groaned out loud, bouncing the heels of her hands on the steering wheel.

'Never mind, Anna. Treat it as if it was meant to happen.' She glared at him.

They walked into the noisy lounge bar. Nick searched the crowded space for Beth and Tim.

'I'm not staying long,' Anna said.

No, Nick thought. You won't stay long; not when you hear what Beth has to tell you.

Beth and Tim waved from the bar. 'Table nineteen,' Beth yelled, pointing to her right.

'Drink?'

'Lemon squash, thanks,' Anna said.

By the time Nick had made his way to the bar, Anna had found table nineteen. She did look worn out—sad and preoccupied, and as if she'd rather be elsewhere. Back home, most likely. He frowned. What had happened in Adelaide? Beth knew more than she was letting on.

The barman asked him twice what he wanted, so intent was he on watching Anna. And why did she keep checking her phone? She wasn't on call.

Beth bowled up to the table carrying two glasses of wine. Tim was on the other side of the bar where the food was ordered. Beth sat down next to Anna. The furrows in Nick's brow deepened when she gripped Anna's forearm, leaned towards her and the two fell into what appeared to be an intense conversation.

Wishing he could lip-read, Nick collected their drinks and navigated his way to the table.

Anna seemed to have lightened up a bit by the time he put the lemon squash down in front of her. Relaxed enough to smile her thanks. A tiny bit of his tension eased.

Earlier, Beth had agreed with him that they'd tell Anna together. Obviously she hadn't reneged on their agreement because Anna wouldn't be smiling at him now if she already knew.

Tim sat down, shoving his credit card into his wallet. 'My treat,' he said when Anna scrambled for her purse. 'I've eaten enough of your food lately.' No-one could argue with that. Nick handed Tim the cash for his meal.

'Put your money away, mate. It won't be long until it's your food I'll be eating as well. At least you'll be able to make sure there's beer in the fridge.' Grinning, Tim nudged Nick with his elbow.

Nick felt the blood drain out of his face. Beth's eyes widened. Anna looked perplexed. 'Are you blokes moving in together or something?' she said. 'That'll be interesting.'

'Oh, shit,' Tim said, colour suffusing his face. 'You haven't told her yet.'

'Told me what?' Anna said, visibly stiffening.

Beth pinned Nick with a meaningful glare. He ignored the silent message, giving his head a small shake. It had been Beth's idea; she could tell Anna.

'I've told Nick he can move into the spare room,' Beth said, the words rushing out on one breath.

'You've what?' Anna said to Beth before directing a death stare at Nick. He met it head on. 'On Saturday my mate told me he needs me out. He's promised to clean up his act, and his girlfriend's moving back in,' he said.

Anna turned to Beth. 'It's your house, your spare room,' she said, appearing indifferent.

Nick knew better. 'Yes, I know, but you live there too.'

Anna pursed her lips. Tim shifted in his seat.

'Anna,' he implored, leaning forward. She would not look at him. He ploughed on regardless. 'It'll only be until I sort out a few things.'

Like what I'm going to do with a homeless and invalid mother, he thought. And what my employment options are when my contract ends, and when the house in Sydney will sell and give me some financial freedom … Then there'd be the divorce.

'It's fine, there's no need to explain,' she said evenly, still not making eye contact with him. Nick wished Tim and Beth would bugger off, leave him alone with Anna so he could explain. And ask her why she was so sad.

Tim gathered up their empty glasses. 'I'll get us another round,' he said.

'Thanks, love,' Beth said, and Nick kicked her under the table, urging her to go with Tim. Instead, Anna leapt to her feet.

'I'll give you a hand,' she said and trotted off after Tim.

When they were out of earshot Nick said, 'Jeez, Beth, can't you take a hint? And what's with Tim and his big mouth? I'll find somewhere else to stay. Snake'll probably let me camp at his place.'

'Snake's a crook. Why do you think he's called Snake?'

'He's all right,' Nick said. 'We've known each other since kindergarten.'

'Whatever,' Beth said. 'It's your decision. But it's my house. It's no palace, but with us all being shift workers, and me spending time at Tim's, I think we can make it work.'

'I'm glad you think so, because I don't think Anna does.'

'Don't stress, Nick. Anna's had a lot on her mind … She'll be fine. And you said you were broke. Be grateful I have a third bedroom I'm prepared to rent for practically nothing.'

'I *am* grateful,' he said, scanning the patrons at the bar until his gaze settled on Anna. She was chatting to Tim as they waited for the drinks. He wished it was him there beside her.

A white sleeveless top showed off her slim, tanned arms; long, shapely legs stretched from the mid-thigh hem of her denim skirt. There was nothing about her he didn't like, or want.

'I'll start looking for somewhere else tomorrow,' he said.

Beth studied him, tutting and slowly shaking her head. 'You know what—' she started, but then the waitress came with the food, and Tim and Anna returned with drinks. Whatever Beth had been going to say was forgotten.

The moment Anna had cleared her plate she pleaded tiredness and stood up to leave. She already had her car keys in her hand.

'I'll come with you,' Nick said, pushing away the remains of his usual hamburger with the lot.

'No,' she said.

'My ute's parked in the driveway.'

'I'll park on the street.'

'You're tired, upset … I'll drive,' Nick said, holding out his hand for her car keys. He wanted her to give him a chance to explain. And he wanted to know what had put the shadows in her beautiful brown eyes.

'Are you serious?' she said.

'Deadly.'

'See you later,' she said to Beth. With a final glare in his direction she stalked off.

'Don't let her get away, mate,' Tim said, doing nothing to hide his amusement as Nick bolted after her.

The night was balmy with just a hint of the coolness to come. In the time it took him to exit the hotel and cross the carpark, she'd started the car, the reversing lights bright. 'Anna, wait,' he shouted, diving for the door handle. When he wrenched open the door, the interior light came on and he saw her eyes were glistening.

'Jeez, Anna, please stop the car. Let me explain.'

Pressing her fingers to her lips, he heard her ragged intake of air. She shook her head. He threw himself into the passenger seat, pulled on the handbrake and shoved the car into park.

'Anna, please turn off the engine,' he said gently but firmly, 'or I'll reach across and do it.'

'What do you want, Nick?' she said, her voice soggy with unshed tears.

'To explain,' he said.

'You have two minutes.' She folded her arms, leaving the car running.

'Anna, that's not—'

She pointedly looked at her watch.

'All right, all right ... Two minutes. Tim and I were talking on Saturday, I told him I had to get out of my mate's place, he told Beth, and you know how she is.'

Anna didn't so much as blink. 'Don't you have to find somewhere for your mother to live? Couldn't you find somewhere you both could stay? With Tim there most of the time, Beth's place is pretty crowded already.'

Nick threw up his hands, letting them drop onto his thighs. 'Until the house in Sydney sells, I'm totally broke,' he said. 'Danny's let me camp on his couch for nothing because he owed me. Beth is a mate and in the past I've helped her out heaps, and now she wants to return the favour.'

'If you're so broke, why don't you sell that flash ute and buy something cheaper. Not that it's any of my business.'

'No, it isn't any of your business,' he said, clenching his fists. 'I worked my guts out to pay for that ute. I'm not selling it. End of story.'

'We don't always get what we want, Nick.'

Nick's mouth twisted with derision. 'No shit? And what is it you want that you can't have, Anna?'

They stared at each other across the console.

'Your two minutes are up, Nick.'

He reached for the door handle. There was so much more he wanted to say. But would it change anything if he did? She was upset and preoccupied by whatever had happened in Adelaide. It hurt that she wouldn't share her worries with him.

But then why would she? His life was a shambles. He had no money, no plans, only short-term employment. Without his mates he'd be living in his car, same as his mother. Standing rigidly by, he watched while she drove away.

20

Anna went flying first thing the following morning, transferring patients to Adelaide. Guess who the flight nurse was? Nick Harrison. She couldn't believe her dumb luck.

The night before, as warned, his ute had been hogging the driveway and she had parked on the street. Something she'd have to get used to when he moved in. Her mouth went dry at the thought of him living in the same house as her.

When she'd spoken to Izzy that night, all she'd got were monosyllabic answers. Frustrated, she'd phoned Teresa, who'd assured her Izzy was comfortably back in her own bed, and not really talking to her either.

Leaving her daughter behind looking pale, unwell and uncommunicative had been one of the hardest things Anna had ever done. But she'd done it and here she was, ready to taxi. Consulting with air traffic control now, nothing could dampen her excitement as she firmed her grip on the control and slowly pushed it forward.

In Adelaide, the patient they'd been booked to bring back to Broken Hill had taken a turn for the worse and they were flying home empty. Conversation between pilot and flight nurse had been clipped, and limited to the job at hand. Although distant with her, Anna couldn't fault Nick's caring professionalism with the patients.

Then the call came in that they were to divert to Elder Creek station for a priority two. The flash of déjà vu Anna felt when they touched down on the dirt strip sent a shudder right through her.

The same station ute with the same taciturn station hand at the wheel was parked alongside waiting for them. She crossed her fingers that this visit to Elder Creek wouldn't be as fraught as the trip weeks before.

As if sensing her disquiet, on the drive into the homestead Nick gave her shoulder a gentle nudge. They were crammed into the cab of the utility, three abreast. The station hand was a lean and sinewy man of indeterminate age named Jim. He smelled of dust and days-old sweat. There was no air conditioning in the ute.

Nick leaned in close and whispered, 'Don't worry, it's a back injury. No blood and gore. All good this time.'

Goosebumps skittered across her skin, more as a result of Nick's breath against her ear than the memory of their last trip. She tilted her head as far as she could in the opposite direction. His lips twitched.

Jim drove straight past the homestead. Following a dusty, rutted track he drove for about another 500 metres, past several sheds and water tanks to a shabby shearers' quarters.

'Matt, your patient, that's his room there,' Jim said when he'd stopped the vehicle, lifting his chin towards the end door. 'Poor bugger can't move.'

'Is anyone with him?' Nick said.

'Nope. I was until I had to come and pick up youse two.'

'Where're Brett and Rachel?' Nick turned to Anna. 'Do you want Jim to take you back to the homestead?'

'Not much point,' Jim intervened. 'There's no-one there. The missus hasn't come home.' He pulled a tobacco pouch out of his shirt pocket.

'What, she hasn't come home since—'

'Nope.' Jim didn't look up from carefully constructing a smoke. 'And not likely to, by all accounts.'

'And Brett?'

'Dunno where the boss is, but I know he won't be up yonder.' His chin jutted in the direction of the homestead, and the unlit cigarette bounced on his bottom lip as he spoke.

'He made the calls about the patient so he can't be far away,' Nick said.

'That he did,' Jim said, 'but there's no telling where he is now. Me and Matt are the only station hands.'

Anna sensed Nick's growing frustration. 'It's okay,' she said. 'I can stay here. You might need a hand.'

He nodded, hoisted his pack off the back of the ute and began the trek to where his patient was waiting.

Jim unloaded the remaining gear onto the cracked cement verandah, mumbled something and then took off in the ute.

Anna searched out a shady spot under the bough of a gnarled old pepper tree. She could hear the murmur of voices—Nick's rumbling baritone and the patient's, wobbly with pain.

Nick emerged twenty minutes later, the rustic-looking screen door slapping shut behind him.

'Where is everybody?' He picked up the evac mattress from where Jim had left it on the verandah. 'Matt's not a big bloke but I'll need a hand to set this up and shift him onto it.'

'Jim said he'd be back.'

'Where the bloody hell is Brett?'

Anna stepped off the verandah and peered down the track towards the homestead. 'It might have been the wind, but I thought I heard hammering or something in one of the sheds a while ago. Do you want me to go and look for him? '

Nick came and stood beside her. She unconsciously leaned towards him.

'Yeah, you might as well,' he said. 'You go look in the sheds and I'll try and raise him on the sat phone. He might be at the homestead, no matter what Jim said. The sooner we get Matt out of here, the better.'

'You're right about that.'

'Don't spend too much time looking, and if you hear Jim's ute, come back. The three of us will be able to move him.'

'Okay,' she said and started moving, only to be pulled up short when his hand clamped on her shoulder. 'Be careful,' he said.

Her heart skipped a beat. 'Do you think there's something wrong?'

He squinted in the direction of the silent homestead. 'I dunno … My gut's telling me something's a bit off. It's probably nothing.' He squeezed her shoulder before dropping his hand to his side. 'But be careful just the same.'

Nick returned to the shearers' quarters to his patient and Anna set off towards the nearest shed, wondering what sort of careful he meant.

The galvanised iron structure was old and rusting, and padlocked up tight. Judging by the height of the dead weeds and the state of the padlock, it'd been a long time since the door had been used.

She walked the 100 metres or so to the next shed, swatting at flies and wishing she'd brought a hat. The sun was fierce. A half-hearted swirl of wind flicked up dust and rattled loose sheets of iron on the outbuildings. A lonely crow eyeballed her from its perch high in a dead tree.

She stopped, listened for the sound of Jim and the ute, or any other activity, but there was nothing except the eerie soughing of the wind through the outbuildings.

The second shed looked more promising. The doors were wide open, and regular traffic in and out had turned the red dirt to powder. It puffed up as she walked, covering her boots.

She went in, eyes adjusting to the gloom. It smelled like dust and grease and diesel, and something else she couldn't quite identify. It was stinking hot.

Workbenches lined one wall and there was an assortment of vehicles, machinery, and 44-gallon drums cluttering the remaining space. The benches were neat and looked well-used.

A disabled quad bike stood precariously on three wheels beside the boarded-over pit. Dark patches on the earthen floor told of generations of oils spills.

Anna called Brett's name several times but there was no response, just the sound of the galvanised iron creaking. Her nose tickled. By now sweat was trickling down her scalp and between her breasts.

She couldn't say what stopped her as she went to leave, but then she was turning back and going deeper into the shed. Anna's pulse thumped in her head, the beginnings of a headache, and her mouth was dry and metallic-tasting.

On an impulse she squatted down and peered under an early model Toyota LandCruiser. That was when she saw the pair of booted feet.

The rush of blood in her head was deafening.

'Brett?' she said, scrambling around the vehicle.

Shock winded her. In an instant the smell she hadn't been able to define earlier was obvious.

He was slumped against a drum, a shotgun in his lap. Anna had only met Brett once, and there wasn't enough left of the man's face to tell for sure it was him.

It took a moment for her to realise the buzzing she could hear was the blowflies. In Anna's horror and haste to get away she caught her shirt on something sharp and felt the fabric rip. All she could think about was getting outside into the fresh air.

The sunlight momentarily blinded her. Gulping in lungfuls of scorchingly hot air, she ran from the shed and didn't stop until she arrived at the shearers' quarters.

The station ute was parked beside the verandah. Voices and cursing drifted out from the building.

Nick was stepping outside to wedge open the screen door when she arrived, bending over to catch her breath beside the ute.

'Anna?' In half a dozen steps he was across the verandah, his hands gripping her arms. 'What's happened?'

She licked her lips, tried to swallow. 'He's dead,' she said, pointing back towards the sheds.

'Who?'

'Not sure, but I think it might be Brett. The smell—' Her throat felt as if it was closing over. 'I need a drink. My bag—'

Nick grabbed her shoulder bag from where she'd left it on the verandah. With trembling fingers she fumbled with the opening and pulled out a bottle of lukewarm water.

Jim came to the doorway of Matt's room. He took one look at Anna, frowned and retreated into the room.

Nick waited while she took a sip, rinsed her mouth and spat onto the ground. And then gulped down half of the water, wiping her mouth with the back of her hand.

'Okay,' he said. 'From the beginning.'

She described where she'd gone and what she'd seen. Nick swore. 'Wait here,' he said. He went inside and minutes later Anna heard

Jim curse too. Nick came out carrying the emergency pack and the satellite phone.

'Jump in,' he said to Anna. He climbed in behind the wheel of the ute. The keys were in the ignition.

Anna glanced at her watch. Barely five minutes had passed since her dash up the track. Nick reversed out in a cloud of dust. She directed him to the shed where she'd found the body.

'Don't come in,' he said, placing a restraining hand on her arm. Anna's relief was visceral. 'I'll check him out and then I'll ring the duty doctor, and he'll call the police and the coroner.'

Anna nodded, and waited. She didn't venture more than a metre from the ute, conscious of every movement and every sound. The crow had flown away.

When Nick emerged from the shed, sweat was pouring down his face and his shirt was plastered to his body. 'I'm sure it's him,' was all he said. He got in the ute and Anna drove them back to the shearers' quarters where Jim was waiting with the patient.

An hour later they were gathered on the verandah. Nick had been in contact with the doctor at the RFDS base. Jim, who was chain-smoking, had had very little to say since Nick described what Anna had found. From Nick's description of the clothes on the body, the old station hand was also convinced it was Brett.

'Jesus,' he'd said, 'I knew the bastard weren't himself, but shit ...'

Elder Creek station was south-east of Yunta, the closest settlement with a police station. But the local policeman was away, so two officers were driving from Peterborough. The doctor agreed that it wouldn't be appropriate to leave Jim on his own with the body to wait for the police.

Matt was stable, and with pain relief on board he was as comfortable as possible. Anna witnessed Jim's relief when Nick told him they'd stay until the police arrived in several hours.

While they waited for the police they moved Matt to the homestead. It was cooler and the amenities better, and there was a landline telephone in the kitchen.

'I wonder where the dog is?' Anna said after they'd carried Matt through to what appeared to be a spare room. It felt weird being in the house. No Brett. No Rachel. Anna couldn't stop herself from casting a nervous glance up the passage to the closed nursery door.

'The dog died,' Jim said, following Anna through to the kitchen. Nick stayed with Matt.

'The dog was old. I reckon he was pining for the missus. The boss took the dog's death hard. What a rotten run of luck.'

'And then some,' was all Anna could find to say. She filled the electric kettle and turned it on. 'What do you reckon'll happen to this place now?' she said, remembering where the tea was.

A chair scraped across the linoleum. Jim sat down at the kitchen table. 'Dunno. I suppose the city folk who own it'll put in a new manager.' He rolled another smoke but didn't light it, tucking it behind his ear instead.

When Anna opened the fridge the contents were sparse. There was an open carton of long-life milk. She unscrewed the lid and sniffed.

'That'd be all right,' Jim said. 'We've been having our meals and smokos here with the boss. Easier that way.'

With bread from the pantry, Anna set about making ham, cheese and pickle sandwiches, more for something to do than because she was hungry.

'You know she hated it here,' Jim said.

Anna looked up from the sandwiches.

'The missus … Rachel.'

'Oh,' Anna said, and went back to her task.

'The boss grew up on stations but she was a townie. She tried, I'll give her that, but the isolation near drove her mad.'

'Is that why she didn't come back after she lost the baby?'

Jim sat hunched over, his ropey forearms stretched on the table in front of him. 'Dunno. A man's not privy to all the goings-on in a marriage, but I wouldn't be surprised if that wasn't a part of it.'

Anna layered on the cold meat and cheese slices. 'Was he a good boss?'

'Mmm, tough, but mostly fair. Although, I reckon he changed some, about a year after they got married. A bloke never knew what sorta mood he'd be in from one day to the next. Went through one station hand after another.'

'You stayed.'

'Yeah,' he said with a phlegmy laugh. 'Nowhere else to go.'

Jim lifted a calloused finger and tapped it against the side of his nose. 'I reckon he knew the missus hated being here, but he had no idea what to do about it. Things got a bit better with a baby on the way, and then …'

'It was tragic what happened,' Anna said, stacking sandwiches onto a plate.

Jim grunted and reached for a sandwich. 'She was lonely. She wanted that baby something fierce. But he—' Jim bit into the sandwich.

'He what?'

Jim chewed thoughtfully, swallowing before he said, 'He never said much about it at all.'

Anna drank sweetened tea but couldn't face her food. Her stomach roiled at the thought. Nick came in and after taking Matt a drink, he sat down at the table and tucked into the remaining sandwiches.

For dessert, Jim found a Lion's Christmas cake in the pantry and it was the sight of the festive wrapping that nearly brought Anna completely undone.

There wouldn't be any Christmas celebrations at Elder Creek station that year.

Grief clogged her sinuses. She lurched to her feet, the chair scraping noisily. Both men looked at her.

'I think I'll go outside,' she said, and took off like the devil was after her.

She met Nick's gaze briefly in passing. She thought he might follow her out—hoped he would, hoped he wouldn't—but then the phone rang and his attention was diverted.

Anna leaned on a verandah post and closed her eyes.

They snapped open in horror. Etched into her mind's eye was the indelible image of Brett Carmichael's body slumped against the drum in the shed. She rubbed at her eyes, forcing the heels of her hands into the sockets. The gory image remained.

Sagging against the post, Anna was overwhelmed by the need to talk to her daughter.

21

'That was the police,' Nick said. Judging by the way Anna started, he realised she hadn't heard his tread on the verandah. 'They're about an hour and a half away.'

'Okay, thanks for the update.'

Hands in his pockets, he stood beside her for several minutes contemplating the homestead garden. If that's what you could call the tangle of mostly dead things.

Anna had a shoulder propped against a verandah post, her arms folded tightly. The breeze ruffled her short, dark hair and Nick wished fancifully that he could be as lucky as the breeze.

When she'd dashed from the kitchen, the bleak expression on her face had hit him like a punch to the gut. Halfway to his feet, he'd been annoyed to the point of anger when the phone had rung.

Now, although she appeared resolute, there was a fragility about her that he hadn't seen before.

'You've torn your shirt,' he said.

Reaching around she fingered the three-corner tear in the heavy cotton fabric. 'Yeah, I caught it on something in the shed.'

Her voice hitched. She fiddled with the tear. 'I should be able to mend it. I'll ask Beth if I can borrow her sewing machine.'

She pressed her fingertips against her forehead, her eyes tightly shut. 'Listen to me will you, going on about mending my shirt when there's a man lying over there with half his head and face blow off.'

'That's not your fault, Anna,' Nick said quietly.

She licked her lips, rolled them together. 'I know it's not, but it's all so bloody awful. First Rachel lost the baby, and now this.' She pushed herself up straighter. 'What about you? How are you doing?'

'I didn't find him, so probably marginally better than you are. I can't wait to put this place as far behind us as possible.'

'You'll get no argument from me.'

'You didn't eat lunch. You need to have something.'

'I have an energy bar in my bag. I'll eat it later.'

'Make sure you do.' Nick paused, rubbing the back of his neck. 'I'm really sorry, Anna.'

She turned his way. 'What for?'

'Sending you to find Brett.'

'You didn't send me, I volunteered.'

'Yeah, but I had this feeling—'

'Not your fault, Nick. It is how it is.'

'Yeah, but don't you always trust your gut?'

Brown eyes met grey. The atmosphere around them shifted. 'Most times,' she said.

Nick ached to touch her. He lifted his hand to caress her cheek. Someone coughed and he dropped his hand, reminding himself where he was.

'I'd better go and check on Matt.'

'You know I had a chat with Jim while I was making the sandwiches. Poor old bugger. Told me he's worked here for twenty-five years. Brett was his fourth boss.'

'I didn't know that,' he said, and they walked inside together, their earlier animosity forgotten.

Two policemen arrived in a dusty 4WD wagon. Nick was tending to his patient so Anna offered to show them to the shed. Jim stood beside Nick on the verandah and squinted at the dust billowing behind the vehicle as they raced up the track.

'Dunno what the rush is. Not as if he's going anywhere.' Jim took off his hat. 'We had breakfast together this morning. I shoulda noticed something was wrong but if anything, he was chirpier than normal.' Clamping the worn and sweaty hat back on, he shook his head slowly, all the while staring towards the shed where his boss's body lay.

'Yeah mate, that's often the way.'

'I'll put the billy on. They'll probably want a brew when they get back,' Jim said, and went inside.

Twenty minutes later, Anna returned to the homestead with the policemen. When she climbed out of the back seat of the 4WD, Nick was thrown by how drained she looked. Pale beneath the tan.

'The police want to take a statement from you, Nick,' she said. 'When you've done that they said we can take our patient and go.'

'Okay, I'll do that right now. Matt's ready to go. And you, go eat and drink something,' he said in a tone that brooked no argument. He gripped her arms and gently propelled her towards the kitchen.

The bloke who took Nick's statement didn't look old enough to be doing what he was doing. He looked about as queasy as Anna had after she'd found Brett. Nick wondered if he'd witnessed anything like this in his short career.

Statements given, Nick and Anna wasted no time. Within an hour they had the patient loaded, the aircraft door closed. Anna had settled into her seat and fastened her seatbelt.

Nick reassessed the patient while Anna ran through the pre-start checklist.

He unconsciously held his breath when she pressed the starter switches to power up the engines. When the engines burst into life, relief flooded through him. He hadn't realised how much he wanted to get out of there.

With one final glance out the aircraft window, Nick saw Jim propped against the bull bar of the ute, arms and ankles folded. Shadowed by the brim of his hat, Nick couldn't read the station hand's expression. He hadn't given his statement yet. He'd be stuck there with the police and the body until the police aircraft arrived to pick it up and take it to Adelaide for autopsy.

Earlier, he'd heard Anna ask Jim if he was going to be all right.

'Yeah,' he'd said. 'I'll give my statement when I get back from dropping off you lot. Suppose the police'll contact the owners. Or I will. And then there's the missus—' He'd turned his head away and sniffed. The station hand obviously had a soft spot for Rachel Carmichael.

Nick trained his gaze forward.

'Right for taxi?' Anna's voice crackled through the headset.

'Cabin secure,' Nick replied and the intercom clicked off.

'We're on our way,' Nick said, giving the patient's shoulder a reassuring squeeze. Matt gave a quick thumbs-up without even opening his eyes. In seconds they were hurtling down the narrow dirt strip.

In the distance the windsock was a welcome sight, billowing in a brisk south-westerly. They touched down in Broken Hill and dispatched the patient to an ambulance before unloading the aircraft. There was a restive refueller standing by. The sun would be setting in half an hour.

'When are you moving in?' Anna said, handing down the last of the equipment.

Nick paused, tamping down the spurt of irritation. They'd agreed Beth would tell Anna the details. Obviously she hadn't.

'I bought a bed and I've already moved in,' he said, stacking the equipment onto the trolley.

'Already? Nobody told me.' She sounded hurt more than annoyed. 'You were at the house last night?'

'Yep. I left early this morning, dropped in to the hospital to see Mum on the way to the base. Had breakfast with her.'

'Right,' Anna said.

They worked quickly and methodically to get everything done, and to Nick her silence said more than any words would have.

Pushing the loaded trolley across to the emergency entrance, he renewed his resolve to start looking for somewhere else to live.

Stopping for a quick word with the refueller, Anna came in minutes after Nick. He'd already started putting away gear. She walked past, heading for the pilots' room.

'Beth's staying at Tim's tonight,' Nick said.

She stopped, spinning on her heel. He didn't miss the way she scanned the area for anyone who might be listening in. 'How do you know that?'

'She sent me a text.'

Anna's eyebrows pulled together, a tiny crease forming between them. 'If she's not there to cook, then I'm getting takeaway.'

'I can cook,' Nick said.

'No need, thanks anyway. I'll get a pizza.'

Nick forced back his frustration. 'All right, I suppose pizza with at least some vegetables is slightly healthier than fish and chips.' He reached for his wallet.

'You want pizza too?'

'Why not?' He handed her his money. Cooking for one wasn't much fun. 'Make mine a vegetarian.'

'Chips? Anything to drink?'

He shook his head, smiling as he put away the wallet. 'You really aren't good for my health, Anna.'

'You aren't good for my health either, particularly my mental health. I'm beginning to expect the worst whenever we fly together.'

'Yeah,' he said, pushing his fingers through his hair, 'I'm not a superstitious bloke, but …'

'At least with the rostering working the way it does we won't fly together very often. I don't think we're rostered together again for about ten days.'

Interesting, Nick thought, watching her stride away. She must have checked to see when they'd be working together. He knew he had. And it was exactly ten days until they were next on a shift.

22

Anna phoned through the pizza order, did her paperwork and picked up the food on the way home. The first thing she did when she went inside, after she'd fed Albert, was shower. She shampooed her hair twice. All her clothes were tossed into the washing machine, the water temperature set to hot.

If only the image of Brett Carmichael, sprawled against that rusty 44-gallon drum, was as easy to wash away as the day's grime.

Neither Izzy nor Teresa answered their phones. Anna left messages. Nick hadn't shown up at home. Convincing herself she wasn't disappointed—and why was she even waiting for him?—she zapped several slices of pizza and ate them standing at the kitchen sink. The leftovers went into the fridge.

She cleaned her teeth and fell into bed, dropping off to sleep immediately.

Three hours later she woke, heart pounding and skin clammy. She'd been dreaming, but what about? Whatever it'd been had left her feeling edgy and upset. Anna untangled her legs from the top sheet and kicked it off. Sitting on the side of the bed she braced herself, taking several long, slow breaths.

With the door closed, the bedroom was stuffy. Yawning widely she slid open the window as far as it would go. Nick's dual cab was parked in the driveway behind her car. She hadn't heard him come in.

Padding back to the bed she perched on the edge. She scanned the two messages on her phone—one from Izzy saying she'd been in the shower when Anna rang, and she was still sore but okay; and one from Nick saying he'd been held up. Wide awake now, and thirsty, Anna opened her bedroom door a crack and listened.

Apart from the whir of the overhead fan, the house was silent. She tiptoed along the passage. Nick's bedroom door was ajar.

The kitchen was bathed in the blue glow of the bug zapper above the fridge. Opening the fridge she took out the water jug to pour herself a drink.

'You can't sleep either?'

She spun around, cold water splashing onto her bare legs. Only then did she see Nick's seated silhouette in the gloom of the dining area.

'Jesus, Nick! Are you trying to give me a heart attack or something?'

'Or something,' he said.

She grabbed a tea towel, mopping up the water. Heart rate settling, Anna filled a glass and refilled the jug, returning it to the fridge.

'You might as well come and sit down.' He had his back to the window and he pushed out the chair opposite him with his foot.

'Do you want water?'

'No, I'm having a beer, or three.'

Anna carried her drink across to the dining table, conscious that a skimpy tank top and cotton boxers were all she had on. She didn't offer to turn on any lights.

'I stayed back and went over the Carmichaels' records to refresh my memory, and reassure myself I'd written everything down about my interaction with Brett. I wanted to see if anyone had followed up with him after I'd tried,' he said.

'And had anyone?'

'The mental health worker left messages, but that's all. Brett didn't ring back, so ...'

'So?'

'So does it mean that he received the messages but didn't want any follow-up, or that he didn't get the messages at all?' He took a mouthful of beer. 'You always feel like you could have done more ... That you should have done more. Was Brett high risk because of what had happened? Should the mental health worker have—'

He stopped, sighing loud and long.

'Shit, I don't know what the mental health worker should have done. What would I have done if I'd been the mental health worker? God knows. You can't force a service on a person, but then how can you assess whether they need the service if you can't see them or talk to them in the first place?'

'I imagine that in a situation like this, no matter what you did, you'd never feel as if you'd done enough.'

'You're right. I don't.' He sounded desolate.

'Nick.' Anna reached out and squeezed his arm. His skin was warm and the hairs on his forearm felt springy under her fingertips. She moved her fingers back and forth, enjoying the sensation. Nick shifted in his seat and their eyes met across the table. Even in the dim bluish light she could see the gleam in his gaze.

She removed her hand carefully and sat on it.

'Don't forget I was there, both times, and I know I'm the pilot and not a health professional, but it looked to me like you did everything you could. And then some.'

The bug zapper crackled. Nick stood up and slid the stubby holder off the bottle. 'Thanks for the vote of confidence, Anna, but it doesn't mean questions won't be asked, and it doesn't make Brett Carmichael any less dead.'

'Tell me about it,' she muttered. 'Finding him like that isn't something I'm going to forget in a hurry.'

'Oh, Anna, I am so sorry. Here I am, bleating on about my miserable self, covering my backside, when you were the one who found him.'

She leaned back in the chair and folded her arms. The hand she'd been sitting on prickled and burned as the blood rushed back. The elusive dream that had woken her earlier was suddenly there in sharp focus.

Bile rose into the back of her throat as she remembered … She'd been in the shed. Her shirt was caught on a piece of wire and she couldn't move and he was advancing towards her, unrecognisable with half his head blown away.

She grabbed the glass of water off the table, and drained it.

'Anna?'

'I wish I could stop seeing him—' She squeezed her eyes shut, screwing up her face with the effort. Then she felt the pressure of Nick's hands on her shoulders, firm but gentle as he began kneading away at the tension.

'You said there'd be no blood and gore.'

His laugh, loaded with irony, was low and throaty, and the sound sent tiny shock waves flitting across her skin.

'I did, didn't I? Shows how much anyone knows about what's around the corner.'

'Or slumped against a drum.'

'You know if you want to talk to someone about what happened, you can see a psychologist through the employee assistance program. Maybe you should.'

'I'll think about it. And I am talking to someone. You.'

The pressure of his hands increased. The rhythmic massaging was soothing and Anna resisted sinking back and resting her head against his abdomen. She'd seen him in Speedos, knew his abs would be rock hard. And then her eyes drifted shut and she leaned back against him anyway.

'Mmm,' she murmured. 'Where did you learn to do this?'

He lowered himself enough for her to feel his breath against her ear and whispered, 'Like I've said before, I'm a man of many talents.'

With that he gave her shoulders one last squeeze and dropped a kiss onto the top of her head. 'You smell nice,' he said. 'I like the way you smell.'

She felt the air shift when he moved away and wished he'd come back.

'Do you want a top up?' he said, the room brightening when the refrigerator door opened.

'No, thanks. I suppose I should get some more sleep.'

She heard the telltale hiss as he uncapped another stubby of beer.

'Don't go,' he said. 'Stay and keep me company while I drink this. I'm on night shift tomorrow night and I'm hoping the alcohol will help me sleep.'

'You should know better than that, Nick.'

She twisted around in the chair but there wasn't enough light to read the time on the kitchen clock. 'What time is it?'

He peered at the microwave display. 'One-thirty,' he said, coming back to the table to sit down.

'I wonder if someone let Rachel know?' It had been bothering Anna since Jim had voiced his concern about that very thing.

'The police told her. Then she rang me. It's another reason why I was late getting here. That, and going through the medical records.'

'How was she?'

'A total mess. Blaming herself. Not that you'd expect anything different in the circumstances.'

'I hope someone's there to support her.'

'She's staying with her mum. Has been ever since she lost the baby, apparently.'

'How come she had your phone number?'

'I gave it to her after she lost the baby.'

Anna frowned. 'Do you normally do that?'

'No, I don't, not ever. But you were there that day, Anna, you saw how she was. Her husband was next to useless. I was speechless when he didn't go with her.'

'Did she call you after that? Did you find out what had happened to make her go into labour?'

'No, she didn't get in touch until tonight.'

Anna was relieved by his answer, and didn't want to analyse why. To be fair, Nick had delivered Brett and Rachel's stillborn baby. He'd been there for what was probably the most traumatic experience the woman had ever had. 'It'd be hard, as a health professional, not to get too involved,' she said.

'Sometimes,' he replied.

Anna stretched and rubbed her eyes. They felt like they'd been sandblasted. She should go back to bed because she was on roster again in about five hours. But then, would she sleep?

When she took her hands away from her eyes, Nick was watching her.

'What?'

'What nothing. I like looking at you. Especially when you're dressed like that.'

Heat flashed through her. Anna blushed, hoping he wouldn't notice in the low light.

A car sounded in the street, strange and loud for this hour of the morning. It stopped close by, then a car door thudded shut. Minutes later, the sound of keys rattling in the front door.

'What the hell's she doing home?' Nick said.

Then the kitchen flooded with light and Anna lifted her hand to shield her eyes. Albert strolled in on Beth's heels.

Because they were sitting in the dining area, Beth didn't see them at first. Anna had a moment to take in Beth's puffy face and her red-rimmed eyes. With a start she realised Beth had been crying.

'Beth?' she said, rising to her feet.

'What are you two doing up in the middle of the night?' Beth said.

'Couldn't sleep,' Nick said. 'We had a difficult one today … Well, yesterday really …'

Albert was rubbing around Beth's ankles. She picked him up and cuddled him. Anna could hear the old boy purring from where she stood.

'More to the point, what are you doing home when you said you'd be staying with Tim?'

Beth buried her face in the cat's coat but not before Anna saw the sheen of fresh tears in her eyes. Anna glared at Nick. He gave a shrug, feigning innocence.

'Do you want a cup of tea?' Anna said, moving towards the electric kettle on the kitchen bench.

Albert leapt out of Beth's arms. She brushed at the cat fur on the front of her navy blue T-shirt. 'Tim and I are history,' she said.

'What?' Anna gaped at her housemate.

'He said I was smothering him and that he needed space.' Beth went to the sink to wash her hands. Anna glanced over her shoulder at Nick. Their eyes met and in that second Anna saw that it was what he'd expected to hear.

'Tim's an idiot,' Anna said. 'He's obviously too stupid to see what an amazing woman you are, Beth.'

Nick came and stood beside Anna.

'Anna's right, mate. He doesn't deserve you.' He put his empty beer bottles onto the sink. 'I'll put them in the recycle bin in the morning.' He hugged Beth, kissing her on the cheek. 'I'm going to bed,' he said. 'Goodnight, Anna. Thanks for the debrief, and don't wake me in the morning.'

The toilet flushed and several minutes later they heard Nick's bedroom door click shut. Beth looked at Anna. 'Sorry, I didn't mean to interrupt.'

'You didn't. We were debriefing about the flight.'

'That's a shame. You guys are perfect for each other.'

Anna snorted loudly. 'Says the relationship guru.'

Beth sighed. 'Yeah, you're right. I didn't go into this thing with Tim expecting it to be a forever kind of arrangement, but I did think it would last a bit longer than ten days. And I like him, a lot. I don't know what it is about me and the men I choose.'

'It's not about you, it's about them.' Anna filled the electric kettle and flicked it on. 'And if you like him a lot, why not try to patch things up with him?'

'I dunno if that's what I want. We had a doozy of a fight and I stormed out. I've been sitting in my car at the lookout for the past hour or so, thinking. Maybe I just need to get out of this place and start over somewhere else. Reinvent myself.'

'Really?'

'Yeah, really. I always imagined I'd work at the hospital until I got married and had kids, and I'd live out my life happy and contented here in Broken Hill. But that's not how it's panning out—I'm not enjoying my job as much as I used to … I'm not far from forty, childless, and now there's not even a prospective partner on the horizon.'

'Tim's a moron.'

'Yeah, well … ' Beth plucked two mugs out of the cupboard and sighed again. 'You know what, Anna? I wish you weren't flying in the morning because now feels like the perfect time to get shit-faced together.'

Before Anna realised what she was doing, she was hugging her housemate.

23

Busy night shifts and days with little sleep meant Nick stockpiled tiredness. The thought of ten or more hours uninterrupted rest was like a carrot dangling just beyond his reach.

On the first of his rostered three nights, they flew twice. The initial flight was early in the night to pick up a teenage boy who'd come off his trail bike and broken his leg.

In bed only an hour and deeply asleep, Nick had been jarred awake minutes after midnight, this time for an elderly man with heart failure. Why couldn't people get sick in the daytime?

As much as he'd have preferred not to, while he was on night shift he'd slept, or tried to sleep, at the base. Beth's house, with Anna there, had begun to feel too much like home—his washing alongside hers on the clothesline, her sneakers on the verandah next to his. Any motivation he'd had to look for another place to live was fading by the day.

But he didn't want to get too comfortable, because when the time came for one of them to move on, and move out, it would be difficult.

On Friday afternoon after a crappy sleep and with one night shift left to work, Nick finally met with the hospital social worker.

Marlene remained an inpatient, but the staff were making noises about discharge. And he suspected she'd been sneaking outside to smoke.

'She can't go back to living in her car,' Di, the social worker, said from behind a desk piled with client case notes.

'You think I don't know that?' Nick said. Di drew back and Nick held up his hand. 'I'm sorry, I didn't mean that the way it sounded. Night shift … Not enough sleep … You get my drift.'

'Yeah, I do. Let's start over. I won't state the bleeding obvious, and hopefully we'll sort out something workable. How does that sound?'

'It sounds like the way to go, thanks.'

Di opened a manila folder with his mother's name on it. She leafed through the papers inside. 'As I told you earlier, we've fast-tracked the aged care assessment, and of course Marlene's eligible for low-level care. The only problem is availability. There's a respite bed free for two weeks from Monday—' She tapped her pen against her lips, perusing the forms again.

'Respite's good but it's only a short-term solution, Di, and we need something long-term. I don't know where I'll be after January when my RFDS contract finishes. I was hoping to have her well and truly settled by then.'

'You know how it is, Nick, being a registered nurse yourself. Aged care facilities can have three vacancies one week, and then nothing for months. Now is one of the times when there's nothing.'

Nick's heart sank. It must have shown on his face because Di said, 'Cheer up. At least there's the two weeks of respite for your mum, and anything can happen in that time.'

Yeah, like he could win the lottery and buy his dream home, with a granny flat, then Anna would move in with him and his mum and they'd all live happily ever after.

The sleep deprivation must be getting to him. He'd never once bought a lottery ticket, and Anna … Best he didn't go there or he'd end up feeing lousier than he already did.

Because he was at the hospital, he could hardly *not* visit his mother after seeing the social worker. His night shift didn't officially begin for a couple of hours.

Anna had a clinic day and she wouldn't land for an hour or more, but if he made it back to the base soon he might 'accidentally' run into her before she went home. Otherwise, he didn't know when he'd see her next.

Marlene was sitting on the edge of the hospital bed, elbows propped on the overway table, swinging her bare feet.

'Mum,' Nick said, dropping a quick kiss onto her parched cheek. His nose wrinkled. 'You've been smoking. You won't be satisfied until you've killed yourself, will you?'

'If I can't smoke I might as well be dead,' she said with a belligerent tilt of the chin that so reminded him of his brother.

'Have you talked to Lachlan?'

'Not since the first time,' she said, quick to add, 'He's busy, he has a job,' when Nick frowned.

'That didn't stop him asking me for money.'

'Give him a go, Nick. It'll take him a bit to get his act together.'

'Whatever,' he said, picking up his mother's chart from the end of the bed and flicking through it. She was on the mend, although her oxygen saturations were nothing to rave about.

'I had a meeting with the social worker,' he said, and sat down in the vinyl visitor's chair. He was tired, antsy, and would have preferred not to have this conversation today, but he wouldn't feel like it tomorrow either.

'They have two weeks' respite available from Monday,' he said and named one of the aged care facilities.

'Why can't I stay here?'

'They need the bed, Mum. You're not acutely sick any more. Not if you can walk outside to smoke.'

Marlene scowled. 'Another day or two and I'll be ready to go home.'

'Home? You call living in your car home?'

'Well, what would you call it? It's all I've got. Where is my car, by the way?'

'In one of Snake's shed's, and don't go getting any ideas.'

Outside the door, the meal trolley squeaked along the corridor towards them. Inside the room, the air could be cut with a knife. Next thing, Marlene's meal tray was dumped unceremoniously on the overway.

'Food's disgusting,' Marlene said. She lifted the plate cover to reveal a blob of mashed potato, and lumps of something in a grey gravy, dotted with orange-and-green flecks. She squinted at the menu slip.

'Shepherd's pie. Or so it says. Smell's more like the shepherd's dirty underwear.'

Nick laughed, easing some of the tension. 'Hospitals aren't known for their haute cuisine, Mum.'

Marlene grunted, dipping the buttered white bread into the gravy. 'You know Anna, that pilot friend of yours ... well, she visited me yesterday afternoon. Took pity on a poor old woman and went out and bought me a Big Mac.'

'Anna came to see you?' Nick sat forward in the chair.

'Don't look so shocked. She seems like a decent sort. Brought me a magazine. That Beth's called in a couple of times, too. She's nosy.'

'No, she's not, Mum. She's a good person.' Nick sat back trying to get his head around Anna having visited his mother and not mentioning it to him.

Marlene fixed him with a steely stare. 'And when were you going to tell me that you and Lauren were a thing of the past?'

'Who told you that? Beth?' He'd kill her.

'No, she wouldn't tell me something like that—too busy pumping *me* for information.'

Anna? Surely she wouldn't have said anything.

'Your brother told me.' Marlene finished the bread, screwed up her nose at the remainders of the meal and pushed away the tray. 'What happened, Nick?' She sounded perplexed more than anything else.

'Lauren wasn't happy with me anymore, simple as that.'

'Were you still happy with her?'

Nick lifted his left foot and rested it on the opposite knee, jiggling it up and down while he contemplated the floor. To give his mother credit, she waited until he was ready to answer.

'Initially I thought I was, but in hindsight my unhappiness at the spilt was more hurt pride than anything else. To be honest, Mum, I probably never should have married her in the first place. Turned out we had nothing much in common. I worked my arse off for three years for zip.'

'Ah, the clarity of hindsight.'

Nick did a double-take. It wasn't often he heard such wise words from his mother's mouth. Maybe part of the reason was he didn't listen often enough or closely enough.

'I'm sorry, son,' she said softly. 'I had wondered why you'd come back. I know you said it was to sort me out, but I sensed there was more to it than that. I'm sorry about the house. I know how much it meant to you.'

'Lachlan was chatty,' he said, but there was a thickening in the back of his throat that felt suspiciously like tears. His mother was actually being a mother. It felt foreign, but not unpleasant.

'Don't blame Lachy. I might not have been the best parent but I'm still your mother, and mothers notice things.'

'Thanks,' he said, for want of anything else to say. 'It'll take a while, but I'll get back on my feet.'

'I know you will, Nick,' she said. She fidgeted and Nick knew he should hug her, or something. But then she said, 'Gawd, I could murder a smoke,' and the moment passed.

Nick stood up, and making the usual excuses about work and sleep, he left, never considering that his mother might have been overjoyed if he'd stayed for a while longer.

24

'I'm getting out of this place for my days off,' Beth said to Anna when she came home late the following Saturday afternoon. 'My friend Gill rang. She lives in Melbourne and is home on her parents' station for a couple of weeks.'

'Is she a nurse?' Anna said.

'Yes, and she wisely left Broken Hill years ago.'

'It's not that bad a place, is it?' Anna said, surprising herself.

Beth stared at her for a moment. 'No, I suppose it's not. To be fair, I have had a good life here. But I still think I need a change or at least a break from the place.'

Beth had been in a funk since the blowup with Tim. A few days away would be good for her. Two hours later she'd packed a bag, thrown it into the back of the ute and was saying goodbye to Albert.

'I won't forget to feed him,' Anna said.

'I know you won't. I'm on afternoon shift Wednesday; I'll be back before then,' Beth said, and headed off.

After she'd left, Anna sat on the edge of the front verandah keeping Albert company. Together they pondered the tiny square of lawn, struggling to survive. Restrictions meant it didn't get any water other than whatever fell from the sky, and it had been a dry winter and spring.

She scratched Albert's throat, feeling the rumble of his purring. Three days without Beth, and three days since she'd seen Nick. You could be fooled into thinking he hadn't moved in at all.

The early hours of the morning after the awful and unforgettable flight to Elder Creek station had been the last time she'd clapped eyes on him. She wasn't sure who'd been avoiding whom. Or if it was because they were both shift workers.

Anna had been sitting there about ten minutes, the cement warm on her backside, when Nick's 4WD pulled into the driveway.

Engine running, he buzzed down the window and she realised there were others in the cab.

'Anna, hi. I'm taking Serena and Mai, the new medical student, up to the Miners' Memorial to watch the sunset. Wondered if you wanted to come along?'

Albert scooted off. Anna stood up, brushing off cat fur as she walked over to the vehicle. She peered in the window past Nick.

From the passenger seat Serena gave her a limp-wristed flick, barely resembling a wave. An attractive girl with dead-straight black hair called out a bright, 'Hi, I'm Mai,' from the back seat.

'Come on,' Nick said, the two words loaded with challenge, and was that pleading?

'All right,' she said after a brief hesitation. 'If you don't mind that I'm on roster from seven. Maybe I should follow you in my car.'

'No,' Nick said, a tad vehemently. 'What I mean is, I can bring you back if you get called out. It's not far.'

'All right. Let me put on some shoes and grab my phone.'

He smiled and her silly heart stuttered. 'I'll wait,' he said.

A few minutes later she slid into the back seat beside Mai. Nick winked when he caught her eye in the rear-view mirror. She looked away quickly, frustrated by the telltale colour coursing into her cheeks.

The drive took less than ten minutes, ending with the climb up Federation Way. Nick parked and they piled out and walked towards the memorial, an immense steel structure in memory of the 800 miners who'd lost their lives since the first mine opened.

They made it to the viewing platform, watching as the sun perched on the horizon before slipping away with another day.

'Awesome,' said Mai, snapping away with her camera.

Anna took a photo with her phone, catching the fiery orb seconds before it disappeared. Overhead the cloudless blue sky faded to pastels, deepening to a golden wash separating earth and sky. Lights twinkled in the darkening cityscape below.

'It's very beautiful,' Anna said to no-one in particular.

'Haven't you been up here before?' Nick said, from close by.

'I drove up the first week I was here, but not at sunset.'

'What about the stone sculptures at sunrise or sunset?'

'No, I haven't been there either. I was always going to, but never have.'

'Haven't what?' Serena asked, bouncing up and inserting herself between them.

'Been out to the stone sculptures.'

'Nick! You *must* take me out there,' Serena said. 'We'll drink champagne and watch the sunset!'

Nick took a step away from Serena. 'Sorry, but during the summer, the park's closed at sunset,' he said.

'Oh.' Serena sounded genuinely disappointed.

'I want to come up here with more time during the day to read the names on the memorial,' Mai said.

'It's interesting reading,' Nick said. 'The men died from all sorts of things. Rock falls and other accidents were common. As were heart failure and lung disease.'

'Follow the boardwalk and read the interpretive signs and you'll get an idea of what it would have been like back in the early days,' Anna added.

They walked to the car a while later. Nick dropped Anna at Beth's.

'Goodbye, and nice to meet you,' Mai said. 'Maybe you'll fly me somewhere while I'm on placement.'

'It would be a pleasure,' Anna said.

Serena didn't look up from her phone, texting furiously.

'Thanks Nick,' Anna said. 'If you hadn't come I'd still be sitting on the step with the cat, contemplating the dying lawn.'

Leaving the engine running he climbed out after her. From the passenger seat Serena glanced up from her phone.

'Where's Beth?'

Anna told him.

'I'll drop off these two and then I'll be back,' Nick said. 'Have you eaten?'

She shook her head and fished in her pocket for the house key.

'What shall I bring for dinner?'

'No need to bring anything. Beth made moussaka last night and there're plenty of leftovers.'

Nick stared at her.

'What?' she said, fiddling with the house key.

'You are so unlike anyone else I know, Anna.'

'What do you mean?'

'You don't ever want anything. It's—'

Whatever he'd been going to say was cut off by the car horn blasting. Nick threw his hands in the air.

'You're being paged. Better not keep the lady waiting.'

'Lady?' He snorted. 'I'll be half an hour, tops.'

'I'll be here. Unless I go flying. It is Saturday night.'

'It is,' he said.

Anna let herself into the house. Why she rushed around and tidied up, she didn't take the time to consider. But on the way to the bathroom to comb her hair and put on some lip gloss, Anna pulled herself up short. Flicking nervous fingers through her hair she retraced her steps to the kitchen and tossed a salad to accompany the moussaka heating in the oven.

Nick was living here. He had to eat. This was her home. She had to eat. This was not a date. Repeat, *This was not a date.*

'Don't they know you're staying here?' she asked Nick when he came back forty minutes later. The table was set, the food well and truly heated. She carried the salad to the table.

'No way. If Serena got hold of that little bit of information, it'd be around the base in no time, but with her take on the facts.'

'But you're Beth's mate. She offered for you to stay, to help you out. And Serena was there when Beth hooked up with Tim.'

'Anna, she's aware that I'm separated from my wife and that you live here too.'

'Oh, yeah, I see what you mean.'

'Never underestimate Serena. I know you well enough already to appreciate how much you value your privacy.'

Poised with her oven-mitt-clad hands on her hips, Anna frowned. 'I hadn't thought about it like that.'

'I had.' Nick went to the fridge and poured two glasses of water.

Anna lifted the moussaka out of the oven. 'This will dry out if we don't eat soon.'

Nick sat down at the dining table. She avoided looking at him, mulling over what he'd said and the implications of him wanting to protect her privacy. Then she reminded herself again that he was married, because it was so easy to forget that.

Resting the baking dish on a cork pot stand, she pushed the food in his direction. Serving up for him would have been way too domestic, although minutes ago that's exactly what she'd intended to do.

'What happened just now, Anna?' he said, after he'd helped himself to the moussaka.

'I don't know what you mean,' she said, concentrating on the salad she was piling onto her plate.

'Yes, you do. Be honest, you're still hung up on me having an ex-wife.'

She dropped the salad servers into the bowl with a clunk. 'Though she's not exactly your ex-wife yet, is she?'

'Only a matter of a few months before I can file for a divorce.'

'And how long does a divorce take?'

'Three months or thereabouts, according to the government website and a couple of mates who've been down that path.'

They ate in silence until Nick put down his knife and fork. He hadn't finished his meal. She looked up.

'Are you going to make us wait that long, Annalise?'

'Nick—'

'Don't pretend you don't know what I mean. I'll wait, if that's what you want. After all, I've been waiting since high school.'

'Don't expect me to believe that!' She pushed away her plate. 'And anyway, you don't even know what you'll be doing in six months. Neither do I. We might not even be here. I could be back in Adelaide, you could be in Sydney—or any place.'

'If it's what we decided we wanted, there'd be nothing stopping us being together here, Adelaide, Sydney, Timbuktu.' He sat back and folded his arms, his eyes on her face.

'You make it sound so easy,' she said, picking at a loose thread on the cotton placemat. 'We hardly know each other.'

'I reckon we're getting to know each other pretty well. Tell me why you think it isn't easy.'

Now was her chance to tell him about Isabelle. It was the perfect opportunity. She opened her mouth, then closed it. If she told him she had a teenage daughter, he wouldn't think it was so easy.

'Anna, talk to me.'

A sudden yank on the thread and the placemat hem started to unravel. She cursed under her breath and pushed the whole thing out of reach. 'What about your mother?'

'Okay,' Nick said, drawing out the two syllables. 'I'll let you get away with changing the subject, for the moment. Yesterday afternoon I met with the social worker about Mum. And I've been doing some serious thinking since.'

'And what have you come up with?'

He stood up. 'Nothing, except that she has two weeks' respite care from Monday, and she can't go back to living in her car after that. I'm going to grab a beer. Do you want more water?'

'No, thanks.'

When Nick came back to the table and sat down, Anna said, 'I don't know her very well, but my guess is that Marlene would hate being cooped up in some aged care facility.'

Nick opened the beer. 'I do know her very well, and you're right, she'll hate it. But she might have to suck it up for a while.'

Anna's mobile rang, vibrating its way to the edge of the table. She dived for it before it hit the floor.

'We have a priority one,' the flight nurse said when Anna answered.

Listening to the flight nurse, Anna glanced at Nick. He was watching her, his expression resigned.

'I'll see you soon,' she said to the nurse before disconnecting, her gaze locked with Nick's.

'I have to go,' she said.

'I gathered that. Be careful. I'll be here when you get back.'

25

Disregarding that he had a bed in the room down the passage, Nick dropped off to sleep on the sofa. After Anna had left he'd tidied up and stacked the dishwasher. The house felt strangely empty without her.

He woke at one with a crick in his neck, wondering where the hell he was. Then he remembered, and went looking for Anna.

A quick walk through the house told him that the only body sleeping in her bed was Albert. He stood on the threshold of her bedroom: it was neat, the furnishings sparse and it smelled like her. He jealously eyed the cat; imagined lying down on the bed beside Albert to wait for her.

Nick was 100 per cent certain of, and comfortable with, his growing feelings for Anna. When he'd first caught sight of her at the base all those weeks ago, the initial punch of lust and longing had been weirdly familiar. It wasn't until later that he realised why—he'd built his eighteen-year-old fantasies around her.

Here she was, back in his life, and he was building man-sized fantasies around her this time. And now as opposed to when he was eighteen, he had the confidence to act on his feelings. That the attraction was mutual he had no doubts. Anna had a bit of catching up to do, that was all.

Heralded by the manic barking of the dog next door, Nick heard Anna letting herself in the front door half an hour later. He was in bed but awake. Only when his body relaxed did he realise how tense he'd been, waiting for her to get home.

Having left his bedroom door ajar, he heard her whispering to the cat and not long after the banging of the water pipes when she turned on the shower. He drifted off to sleep, happy she was home safely.

The sound of shattering glass had Nick bolting upright in bed. His heart slammed against his chest wall. It was pitch black. Had he been dreaming?

Pounding feet, rapid panting, closely followed by a dull thud and a yelp. Not dreaming. He leapt out of bed and flung open the bedroom door.

Anna streaked out of the sitting room into the passage, all legs and see-through cami and skimpy boxers. His heart slammed in his chest again, for an entirely different reason.

The house was lit up like a Christmas tree.

'It's that effing dog from next door,' she cried.

'What?' He stood in the bedroom doorway, trying not to stare.

'Hercules. He must have got out and squeezed in through the cat flap.'

Albert howled, the dog growled, there was another thud and Anna darted off. 'You go for the dog, I'll try for the cat.'

It wasn't a big house, but it was cluttered. Nick took off in the direction of the kitchen, swearing loudly when he stubbed his toe on the bookcase in the passageway.

'Watch out for broken glass,' Anna warned. 'They've knocked a vase off the sideboard. Beth'll be so pissed. It was her great-aunt's.'

Nick looked down at his bare feet. 'Shit,' he muttered as the mongrel of a dog shot between his legs, Anna in hot pursuit.

'I thought you were going after the cat!'

'The cat's up on top of the pantry cupboard. He'll stay put.'

Sure enough, Albert was hunched on the highest piece of furniture in the house, hissing and spitting when the dog spied him from below. Yipping at the cat, quivering with excitement, the dog's claws scraped at the vinyl flooring.

Anna stood poised in the kitchen. Nick waited in the archway between the dining area and the sitting room. He had shut the door from the sitting room into the passage on his way through.

'I'll grab the dog,' he said, tiptoeing towards it. Hercules took no notice, his attention focused solely on the out-of-reach feline.

'I don't think you need to tiptoe, Nick.'

Diving for the dog he said, 'If it bites me, I'll kill the little fu—'

He had it by the hair, the muscly bundle squirming in his arms. He grinned at Anna, took his eyes off Hercules, and the dog hurled itself out of his arms, scrabbling for purchase on the slippery floor. Nick swore. The dog streaked into the sitting room, spinning around when it realised its escape route had been cut off. The cat yowled from its lofty perch.

Nick lunged, missed, and the dog scrambled up over the back of an armchair and into the narrow corner space between the wall and the chair. When Hercules realised he was trapped, he freaked, yelping in distress.

Together, Nick and Anna wrenched the piece of furniture away from the wall. It came away quicker than expected and Nick stumbled against the corner of the adjacent sofa. On reflex Anna reached out to stop him falling, he grabbed her outstretched hand and they went down together.

The dog flew over the tangle of their bare legs.

'What the—' Nick spluttered, momentarily winded. Anna's face was only centimetres from his own, eyes wide and the colour of dark chocolate. Her barely clad body, warm from exertion, rested on his—unfettered breasts achingly soft against the wall of his chest; bare thighs pressed against the increasing hardness of another part of his anatomy. Like slow-moving lava, heat rolled through him. A low, inarticulate sound rumbled from his throat.

'Nick? Are you all right?'

'Yes,' he said, 'I'm better than all right.'

She made no immediate move to lever herself up.

'You have amazing eyes, and the most gorgeous eyelashes,' she whispered. Pink spots of colour burst onto her cheeks.

'You're perfect,' he replied, and reached up to stroke the backs of his fingers across the silkiness of her skin. 'And I love it that I can make you blush.'

The colour in her face deepened, she averted her eyes and started to move, preparing to push herself up and off of him.

'Annalise,' he said gently, hoarsely, and cupped her face with his hands.

Her eyes flashed back to his and her body tensed. He swiped his thumb slowly across her bottom lip.

'Relax,' he said. 'Please let me kiss you.'

The tip of her tongue darted out to wet her lips. He nearly groaned out loud.

'Okay,' she breathed, and then he did groan out loud.

Their lips met—a tentative touch, a tantalising taste. She pulled back. Her eyes were wide and hesitant.

'I haven't kissed a man for a very long time,' she said, and Nick's heart swelled.

He went in for a deeper taste. Her lips parted and he let himself sink into the most amazing kiss he'd ever had. And all of her skin was soft and silky, not only her face. The way she shoved her fingers into his hair, anchoring herself to him, was enough to drive him off the deep end.

And then, something penetrated his lust-saturated brain, bringing to a halt what until moments earlier he'd only dreamed about since first seeing Anna again. She must have heard it too because she stilled, and then peeled her lips from his.

'What was that?' she said, looking over her shoulder towards the kitchen. 'Where's the dog?'

In one agile movement, she'd rolled off of him and sprung to her feet. She stood gazing down at him and his blatantly obvious state of arousal. 'Wow,' she mouthed. Her hair was mussed, her mouth swollen.

'Wow yourself,' he said, eyes irresistibly drawn to the front of her sheer camisole top.

Then it came again, a rattling, clunking sound. Nick pushed himself to his feet. Anna disappeared into the kitchen. He followed her, at a much slower, stiffer pace. As he passed the pantry cupboard he looked up and threw the cat a grateful glance. Comfortable on top of his world, Albert stared down through slitted eyes.

Light flooded the backyard then the screen door slapped shut.

That rattling sounded again. Nick stopped. Ducking back to his bedroom, he grabbed a pair of shorts and pulled them on over his jocks as he made his way towards the front door. He turned on the verandah light. Now, except for the bathroom, every light in the house was on. He peered out the door. A shape emerged from the carport side of the house.

Coming further into the light the shape transformed into an elderly woman. She was thin, her hair a helmet of tight, white curls. Incongruously, her feet were thrust into a pair of bright pink Crocs.

'I'm Josie, from next door. You have Hercules,' she said. 'My dog.'

Nick cleared his throat. 'He was here, yes,' he said. 'We didn't exactly *have* him, and I haven't a clue where he is now.'

'He's in your backyard. I heard him whimpering. I was trying to open the gate to let him through.'

That explained the rattling sound Nick had heard. But then he heard it again. He glanced at the woman. They both moved towards the carport.

The galvanised iron gate that separated the carport from Beth's backyard swung open. Like a bullet, Hercules shot through.

'You come here, you little bastard,' Anna hissed, hard on the dog's heels.

Disinclined to do so, Nick prepared to launch himself at the dog again. Josie put out a staying hand.

'It's all right. He'll go home. I've left our gate open.'

'I found the place he got in,' Anna said. 'He dug under the fence.'

'Oh dear. It's the cat, you know.'

'We know,' they said in unison.

A light came on in the house across the street.

'Look, it's four in the morning, and we're waking the neighbours.' Anna said. 'You'll have to keep Hercules inside for what's left of the night. I'll block up the hole in the morning.' Anna stalked off towards the gate, closing it behind her.

'You heard the lady,' he said.

Josie sized him up through glasses that made her eyes look much bigger than they were. 'Are you Beth's or that dark-haired one's boyfriend?'

The inside lights were flicking off. Nick flexed his fingers in frustration. His chances of picking up with Anna where they'd left off were slipping past by the second.

Josie waited expectantly.

'Goodnight … Or good morning, whichever,' he said and hoped he didn't sound as irritated as he felt.

With relief Nick heard the crunch of Josie's Crocs on the gravel footpath as he let himself in the front door.

Anna's bedroom door was shut, and except for the passage light the house was in darkness. Without thinking he tapped on her door. There's no way she could be asleep already.

'Anna?'

No answer.

'Anna, I know you're awake.'

'Go to bed, Nick.'

'We need to talk, about what happened.'

'No, we don't.'

He frowned. That effing dog. He wanted to kill the little bastard. Harsh, because without the dog there wouldn't have been that mind-blowing kiss. One taste of Anna and he was completely hooked. Nick leaned his forehead against the door, his fingers curled around the handle.

'Anna?'

'Nick, it's not going to happen, so go to bed,' came the muffled reply.

'Why not?' He was past caring if he sounded desperate. He was.

'Because I had the chance to think, before I did something stupid.'

'Why would it be stupid? I want you, you want me … What's stupid about that?'

'Arrrgh! Can't we discuss this in the morning? I've been up most of the night, and I'm totalled. I have two more night shifts.'

He closed his eyes and soundlessly bumped his forehead against the door. The unexpected opportunity he'd been handed to move their relationship a step in the right direction had slipped out of his grasp.

For now. Nick straightened away from the door. There would be other opportunities, and he wouldn't let the next one get away from him. He would make certain of that.

'Goodnight,' he said, and didn't wait to hear if she replied.

26

It was mid-morning and the house was eerily quiet. Anna climbed out of bed and peeked through the curtains. Nick's dual cab was gone. She touched her lips. Her heart rate steadied.

Regardless, before she ventured out she pulled on shorts and a T-shirt. In the aftermath of what she'd already dubbed 'the dog incident', Anna wouldn't be wandering around the house in her pyjamas.

Hercules was barking next door when she walked into the kitchen. Albert was absent but his food bowl was empty.

Being Sunday, in the distance the whine of trail bikes could be heard, bashing about in the saltbush somewhere over the back fence.

Nick had swept up the broken vase. She peeked into the sitting room to find all the furniture back in place. Her gaze dropped to the spot on the carpet where they'd landed, her on top of him.

Thank God Josie had come looking for her dog. Anna's breath hitched and her body pulsed at the thought of where it would have ended if she hadn't … Damn Josie for coming looking for her dog.

Anna massaged her temples. This whole thing with Nick had her tied in knots. In the perpetual, *Do I? Don't I?* argument going on in her head, at the moment, the *Don't I?* was losing. One kiss and she'd been good to go.

Her phone pinged—a text from Izzy. Reality quickly shoved the *Don't I?* side of the argument back into top place. She rang and chatted to her daughter.

Disconnecting fifteen minutes later, Anna renewed her resolve to keep things with Nick strictly platonic, which would be even more difficult now because that kiss had shown her exactly what she was missing. But in reality nothing had changed, except for Anna feeling that her life was spinning out of her control.

And then he came home.

It was hot. Anna was watering Beth's pot plants on the back verandah when she heard his ute. Funny how out of all the thousands of vehicles in Broken Hill, she could already identify the sound of his.

He came in via the carport, letting himself through the gate. Dropping the *Sunday Mail* onto the outdoor table he said, 'I blocked up the hole under the fence earlier, but there's no reason why the dog couldn't dig another one and get in.'

Anna looked up. Her gut clenched. Nick in the flesh was way more potent than the fantasy. Stunned by the physical force of her yearning, she tore her gaze away. Following the hose back to the tap, she turned it off. His steady scrutiny was like a slow burn on her skin.

'I'd noticed that you'd blocked it up. Thanks. Beth might want to do something more permanent in the long run,' she said, wondering how she managed to form coherent sentences.

What was happening to her? She'd convinced herself she wasn't a sexual person—her libido shrivelling after a few brief and unsatisfying entanglements, and the responsibilities of single parenthood. Now, she only had to think about Nick and her body reacted.

'I haven't seen Albert,' she said.

'He was here earlier.'

She nodded, fidgeting. He took several steps towards her but must have read the uncertainty in her eyes because he stopped.

'Do you want to talk about what happened, about where we go to from here?'

Did she want to talk? And if she did, what would she say? Should she ask, Was that the best kiss you've ever had? Should she tell him, I could have strangled Josie for interrupting like that. Or, Please, kiss me again, *now*.

Imagining his response, amusement bubbled up into her throat, cutting off speech.

Nick reached for Anna's hand and she let him lead her out of the sun to the swing seat on the verandah.

'Sit down,' he said.

This is ridiculous, she thought. *I'm ridiculous.* But she sat, trying to get into perspective what was happening, to claw back some of her usual composure.

'Nick, I am so not good at this sort of stuff,' she said. The seat wobbled when he sat down beside her.

'Tell me why you think that,' he said.

Here was another opportunity to tell him she'd never been in a relationship and she had a fifteen-year-old daughter; that the first time she'd ever had sex, she'd found herself pregnant; that the father had been married, and he'd denied it and in her teenage naivety she'd believed him; that her parents hadn't supported her decision to have the baby, and as a result she'd learned to be fiercely independent; and that she recognised she still had issues with trust.

'I suppose I haven't had much experience at it,' she said, and then wanted to stamp her foot, disappointed with herself because those weren't the words she'd needed to put out there.

'What I mean is that with my job, and everything else … '

She slumped back in the seat. Why couldn't she do it? Why couldn't she tell him?

'What everything else?' Nick asked gently.

'You know,' she said, and lifted her shoulders.

'No, I don't know. I'm asking you to tell me.'

When she didn't elaborate, he sighed with frustration. 'Did a boyfriend give you a hard time or something? Help me out here, Anna.'

'Something like that, but please, can we leave it now, Nick ...?' She sprang to her feet, suddenly desperate for space. 'Let's accept that for us, the timing is wrong. You're still attached—' he opened his mouth to protest but she held up her hand and barrelled on, '—we work together, you have responsibilities where your mother's concerned, and after January you don't even know how long you'll be here. And I have commitments and responsibilities in my life in Adelaide.'

The swing seat creaked as he stood up. 'That's a cop-out, Anna, and you know it. My marriage is over. Like I've said before, the moment I can file for a divorce I will. Mum's situation will sort itself out, one way or the other. And beyond January and this RFDS contract, I'm sure something else will turn up. It always has.' He shoved his hands into his pockets. 'I'm yours for the taking,' he said, his eyes never leaving hers, glittering with challenge.

How could he do that? Take the rug out from under her with a few words. Make it all sound so simple when she was certain it wasn't.

Leaning in, he kissed her, hard and fast. 'Ball's in your court, sweetheart,' he whispered, a hair's breadth from her mouth.

He left her standing there, stunned and off balance.

27

Over the next few days, whenever they were at home together Anna kept Nick at arm's length. She wasn't sure how to act when he was around and she sensed he was amused by that. Without Beth as a buffer, Anna felt exposed.

However, she discovered he was amazingly patient, and as self-sufficient as she was.

Marlene Harrison moved from the hospital to the residential aged care facility and began the two weeks of respite. After her first meal, she told Nick that the food was worse than the hospital. Anna decided she'd visit Marlene soon, take her another Big Mac.

Beth returned on Wednesday after three days away, and they settled into a vague routine, their work rosters fixed to the fridge door. Anna went swimming most mornings; Nick went for a run. Rarely out of bed before ten if she wasn't on a day shift, Beth said they were both crazy.

Anna had three days off after night shift. Izzy was convalescing from her appendicectomy, and November was history. Christmas was only weeks away.

After Anna's unplanned trip to Adelaide when Izzy was in hospital, she had had to postpone the planned weekend trip home at the beginning of December.

On the first Friday in December, Anna had a day shift with Nick. They were taxiing by eight-fifteen, transferring two stretcher patients to Adelaide. They would be carrying one stretcher and one sitting patient on the return journey. The sky was clear and the wind sock flaccid when they took off.

Anna had reached the top of the climb and was settling in to enjoy the flight when Nick's voice came through the intercom.

'Are you okay to talk for a sec? Both patients are dozing.'

'Sure,' Anna said.

'First, thanks for visiting Mum on Wednesday. She couldn't stop yapping about how you'd taken her a Big Mac and fries.'

'She ate every last greasy mouthful.'

'The other thing I wanted to tell you is that Brett Carmichael's funeral is this coming Monday afternoon.'

'Oh. Are you going?'

'I'll be in the middle of three night shifts.'

'I have a clinic day.' Anna scanned the instruments and then gazed out into the infinite nothingness of the troposphere. The image of Brett Carmichael slumped against the drum was only ever a thought away. Maybe going to his funeral would bring some sort of closure.

'Do you ever go to patients' funerals?'

'Very occasionally. Only if it was a person I'd really liked and I'd looked after them for a long time, got to know their families.'

'Maybe I could swap. I'm off Sunday.'

'Hang on a tick, I need to check these patients.' The intercom went dead. Anna twisted a look over her right shoulder. Nick had taken off his headset and was leaning forward over the first stretcher patient. Anna went back to enjoying the scenery.

His voice crackled through the intercom a few minutes later.

'Everything all right?'

'Yep,' he said. 'Do you want to go to Brett's funeral?'

'Yes, I think it might help me—' She paused. She hadn't shared with anyone how much she still thought about that Tuesday afternoon ten days ago.

'Find some kind of closure?' Before she could answer there were some ominous and muffled sounds. 'Sorry, but we'll have to finish this later,' he said, and the intercom went dead again.

When she glanced back into the cabin, one of the patients was heaving into a vomit bag.

It was late afternoon before they picked up the conversation again. They were home in Broken Hill, unpacking the aircraft after the two patients had been waved off in the back of the waiting ambulance.

'About Brett's funeral,' Nick said as he passed down bags of equipment and Anna stacked them onto the trolley. They always took more than they needed in case they were diverted. 'If you can swap shifts, I'll go with you.'

'Would you?'

'Yes, if you want me to.'

'Thanks, I would like that. The more I've thought about it, the more I want to go, and it'll be heaps easier if I'm not on my own.'

Since they'd landed the wind had increased and cloud was rolling in from the south-west. A change had been forecast. Anna recharged the onboard oxygen and the refueller moved in as soon as she'd finished. If the wind increased much more, the engineers would tow the aircraft into the hangar.

Anna met Nick in the staff carpark forty-five minutes later. Making the most of the rare occasions they worked a shift together, they'd car-pooled that morning.

'Has Rachel Carmichael called you any more?' Anna asked when Nick was reversing out of the carpark. It had been playing on her mind since Nick had offered to go to the funeral with her.

'It was Rachel who told me about the funeral,' he said.

'Oh.' It shouldn't bother her that Nick had been in touch with Rachel, but it did.

'Oh, nothing,' Nick said.

'Has she called you very often, you know, since—'

'She has, several times.'

That bit of information had Anna chewing on her bottom lip. 'I suppose she's not in a very good place right now.'

'No, she's not. Last time I spoke to her I gave her the name and contact details of a brilliant grief counsellor.'

He took his eyes off the road for a moment to glance Anna's way. When he had her attention he said, 'She has called again since, but I didn't pick up. I don't want to give her the wrong idea about anything.'

Anna acknowledged this with a brief tilt of her head. What a bizarre situation Nick was in, she thought, idly watching the scenery whiz by.

They were halfway home before she broke the silence again. 'I can understand why she'd want to talk to you, Nick. You were there and you're a good listener, and you're very kind and compassionate.'

'Don't forget witty, intelligent, good-looking and sexy,' he said, with an exaggerated wink.

'That too,' she said lightly, and the mood inside the cab lifted for what remained of their journey.

Nick's mobile rang as they pulled into the driveway at Beth's. 'This better not be the base,' he said. He dragged it out, frowning at the caller ID. 'It's not a call-out.' His voice was flat, and he made no attempt to answer the phone.

'Okay,' Anna said, unclipping her seatbelt and reaching for the door handle. It was personal and he wanted her out of there.

'Sorry,' he said, and she could see he meant it.

She grabbed her things and climbed out, closed the door, but not before she heard him say, 'What do you want now, Lauren?'

About ten minutes later Anna heard Nick's ute reverse out the drive, the tyres screeching when he took off.

He didn't return for several hours. Beth was on an afternoon shift. Anna kept telling herself it was none of her business where Nick had gone, or what he was doing.

In need of hearing a familiar voice, she phoned Izzy, but her daughter didn't answer. Anna wondered what she would be up to at six-thirty on a Friday evening.

Then she heard Nick's key in the lock followed by the squeal of the front door hinges, and her whole body contracted in anticipation.

He stopped at her open bedroom door. She was sitting on the bed, balancing her laptop.

'The nursing home contacted me,' he said.

He must have taken another call after the one from his wife. They might be separated, but Anna remembered how many times Teresa and her husband had been on and off before they'd actually divorced. It'd been an emotional rollercoaster for her sister.

'Mum had absconded.'

'I didn't think she'd be well enough to do that.'

'Neither did I.'

With his eyes closed Nick rubbed the back of his neck. He looked tired—tired and worn down.

She put the computer on the bed beside her. 'Is there anything I can do to help?'

He shook his head.

'I would have come with you, helped look for her.'

His eyes snapped open; they were the stormy grey colour she was beginning to recognise meant he was angry.

'Oh, I didn't have to look far, I knew where she'd be. And trust me, Anna, you wouldn't be calling me kind and compassionate if you'd seen the way I had to "coax" her out of the workers' club.'

Anna could feel the tension coming off him in waves.

'I wouldn't have minded, Nick. It's not as if I've never met her.'

'Anna, it was embarrassing enough without having you there as a witness.' Nick's hand dropped to his side. 'I'm having a shower and then food.' He turned to go.

'How did she get there?'

He paused. 'She called a cab. But it's only a matter of time until she liberates her car from Snake's shed.'

With that he disappeared. Anna sat on the bed until she heard the shower running. How would you deal with a recalcitrant parent? What would she do in the same situation? She had no idea. She couldn't imagine her mother ever going near a poker machine. And the thought of her mother or father living in their car? It was out there with pigs flying.

Anna chuckled out loud at the thought of Izzy having to deal with her the way Nick did with Marlene. But her amusement dissipated as quickly as it had risen. It was as if Nick had become the parent, and Marlene the delinquent child.

Anna slid off the bed and went to feed the cat, and find something for her own dinner.

28

Chastened after her escapade, Marlene behaved like the perfect resident over the weekend. Nick suspected the excitement and exertion of her little excursion had left her feeling sick and exhausted. Not to mention the cigarettes and alcohol she'd consumed. It was just as well she was behaving herself because his patience was running out.

A solid night's sleep was fast becoming a fond memory. Nick placed part of the blame squarely, if not fairly, on Anna. Since their kiss, his body wouldn't let him forget the feel of her body, skin to skin with his.

The moment his head touched the pillow each night, all he could smell, taste or think about was her, only two closed doors and six steps away down the passage.

Between his increasing sexual frustration, his diminishing confidence in finding palatable alternative accommodation for his mother, and the reality of being on night shift again, Nick felt like he was as close to snapping as he had been for a long time. And that was without taking into consideration Lauren's phone call.

Nick yawned and his jaw cracked. Lauren said there'd been an offer on their house, pending an engineer's report and the buyer coming up with finance. The money they were offering was rock bottom. What should they do? Take whatever they could get or hold out for the auction? Over the weekend he'd thought about it and was no closer to a decision.

He'd been flying in the early hours, creeping in before dawn so as not to disturb Anna or Beth. Now, five hours of restless sleep later, Nick's head throbbed and his eyes felt like sandpaper. He would have slept at the base but this afternoon was Brett Carmichael's funeral and he'd promised Anna he'd go with her.

The fan on the chest of drawers pushed warm, stale air around the small room. There was nothing as flash as an overhead fan in this room and even with a blanket hanging up at the window, the space was far from dark. The mongrel from next door started barking; someone started up hammering. He wrapped the pillow around his head but knew more sleep was out of the question.

'I know we're going to a funeral, but you look awesome,' Nick said when Anna met him in the passage.

Anna glanced down at the simple sleeveless black dress. 'Thanks. My wardrobe was sadly lacking so I went op-shopping this morning. Five dollars,' she said, smoothing a hand down the front of the dress, looking pleased with herself. 'And it still had the tag on it.' She crinkled her nose. 'It's a bit short though, don't you think?'

Nick openly ran his gaze up and down her legs. 'No, not from where I'm standing,' he said. The black high heel sandals meant he'd hardly have to tilt his head down to kiss her. 'You know, you didn't strike me as an op shop kind of girl.'

A snort was the only way he could describe the sound that Anna made. 'They know me by name at the op shops near where I live in Adelaide.'

Nick raised his eyebrows, only mildly irritated when she swerved around his curiosity with a flippant, 'Never thought I'd see you in a suit. You look pretty hot yourself.'

Should he tell her it was the only suit he'd ever owned? And the one he'd worn at his wedding? Nah, he'd save that for some other time. Maybe never.

'Let's get going,' he said, and she scooped up the black shoulder bag sitting at the foot of her bed. He followed her outside, locking the front door.

'Where's Beth?'

'I don't know. Said she was going out,' Anna said. Nick slipped on a pair of sunglasses. 'She's certainly not her usual bubbly self since the Tim episode.'

Nick's ute was parked at the kerb. He opened the passenger-side door for her, amused by her consternation at this simple act of chivalry.

When they were on the move he said, 'Tim's being a complete pain in the arse. He's definitely not his usual bubbly self, either.'

'Maybe we could—'

'Not going to go there, Anna.' Nick was slowly shaking his head. 'I have enough to deal with in my own life without poking my nose into other people's business.'

'You don't even know what I was going to say!'

He peered at her over the top of his sunglasses. 'I can guess.'

She folded her arms, angling herself away from him. He happily noted that the change of position had her dress hiking further up her thighs. Down boy, he thought, and focused his attention on the road.

The chapel was packed and overhead fans were churning the air. They squeezed into a pew three rows from the front. With no room to spare, Nick flashed her a 'not my fault' smile when his thigh slid firmly against the length of hers.

When everyone was seated, the bereaved family and close friends filled the front pews. Anna's eyes didn't waver from the flower-swathed coffin. Nick suspected she was seeing Brett's bloody, mangled face and head. When she shifted on the seat so she didn't have to face the coffin, Nick reached for her hand, linked his fingers with hers and squeezed. She returned the pressure, clinging onto his hand like it was a lifeline.

Dark glasses covered Rachel's eyes, her blonde hair hanging limply down her back. What he could see of her face was pale, hollowed out by grief. And any wonder—two funerals in the space of a month. First her stillborn baby, and now her husband. It was more than anyone should be expected to bear.

'God, I can't believe how much weight she's lost,' Anna whispered from beside him. 'Only five weeks ago she was married, and pregnant.'

Emotion tightened Nick's chest. With discipline, and the experience gained over a long nursing career, he'd managed to mentally file away the events encountered on both visits to Elder Creek station. But seeing Rachel Carmichael in the flesh now cracked open the drawer on those memories.

Anna's grip on his hand didn't loosen. When he glanced sideways she gave his hand a reassuring squeeze. He swallowed, the tightness in his chest easing.

Jim, the station hand from Elder Creek, sat on the other side of the aisle, directly behind Rachel Carmichael. He was clearly uncomfortable in a tie and jacket. Coarse grey hair scraped his shirt collar and his weathered face looked chafed from too close a shave.

Nick noticed that over the course of the service Jim's focus rarely shifted from Rachel. And later at the graveside the old station hand was never further than a step away, ready to be leaned on if necessary.

There was a paucity of shade at the cemetery, the sun unrelenting. Nick left his suit coat in the car and rolled up his shirtsleeves.

The minister, his face the colour of beetroot, took pity on the sweltering crowd and the words said at the interment were brief ... A life lost in tragic circumstances ... Grieving and bewildered families urged to seek comfort and support.

A middle-aged man with thin lips stood rigidly on the opposite side of the grave. Beside him a woman wept, her tears coursing down a face corrugated with wrinkles. A younger, heavy-set man with a bushy beard made an awkward attempt to comfort her.

Anna leaned into Nick and he tilted his head closer. 'Are they Brett's parents?' she said softly, her breath tickling his ear.

He nodded. 'And his brother. He flew in from some remote place in Asia. They didn't want to bury Brett until he got here. The parents were station people, but live in Broken Hill now. Rachel told me all about them, says they blame her.'

Above her sunglasses, Anna's brow furrowed. Her attention shifted back to Brett's family.

The minister finished, and the coffin was lowered. Friends and relatives began to file past the grave murmuring their final goodbyes.

'Do you want to pay your last respects?' Nick said.

'No, I feel like a bit interloper as it is,' she said. 'But I'm glad I came. It was like I needed to be here.'

'Yeah, I understand.'

'And thanks for coming with me,' she said. 'I can't imagine what it would have been like on my own.'

'Anytime you need someone to hold your hand, I'm your man.'

Nick scanned the thinning crowd. There were several familiar faces.

'I feel like I should say something to Brett's family, and to Rachel,' Anna said.

'Are you sure?'

'Yes, I think so.'

'I'll come with you,' he said, and tightened his grip on her hand.

People had begun wending their way back to the cemetery car-park. Brett's family had disappeared. After searching for several minutes they gave up, found some shade and waited while Rachel finished her conversation with the minister. The two women standing with Rachel began to guide her towards the carpark, but she shook their hands off and wobbled across to where Nick and Anna were standing.

'I was hoping you'd come,' Rachel said, sliding off her sunglasses, her attention solely on Nick.

He shifted from one foot to the other. 'You've met Anna,' he said, draping an arm around her shoulders, pulling her into him. He didn't care how hot it was, and Anna didn't seem to mind either.

Rachel's eyes were swollen and bloodshot. She squinted at Anna. 'Oh, yes, you're the pilot. Aren't you the person who found my husband?'

'Yes, I am. Please accept my condolences, Rachel. No-one should have to go through what you've been through.'

Rachel's eyes filled with tears and she dabbed at them with a wadded up tissue. 'Brett's family blames me, and I can't help but think it was my fault. But that place … I told them I wasn't going back. If only Brett had—' She stopped, curled her fingers into a fist and pushed them hard against her mouth.

'Had what?' Nick prompted, his voice quietly firm.

Rachel shook her head, quick, jerky movements. 'Nothing,' she said. 'It was nothing.'

'Rachel? Sweetie?'

A woman Nick assumed to be Rachel's mother materialised beside her. The black outfit she wore accentuated the deep shadows beneath her eyes. She frowned at Rachel and threw an irate glare in their direction.

'Mum. This is Nick and Anna ... This is my Mum, Trish Campion.'

The older woman's expression mellowed slightly.

'Nick is the nurse who delivered Matilda,' Rachel said, pressing her lips together, focusing on the tissue she was shredding. 'She found Brett.'

Trish's face crumpled. 'Oh, dear,' she said, sniffing, rooting around in her handbag for more tissues. 'I am so sorry. For all of us. It's such a God-awful tragedy.' She handed the tissues to her daughter. Rachel sniffed and took them. 'One wonders if you ever recover from something like this.'

Nick and Anna murmured in agreement.

Rachel conjured up a watery, over-bright cheerfulness. 'We're going for coffee, or a drink if you'd prefer,' she said, naming a popular local watering hole. 'Jim, and a couple of the others will be there. You'll come won't you, Nick?'

Nick lifted his hand, Anna's fingers tightly entwined with his. Trish nudged her. 'Oh, and you too, Anna,' Rachel said.

Nick tipped his sunglasses onto his forehead, raised his eyebrows to Anna.

'Thanks Rachel, Trish. But no, we won't intrude,' Anna said, and Nick silently thanked her for reading his mind. Anna had needed to say goodbye to Brett, to get closure, but as far as he was concerned there was no reason for them to prolong the experience. He wanted out of there, now.

Rachel stepped back, slipped her sunglasses into place. Her mother took her hand. 'Come on, love,' she said.

'You take care, Rachel,' Anna said, and Rachel nodded, stiffly. 'Bye Trish, lovely to meet you.'

'All the best, Rachel,' Nick said. And then in a blur of movement, Rachel launched herself towards him, inadvertently elbowing Anna out of the way.

Nick was given no choice but to return the hug, gingerly patting her on the back. Like a limpet Rachel hung on, stumbling when he purposefully disentangled himself. She was crying now, loud, hiccoughing sobs. Trish threw Nick and Anna a strained smile before reaching for her daughter and gathering her into her arms.

Nick turned to Anna. 'Are you okay?' he asked quietly.

'Yep. You?'

'All good.'

From behind Rachel's back, Trish flicked her wrist, waving them off.

Nick grabbed Anna's hand. 'Let's get out of here,' he said under his breath.

Anna didn't need to be told twice, and they fled as fast as her high-heeled sandals would let them.

Safely ensconced in Nick's dual cab minutes later, the engine on and the air conditioner cranked up to high, he turned to Anna. 'I'm sorry about that,' he said.

'Why? What's there for you to be sorry for? It's awful what's happened. I can't begin to imagine what it must be like for her.'

'No,' he said, and slowly reached for his seatbelt.

'She's grieving, you offered support and comfort, maybe in her fragile and mixed-up state she's confused that for something else. Who knows?'

There was no confusion in his mind about the way Rachel had thrown herself at him, and then ground her body against his.

'You're probably right. She's grieving. She's confused.'

His phone pinged with an incoming message. He put the ute in park again and reached for his phone.

'Oh no, it's her. Begging me to come for a drink. Without you. She wants to thank me *properly*.' He pinched the bridge of his nose. 'I don't believe this.'

'Drop me off if you need to go.'

'Anna,' Nick said through clenched teeth. 'I will not drop you off. I am not going anywhere near her. I came because there was no way I was letting you come on your own. End of story.' He threw the phone onto the console. 'I wish you'd get that.' He pounded the steering wheel with the heel of his hand.

'I do,' she said quietly. 'But I thought maybe there was something you needed to say to her without me there. Or something … ' Her words petered out and she slumped in the seat.

They sat in silence for several minutes, each lost in their own thoughts. Then Anna said, 'Let's go for a drink. Or three.'

'Let's,' he said.

29

Nick took Anna to The Palace Hotel on Argent Street.

'You ever been here before?' he said, holding open the door for her.

'No, I haven't,' she said, entranced by the huge, colourful murals on the foyer walls. 'Isn't this the pub that was in *Priscilla, Queen of the Desert?*'

'Yep. You'll have to come to Drag Bingo one night,' he said.

She looked at him, her mouth a perfect O. He grinned. 'It'll be worth it, if only to watch your face.'

They sat at a table in a quiet corner. Anna checked the time, quickly calculating the hours until she'd fly.

'I'll have a beer,' she said.

Nick came back with a beer for her, a squash for himself and a packet of peanuts. Anna emptied them into the bowl and scooped up a handful.

'I keep forgetting you're rostered on tonight,' she said.

'With a bit of luck, all I'll do is sleep. I'm totally knackered.' As if on cue, he yawned.

The bar was dimly lit and deliciously cool. They people-watched, although there wasn't much happening: a handful of seasoned drinkers were nursing drinks and the barman was leaning on the bar watching the television. But within an hour or so the after-work crowd would swell numbers.

'What are you doing for Christmas?'

'I'm working,' Anna said, crunching on several peanuts.

'I thought you'd be heading south.'

'I will for the three days I have off before Christmas. I'm back Christmas Eve. What about you?'

'I'm on nights, believe it or not.' He stretched, tilting back in the chair. Anna's eyes were drawn to the breadth of his chest, the way the buttons of his dress shirt pulled at their buttonholes.

'Any update on accommodation for your mum?' she asked in an effort to distract herself.

'Nah,' he said and then drained his glass. 'Another one?'

'Why not?' She finished her drink, handing him the empty glass.

He went to the bar and she watched him chatting with the barman. Given their easy familiarity Anna wondered if they knew each other.

'Thanks,' Anna said, accepting the cold, frothing glass of beer.

Halfway into the second drink, Anna felt the knot in her belly begin to loosen; the tension from the funeral and what had happened afterwards was beginning to ease. She rarely drank alcohol, and she'd be the first to admit she was a cheap drunk.

'Do you know the barman?'

'Trevor Miller? You don't remember him?'

Anna contemplated the tall, rangy man behind the bar. Tattoos covered every available space on his forearms. 'No. Should I?'

'He was in the same year as us at school.'

'Nick! It's years ago. I don't remember anyone.'

'I remembered you.'

'Yeah, but not right off. And I did admit there was something vaguely familiar about you.'

His smile was infectious and Anna found herself smiling back.

The sport on the television above the bar snagged Nick's attention, while Anna studied the barman. No, she definitely didn't remember Trevor. He looked older than Nick, but that could have been lifestyle-related.

'You know what?' she said, and Nick shifted his attention from the TV to her.

'What?'

'These sandals are killing my feet.'

Nick bent sideways to look under the table at the offending footwear. She wiggled her toes.

'They're too small. They didn't have anything my size in black.'

'Op shop?'

She nodded. 'Only wasted seven dollars, because I'll never wear them again.'

'That would be criminally negligent, unfair to all red-blooded men.'

'You know that's an incredibly sexist thing to say.'

'It was meant as a compliment, Anna. You have breathtakingly beautiful legs and wearing those sandals …'

Anna knew her mouth was hanging open but she'd lost the power to close it. The way Nick was looking at her sent a flash of heat straight to her core. In her hand, the beer glass felt cold and slippery. At the bar someone shouted. Nick picked up his glass and drained it.

'Finish your drink and let's get out of here,' he said, in a voice she didn't recognise.

She downed the last mouthful, hitched her bag over her shoulder and on shaky legs, followed him out.

The drive home was mute; the atmosphere crackling. When they arrived at the house, Beth's ute wasn't in the driveway, or on the kerb.

They climbed out. Car doors closed simultaneously followed by a clunk and a flash when Nick hit the remote lock.

Anna opened the screen and held it while Nick unlocked the front door. He stepped back for her to enter. The moment she crossed the threshold her shoulder bag hit the carpet with a resounding thud. She lifted her right foot and slipped off the sandal with a groan of satisfaction.

Teetering on one foot she lost her balance, yelped, and would have fallen if Nick hadn't been right behind her.

Her bottom connecting with his groin added oxygen to the fire that was already smouldering. One second she was falling, and the next she was pressed hard against the passage wall, Nick's mouth crashing down onto hers.

Leaving behind a decade of frustration and self-denial, Anna sank into the kiss. Lips bruised, teeth scraped against teeth, tongues mated in an age-old rhythm. Determined to get closer, she twined a leg up and around his hip. With a feral growl his hand skimmed up her thigh, fingers finding the elastic of her knickers.

'Anna—' Nick's breath was hot and ragged against her lips. 'If you don't want this to move to its inevitable conclusion, you'd better say so, *now*.' He tipped back far enough to look at her. 'This is what I want but you need to be sure it's what you want.'

'Yes, I'm sure.' And at that moment, her body hot and heavy with desire, she was 110 per cent sure; sure that if they didn't get on with it she'd implode. Whether she'd be so sure tomorrow, or even in an hour's time—well she'd have to deal with that then.

'I'm not on the Pill.'

'I have condoms.'

'Whose room?'

'Yours. Things are going to get even hotter and you have an overhead fan,' he said, nuzzling kisses the length of her neck whilst backing her towards the bedroom door.

She turned the fan on high and he pushed the door closed with his foot. The last thinking thing she did before she landed on the bed with Nick on top of her was reach to flip over the picture on the bedside cupboard, the one of her and Izzy. The frame toppled, and then slid noiselessly down between the bedside cupboard and the bed.

'What are you thinking?'

Anna's head swivelled sideways on the pillow. 'I thought you were asleep.'

'I was, but your thinking woke me.' He pushed himself up onto one elbow. 'What time is it?'

'My phone's in my bag, and my bag's out there.'

Nick grunted, scanned the room for his discarded clothes. 'I think mine's in my trousers.'

Anna's eyes travelled the length of his naked body as he bounced out of bed and grabbed the trousers lying in a crumpled heap on the floor alongside his wallet.

Like fireworks, hot spots erupted across her skin as she remembered what that body could do, and why the wallet was there. They'd find a torn foil packet somewhere.

'Damn,' he said, phone in hand. 'It's nearly seven.' He yawned, and stretched. His night shift started at seven.

Anna inched the bedsheet higher, covering herself completely, all the while envying him his unselfconsciousness.

He put the phone and wallet on the chest of drawers and returned to the bed. 'So,' he said, 'back to my original question. What were you thinking about?'

She pushed herself upright, careful not to let the sheet slip. 'Noth—'

'Don't you dare say nothing, Anna. I could feel you over-thinking what's happened here.'

Opening her mouth to rebuff him, he cut her off for the second time.

'And if you say it was all a mistake—'

'No,' she said, her head moving repeatedly from side to side. 'It was never going to be a mistake, Nick. We both know it's been there between us from the beginning. But we can't let it happen again.'

'Right. Not a mistake, but it can't happen again. Why not?'

Closing her eyes, she asked herself the same question. Why not?

The answer? She wasn't sure any more. She knew that if they did it again she wouldn't want to stop having sex with Nick, and then her life would get even more complicated.

He stroked a lazy finger down her arm. 'Why not, Anna?' he repeated, his warm breath feathering across her lips. He propped himself up and tugged at the sheet. She shivered as his thumb grazed her breast.

'Please don't,' she begged, opening her eyes to stare into his.

'Why not?' He brushed his lips against hers.

'Because—' she said, putting the flat of her hand on his chest with the intention of pushing him away. And then she froze when she heard voices out the front. Someone coughed.

'It's Beth,' she hissed, and shoved him. He sprawled back onto the mattress.

'I didn't hear a car.'

'Well, we were a bit preoccupied.'

She scrambled down the bed. Nick gave a growl of approval. Footsteps crunched up the gravel pathway. She glowered at him over her shoulder, diving for the door handle. Scuttling into the passage she retrieved her shoes and shoulder bag and shot back into the bedroom.

Simultaneously, the bedroom door closed with a click as a key slid into the front door.

Anna pressed her back against the door, sandals and handbag hugged to her heaving chest. Propped up against the headboard, Nick grinned. She lifted a finger to her lips to shush him, and almost took out an eye with a sandal heel.

She heard Beth pause in the passageway, then the clank of car keys as they lobbed into the pottery bowl on the bookcase.

'Is your bedroom door closed?' she mouthed, gesticulating wildly.

'I can't remember,' Nick mouthed back, still grinning.

Anna tiptoed towards the bed. 'We'll have to wait, and listen, and when the coast's clear you'll have to go back to your room.'

'Why?' he whispered.

'Beth can't know about this—' she spluttered.

'Why not?'

Anna stilled, her eyes not leaving his. 'Humour me,' she said.

They stared at each other for what seemed like an age. Nick's grin vanished. 'This time,' he said. 'But I'll need a better answer than that in the near future, Anna.'

She shifted from one foot to the other. 'Okay,' she said.

Zeroing in on the handbag and shoes still clutched to her bare chest, something sparked in Nick's eyes.

'But before I go, would you mind doing me a small favour?' His tone brimmed with reasonableness. Her eyes narrowed.

'What?'

'Slip on your shoes. I want to see you in them naked—' He covered his head with his arms as a tangle of leather sailed through the air and landed on top of him.

Anna turned her back and dressed quickly in a T-shirt and shorts. Snickering under his breath, Nick pulled on his jocks and trousers. He didn't button up his shirt.

'Where're my shoes?'

Anna dropped to her knees and hauled them out from under the bed. 'Here,' she said and thrust them at him.

Shoulder to shoulder they faced the bedroom door, Anna with her ear towards it. She eased it open, darted her head out and back. 'She's in the kitchen, talking to Albert.'

Nick nodded. Anna backed away so he could get past.

'Wait!'

He halted. 'What?'

'Don't forget these,' she said and held out his wallet and mobile phone.

When he went to move again she grabbed his arm. 'Maybe I should go out first, distract her?'

'You might want to turn your T-shirt in the right way before you do.'

Anna glanced down. 'Oh, shit.' In one fluid movement she stripped off the garment, then slipped it on the right way out. 'Better?'

'I liked you better without it,' he said, not giving her a chance to respond, his lips hot and possessive against hers.

'That'll have to do, for now.' He emphasised the final two words.

Head spinning and lips tingling, Anna opened the door and dashed out in search of Beth, and her own equilibrium.

30

'Hey, Mum. What ya been up to?' Izzy's beaming face on the laptop screen put a smile on Anna's.

'Not much. I went to a funeral this afternoon.'

'A funeral? Who died?'

'A man I met on one of the stations. It was very sad.'

'Are you all right? Was there someone there who could give you a hug?'

'I'm good, and yes, someone, er, gave me a hug.' Anna pinched herself hard hoping to halt the blush she knew was coming. This was her daughter she was talking to.

'Wicked, Mum. Tell me all about him. What's his name? Is he hot? When do I get to meet him? Has there been more than one hug?' Izzy gave an exaggerated wink and bounced up and down on her bed.

'Whoa,' Anna said. 'You'll make me seasick.'

'Tell me, tell me, tell me,' Izzy chanted.

'There's nothing to tell. Nick is one of the flight nurses and because he knew the man as well, we went to the funeral together.'

'Oh, is that all? You need a boyfriend, Mum.'

'What do I want with a boyfriend when I have you?'

'I won't be around forever.' Izzy leaned in closer to the camera and continued earnestly. 'I'll be in Year Eleven next year. Two years from now I'll be getting ready to go to uni, and then who knows? I could travel or anything. You'll be all on your own.'

Anna sat up straighter. Mother and daughter stared at each other.

'Aunt Tee says you should have a boyfriend. She says you're young enough to have more kids, if you want to, that is.'

Anna folded her arms. 'Maybe my daughter and my sister should worry less about my life, and concentrate more on their own lives.' Anna knew she sounded snippy and unreasonable, but she didn't care. She was tired. It had been a rollercoaster of a day.

'Just saying, Mum.'

Anna's pulse echoed in her ears. Inexplicably, she felt like bursting into tears.

'So,' she forced herself to say. 'How's everything at your end?'

'Cool. Exams are over and it's only nine days until school finishes. Woo hoo!'

'Only nine days?'

'Don't look so shocked, Mum. It's less than three weeks to Christmas Day.'

'You're joking?' Anna grabbed her phone and opened the calendar; sure enough, there were less than three weeks until Christmas. When had that happened?

'You remember that I won't be there on Christmas Day? My days off are just before. I'll drive down and we'll have our Christmas a couple of days early.'

'Then I can go to Clara's for Christmas Day.'

It wasn't a question and Anna frowned. 'Clara's? What about Aunt Teresa? I thought Miranda was coming home.'

'Nah, she has to work, or so she told Aunt Tee. But I reckon she's got a boyfriend and she wants to have Christmas with him.'

'Did Miranda tell you that?'

'No, not in so many words,' Izzy said, scrunching up her face into the look Anna always read as *You really are thick sometimes, Mum.*

'But Clara's? Christmas is a family time, Iz. What about Aunt Tee?'

Izzy looked away from the camera, definitely evasive, and Anna's parent alarm clamoured.

'Did Clara or her parents ask you?'

'Clara asked me but she said it would be okay with her parents.'

'Izzy,' Anna said and shook her head slowly. 'We've discussed this before. Any invitations need to come from Clara's parents.'

Her daughter looked up, her eyes filling with defiant tears. 'That's all right for you to say. You'll be up there and I'll be stuck here at Aunt Tee's on Christmas Day!'

'Izzy, we'll still have our Christmas together, just not on the twenty-fifth. I'm sorry I won't be there with you on the day. I bet Teresa has something special planned.'

The tears dried up but Izzy's expression remained defiant. 'Probably. But if she does you can be sure her new friend will be invited.'

'Have you met him?'

'That's assuming it's a him.'

'Really?'

'What do you think, Mum?' Izzy replied, and Anna didn't know what to think. Izzy gave an exaggerated shrug.

'You little tease,' Anna said. 'I love you Iz, and although I won't be there on the actual day, we'll have fun, I promise.'

'Yeah Mum, I know we will. It's just that we've never missed being together on Christmas Day.'

'I know we haven't, but this is my first Christmas here and that makes it my turn to be on call. I promise that next year we'll do Christmas together, no matter where we are.'

When Anna disconnected she tried Teresa's mobile but the call went to voicemail. Anna left a message asking her sister to phone back.

Counting up on her fingers, Anna discovered that it'd been thirteen days since she'd spoken with her sister. They'd messaged and relayed information through Izzy, but they hadn't actually spoken.

Disconcerted, Anna sat back on the bed. Thirteen days—a day shy of a fortnight. It was many moons since they'd gone that long between chats. Reaching for another pillow to prop behind her back, her hand stalled. It hovered over the pillow on the bed beside her.

There was a dent where Nick's head had lain not two hours before. Conflicting emotions vied for space. Her hand dropped, her shoulders fell, and tears welled in her eyes. The empty house echoed around her.

If Beth had noticed anything different with either of her tenants when they'd emerged from their respective bedrooms earlier, she hadn't mentioned it. They'd talked about the funeral, and how devastating the circumstances were for Rachel.

Anna had let herself relax a little, grateful to have Beth there as a buffer. And then in a whirlwind, Beth had showered, changed and disappeared in a cloud of perfume.

Envisioning an evening alone with Nick following Beth's exit, Anna's tension had escalated. In her lust-saturated state, she couldn't trust herself—she knew they'd end up in bed. Then he'd been called out on a priority two.

Simultaneously giddy with relief and sick with disappointment, Anna convinced herself that a few hours alone would do her good.

It would give her a chance to strengthen her resolve before she spent any more time alone with him.

Hugging the pillow, Anna slid down the bed. Without the light of the computer screen, the room was dark. It was late. Unable to resist, she pressed her face against the cotton pillowslip, savouring the lingering scent of Nick's aftershave.

But it did nothing to calm her. Instead, it had the opposite effect. The sensation that her two lives were diverging, pulling her in opposite directions more rapidly with each passing day, had her heart racing and her mouth going dry.

She must have dozed off because when her phone rang she spent seconds wondering where she was, and why she was desperately clutching a pillow.

Anna pushed the pillow sideways and reached for the phone on the bedside cupboard. It was her sister.

'Hi, Anna. Hope I haven't woken you, but your message said to ring back anytime and life's been hectic.'

'That's okay,' Anna said, levering herself into a sitting position. 'We haven't talked for nearly two weeks—'

'I know, I'm sorry, and I've been meaning to ring. I'd like to take some time away over Christmas and New Year. I was wondering if Izzy could come to you.'

'Right.' Anna drew out the word slowly, giving her sleep-fuddled brain time to process what Teresa had said. Then her thoughts flew in a hundred directions at once.

Where would they stay? There wasn't enough room at Beth's. What would Izzy do while Anna worked? Who'd look out for her? She was only fifteen. What would she tell Nick? And everyone else …

'Anna? You haven't gone back to sleep?'

'No, I haven't. I was taking it all in. When did you want to leave?'

'Christmas Eve, and I know it's short notice, but I was hoping we'd be able to work something out. If not—'

'Is this anything to do with your new friend? The one Izzy hasn't met and you've studiously avoided telling me anything about.'

Silence, except for the sound of Teresa breathing. Anna repositioned the phone, peeling it off her sweaty cheek, unaware she'd been pressing so hard.

'Teresa, you don't have to tell me anything if you don't want to,' she said. 'And I'll sort out something for Izzy.'

'I'm really, really happy when I'm with her,' Teresa said, tentatively.

'Who, Izzy? I know you are but you deserve to have your own time, and I don't begrudge you that. Not one little bit. You've always been there for us—'

'Anna, I don't mean Izzy.'

'Ah, I see.' Izzy's mentioning the gender of Teresa's new friend came rushing back. What had her teenage daughter picked up on that Anna had so obviously missed?

'I hope you do see, Anna. This isn't just about dating and sex; it's about friendship, common interests, not being lonely anymore.'

Anna took a moment to consider her sister's words and then said, 'I remember Mum shouting at Dad once, saying she could understand why a woman might choose another woman over a man, because most men had no clue what a woman really wanted, or needed.'

'Our mother said that? What did Dad say?'

'I can't remember because I was too busy trying to get my head around Mum being a lesbian.'

'That is so funny. What were you thinking?'

'I know, but I was only thirteen at the time.'

'Well, my friend's name is Vanessa. I've been doing some consulting for a company in Sydney and she's the CEO. That's how we met. Vanessa's also been in heterosexual relationships all her life. She's a divorcee like me and has three grown-up children. It turns out we've both been on our own for a long time.'

'You've had Tom and Miranda, me and Izzy,' Anna said, unrepentantly petulant.

'I know, and I've enjoyed every moment. I love you all, but it is time for me to devote some time to me.'

'Have you told Tom and Miranda?'

'No, not yet. I'll tell everyone in the new year. That's what this trip, if it comes off, is all about—to see if we can be together longer than a day here and there. We're going to see the sights, go to the Opera House, cruise on the harbour … It'll be wonderful.'

Anna couldn't ignore the excitement in her sister's voice.

'I feel comfortable with her, Anna. She's six years older than me, but we have so much in common. And don't worry, I was as gobsmacked as you are. I guess if I didn't have any reservations myself, I would have shared it with you sooner.'

'I'd be a liar if I said you hadn't totally surprised me. Izzy hinted, and I thought she was teasing.'

'She must have been teasing. There's no way she could have known. Vanessa's never been here when Izzy was home—'

'It's fine, Teresa. You don't have to explain. I know you've always looked out for Izzy. And you're right, you deserve time for yourself.'

'I'm as nervous as hell. Excited, but nervous. I've lost more weight … These ten days away together—'

'Will be perfect. I'll look forward to meeting Vanessa sometime. And if it doesn't work, I'll be there for you.' Anna's throat thickened with emotion. 'I love you, Teresa. I couldn't have asked for a better sister.'

'Thanks, sweetie. I love you too. Now, what about Izzy?'

'Oh, before we move on to Izzy, what's the plan if the holiday goes well?'

'There's no plan as yet. It's still early days.'

'Yes, but I know you, Teresa, and you would have thought this through from every angle. Let's not pretend your business couldn't work from a home office anywhere.'

Teresa sighed. 'You're right on both accounts.'

'So what to do about Izzy is not just about Christmas.'

'In this instance, yes it is, Anna. I made a commitment to you and Izzy and I have no intention of walking out on it. We'll deal with things when, and if, they arise.'

'That sounds more than reasonable,' Anna said after a moment, sounding reasonable herself, when what she really wanted to do was swear, and stamp her foot like a two-year-old. Her sister, her rock, the person who'd always been there for her, had found somebody else to be there for.

'All I can say is, life is short, Anna. Good things don't come along very often. When they do, you need to grab them with both hands. You hear me?'

'I hear you,' she said, and they turned their attention to Izzy's needs, and the here and now.

31

Nick felt as if he was doing everything in slow motion. At four in the morning, the body's circadian rhythms meant energy was at a low ebb. That good night's sleep he'd hoped for? Maybe it'd happen tonight.

They were on their second flight for the shift. As luck would have it, he'd been in a deep sleep when the duty doctor had rung and woken him with details of the second call. He couldn't believe his luck. The flight nurse who'd been rostered on nights before him hadn't flown at all.

Now they were in flight to Adelaide via the oil and gas fields. Nick's brain felt like mush. It'd be sun-up before they touched down in Broken Hill and he could go to bed at last.

The patient, a field operator, had rolled his 4WD vehicle and it'd been several hours before he'd been retrieved by the paramedics and taken to the oil and gas field's casualty centre. The paramedics had shown Nick a photo of the 4WD utility: the patient was lucky his injuries were limited to a few fractures and a headache.

The man on the stretcher moaned, the sound muffled by the oxygen mask. He clumsily lifted his hand to pry at the soft collar around his neck.

'What's up, mate?' Nick said, raising his voice to be heard over the drone of the propellers.

'Gotta lot of pain,' the patient said. 'Are we nearly there?'

Nick paused in his assessment of the man's splinted, severely fractured arm. He leaned towards the window, taking in the distant lights twinkling below.

'My best guess? Half an hour and you'll be in the back of an ambulance and on your way to the hospital.'

'My wife … Did anyone contact my wife?'

'Yep, the paramedic at the casualty centre did. Your wife will be waiting for you in A&E.'

The man nodded as best he could with the restriction of the soft collar. Nick administered more analgesia. The patient's eyes drifted shut, his whole body sighing as the painkillers rushed to their destination.

Nick sat back. He threw a glance over his right shoulder, disappointed for the hundredth time that it was Kyle Peterson's bulky frame crammed behind the controls, not Anna's slim, toned, incredibly flexible—

With a sharp indrawn breath Nick redirected his thoughts. He needed every drop of his sluggish blood supply up top, not down below. But he couldn't stop the smile when he thought back to the evening before and Anna's reaction when Beth had come home.

She couldn't get him out of her bed fast enough, making him sneak back to his room while she distracted Beth.

When he'd shown his face ten minutes later, they'd both been in the kitchen. Beth had looked at him, raised a well-plucked eyebrow, and then glanced towards Anna, who'd been conscientiously refilling the cat's water bowl.

He'd wanted to grab her and take her back to bed. But Nick had kept his expression neutral, because he knew that that was what Anna wanted.

But his bedroom door had been wide open, his room patently unoccupied. And Beth knew how much he was attracted to Anna.

Now to convince Anna that she felt the same way about him. Nick knew she did, it was only that she hadn't admitted it to herself yet—there was no denying the way she'd wrapped those gorgeous legs around him and lustily welcomed him into her body. But Nick wanted her for way longer than one afternoon's tumble between the sheets. The rest of his life probably wouldn't be long enough.

The patient stirred. Nick cleared his ears. They were on their way down. A few more hours and he'd be able to go to bed. The thought of a dark room and cool sheets left him lightheaded with anticipation. How sad was that?

He started preparing the patient for transfer to the ambulance. He'd organised it in transit and hoped it'd be standing by at Adelaide airport.

After a smooth patient transfer they were in the air again, but headwinds slowed them down and they were back at base later than expected. The new day was well on its way. Doors were unlocked, lights on, and the cleaner's trolley parked in the corridor. The local station blared from a radio inside the hangar.

Nick hurried to unload and restock and get home before Anna left the house. He needed to see her, talk to her. He was off for three days now, and she was working every one of them. Knowing his luck, they'd probably pass on the highway.

When Nick hit the staff carpark he wanted to shout with frustration when he spotted her Commodore already there.

Nick's intuition told him that the less time allowed to elapse before he spoke with Anna, the better his chances of moving their relationship in the direction he wanted it to go. The longer she had to think about it the more likely she was to come up with a thousand reasons why that direction was wrong.

He contemplated going back inside and finding her. But even if he did, they'd have no more than a few minutes and no privacy at all. Disappointed beyond belief, he drove home with the windows down and the radio pounding.

The house was blissfully quiet. Nick showered and crawled into bed, resigned to spending the majority of this day off sleeping. He was out to it before his head hit the pillow.

On Thursday afternoon, the last of his three days off, Nick was driving downtown after visiting his mother and meeting the social worker when he espied Anna exiting one of the several real estate offices on Argent Street.

'What the hell—' he muttered, slowing down and peering into the rear-view mirror. Yes, it was definitely Anna.

He pulled into the first vacant parking bay without indicating, the motorist behind him giving an indignant blast on their horn. Nick lifted a hand in apology.

By then Anna was nowhere to be seen. But her unmistakable red Commodore was parked several spaces further up. He'd wait. She'd have to walk past him to get to her car.

She did, ten minutes later. Nick climbed out and locked the ute.

When he fell into step beside her, so focused was she on a brochure in her hand that she didn't notice Nick until he spoke. Heat blistered the bitumen and blasted back at them from the buildings.

'Buy you a coffee?'

Her head snapped up. 'Where did you come from?' she said, glancing over her shoulder at the deserted footpath.

Telltale colour highlighted her cheekbones. She was up to something.

'I saw your car—knew you wouldn't be far off. What have you been up to? Besides avoiding me.'

'I've been busy,' she said, stuffing the brochure into a white manila folder, but not before Nick read the heading: *All You Need to Know about Renting & Leasing.* He reached for the folder but she whipped it away, tucking it under her other arm.

They'd arrived at her car. She had her keys in her hand and a stand-offish expression on her face. Nick wouldn't let either put him off.

'So, what about coffee or a drink?'

Fidgeting with her car keys, she looked at her feet and then up the footpath. She was going to say no. She'd been avoiding him since they'd had sex and they both knew it.

And now, if his two and two made four, she was looking for another place to live.

'I can fill you in with what's happening with Mum,' he said, counting on her concern and fondness for his mother winning out over her desire to steer clear of him.

She looked longingly at her car, and then sighed. 'All right, where do you want to go for coffee?'

'The Silly Goat,' he said, a popular cafe nearby. 'It'll be quiet this time of day.'

She put the folder in her car. They crossed the road and walked side by side, Nick's hands pushed into his pockets and Anna with her arms folded tightly.

'Where'd you fly to today?' Nick said, when he couldn't bear the silence any longer.

'Nowhere, as it turned out. We had to cancel a booked transfer because the landing gear was broken. If it's fixed, they'll go tonight.'

'If not, I'll get it tomorrow.'

'You will. I'm on clinics.'

Nick knew she was. He'd compared their rosters, knew them off by heart, and they weren't working a shift together until the weekend. They didn't have a day off together until January. He couldn't let that discourage him.

He held open the coffee shop door as Anna slipped past him. She smelled divine, a heady mix of her unique scent and the body lotion she wore. Nick followed, let her choose the table.

'Iced coffee, please,' she said, swiping at the tiny beads of perspiration forming along her top lip. He'd willingly lick them off, if she'd only let him …

He ordered and sat down opposite her. She had her back to the street. Their knees touched under the table. When she didn't shift he gave a mental fist-pump.

'Have you found somewhere for Marlene to stay?' Anna leaned forward, brown eyes wide with curiosity. Her tongue flicked out to lick at her bottom lip.

Nick almost whimpered. Anna blinked, her thick, straight, black lashes sweeping across flawless skin.

You are beautiful, he thought, and when she drew back, obviously disconcerted, he realised he'd said the words out loud.

But he couldn't be sorry because she was stunning, from the tips of her espresso-coloured curls to her unpainted toe-nails.

And he wouldn't let himself dwell on what he couldn't see, hidden by the shapeless chambray shirt and trousers of her uniform. He was besotted and knew it was plastered all over his face.

'Don't say stuff like that, Nick.'

'Why not? It's what I think … How I feel.'

She looked away. Her chest rose and fell slowly. She feigned interest in the plethora of posters covering the walls.

The waitress came with their drinks. Anna took a sip and ice clinked against the glass. Nick gulped his long black, scalding his tongue. He was in love with her. The enormity of it filled the space between them.

When he braced himself to look at her again, the uncertainty in her eyes was at odds with her outward calm. What should he say? He didn't know so he went for something safe.

'They might have a permanent bed for Mum at the residential aged care facility. One of the other residents died yesterday. The social worker said that before they allocate the bed, they'll look at everyone on the waiting list and consider who has the greatest need.'

'That's positive news.'

'Maybe, but Mum doesn't have any money for a bond and unfortunately, these days it's often down to the money.'

'What'll you do if that doesn't work out?'

Nick leaned back, stretching out his legs either side of hers. 'There's hostel accommodation. She might stay, if I help pay. But there's a waiting list.'

'What about your brother? Couldn't he help out?'

'Lachlan? They're peas in a pod. Neither of them can manage money, not that they've ever got any, and they have no concept of responsibility. Lachy says he has a job, but that's more than likely all bullshit. It wouldn't be the first time he's told Mum what she wants to hear, regardless of the truth.'

'Families, eh,' Anna said, not without irony.

'Oh no,' Nick groaned, sliding down in his seat.

'What?' Anna started to twist around to see who he was trying to avoid.

'Don't look now but Serena is walking past outside,' he said. Anna spun back towards him, a look of horror on her face. Nick grinned. But the grin faded when the cafe door opened.

'Nick! I thought it was you,' Serena shrilled across the room, not acknowledging Anna.

He smiled through stiff lips. When Anna started to push back from the table he hooked his foot around the leg of her chair. 'Don't you dare leave me here with her,' he hissed.

Serena wove her way past the empty tables and chairs to where they sat. She purloined a stool and set it down at their table. 'I'll go order. Nick, can I get you anything?'

'Why don't you join us, Serena? And no, nothing for me,' Nick said, heavy on the sarcasm.

Anna lifted her empty glass. 'I'll have another one if you're buying. Iced coffee. Decaf this time round, with ice cream. Thanks, Serena,' she said, beaming, and Nick could have kissed her.

He would have kissed her, except Anna would have hated the public display of affection, and God knows what Serena's reaction would have been.

Twenty minutes later, his head echoing from Serena's mindless chatter, he walked with Anna the short distance to their respective cars.

'I reckon that girl's got a Nick radar,' Anna said.

Nick pressed his lips together. Anna punched him playfully on the arm. 'Ah, poor Nick,' she said.

He grabbed her hand, his heart skyrocketing when she willingly linked her fingers with his. What had changed? He didn't ask, keeping his fingers firmly linked with hers.

And again that night Nick didn't ask when, after Beth had left for a night shift, Anna tapped on his bedroom door and soundlessly climbed into bed beside him.

32

The following Saturday morning Beth, Nick and Anna were sitting around the table on the back verandah. Beth had not long been home from a night shift, and Anna was trying to ignore Nick playing footsies with her under the table. Heat already shimmered off the roof of the old shed in the back yard, but vestiges of the night's coolness lingered in the shadows of the verandah.

Without preamble Beth put down her cup of tea and said, 'I'm seriously thinking about moving to Melbourne, looking for a job there.'

'You are? I knew you were a bit fed up but I didn't realise you were serious about moving,' Anna said.

'When Gill was at her parents and I went to visit, we got talking. Gill said I can stay with her until I find work. And I am totally over this arsehole of a place.'

Nick raised his eyebrows.

'Even before the Tim debacle, the idea of making a fresh start somewhere else had occurred to me. My job's been getting to me—there's never enough staff and I'm always on night shift. If you hadn't come along when you did, Anna, I probably wouldn't be here now.'

'You'll be back,' said Nick.

'Not in the foreseeable future, I won't.'

'That's what we all say, but then we come back.'

'Not me! You'll see. I've wasted enough of my life in this poxy city.'

While Nick and Beth bantered back and forth, Anna's thoughts rushed headlong into the implications of what had just been said.

Would Beth put her house on the market? How would Anna ever afford to rent on her own, run a car and cover all the other living expenses, and keep Izzy at private school? Izzy would be a full-time boarder if Teresa moved to Sydney. Anna felt sick. Saving for the deposit on a house would slip further from her grasp.

In light of Izzy's pending visit, Anna had been researching Broken Hill's short-term rental market. The results had been downright depressing. Accommodation was expensive and geared to tourists. Izzy would have to bunk in with Anna. Not ideal.

'Earth to Anna,' Nick said, and nudged her under the table. She tuned in to find Nick and Beth regarding her closely.

'What will you do with your house?'

'I told you she wasn't listening.'

Albert stretched out on Beth's lap, purring loudly.

'I'll be putting the house on the market. I've already had an agent in to look. I'm sorry, but I need to break all ties with this place. I should have done it months ago.'

Damn. Beth would sell the house to the first person who looked at it, and Anna would be homeless. Teresa would move to Sydney, sell her house, and Izzy would be homeless. Maybe she'd ask Marlene if there was room in the scrub for her car as well.

'Anna? You've drifted off again.' Under the table, Nick massaged his bare foot soothingly up and down her shin. She shivered but purposely looked everywhere but at him. Difficult to do when he was sitting directly opposite her.

'Fine, I'm fine,' she said, conjuring up a positive tone. 'And please Beth, you don't need to apologise. We all do what we have to do. It's been great living here. How long before I'll need to find another place?'

Beth moved and Albert jumped off her lap. 'There's no rush. Real estate's not known to move fast in this place. You can both stay put until it sells.'

'I bet you find a job in the first week,' said Anna. 'Oh! What about Albert?'

'Maybe Josie next door will take the cat,' Nick said, tongue-in-cheek. And as if the dog had heard and understood, Hercules started barking.

'Ha ha,' Beth said. 'Don't be mean. Carol said she'd take the cat. He's too old to uproot.'

'When are you thinking of going?'

'First thing in the new year, I reckon. I'll give a fortnight's notice at work. Gill said I can come anytime.'

As much as she was trying to downplay it, she could see Beth was vibrating with excitement. Anna pushed her own worries to one side.

'It's a huge decision to make. I'll miss you but I'm pleased for you, and I hope it all goes well and you find what you're looking for,' she said, and meant it.

Beth's unconditional friendship had filled a gaping hole in Anna's life. A hole she hadn't realised existed until she'd rung Beth's doorbell in response to her ad for a room to rent.

Anna stood up. 'I'm going to the swimming pool.'

'Do you want company?' Nick said, getting to his feet.

'No,' she said bluntly, softening the answer with a quick, 'Thanks.'

She needed time to process this. And make plans. When Nick was around she couldn't think about anything else but him.

Her empty coffee mug went into the dishwasher on her way through to change into swimming gear. When she opened her bedroom door, a blast of sultry, sex-scented air enveloped her. Their second night together had been spent in her bed, some of it sleeping. They'd taken advantage of Beth's last night shift, and the overhead fan in Anna's room.

Anna sank down onto the edge of the bed, dropping her head into her hands.

She'd managed to resist Nick for three whole days. But Teresa's words had been playing over and over in her head during that time. And when Nick had ambushed her on the street, invited her for coffee, made no secret how he felt about her, she'd done what Teresa had recommended and grabbed him with both hands.

Because good things didn't come along often.

Anna thought she'd experienced desire before, but found she had no reference point for the hunger that consumed her whenever Nick entered her thoughts or her space. It was terrifying and invigorating at the same time.

Lifting her head, Anna's eyes fixed on the empty spot on the bedside cupboard; the spot where the photograph of her and Izzy had taken pride of place. Her gaze shifted to where the picture lived now, tucked away in the top drawer under the tissue box.

On a wave of emotion so intense it took her breath away, Anna reached into the drawer and lifted out the photograph. Seconds ticked by as she stared down at her daughter's smiling face.

Carefully, Anna placed the frame on the chest of drawers, behind the pump pack of body lotion. She could never let herself forget she was a parent, first and foremost.

The rain started during Anna's seventeenth lap in the water. Big, fat drops plopped into the pool as she swam, the bright day fast becoming gloomy. Thunderstorms had been on the radar.

She cut the swim short, but was the last person to pull out of the pool. The rain drops were warm on her cool skin. Thunder rumbled.

The attendant rushed about stowing pool paraphernalia. A sharp gust of wind sent ripples across the water.

Dragging a T-shirt over her wet torso, Anna thumbed open her phone, checking for missed calls. The screen was empty. She was on roster for the day with Nick. One look at the sky told her they wouldn't be flying anywhere until the weather cleared. She packed up her belongings and headed home.

Ambling through the aquatic centre gate and onto the footpath, her thoughts a million miles away, Anna jumped when Nick said, 'Get in,' through the open passenger door of his ute, the engine idling.

'I'm wet,' she replied, looking down at her dripping form. 'I left my towel at home.' She rolled her eyes upwards. 'And it's raining, in case you hadn't noticed.'

'Get in, Anna,' he said, and tossed a dry towel, her towel, onto the seat.

She hesitated, then spread the towel over the seat and climbed in. Raindrops splattered onto the windscreen. 'Thanks,' she said, 'but you didn't have to pick me up.'

'I know I didn't, but I did any way,' he said, and he sounded anything but happy.

'Nick?' she said, jumping when he slapped the heel of one hand against the steering wheel.

He pivoted round in the seat. 'You keep shutting me out, Anna, and I hate it. Why didn't you want me come for a swim with you?'

She swallowed, forced her eyes to the front. 'I needed time to think.'

'About what?'

She lifted her hands, let them flop onto her thighs. 'Where I'm going to live … How I'm going to afford it … What I'm going to do about—' She broke off, heart pounding.

Nick waited. Resolutely, she kept her focus forward. When she didn't continue, he said, 'Beth knows there's something going on between us.'

'You told her?' She swung around to meet him head on.

'I didn't have to. She's not blind.'

'What did she say?'

'That we were meant for each other.'

'She did not,' Anna retorted, pushing her hand out defensively.

'She did,' he said, capturing her wrist, tugging her towards him. A second was all the notice he gave that he was going to kiss her. In broad daylight, outside the swimming pool.

His lips were hot, slick, and he tasted like toothpaste. His hunger was a match for hers. Rain pelted on the roof and the windows began to fog up. At first Anna didn't feel the console between the seats digging into her tummy.

A car horn tooted, followed by the thud of car doors closing. Anna pushed against Nick's chest with the flat of one hand. With a low and feral sound he peeled his mouth from hers.

'You taste like chlorine,' he said, his forehead resting against hers.

Under her palm Anna felt his heart hammering in rhythm with hers. Her body ached for what it'd been denied. She eased back into her seat, away from Nick. The cabin was muggy, but Anna felt cold. Conscious of Nick's scrutiny, her skin prickled.

'You're doing it now, Anna,' he said, voice tight.

'Doing what?'

'Closing me out.' He reached for her hand. His fingers were warm, his grip sure. For a heart-stopping moment Anna imagined curling into him, telling him everything, losing herself in his heat and strength.

The moment passed and she tugged her fingers in an effort to free her hand.

'Please don't pull away from me, Anna. What we have together is too good to let go,' he said, his grip tightening.

'Lust … Chemistry … Call it what you like. It'll burn itself out in due course, and you'll go back to your life and I'll go back to mine. We'll have some nice memories.'

Rivulets of rain ran down the windscreen. The air crackled with electricity. Thunder rumbled close by.

'*Nice?*' Nick's face twisted with derision. His head moved slowly from side to side. 'You don't have a very high opinion of men, do you? Tell me what happened, help me to understand.'

Anna wrenched her hand free. This time he didn't try to stop her. Shivering, she reached for the seatbelt, clicked it into place. 'Let's go,' she said, hunching into the seat.

She wouldn't look at him. She couldn't look at him. If she did she'd spill every sorry detail of her past, her uncertainties about the future, and then probably burst into tears.

'This isn't still about me being separated? I thought you'd got over that little stumbling block.'

Her shoulders jacked up slightly. 'Maybe it's still part of it,' she said.

'Then what's the other part? I don't get it. You're single. My divorce is only months away. But if you want for us to go into a holding pattern until then, I'll do that. It'd nearly kill me to be near you and not be able to touch you, but I'd do it, if that's what you want.'

'You'd do that?'

'Why is it so hard for you to understand that this thing between us is something special that can only get better if we let it? It isn't only lust and chemistry from where I'm sitting. I don't want to lose you, so yes, I would do that.'

'You let me off too easily,' she said quietly.

He studied her for an endless moment, and then turned the air conditioner to high and de-fogged the windscreen with the back of his hand. 'Whatever it takes,' he said quietly.

Putting the ute into gear, he pulled away from the kerb and then stopped to let a group of teenagers straggle across the road. They'd been at the swimming pool and were laughing, pushing and shoving each other. One snatched another's towel, balled it up and threw it into the air. It landed on the bonnet of Nick's 4WD. When Nick shook his head, the boy, who looked about thirteen, gave him the finger before grabbing the towel.

'Jeez,' Nick hissed, accelerating sharply when the road was clear. 'Who'd have kids.'

Anna glanced at his rigid profile before shifting her gaze to stare at the passing scenery, without really seeing any of it.

33

The thunderstorms retreated, leaving the pavements steaming. For no other reason than her not wanting to disturb Beth's post-night duty sleep, Anna showered and changed and went to the base. Perhaps being in her comfort zone would help get things back into perspective.

The short trip home from the swimming pool with Nick had been made in a tense silence. He'd muttered something about having stuff to do, and taken off. They hadn't resolved anything.

What had happened to her simple life? She had been on her way up, but then she must have banked too hard and stalled, because now she was on the way down. Fast. She'd crash and burn when Nick found out about Izzy.

Arriving at the deserted base, the first thing Anna did when she let herself into the pilots' room was ring Izzy. But Izzy didn't want to chat.

'It's Saturday, Mum,' she said. 'We're at the shops trying on jeans.'

'Don't you have enough jeans already?'

'Mum—'

Anna wanted to ask when would be a good time to talk, but her daughter had already disconnected. Dropping her shoulder bag onto the desk with a despondent sigh, Anna sat down and logged onto the computer, and then into her email.

A name she hadn't seen for months appeared in her inbox: Rod Stilwell, her former boss.

'I wonder what he wants?' she said out loud. They hadn't parted on the best of terms when she'd been made redundant.

Although, to be fair, Rod had given her a solid reference and it had helped her secure the RFDS position.

She clicked on the email. *Ring me,* it demanded. Apparently Rod had an offer she wouldn't be able to refuse.

Anna leaned back from the desk. Unscrewing the lid on her water bottle she took several slow sips, re-reading the email. She put down the water bottle and reached for her phone, tapping in Rod's number. If nothing else, she'd ask why she'd been made redundant earlier that year. She had her own theory about it.

Neither of them were up for idle chitchat and their conversation got quickly to the point. Rod wanted her to come back and work for the regional airline. He'd lost two part-time pilots and he was offering her a permanent contract with more money and better hours. She could start whenever she wanted—the sooner the better.

'So Rod, if you want me back, why did you let me go in the first place?'

'Nothing to do with you as a pilot, Anna,' he said in his characteristic clipped tone. 'Times were tough and we had to cut back.'

'And it had nothing whatsoever to do with me being a woman and a single parent?'

He barely missed a beat before coming back with, 'It wasn't my decision alone, you know that.'

'Rod, I took one-and-a-half days of parental leave in eighteen months, and only then because my daughter was sick and my sister was away. I was more reliable than the others, you know that.'

'I know Anna, that's why I'm asking you to come back.'

'But what if things get tough—'

'You have my word that if you come back *I'll* make certain your contract is watertight. Tell me you don't want the flying experience on offer, and that you don't want to come home, and I won't bother you again.'

'How long do I have to make up my mind?'

'As long as you need.'

'How long, Rod?'

'A couple of weeks, and then we'll have to advertise because I need someone to start as early in the new year as possible.'

Her pulse was tripping over itself by the time she hung up. Was this a way out of her increasingly complicated life? Her mind went into overdrive.

Teresa would be thrilled to have Anna home again; it would mean she and Izzy could housesit and Teresa could move to Sydney—if things worked out with Vanessa, of course. Anna's accommodation problems would be resolved; Izzy wouldn't have to board; and the savings would be significant. Maybe, just maybe, Anna would be able to put more towards that elusive home loan deposit. The idea had her bubbling with possibilities.

A feeling that promptly fell flat when she thought of what she'd leave behind: she had a job she found challenging and rewarding; Broken Hill wasn't as bad as she'd expected; and there was Nick. As much as she pretended otherwise, her feelings for him were developing into much more than chemistry and lust.

Realistically, there'd always be another job. It was only a matter of time before an RFDS vacancy came up in Adelaide. But would there ever be another Nick?

How long she would have sat there staring at her phone Anna didn't know, but it rang and she flinched, fumbling and then catching it before it flew through her fingers and crashed to the floor.

It was Nick.

'We've got a priority two to Mount Sabrina station,' he said. The sound of his voice was all it took for her body to surge with longing. She clamped her legs together.

'I don't think I've landed there before,' she said, hoping her voice sounded normal. Sandwiching the phone between her cheek and shoulder she sorted through a stack of folders until she found the airstrip guide.

'I know I haven't. Where are you now?'

'I'm at the base,' she said, flicking through the guide until she found the airstrip specifications for Mount Sabrina station.

'Are you okay? You sound distracted.'

She was distracted. By him, and by a phone call offering her the chance to return to an uncomplicated life, a life without Nick.

'Yeah, I'm okay,' she said, eyes fixed on the guide, a stone settling in her stomach.

'If you say so,' Nick said. 'See you shortly.' He disconnected.

'Arrrgh,' she wailed, throwing her phone onto the desk. Then, taking a deep breath, she set about preparing for the flight.

After rechecking the weather forecast Anna rang Mount Sabrina, and was pleased that she did. The earlier band of thunderstorms had dumped twenty millimetres of rain on them the hour before. The station manager was on his way to assess the state of the strip.

'The strip's solid but there're a couple of boggy patches off to the side,' he reported ten minutes later.

'How's the weather looking now?'

'Clear. The storm passed as quickly as it came. A few hours of this heat and you won't even know we had rain,' he said.

All the same, Anna carefully calculated her fuel requirements on the off chance they'd need to divert around any bad weather.

When a knock on the door broke into her concentration, Anna didn't glance away from the computer screen, calling, 'Come in.'

'Are we okay to go?' Nick said, opening the door. 'Tim's the duty doctor and he thought the rain might hold us up.'

'All good to go. The station manager says the strip is sound. I'm almost finished here.'

'Right. I'll let Tim know,' he said, but she sensed him still hovering in the doorway.

'Was there something else?' she said absently, finalising the takeoff data.

'No, nothing at all,' he said coolly and succinctly, backing out the door.

It had almost closed when the tone of his comment registered.

'Nick!' Spinning the chair around she surged to her feet. It rolled backwards, smacking into the map table. 'Wait,' she said, halfway to the door. 'I'm sorry. About this morning. At the pool.'

He nodded, his expression softening.

Anna breathed, letting her shoulders relax when he smiled. The door clicked shut as he left.

With the walkaround checks completed and everything up to speed, Anna sank into her seat in the King Air. They had only minutes to spare of their priority two deadline. Buckling up and positioning her headset, a sense of calm descended over her. Here, Anna was in control.

Life's dramas, emotional upheavals and job offers could be put on hold; for the next few hours her total focus would be on getting the aircraft and its crew safely to their destination, and then home again. Calmly, she went about the pre-flight routine and start-up.

Minutes later her lips brushed the mic. 'Right for taxi?'

'Cabin secure,' came Nick's brisk response.

They were on their way. Cumulonimbus clouds foaming on the eastern horizon were the only evidence of the passing storm band.

'Did you get any lunch?' Nick asked when they'd reached cruising altitude, nothing to see now but endless blue above.

'An apple and a protein bar. You?'

'Nah. Didn't have time.'

'I've got another protein bar in my bag if you want it.' She found it and passed it over her shoulder.

'Thanks,' he said, unclipping his seatbelt to take it. 'I'll buy you dinner tonight.'

Knocking him back was almost a reflex, but then she thought, Why not? So instead of refusing she said, 'Thanks, I'd like that. And I have another apple here if you want it.'

He laughed, a low rumble that sent shivers all the way down her spine. 'This'll do for now,' he said.

While they cruised at 10,000 metres Anna refreshed the Mount Sabrina airstrip specifications. Narrower airstrips could appear deceptively long. With the recent rain there was no margin for error. Getting bogged wasn't on her list of things to do that day.

Because she'd never landed at Mount Sabrina before, Anna flew over first to be sure the approach and overshoot were clear, and the strip was safe. When they'd heard the aircraft overhead, the station folk would have run the strip for stock, emus, kangaroos and any other wildlife. Satisfied, she made her approach.

The main landing gear hit the strip hard. There was a thud, the aircraft pulled sharply to the left and icy fingers squeezed at Anna's insides.

With a muttered curse she applied the brake on the starboard side, pushing down on the right rudder.

'Keep it straight, keep it straight, keep it straight,' she repeated through clenched teeth, as the saltbush flew past.

Another 30 seconds, which felt like 30 minutes, and they'd come to a complete stop and she shut down. Anna's hands were clammy on the control. She flexed her fingers, fumbled with the release on her seatbelt and removed her headset.

A 4WD ute was racing through the saltbush towards them. Climbing between the gap in the seats her eyes met Nick's.

'Sorry about that. Are you okay?' she said.

Nick nodded.

'My guess is we've blown a tyre. I'll go and have a look.'

'I'll get the door,' he said, unclipping his belt and standing up. When she bumped up against him in the narrow aisle, his gaze swept over her face. 'More to the point, how are you?'

'All in a day's work,' she said, ignoring her jelly legs.

'You did good.' He rubbed a steady hand up and down her arm.

'I'd have never lived it down if I'd gotten us bogged as well.'

The port-side tyre had blown and Anna used the satellite phone to contact the on-call engineer. They'd fly him out to change the wheel. In the meantime, they were stranded at Mount Sabrina for at least several hours.

Luckily, the ground immediate to the strip where the aircraft had come to a stop was firm. Anna could see several boggy patches only metres away. With help, she would have to move the aircraft off the runway so whoever came to their rescue could land.

The station hand introduced himself as Mark. When he was satisfied they were all in one piece, he helped Nick load the medical gear onto the back of the 4WD.

'I'll drop off Nick at the homestead, grab a couple of the other blokes and we'll be back in half an hour or so to help you shift the plane off to the side,' Mark said. He swung into the station vehicle and it rattled to life, belching diesel fumes.

'Are you sure you won't come in with us?' Nick said.

Surveying her surrounds, Anna held up a hand to shade her eyes. 'You go,' she said. 'I'm going to walk down the strip, take a look.'

'Put on a hat or you'll give yourself sunstroke.'

'Yes, sir,' she said with a mock salute.

Nick got in beside the station hand. Anna watched them drive away, peeling off to the right. In minutes the only evidence of them ever being there, was a plume of dust. Like the manager had said, you wouldn't even know it'd rained.

She turned around slowly. The view was the same in every direction.

It was hot and humid, the sun high in a dense, powder-blue sky. The flies were a nuisance. There was no shade except under the aircraft wings. Inside, it was heating up. Within fifteen minutes it'd be intolerable. With a sense of purpose Anna searched out a hat, fixed it firmly on her head, and set off down the dirt airstrip.

34

The patient's name was Eileen. She was the station manager's wife, forty-six years old, and right now she looked every one of them, and then some. She'd been vomiting for the past three days.

'Has anyone else been sick?' Nick asked, and she shook her head, clutching an empty ice cream container in one hand and a fistful of tissues in the other.

The bedroom was overly warm and the blinds closed. A pedestal fan at the foot of the queen-sized bed worked hard to churn the thick, vomit-scented air.

Nick kept swallowing the saliva that pooled in his mouth, grateful now that all he'd had to eat was a protein bar.

Eileen sat forward, retching. Her collarbone protruded sharply above the neckline of a washed-out pink nightie. Fine, dirty-blonde hair snaked down her back in a limp plait. She spat into the container and swiped at her mouth with the wad of tissues before sinking back onto the pillows.

Nick examined the contents of the bowl, and didn't miss the flecks of fresh blood. He finished taking her vital signs, jotting them down. She was in sinus tachycardia, and her blood pressure was on the lower end of normal, as was her oxygen saturation. Nick readied an IV infusion and drew up an antiemetic.

His thoughts drifted to Anna alone out at the airstrip. He hadn't wanted to leave her there.

Blowing a tyre had given him a jolt, and a brief dose of white-knuckle syndrome. But not for a moment had he doubted her ability to deal with whatever was happening.

He glanced at his watch. It was stinking hot, and the humidity hanging around would make for more discomfort. Surely, Mark and the other blokes would be with her out at the airstrip by now. Funny how he'd never given the wellbeing of the pilot more than a cursory thought before Anna.

Eileen moaned. Nick looked up from his notes in time to see her sit bolt upright, and then proceed to projectile vomit a copious amount of bright red blood. It sprayed across the bedsheets and onto the floor. It even hit the fan.

He silently swore, spinning around and grabbing a towel from the chest of drawers. Eileen collapsed back against the pillows, her eyes closed, sinking further into their sockets. Beneath the sun damage her skin was pasty grey.

Speaking quiet words of reassurance he quickly mopped up as best he could and focused on getting the IV line and some fluids into her. When he got around to taking her blood pressure again, it hadn't changed. But Nick knew if she continued to lose blood her body wouldn't be able to compensate indefinitely, and her blood pressure would plummet.

In the time since his arrival Eileen had deteriorated significantly. She was fast becoming a priority one, and their aircraft was disabled on the runway.

'How is she?' came a gruff voice from the doorway. It was Jack, Eileen's husband.

Jack moved into the room and before Nick could warn him, he saw the blood. His eyes bulged. 'Jesus! What the hell's going on here?' he said, the colour draining from his face. For a moment Nick thought he'd have two patients on his hands.

Concern etched into his craggy face, Jack lowered himself down onto the chair beside the bed, reaching for his wife's hand.

'Eileen? Love?' he said, but she didn't open her eyes; it was as if she couldn't muster the energy to do it. Cracked, dry lips moved but no sound emerged.

'I could use a bowl of warm water, soap and as many face washers as you can spare,' Nick said, opening up the IV line to let the fluid pour into her vein. 'And more towels would be good.'

Jack pushed himself to his feet, eyes on his wife's ashen face. 'You got it,' he said, and lumbered out of the room.

Nick dragged out the satellite phone. Tim Carpenter, the duty doctor, answered on the third ring. 'Heard you had a bumpy landing,' he said. News travelled fast. 'Lucky she kept it out of the mud.'

'Yeah, and things have got even bumpier, and stickier,' Nick said, his back to the patient.

'How so?' Tim said, sobering immediately. 'Is Anna all right?'

'Yeah, she's fine. It's the patient—' Nick followed with a summary of Eileen's condition and what he'd done so far. Tim listened, asked a few questions, and gave several instructions.

'I'm at the base,' Tim said. 'They haven't taken off yet with the new wheel. I'll come with them and bring blood. Anything else we might need?'

Nick glanced over his shoulder towards the patient. 'Nothing that I can think of,' he said. 'Get your arses in gear and get here.'

'Alrighty! I'll give Kyle a hurry on, make his day. I'll phone through an ETA. Ring me if you need to. See you soon.'

Nick blew out a relieved breath. He had a bad feeling about this patient and two pairs of hands were always better than one.

Eileen started to retch and Nick watched helplessly as more bloody vomit splattered into the vomit bag he'd replaced the ice cream container with. He opened the IV line wider, and then pumped up the blood pressure cuff: eighty-five on fifty. Eileen's blood pressure had dropped significantly. Nick's blood pressure rose.

He administered the drugs Tim had ordered, writing down the times and doses. As best he could he washed Eileen and cleaned up the remaining blood. Jack rummaged through the linen press and found a fresh top sheet.

Eileen dozed. Jack made tea. It was milky and sweet but Nick drank it anyway. It could be another hour and a half before the others arrived. Nick mentally crossed his fingers and toes that Eileen wouldn't deteriorate any more before Tim got there.

Dogs barked and car doors slammed. Then the sound of voices.

'That'll be the boys back from dragging the plane off the strip,' Jack said, and then the station hand Mark appeared in the doorway.

'How's Mum?' he said, and Nick berated himself for not picking up on the family connection earlier. Mark had the same deep-set eyes and dirty-blond hair as his mother.

At the sound of her son's voice, Eileen's eyes fluttered open. She lifted a beckoning hand and Mark sat down gingerly on the bed beside her.

'How are you, Mum?'

She tried for a smile, but it came off more like a grimace. Jack stood up, and without a word he left the room. Nick saw that the older man's eyes were glistening with tears. Mark moved to the chair his dad had vacated, picking up his mother's hand.

'How'd you go at the strip? Did Anna, the pilot, come back with you?' Nick said, and Mark nodded.

'She's in the kitchen making a coffee and having something to eat. She did a bloody first class job not to have spun off the strip completely and ploughed into the saltbush. Could have done a hell of a lot more damage.' Nick didn't miss the admiration in the younger man's voice.

'And she'd collected up any shredded rubber from the tyre. Had it in a pile ready to dump. She said she'd found a shallow washaway in the touchdown zone that she hadn't seen on the fly over. Probably came in a bit hard on that and the tyre blew. I reckon she's a bit of alright,' Mark said, and grinned.

'I'm always comfortable flying with her.'

After he'd taken Eileen's vital signs again, and started a new bag of IV fluid, he said to Mark, 'Do you think you could ask Anna to come up here for a minute? I need to have a word with her and I can't leave your mum.'

'Yeah, no worries, mate,' Mark said, and shot to his feet.

Anna materialised in the doorway minutes later. She hung back, and Nick could see from the look on her face that she had no desire to enter. He didn't blame her. Their shared experiences at Elder Creek with Brett and Rachel Carmichael would still be fresh in her memory. They were in his.

He went to the bedroom door, keeping one eye on the patient.

Anna retreated further into the hallway. 'What's up?' she said, her voice low.

'Have you heard anything from the others?'

'I spoke to Kyle about fifteen minutes ago. He said we'd been upgraded to a P1.' She frowned. 'They'll be in the air any time now. I'll get Mark to take me back out to the strip in about three-quarters of an hour. When they get here, it'll take us an hour or so to change the tyre. Hopefully, there's no other damage.'

'I suppose if there is we'll have to take the clinic plane.' Nick threw a quick glance towards his patient.

'We will. They've taken out seats and put in a stretcher, just in case.'

'Shit,' he said, scrubbing at his face with his hands. They both knew the aircraft they'd flown in was the flying intensive care unit, and that's what was needed for this patient.

'Tim will be on board.'

'Get Mark to bring him here first, before he does anything else.'

'Will do.'

Their gazes locked, and held. They were both remembering Elder Creek. Both trips. And the night flight with Serena when the patient had arrested and died at the nursing outpost.

'Probably best that we don't fly together that often,' Nick whispered. 'Our flights always end up with some kind of drama.'

'Yeah,' Anna said. 'How are you? Do you want coffee? Cold water? Something to eat?'

He shook his head.

'You look a bit hot and bothered.' Surreptitiously reaching for his hand, she gave it a squeeze. 'I'd give you a hug, but I know it wouldn't be appropriate.'

Nick felt a fraction of the load lift from his shoulders. 'I'll consider myself hugged,' he said.

From inside the bedroom the patient moaned.

'Gotta go.'

In a few strides he was back at the bedside. Eileen was struggling to lever herself into a sitting position. 'I'm going to be sick again,' she said, her eyes watering.

Nick reached for the disposable vomit bag on the bed beside her. He held her steady while she threw up more blood. He'd be counting the minutes until backup and blood arrived.

'What took you?' Nick said when Tim hustled into the sickroom, loaded down with equipment.

Anna had popped her head in and said goodbye before she'd headed out to the airstrip to wait, and that had been over an hour ago.

Tim raised his eyebrows. 'How's the patient?'

Nick swallowed his frustration and summarised her condition, with an estimation of how much blood she'd lost and details of the IV fluid replacement he'd given. 'Her blood pressure hasn't bounced back with the IV fluid as much as I'd hoped,' he finished.

'I'll examine her and we'll go from there.'

Nick nodded. They both turned to the woman in the bed. Her eyes were closed and she appeared to be dozing. Tim glanced at the cardiac monitor before pulling a stethoscope from his bag and moving towards the patient.

'So, back to the original question, what took you so long?' Nick said, when the first bag of blood was flowing into Eileen's vein.

'Kyle got us bogged,' Tim said.

'What?' Nick's eyes moved from the patient to Tim, and back again. He stepped away from the bed, out of earshot, dragging Tim with him. 'Do you mean to tell me we have a critical patient and both aircraft are disabled?'

'That about sums it up.' Tim glanced at his watch. 'They were going to change the tyre first. Let's hope there's nothing else wrong with that aircraft.'

'Yeah, let's hope,' Nick said, and went about taking the next set of observations on the patient. When he'd finished, Tim said, 'Why don't you go stretch your legs, grab a coffee. As soon as we know one of the aircraft is good to go, we'll intubate the patient ready for the flight.'

'Thanks, I'll be back in ten minutes. And I'll send her husband Jack in and you can explain it all to him.'

'Do that,' Tim said, and Nick left in search of a bathroom and a coffee.

Jack was in the kitchen. He filled the electric kettle and pointed Nick in the direction of the coffee jar and biscuits, and then lumbered off to the bedroom to talk to Tim.

The kettle had boiled when Nick heard a vehicle, followed by voices. In a matter of moments Anna appeared in the kitchen doorway.

'What a day! Poor Kyle.' She shrugged. 'It could have happened to anyone.' Her face was red, her clothes dusty and her boots splattered with mud. No-one had ever looked so good.

'Tyre's changed, there was no other damage so we can go whenever you're ready. I came in to give you a hand moving the patient. I thought you might need it.'

Nick let go of some of the tension that had been building over the last few hours. 'Thanks,' he said and smiled, and she smiled right back.

When they landed back in Broken Hill, it was dark and Nick was numb with fatigue. The patient's condition had been stable when they'd handed her over to the paramedics in Adelaide. There'd been no more bloody vomits on the trip.

Restocking had been a mammoth task. It had taken longer than it should have because he'd been fuzzy with exhaustion. The night duty flight nurse offered to come in and help but Nick knew exactly what needed replacing so he plodded through on his own.

Anna had left long before. When his phone rang on the way out to the carpark he expected it to be her or Beth asking him to bring home milk or cat food. Or pizza.

He didn't expect it to be the aged care facility where his mother was on respite. He'd visited her … When? Had it only been that morning?

'Sorry to bother you, Nick, but we can't find Marlene anywhere. We think she's been gone for about three hours,' the RN said.

'You *think* it's about three hours,' Nick said slowly, trying to get his weary brain around what she'd said. 'Has anyone been to visit her today?'

'Not since I've been on duty. We think maybe she rang a taxi.'

'Right. Why do you think that?'

'There was one parked out the front and no-one knew who'd called it. And then it went—'

'And that would be about three hours ago?'

'I'm afraid so. We can't lock her in or restrain her, you know that. At least this time she's taken her puffer.'

Nick leaned against the door of his ute and closed his eyes, the phone pressed to his ear. All he wanted was a shower, a beer, some food, and then to go to sleep beside Anna.

'Are you still there?' squeaked the RN.

'Yep, I'm still here. I will go and find her. If I can't, I'll get back to you.'

'Thanks,' she said, with a relieved sigh.

He disconnected and rang Anna. The call went through to voicemail. He left a short message: *I've been held up. I'll see you when I see you.*

With a pithy curse he unlocked the ute. One more day and Marlene's respite would be finished, and there'd been no news from the social worker. Not that he'd expected to hear from her, because Nick doubted his mother's situation would have taken precedence over others. Frustrated, he reversed out of the park and went in search of his mother.

35

Anna was in the shower when Nick rang. She didn't get to it in time, the beep telling her she had a message. Beth was out with friends.

After she'd listened to Nick's message, she worried. What would have held him up but trouble of some kind?

He arrived home an hour later. Anna was in kitchen when she heard the front door. She stopped, listened, and winced when his bedroom door slammed. It sounded like whatever had held him up hadn't gone well.

Not long after she heard the shower. She was still standing at the kitchen sink when the bathroom door opened. She held her breath. Nick's bedroom door clicked shut.

She waited for him to come out of his bedroom, but he didn't. Chewing on her bottom lip, Anna dithered about her best course of action. If work had held him up, it wasn't her business, not really. If it was personal? Well, then it wasn't really her business either. Or was it?

It wasn't in Anna's nature to dither, but what part of his business was her business? She cared about him. This vague no-man's-land of a relationship that wasn't really a relationship was beginning to get to her.

If it wasn't a relationship, then what was it?

In the end she marched through the house to Nick's door. Relationship or not, as a friend she had a right to know that he was okay. She rapped on his door. Silence. She knocked again, making her knuckles sting.

'Nick? I know you're in there. What's happened? Please talk to me.'

More silence.

Lifting her hand to knock again, the door flew open and he caught her fist before it pummelled his bare chest.

'What's happened?'

He dropped her hand and folded his arms across his chest. His face was expressionless, but his eyes gave him away. They were the colour of a roiling, stormy sea. He was upset, and angry.

'What do you think happened?'

'I have no idea. And if it is none of my business, tell me and I'll back off.'

'Mum took off from the aged care home again. I found her at the club, in her trackie daks this time, beer in hand, playing the pokies. When she'd finished her drink, she reluctantly came with me. And that wasn't until after she'd had another smoke. We argued, as per usual. I took her back. End of story.'

'Is she all right?'

Nick's eyebrows shot up. 'Is *she* all right? Of course she is, firing on all cylinders. She'd won fifty bucks.'

'What would have happened if you weren't around to go looking for her?'

'The RN on duty would have called the police.'

'The police? That's a bit extreme, isn't it?'

'What else are they going to do? It's not the aged care facility's responsibility to go looking all over town for her, even if they had the resources. I'm her next of kin. I've lost count of the number of the times I've picked her up, no money for a taxi fare home. And that's when she had an address for the taxi to drop her off at.

'You wonder how I got to know a lot of the bar staff around town? They'd ring me, tell me to come and get her. They'd make like it was no big deal, but I was always embarrassed. When I left, my brother would pick her up, if he was around—and sober.

'The day after tomorrow the respite care is over, I haven't heard from the social worker. Or anything from the hostel. I have no idea what I'm going to do with Mum.'

Anna stared at him, mouth slightly open. She'd had only a sketchy idea of the complexity of Nick's situation until now.

Judging by the rigid set of his shoulders, the last thing he'd want was her sympathy, which he'd only interpret as pity. So she said, 'Do you want a cup of tea? A glass of water?' She raised her eyebrows. 'A beer?'

He relaxed. 'What about that hug you offered earlier?'

Anna folded her arms, contemplating him. 'You look exhausted. Have you eaten anything? Rehydrated? Because if you haven't, you need to do that first. I wouldn't want your stamina compromised.'

Grinning, he reached around for his T-shirt on the end of the bed, shrugging it on. Anna watched unashamedly.

'What were you doing in here? Why didn't you come and talk to me when you got back?'

'I was totally, totally pissed off. I needed to get a grip before I talked to you. There's no way I want any of this to impact on you, on us.'

Anna stilled. 'We all have stuff in our past that creeps into the present,' she said.

'Yeah, but there's stuff, and then there's other stuff. My seriously dysfunctional family is that other stuff.' He reached for her. Warm fingers encircling her upper arms, he leaned in and dropped a kiss onto her forehead. 'Thanks for flushing me out. I was well on the way to a full-blown self-pity fest. The only thing I was missing was the booze.'

Turning her around, he propelled her forward and towards the kitchen. 'What is there to eat? I know it's late but now that you mention it, I'm starving.'

'There's cake. Beth has been baking—motivated by guilt, I'd say, for dropping her bombshell this morning, forcing us both onto the street. If you want healthy, there's chicken risotto.'

'I reckon you might be right about the baking.'

Nick filled a small bowl with risotto and heated it in the microwave.

Elbows on the table and propping her chin on her hands, Anna watched him eat. All the while dreading to think what he'd make of her far-from-functional family and 'other stuff'.

With acquaintances and work colleagues, the act of not telling them about something important in your life was no big deal. It was a choice you had. But if you became friends with an acquaintance or work colleague, and then the friendship deepened into something more than a friendship, that thing you hadn't told your friend-who-was-now-your-lover became a secret you were keeping from him.

It blew her mind how insidiously a perfectly reasonable omission had, overtime, morphed into a deception. Owning up to being a single parent was becoming harder by the day.

'Are you okay? You've gone all pale.' Nick put down his fork and reached for her hand, practised fingers gliding over the pulse point in her wrist. 'Anna? Your heart's racing!'

Withdrawing her hand, she pushed back from the table and stood up. 'I'm pretty tired, that's all,' she said. 'Busy day. Lots of drama, and it's almost midnight. I think I might go to bed.' She yawned.

'You sure that's all it is?'

'Yep, I'm bushed,' she fibbed, to herself and to him.

He tilted his head to the side. 'Okay. And are we still pretending Beth doesn't know we're sleeping together?'

Timely question. Beth was back on day shift and would be home from her evening out any time. But a night without Nick? The speed at which she'd got used to sharing a bed with him made her head spin.

'You decide. You know her better than me. You know if she'll be discreet.'

'I think she's got enough going on in her own life to be bothered about what we're doing. But if you feel uncomfortable about her knowing—'

'I'm sure Beth's okay. But I worry what our work colleagues would think if they knew. Especially if they heard it from Serena Morris. As you've pointed out, she's no fan of mine, and she knows a lot about … Things.'

'Yeah, Beth's good, but I know what you mean about Serena.'

'So, are we in a relationship?'

Nick pushed away his plate, studying her carefully. 'Do you want us to be?'

'What if it's a rebound thing for you? Have you thought about that? You know, a marriage breakup, seeing if you've still got what it takes to—'

He was out of his chair and in her space before she could finish. Sliding his arms around her waist he pulled her hard against him.

'This is not a rebound thing, Anna,' he said. 'I know you know that. I don't know why you keep trying to sabotage what's happening here.'

Is that what she was doing? Sabotaging their fledgling relationship? Why? To assuage her own guilt? The guilt she felt because these days she spent more time thinking about the man holding her than she did about her own daughter, the one she hadn't told him about …

Nick's lips touched hers in a gentle, whisper of a kiss.

'Go to bed,' he said, his mouth moving against hers. 'I'll be there in a while.'

Mutely, Anna nodded. At that moment, surrounded as she was by him, his warmth, his scent, his strength, she was powerless to do anything else.

36

On Monday morning, Marlene took her ongoing accommodation issues into her own hands. She booked a taxi to take her from the aged care facility to where her car was parked in Snake's shed. Using a crowbar and her spare set of keys, she liberated her home.

Anna had the day off, and Nick was flying. Mid-morning, a breathless Beth rang Anna from work.

'Marlene's flown the coop,' she said. 'They rang me when they couldn't get Nick.'

'Her respite finished today. She couldn't stay there anyway.'

'So the RN said.'

'I don't know if Nick had planned to pick her up. His mother's situation can be a touchy subject with him.'

'I know,' Beth said. 'And you're right, the facility doesn't want her back. The respite bed is booked out, and they've decided on another person for the permanent bed. I bet they'll say she discharged herself. Bev, the RN who I know, told me more than she should have, and she was quite blunt about it. But then, Marlene can be difficult.'

'Did she leave any belongings there? I could go and pick them up if she did.'

'I'm sure Nick would appreciate that. Anyway, I need to go. Two in labour with one ready to push. It's her fourth so a cough is all it'll take. And as usual, there's not enough staff.' Beth disconnected.

An hour later Anna drove to the aged care facility.

'I've come to collect Marlene Harrison's belongings. I'm a friend of Nick's,' she said to the receptionist. The woman looked her up and down, and then made a phone call, turning away from Anna and speaking in a hushed tone.

A nurse appeared just as Anna was beginning to think they'd forgotten her. She was dumbstruck when the woman pushed a bulging black plastic garbage bag into Anna's arms and said, 'Good luck with her, darl. You'll need it.'

Anna found Nick's mum parked in her usual location in the scrub. It was midday and already nudging 34 degrees, the heat clear and dry. The forecast was for 38 degrees by mid-afternoon.

When she pulled in, Marlene was sitting under a scrubby-looking tree in a folding canvas chair reading the *Barrier Daily Truth* and swatting flies. She was wearing a well-washed but still colourful cotton shift, her hair its usual fly-away halo around her head.

'Hello, love,' she called. 'I see you've brought me my Louis Vuitton luggage. I bet they couldn't get rid of it fast enough, even though I'd told that sour-faced nurse I'd be back later.' Her throaty laugh ended in a chunky cough. There were several cigarette butts in the sand by her slippered feet.

'Where do you want me to put it?'

'Throw it on the back seat. I'll see to it later.'

When Anna opened the car door the interior was not as she'd expected. Although, Nick had cleaned the car before he parked it in Snake's shed.

It smelled a bit smoky and stale from being shut up, but the clothes, towels and various items were stacked neatly. There was a sleeping bag and two pillows on the front passenger seat, the pillowcases faded but clean.

She put the garbage bag on the seat and closed the door. Sad that all of Marlene's worldly possessions fit so easily into a car.

Anna's own meagre collection of furniture and household goods were stored in Teresa's back shed. It was a bit more than would fit into her car, but almost as pathetic.

'I bought us coffee,' she said, collecting a cardboard tray from her car, 'and doughnuts.'

'Ah, you are a sweetheart. I can see why my boy's smitten. Pop the boot, would you. There's a stool in there. Take a load off.'

Anna ignored the remark about Nick, and found the folding stool. She settled in the shade beside Marlene. Close up the older woman looked tired, and frail, but wasn't clawing for each breath like she had been in the hospital. Frail or not, she exuded an air of contentment.

'So where to from here?' Anna said, after they'd eaten the doughnuts and downed the coffee.

At first Marlene looked puzzled, and then she sighed with comprehension. 'Ah, you mean Nick. He won't like that I've taken matters into my own hands, will he?'

Anna shook her head. 'You can't really blame him either.'

'And I don't.'

'What if a permanent place did come up for you? Your own room where you could have all your things?'

'What, some old codger has conveniently snuffed it and I can have the room? If I wanted to, which I don't—'

Anna opened her mouth to interrupt but Marlene barrelled on.

'—and anyway, do you think they'd pick me above some well-heeled fossil with a load of money in the bank? I know how it all works.' She tapped the side of her nose with her finger. 'And a place to put my things?' She cackled with mirth. 'In case you hadn't noticed, pet, I don't have any things to put in a room.'

'You could get a TV, and a nice chair. A bookcase ...' Anna began decorating a room for Marlene. 'There're op shops and second-hand furniture places where you can get real bargains. A good clean-up and a coat of paint—'

'Anna,' Marlene said and patted Anna's arm. 'I've had plenty of things. I know Nick thinks I was irresponsible to let them go. But not having my life cluttered with useless possessions doesn't bother me one iota.' Then Marlene's face scrunched into a sudden scowl. She looked at Anna. 'Do you think I'm being reckless?'

Marlene's scrutiny was intense, as if Anna's response really mattered. Buying time, Anna crumpled up the greasy doughnut bag and stacked their empty coffee cups.

'No,' she said, 'I don't think so. We all have the right to choose how we live our lives. As long as we don't cause any harm.' Marlene nodded as if satisfied, and Anna felt compelled to add, 'But I also understand why Nick feels the way he does. You're his mother. You're unwell. He cares about you and he wants what's best for you.'

Marlene sighed. Using one hand she flapped the hem of her dress, exposing white, knobbly knees, the skin dry and flaking. Then she rolled up the newspaper and started swatting at the flies, grinning when she hit one.

Anna's attention was caught by three bull ants dragging a struggling moth through the red sand. She gave up trying to remember how many times their own weight ants could carry.

The heat was building, the air redolent with eucalyptus. Sweat prickled in Anna's hair, her blouse sticking to her.

Discarding the newspaper, Marlene took out a cigarette but didn't light up. She tapped a disposable cigarette lighter rhythmically on the wooden arm of the chair. Finally she said, 'Nick'll only be happy if I go into that bloody place for good.'

Anna looked up from the struggling ants. 'I'm not sure he'd be *happy*, but he'd know you were safe and being looked after.'

'Yeah, if you didn't count being bored shitless, and slowly poisoned by the food.'

'There is that,' she said. 'And I can kind of see the appeal of living like you are. No rent, no housework, no home maintenance, no bills, no ties. I imagine it's okay when the weather's good. But it gets pretty damned cold here in the winter and it can't be safe. Aren't you scared out here on your own?'

Marlene put the cigarette into her mouth then took it out again, tucking it behind her ear. 'I've lived in the Hill all my life. Everyone knows I've got nothing to pinch. No-one bothers an old duck like me.'

A discarded McDonalds wrapper cartwheeled on a gust of wind. The ants stoically wrestled with their load; they hadn't given up, but the moth had.

Marlene sucked in a wheezy breath. 'I sometimes think Nick treats me like a child.' Her voice was sad. 'In my own way I get along, but not how he thinks I should. I'm sorry if that makes him unhappy.'

'What if he found you a place to live that wasn't a nursing home? Surely in a town this size there's got to be something suitable. I know! What about a caravan?'

Marlene's face brightened momentarily, but then she said, 'Where's a caravan going to come from? I haven't got any money saved. I know Nick has the house to sell, but I don't think there'll be anything left after his grasping wife finishes with him. Not that I'd want his hard-earned cash.'

Anna leaned forward, didn't give herself a second to rethink before saying, 'What's she like, his wife?'

'Lauren? A real looker, and I liked her at first. But then each time Nick came home he was more miserable than the last, although he'd never admit it. He tried to convince everyone he was living the dream or some such bullshit.

'She came with him the first couple of times, and then he started coming on his own. Always had some excuse why she couldn't join him.'

'Did you expect them to split up?'

'Nah, not really. Nick's not a quitter. When I heard I was disappointed for him, and for myself in a weird way. Nick says he doesn't want children, but I'd kind of hoped that one day he'd change his mind. Not that they'd have ever let my grandkids stay with me in my palace on wheels.' She swiped at the persistent flies. 'Lachlan will never settle down and Nick was my only chance. He's always been the responsible one. More like his dad.'

Anna's phone rang. Damn. The conversation was getting interesting. She stood up and wrangled the phone out of her pocket. It was Izzy.

'I need to take this,' she said, and Marlene nodded, waved her off. Anna walked to the other side of her car giving herself a modicum of shade and privacy before she took the call.

'Hello, sweetie,' she said.

'Mum, you are there. I thought you weren't going to answer.'

'How come you're not in class? Is everything okay?'

'Why do you always think something's wrong? Anyway, it's lunchtime and we break up at the end of the week so there's not much happening. Grandma has—'

'What wrong with Grandma?' Anna interjected, her heart thudding.

'There you go again, Mum. Nothing's wrong. If you give me a chance, I'll tell you!'

Anna paced the length of the car, swapping the phone to the other ear. Mention of her mother always made her palms sweaty.

'Okay, sorry for interrupting. Over to you.'

'Grandma emailed last night with a plane ticket for me to go and stay with her over Christmas.'

Cold fury sliced through Anna. How like her mother not to ask Anna first, not to consider that they might have plans. How hard would it be for Tina to pick up the phone and talk to her youngest daughter?

'Mum? Are you still there?'

'Yes, I'm still here,' she said, her jaw so tight it hurt.

'I knew you'd be angry.'

'I'm not angry, and what about *our* plans?'

'What plans? You're working, remember?'

'I'll be coming home for those three days before Christmas. We were going to have our celebration together then.'

'Mum, we can still do that. You're coming down from the twenty-first to the twenty-third and I'm going to Grandma's on the twenty-fourth,' Izzy said, as if explaining to a six-year-old.

'Oh, so you are going to your Grandma's. Exactly when were you going to ask me if it was okay?'

'Aunt Tee said—'

'She's not your mother, Isabelle, I am.'

'I can't help it if you're not around to ask,' Izzy said, and Anna gasped, recognising her own petulant tone of moments before.

She pressed the heel of her free hand to her forehead. 'Izzy,' she said. 'Let's not argue. How long has your Grandma asked you to stay?'

'Until the thirtieth because Grandma and some bloke are going on a cruise on New Year's Eve.'

'Oh, I see,' Anna said. Tina had never remarried after the divorce but Anna had wondered if there was a man lurking about somewhere.

'I was going to bring you back to Broken Hill with me for the rest of the holidays. It was going to be a surprise.'

'Because Aunt Tee wants to go to Sydney?'

'You know about that?'

'She was Googling airfares.'

'Oh, well, if you're going to Grandma's, we'll have to change your return flight to Broken Hill instead of Adelaide.'

Izzy coughed and cleared her throat. 'Grandma only sent a one-way ticket,' she said quickly, the words running together.

'Say that again.'

'Sorry, Mum, but the ticket is only one way.'

Anna's fingers curled into a fist. Never before had she had such an overpowering desire to hit something. She kicked the front tyre, wincing when it hurt.

'Mum?' came Izzy's tremulous voice. Gone was her excitement about spending Christmas with Grandma on the Sunshine Coast.

Anna stopped pacing, closing her eyes. 'I'm still here, Iz. It's very generous of Grandma to invite you. I'll book your return flight to Broken Hill on the thirtieth. I might even be off that day. I need to check the roster.'

'Does that mean I'll be staying with you until school goes back?'

'I'll be honest Iz, I'm not sure. It'll depend a bit on what Aunt Tee does. Don't you want to be home for some of the holidays?'

'Home?' Izzy snorted. 'Aunt Tee's isn't my home. I don't have a home. And if Aunt Tee goes off with her friend, I won't even have a place to stay on weekends and holidays.' Izzy's voice rose as she spoke. 'At least if I was up there we'd be together.'

Poleaxed by her daughter's words, Anna slumped against the car. The doughnuts and coffee threatened to reappear. She couldn't speak, not that she had any idea what she'd say to her daughter if she could.

'Mum?' Now Izzy's voice was teary. 'I'm sorry. I should never have said that. I know how hard you work. Only sometimes I wish we had a proper home.'

'I know, Izzy. And I'm sorry. For everything.'

Neither of them spoke, each aware of the minefield they were tiptoeing through. Now wasn't the time for a deep and meaningful tete-a-tete about absent fathers and single-parent families.

'It'll be okay, Izzy. We'll work something out. I promise.'

Izzy spoke but her words were muffled and Anna realised she was talking to someone else. When she came back she said, 'Clara's here, Mum.'

'Okay. We can talk again later.'

'Sure. Gotta go. See ya.'

She'd disconnected before Anna could say goodbye.

'You all right, love?'

Snapped out of her funk, Anna blinked at Marlene, who was almost up in her face and regarding her with concern.

'Yeah, yeah, I'm fine. Frustrating family stuff,' she said. *Frustrating!* There was the understatement of the year.

Marlene sniffed. 'Like they say, you can pick your friends but not your family,' she said. 'Ask my boy Nick.'

Anna gave a humourless laugh. Hadn't she said that very thing to Nick recently?

Her head throbbed and perspiration trickled between her breasts. Marlene shuffled back to her canvas chair, shifting it deeper into the shade. Moments later the air was tainted with the acrid smell of cigarette smoke.

'Marlene, let's go to the pub for lunch,' Anna said.

Anything to get out of this heat and pretend her life wasn't in a tailspin.

37

The moment the wheels hit the tarmac late Monday afternoon, after a long and tedious day of patient transfers, Nick turned on his phone to find four voice messages waiting. He expected at least one to be from Anna.

Last night, when he'd stretched out beside her well after midnight, she'd been asleep. Too tired to do anything but sleep himself, he hadn't disturbed her. It was enough to be there with her.

This morning when his alarm had sounded, the bed beside him had been empty and Anna's swimming gear missing. In vain he'd waited for her to come home from the pool before he left for work. As a consequence, her suggestion that this was a rebound thing had nagged at him all day.

The first message was from Di, the social worker. She was sorry but the aged care bed had been allocated to someone else and 'Could Nick please make another appointment to talk about their other options for Marlene.' What other options? They could talk until they were hoarse and it wouldn't change anything. He moved on to the next message.

It wasn't from Anna either. It was from a haughty-sounding administrator at the aged care facility. 'Your mother is no longer with us. Please collect her belongings at your earliest convenience.' Nick stabbed at the phone, deleting the message, wondering where his mother was right now.

Lauren, his ex-wife—notice how he didn't have any problem thinking of her as his *ex*-wife—was the next caller, leaving a curt message, 'Call me. It's urgent.'

When he came to the fourth and final message he was taken aback by the sharpness of his disappointment when it wasn't Anna's voice he heard. Instead it was the nasal twang of Neville Abrahams, the senior flight nurse, saying he needed to talk to Nick, like yesterday.

Nick disconnected and barely resisted the urge to throw the phone across the cabin.

'Not the news you were hoping for?' Bruce, one of the other pilots asked as he stepped through from the cockpit, leather satchel under his arm. Nick hadn't even noticed they were parked on the apron in front of the hanger, the propellers stationary.

'You could say that.'

Bruce clapped him on the shoulder. 'Shit happens, mate. Let's unload and then you go home and have a couple of beers. It'll all look better after that.'

Nick unclipped his seatbelt and stood up, shoving the phone into his pocket. He doubted a couple of beers would turn things around, even in the short-term.

In the distance a regional airlines plane touched down. The runway seemed to float in the heat. Bruce disappeared into the hangar. Nick didn't waste any time unloading on his own.

In no hurry to hear what Neville had to say, Nick wasn't quite quick enough getting out of the door when he'd finished the restocking and paperwork.

'My office,' Neville said, standing in the corridor leading to the admin block, hands on hips.

The officious little so-and-so, Nick thought, following him through to his office.

Neville was mid-forties, a nugget of a man with a crew cut and an inflated sense of his own importance. But in the few dealings he'd had with him, Nick had always found him to be fair.

'Close the door,' Neville said, and sat down behind a scrupulously neat desk.

Nick's apprehension increased as he followed orders and closed the door. Must be more than a rostering issue. He fast-forwarded through his last few shifts, certain he hadn't stuffed up in any major way. Uneasy now, he perched on the edge of the visitor's chair, his earlier fatigue forgotten.

'I'll get straight to the point. Brett Carmichael's parents have made a formal complaint. Basically, they don't think we did enough to prevent their son taking his own life. I'd be interested to hear what you think.'

Nick eased himself further into the chair. 'They're grieving, angry, looking for someone to blame.'

Neville gave an impatient shake of his head. 'Tell me something I don't know. You dealt with Brett and his wife from the get-go. Did we do enough?'

What he really meant was 'Did *you* do enough?' Nick swallowed and moistened his lips, carefully picking his words.

'I'd never met Brett Carmichael until the day I delivered their stillborn baby, and I didn't ever see him alive again.'

'How did he seem at the time?'

'How do you think?' Nick frowned, tempered his speech. There was no value in coming across as defensive. 'He didn't say much, didn't ask any questions, didn't seem to want to be in the room with his labouring, and distressed, wife. At the time I thought it was unusual, but people in traumatic situations deal in different ways.'

'And afterwards?'

Nick corralled his thoughts, casting his mind back to the afternoon at Elder Creek station. He recalled the look on Anna's face when he'd asked for her help, and how tender and compassionate she'd been with Rachel.

'I'll admit I was taken aback when he refused point blank to accompany Rachel and their baby in the aircraft. But, like I said, people deal in different ways, and my focus was on the patient. She was devastated and she'd lost a significant amount of blood—' Nick lifted his hands, let them drop onto his thighs. 'It's all there in my nursing notes.'

'Didn't you think to follow up with him?'

Neville sounded accusatory and Nick bit back the first impulsive, angry response that came to his lips.

'Yes,' he said in a measured tone, 'I did think to follow up. I was concerned and looked on the patient database to see if he had an active record. As far as I could see he'd never been a patient with us. I rang him twice and left messages asking him to phone me back. He didn't return either of my calls. I talked to the mental health worker and made a referral. I know someone from the team tried to contact Brett, but he didn't return their calls either.'

'Of course there has to be an internal investigation. The parents have given us the opportunity to do that before they take their complaint any further.'

'I haven't met the Carmichaels. I was going to introduce myself at the funeral—'

'I heard you went to his funeral. Why?'

'As you know, the pilot, Anna Kelly, found him. She wanted to go to his funeral, and I went along as moral support. Rachel

Carmichael called me a few times after Brett's suicide. She had unanswered questions and was looking for support. She's staying with her mother. My understanding is she refused go back to Elder Creek after she lost the baby.'

Neville frowned. With stubby fingers he squared up the already square desk blotter. 'You appear to have become quite involved with Mrs Carmichael.'

Nick drew back. He didn't like the inflection Neville had put on the words *Mrs* and *involved*.

'Mrs Carmichael was extremely traumatised and distressed. I'd delivered her dead baby. After her husband killed himself, she called me, several times. I was someone familiar.'

'How did she know you were at Elder Creek after her husband died?'

'She said the station hand had told her. I urged her to seek help, talk to a grief counsellor, and I gave her the contact details of a person who comes highly recommended. And I asked her not to call me anymore. I didn't want to give her the wrong idea about anything.'

Nick didn't move a muscle, not so much as a flicker of an eyelid under Neville's cool, probing gaze.

The whole episode could only be described as a tragedy. Nick knew he'd done his job and acted professionally both times. He'd documented everything punctiliously, because he'd had a feeling this one could come back to bite him.

'And how is the pilot, Anna, dealing with it all? Finding him like that … Not something the person who flies the aircraft should have to confront.'

'That's something you'd have to ask her. But as colleagues involved in a traumatic incident, we did the usual debriefing—at the scene and then afterwards. She was great, the consummate professional.'

'Was she offered any counselling? Did she take it up?'

'Once again, you'd have to talk to her about that. I mentioned the employee assistance scheme to her.'

Neville's chair creaked as he reclined as far as it would let him, folding his hands across the beginnings of a paunch. 'You're separated from your wife, aren't you? You live with Beth Samuels *and* Anna Kelly, I'm told.'

'I share a house with them, yes. And?'

Neville nonchalantly lifted his shoulders. 'Plenty of opportunities for *cosy* little chats with Anna Kelly.'

'I'm not sure where you're going with this, Neville, or how relevant it is to the issue. But if your intention is to speculate about my personal life, I think I'd like the union rep to be sitting in on any further conversations.' Nick pushed himself to his feet.

'Sit down, sit down,' Neville said, waving him back into the chair. 'No harm intended. I was following up on a comment Mr Carmichael made about the appropriateness of your relationship with his daughter-in-law Rachel. And Mrs Carmichael mentioned that at the funeral you seemed very "close" to Anna Kelly.'

Nick sat. His stomach felt like it'd been doused with petrol and had a match thrown onto it. His mouth tasted sour.

'How would she know who I'm close to or not? I've never met the woman.'

'I've no idea how she knows or who she talks to, I'm repeating what she said to me when I contacted them about their letter of complaint.'

'I like and respect Anna. She's good to fly with,' he said, careful with each word. 'We've become friends. An experience like she had would have been tough for anyone.'

'You're right,' Neville said after studying Nick for what seemed like several minutes but was probably only seconds. Then, as if he'd made a crucial decision, he hoisted himself up in his chair.

'We need to make certain we dot the i's and cross the t's in this investigation, and I'll need your full cooperation,' he said. 'I think if we do it comprehensively the Carmichaels will be satisfied and won't want to take the complaint any further. They seem like reasonable people, and like you said, they're grieving and looking for explanations.'

The fire in Nick's gut died down a little, but didn't go out completely. Assuming the interview was over, he stood up, turned towards the door.

'Oh,' Neville said, pulling him up sharply. 'If you feel like you need time off until this blows over—'

Nick frowned. 'Why would I need time off?'

Neville pushed back from his desk. 'Just putting the offer out there, mate.'

Mate?

Neville smiled benignly, and Nick was struck by how much the man irritated him, fair or not. And someone should tell him to trim the hairs in his nose.

Nick shoved his hands in his pockets and legged it.

'See ya,' the receptionist called. Nick waved absently as he walked past. The automated door slid shut behind him.

He slogged across to the carpark. His line manager had just tried to set him up to take the fall for the organisation if they'd failed their duty of care to Brett Carmichael. A failure that later led to his suicide. Blindsided best described how Nick felt.

And then the squirrelly little bastard, suggesting he might want some time off. What was that all about?

Nick tried to moisten his lips but his tongue stuck to the roof of his mouth. Reaching for the bottle of lukewarm water in the console he sucked down half of it in one gulp.

He was back at Beth's. He'd made the trip on automatic pilot, lost in his thoughts, mulling over the recent interview.

How long had he been parked in Beth's driveway? A while because the cabin of the ute was like an oven.

Fresher and marginally cooler air rushed in when he opened the car door. Paranoia aside, the only conclusion he had come up with was that as senior flight nurse, Neville had a job to do, and he was doing it. It didn't make Nick feel any easier about the conversation though, or its implications.

The carport was empty and there was no familiar red Commodore parked on the kerb. He'd have the house to himself, which wasn't a bad thing because Nick's mood was low. And he needed to return Lauren's call, which wouldn't improve his mood any.

Halfway to the front door it dawned on him that he didn't have a clue where, or how, his mother was. Preoccupied, he hadn't noticed if her car had been parked in the scrub when he'd driven past.

He glanced at his watch. It was almost four. Unlikely she would have been there anyway, at this time of the day. Too hot. She would have sought the air-conditioned comfort of one of the pubs or clubs—or Macca's.

Nick cursed and retraced his steps, unlocking the 4WD. A shower, a cold beer, and returning Lauren's call would have to wait a while longer.

38

Sliding into the driver's seat, Nick threw the plastic carry bag down beside him. Mission accomplished, and the mobile phone hadn't cost him as much as he'd expected. From now on his mother would be at the end of the phone when he needed to reach her; he wouldn't have to drive around the streets looking for her anymore. Except for this time.

After a circuit of the pubs and clubs, he found Marlene's car parked in its usual place in the scrub. It was in the shade but it was deserted. Nick didn't know whether to worry or not.

To put his mind at ease before he did another round of the city's watering holes, he sat in the ute with the aircon blasting and called the hospital. No, she hadn't been there. The staff at the doctor's surgery hadn't seen her either.

Resigning himself to another fruitless drive around town, he frowned when a red car drove up, stopping alongside his mother's car. The driver's side door opened. It was Anna. He'd recognise those legs anywhere. When his mother emerged from the passenger side his relief was quickly overtaken by annoyance.

He threw open the door, nearly tripping over his feet in his haste to get out. 'Where the hell have you been?' he said, glaring at his mother over the bonnet of the dual cab.

The two women looked at each other, and then their gazes both swung to him.

'Hello, Nick. We had a late lunch at the pub and then I took your mother to Macca's for a thickshake,' Anna said, her reasonableness ramping up his irritation.

'I won sixty bucks on the pokies,' Marlene crowed.

Nick threw his hands in the air. 'Well, bugger me, and you didn't think to ring and tell me, either of you?'

'What, that I'd won sixty bucks? You don't usually want to know.'

'Mum,' Nick growled.

'I knew you were flying,' Anna said, slipping on her sunglasses. 'I'm sorry if you were worried.'

'Nick worried?' Marlene snorted, and then she promptly unlocked her car and disappeared inside.

'How is she?' Nick said to Anna, pulling the plug on his irritation. It was good to see her.

'A bit frail, although she's pretending to be fighting fit.' Anna pushed her sunglasses onto the top of her head again. 'I picked up her gear from the nursing home and then found her here. I couldn't leave her in this heat, Nick.'

'Thanks. I owe you,' he said, scuffing the ground with the toe of his boot. 'I don't know what I'm going to do with her. The social worker left me a message—she wants to see me again, but I'm not counting on her having any answers either.'

Anna scanned the scrubby, semi-secluded spot. 'Why hasn't the council moved her on from here?'

Nick propped himself against the side of his vehicle, crossing his ankles. The shadows were lengthening, high cloud streaked across the sky, but the heat sat like an immovable object.

'This is private property,' he said. 'Snake owns the land and he doesn't mind Mum parking here. If it was crown land you're right, she would have been moved along months ago.'

'I wish I had some suggestions for you, Nick, but I don't have any that don't need money.'

'Yeah … Money … Everything needs money. Thanks for babysitting her today.'

'It didn't feel like babysitting, and I didn't mind,' Anna said, swiping at flies. When she propped herself beside him, he hoped it wasn't only because the 4WD was in the shade.

'I missed you this morning,' he said, nudging her shoulder with his. 'I was hoping you'd get back from your swim before I left for work.'

'The pool was packed. I had to wait for a space, which is unusual for a Monday. Must be the heat.' She leaned in, examining his face. 'You look beat.'

Nick swallowed. 'Busy day. Crap day, if you want the truth.'

'What happened?'

'Oh, some work stuff,' Nick said, immediately regretting he'd said anything.

Anna wouldn't like the things Neville Abrahams had alluded to. And rightly so; Nick didn't much like them himself.

'What sort of work stuff?' she said, peering at him intently. 'Maybe I can help.'

He shook his head and gave what he hoped was a nonchalant lift of his shoulders. She drew back, a worry line appearing between her eyebrows.

'No, you can't—' he started, distracted when Marlene chose that moment to back out of the rear door of her car clutching a water bottle.

'You two still here?' she said, holding up a hand to shield her eyes from the lowering sun. She stared at them briefly, tutted loudly and set about erecting the rickety folding chair.

Nick glanced at Anna. 'I'll go,' she said, her sunglasses back in place, effectively blocking him out.

'Before you do,' he said, retrieving the plastic shopping bag from the ute, 'follow me.' He walked over to where Marlene was sitting. 'Mum, I've got something for you.' He passed her the bag. She opened it, peeked inside, grunted and then shoved it back at him.

'I told you I didn't want one of those bloody things,' she squawked, flapping her hands when he tried to give it back to her.

'I know you did, but I bought it for you anyway. I'll feel better knowing you have it.' He took the mobile phone out of the bag. 'It's been charged up and is ready to go. I'll show you how to use it. It's simple. I've put in my number, and the hospital and the doctor's surgery.'

'Here, I'll add my number.' Anna reached for the phone.

'Thanks,' he said, handing it to her.

Marlene scowled, sat back and folded her arms across her bony chest. Nick glared at her; she glared back. Anna glanced from mother to son.

'Marlene, we'll be able to keep in touch if you have a mobile phone. There're plenty of places you can charge it.'

Marlene stared at the phone in Anna's outstretched hand as if it was poisonous.

'And who's going to pay for it?'

'It's paid for, Mum. It's in my name and I'll keep paying for it as long as you promise to keep it with you and use it if you need to.'

Marlene glowered at Nick and then the phone.

'Here, I'll show you how easy it is.' Anna handed the new phone to Nick and took out her own phone. 'What's Marlene's number, Nick?'

Nick rattled off the number and Anna dialled. The phone rang. Nick demonstrated how to answer it and Marlene tentatively pressed it to her ear, smiling reluctantly when she heard Anna's voice.

A few more practice calls and Marlene was a pro. Well, sort of. Nick let himself relax, a fraction. 'You need to keep it charged and with you,' he said. 'And don't let anyone pinch it—'

'Nick,' Anna said, placing her hand on his arm. 'Your mum will be fine with it, won't you, Marlene?'

'Yes, I will,' she said, 'I might be old, but I'm not a complete duffer.'

Nick rolled his eyes. Anna made for her car. 'I'll see you, Marlene,' she said.

'You will darl, and thanks for dropping off my gear and shouting me lunch.'

'You're very welcome. Bye, Nick.' She waved, and after a perfectly executed three-point turn, took off in a cloud of dust.

Nick turned to face his mother. 'What?' he said, her expression smug.

'Lovely girl,' Marlene said. 'She must think the world of you to babysit your feisty old mother for the best part of a day.'

'You reckon? I'm never sure what she thinks.'

Marlene's face rumpled thoughtfully. 'There's something familiar about her … But I can't put my finger on it,' she said.

'She went to Broken Hill High, we were in Year Twelve together. Her father was the principal. Max Kelly.'

'Might have seen her about. Don't remember him.'

'No, you wouldn't—' Nick stopped, closed his mouth. The past was the past. What did it matter now that neither of his parents had ever darkened the doorway of any school he or Lachy had attended?

'If there's nothing else I can do for you, I'm off. Ring if you need anything.'

Marlene nodded vaguely, not saying anything, lost in her own thoughts.

As he drove off Nick glanced in the rear-view mirror. She hadn't budged.

39

Anna arrived home two days later, after a never-ending shift flying patients to and from Adelaide, to find a *For Sale* sign hammered into the front lawn. Fleetingly, she thought she'd stopped in the wrong driveway. Then Albert strolled down the path.

The day had seen one frustration after another—a grumpy flight nurse, a dust storm, defective equipment and a long wait at Adelaide airport while the plane was repaired. Seeing the sign on the lawn topped off the day nicely.

That morning Beth had flown to Melbourne for a nursing agency interview. She was overnighting it with her friend Gill.

Anna had wished Beth luck and meant it. But now, seeing the bright yellow cardboard sign in reality, the implications of Beth getting a job in Melbourne and selling the house hit home with the suddenness of a wind shear.

Anna dropped her bag onto the verandah and sat down beside it, her thoughts spinning.

Nick was on nights. She knew he'd flown sometime during the previous night because she'd woken at two to find the space beside her cold and empty.

When he didn't return, and his ute was already parked at the base when she arrived at work, Anna surmised he'd chosen to sleep there and not wake her.

Personally, she wished he had come home and woken her; professionally, she was glad he hadn't. She needed her sleep too.

At knock-off time Nick's ute was gone from the staff carpark. Anna hurried home to see him, but he wasn't there.

Using her phone to snap a photo of the sign, Anna texted it to Nick with the accompanying message: *Have you seen this?*

Seconds later a reply whooshed back: *No, but it's what she said she'd do.*

But so soon!

Beth's on a roll, came Nick's reply.

'I suppose she is,' Anna said out loud.

The cement was hot, even through her heavy cotton drill trousers. The sun wouldn't set for a couple more hours. Albert jumped up onto the verandah, rubbing along her thigh, leaving a fuzz of fur. He purred loudly when she scratched him behind the ears.

'What are we going to do, Albert?' she said, and the cat nuzzled into her hand. 'At this rate we'll be out on the street before we know it.'

Despondent, she thumbed back a message to Nick. *I'm cooking. Chicken stir-fry. What time will you be back?*

Nick's reply was immediate: *Patient transfer at 8 pm. Few things to catch up on at base. Sorry.*

So, he wasn't coming home at all. Her shoulders slumped. She started to compose a return message then thought, bugger it, and rang him.

'What's up?' he said.

'What's up? I guess seeing the sign gave me a bit of a jolt.'

'It's what she said she'd do.'

'Yeah, I know—'

'Anna, it mightn't sell for months. We'll find something else. Didn't you pick up rental info the other day from the estate agent? What was that about?'

They both knew she'd visited the real estate agent before Beth's news. This was the first time Nick had mentioned it.

'Were you planning on moving out because I'd moved in?' he said.

'It had crossed my mind. But no, someone I know wants to visit,' she said. 'I was getting info about holiday rentals.' Sort of the truth. She closed her eyes, held her breath. She had to tell him about Izzy but not now, not on the phone while he was at work.

'Beats me why anyone would want to holiday in this place.'

'Yeah,' she said, letting go of her breath. 'Go figure.'

'I've got to go. Don't worry about the house, something will come up. If all goes well and we don't get diverted, we'll be back by midnight.'

'Will you sleep there?'

'You're working tomorrow and I'll only wake you if I'm late.'

'Wake me,' she said. 'Please?'

'If you insist,' he said.

They disconnected. She bounced the phone on her knee. The cat stretched out beside her on the cement. Absently rubbing his stomach she said, 'Albert, did I just beg him to come home?'

Albert's eyes opened to narrow slits, vibrations of contentment rumbling through him.

'Yep, I reckon I did.' She stopped rubbing and Albert swiped her with his paw. 'I'm in deeper than I realised.'

They had been on opposite shifts that week, and Anna had seen little of Nick. When she had, he'd been distant and preoccupied. What had happened on Monday was obviously still troubling him.

'I know he doesn't have to share with me,' she said, and Albert's ears twitched. 'But it would be helpful if he did …'

The same as it would be good if her daughter found the time to have a proper conversation with her, and she didn't have to stalk her on social media, and her sister—

Anna rested her head in her hands. A girlfriend named Vanessa. Who knew?

To top things off, Christmas was only a week away. Rod Stilwell's job offer needed to be dealt with; Anna had to decide what to do with Izzy over the holidays and where they'd stay; and she had no clue where this thing with Nick was going.

Or if in fact it was him who was going—back to Sydney when his contract finished in January.

The only certainty that Anna had was that Izzy would be in Broken Hill after new year, and she had to tell Nick about her before then. And she had to tell Izzy about Nick.

Anna's backside and brain were both numb when she finally stood up and stretched. The front yard was in shadow, the blue fading out of the sky as day transitioned to night. Albert had wandered off, and she was no closer to any solutions.

Her stomach rumbled and she remembered she'd been ravenously hungry earlier. Albert reappeared and pushed his way past her into the stuffy house, making a beeline for his empty food bowls and meowing plaintively. Anna fed him, and then stood under a cool shower.

Drying herself and smoothing in moisturiser, Anna examined the small bathroom: the pink and grey tiles, the sagging door on the vanity unit, the mould ingrained into the shower recess.

Regardless of its state, she liked the house; she liked living there. A day's work would be all it'd take to dig out the bathroom grouting and silicone and refresh it. The vanity needed a new hinge and a coat of paint.

Dream on, she thought, stepping into shorts and a clean T-shirt.

Beth wouldn't be home until the following day so with only herself to feed, Anna settled for grilled cheese and tomato on toast. Albert would enjoy the chicken breast strips thawing in the fridge, and the vegetables she was going to stir-fry would keep for another time. Maybe she'd cook tomorrow night.

Nick didn't wake Anna. He didn't come home at all. Anna tossed and turned, and in the grey light of pre-dawn she rolled over, contemplating the empty bed beside her. In that moment she knew, job offer or not, she wouldn't leave Broken Hill without first seeing if this thing with Nick could work. They had a month until his contract finished. Surely in that time they'd know.

But what if he baulked, and walked, when she told him about Izzy? He'd voiced his views on parenthood on several occasions, clearly stating he was in no hurry to be a parent.

Regardless, she tried to imagine how she'd feel if the situation was reversed and he was the one with a teenager. A teenager who he hadn't told her about. She couldn't imagine feeling anything other than hurt and anger. Extreme hurt and anger.

Shit. Punching the pillow she squeezed her eyes shut. For such a practical and sensible person, she had got herself into one hell of a mess.

40

Beth returned from Melbourne pulsing with energy. 'I'll get more work than I want through the agency,' she said. 'And Gill can't wait for me to come and stay.'

Home barely an hour and she'd organised a rubbish skip to be dropped off the following day.

'I know the house might not sell for months, but the last thing I'll want to do is come back from Melbourne to clean it out.'

Grinning from ear to ear, Beth waved an expansive hand at the table on the back verandah, already piled high with household odds and ends. 'I'm going to chuck everything I don't want. If I have to get the skip emptied more than once, so be it.'

'Don't forget the op shop,' Anna said, running her fingers over a lumpy, brown pottery vase.

Beth flicked her wrist at the cardboard cartons stacked on the verandah. 'That's what they're for. What's not junk is for the op shop, and the rest goes into storage. Carol Petrucci gave me newspapers to use for packing. And Mario has heaps more cartons.'

'Trust me, you'll need them. What can I do to help?'

'You'll help? Even though I'm virtually throwing you out of your home?' Beth said, with characteristic bluntness.

'Mmm … Like you said, the house might be on the market for months, and a lot can happen between now and then.'

'You're right, a lot could happen,' she said. 'By the way, where is Nick?'

'Nights, and he must have slept at the base.'

Anna hadn't seen him for more than thirty-six hours and couldn't get past the crazy notion that he was avoiding her. Common sense told her she was being paranoid. Nevertheless, her newly enamoured heart was fragile, and highly reactive to the most irrational of suggestions.

Beth didn't comment before going inside. Anna was shuffling through a stack of vinyl records when she returned with two beers encased in stubby holders. 'Here,' she said, handing one to Anna. 'You look like you could do with this.'

'Thanks,' Anna said. 'I think something happened at work a few days ago. He won't tell me what, but I know it's bothering him.' The cap on Anna's stubby twisted off with a loud *pfft*.

'He'll get over himself,' Beth said, raising her drink in a toast. They clunked stubby holders, before guzzling down the cold brew.

For the next two hours, while moths and bugs circled pointlessly around the verandah lights, Beth kept Anna busy, and entertained. Every weird possession had a funny anecdote to go with it: how she'd come to own a mini piano accordion, a fondue set, and a selection of Cat Stevens' vinyl records, and why she wanted to keep them.

Whether it was the funny stories or the beer they were drinking, Anna didn't care: it took her mind off Nick, and she hadn't laughed as much since … She couldn't remember.

At about ten-thirty Beth surveyed the backyard and swore. 'The shed,' she said, yawning widely. 'I haven't been out there for so long

I've forgotten what's in it.' She pulled a bunch of keys out of her pocket, searching through them, finally settling on one. 'No time like the present.'

'Wouldn't it be better to look in the daylight?'

'Yeah, but there's power's on down there and if I do a reccy now, I can be thinking about what I'm going to do with it all.'

'That sounds ominous.'

'Nah, not really.' She flicked on the floodlight. Hercules started barking. Albert streaked past and into the house through the cat flap. Beth set off across the lawn towards the shed, tucked away in a corner of the backyard.

'As you know, I bought this house from one of Mum's aunts. I'm embarrassed to say that in all the time I've lived here, I haven't touched the stuff in the shed. Most of it was hers,' she said when Anna caught up with her.

It was about double-garage size, the corrugated iron exterior dulled by the relentless sun and the gutters scarcely hanging on. A modular steel rainwater tank, pockmarked with rust, leaned precariously against the end wall.

Once upon a time, someone had planted a border of rosemary bushes; now they were gnarled and sparse, woody with age.

When Anna had moved in with Beth, she'd wandered around the backyard and pressed her face to the grimy shed window. All she'd seen through a tear in the blind was the front wheel of a bicycle leaning against something bulky and covered with a dusty sheet.

The sound of metal on metal as Beth wrangled the lock, and then buttery-coloured light fell from the open doorway.

'What *am* I going to do with all this shit?'

'Yeah,' Anna said, giving the cluttered space a once-over. 'You'll need that skip emptied more than once.'

The interior of the shed was lined, the paintwork peeling. A vintage air conditioner protruded from the wall.

To the left of the door there was a compact kitchen alcove; and an empty space where a fridge would have been.

'Is that a bathroom?' Anna said, pointing to the walled off area adjacent to the kitchen.

Beth's cheeks puffed out a tired breath. 'Yep, it is. Shower and toilet.'

'What, all plumbed up and everything?'

'Sure is. Lenny, my great-aunt's son, lived out here. He never married. He used to work at one of the mines until he had an accident and was invalided out. Ended up with a metal plate in his head. He was already mildly intellectually disabled. An acquired brain injury made it harder for him. As kids, we weren't always kind.'

'What happened to him in the end?'

'He started having seizures and was admitted into hospital for investigations. The nurses found him dead in bed the next morning. Cerebral bleed. His mum buried him, sold the house to me and moved to the Clare Valley to be near her daughter. That'd be almost ten years ago. My great-aunt died last year.'

'Oh, I'm sorry.'

Beth lifted a shoulder, let it drop. 'She was old.'

Together they silently contemplated the jumble of old furniture covered with threadbare sheets and curtains. Dusty boxes of books, newspapers and magazines were stacked haphazardly against the walls. There was a battered trunk, the bicycle Anna had seen, and a derelict treadmill and other gym equipment—all of it decoratively laced with cobwebs and speckled with mouse droppings.

'The bike and some of the books and magazines are the only things that are mine.'

'What, the gym equipment doesn't belong to you?' Anna said, smirking.

'Ha ha,' Beth said. 'I can't believe I've never done anything about this before now. I promised I'd sort it out when I moved in. Then I kept putting it off, and conveniently forgot about it altogether.'

'Didn't she want any of the stuff?'

'Nope, she said to sell what I could and dump the rest. By then she was elderly, frail. She sold the place to me for a song. Clearing out Lenny's things was the least I could have done for her, if only I'd done it.'

Beth reached for the light switch and plunged the shed back into darkness. 'Let's go. This is too depressing.'

Anna stood by while Beth locked the door. There wasn't a breath of wind. Flattening her hand against the shed wall, Anna felt the warmth still radiating from the galvanised iron. 'Maybe whoever buys the house will take the furniture,' she said, and Beth's only response was a distracted grunt.

After a shower Anna propped herself up in bed with the overhead fan on high, scrolling through Izzy's social media sites.

Earlier that evening her daughter had blown her off yet again when she'd suggested via text that they FaceTime later. Something was up and Anna had no inkling of what, except for an underlying unease. And it seemed that Teresa, caught up in her own happiness, for once couldn't be relied on to notice if anything was amiss.

Thumbing her way through the photos and comments—most of them innocuous, some amusing, and some that read like a foreign language—she wondered whether Izzy's friends did anything other than wile away their waking hours on social media.

When she put down the phone and turned off the bedroom light, she was none the wiser as to what had her spidey sense twitching.

But her mind kept going back to one photo … Izzy, Clara and several other teenagers having fun somewhere, and at the side, almost out of the frame, a grinning Damien.

An hour later Anna woke with a start when the bed beside her dipped. A large, familiar hand was sliding across her bare stomach, a sand-papery chin nuzzling into her neck.

'Are you awake?' Nick whispered.

'I am now,' she said.

'Sorry I didn't make it last night, but it was late … ' He trailed off, his hand moving steadily upwards to fondle one breast. Her slumberous body reacted with gobsmacking intensity and she felt the vibrations of his amusement.

Anna wanted to shove his hand away, ignore her traitorous body, demand to know why he'd been avoiding her; and just as desperately she wanted to draw him closer, let him sink into her, lose herself, if only for a while.

'Anna?'

As if tuned in to her inner turmoil, Nick eased his hand away from her breast, let it rest lightly on her abdomen.

'Have you been flying?' she said, straining her eyes in the gloom to make out his expression. She could only feel his weight and warmth against her.

'No, I haven't,' he said, and the bed undulated when he rolled onto his back.

Her skin tingled where his hand had been.

A hundred thoughts flitted through her brain, too fast for her to grab hold of a coherent one. 'You've been avoiding me,' she said, the words heavy in the darkness.

He sighed. 'Not intentionally, Anna, please believe me. Work has been—' He paused and she heard the rasp of his hand cross his jaw. 'Challenging,' he said.

She swallowed, didn't move or make a sound, hoping he'd fill the silence with an explanation. He did.

'The Carmichaels put in a complaint saying we—I—didn't do enough to prevent their son taking his own life.'

Anna made a strangled sound, groping around until she found his hand, linking her fingers tightly with his. He returned the pressure before relating the salient points of the story, finishing with how, over the past few days, he'd spent hours going over every interaction he'd had with Brett and Rachel. He'd made copious notes detailing everything he could remember, checking and rechecking that he hadn't left out anything.

'Neville Abrahams, and the bosses up the food chain, don't want this to blow out and for the Carmichaels to take their complaint higher. We're going through everything, over and over … You get my drift?'

'I do,' she said. 'I wish you'd shared this with me when it happened.'

'I wanted to keep you out of it for as long as I could. As it was, you were more involved than you should have been. Neville and the chief medical officer will want to talk to you, eventually.'

'Bring it on. I was there. I'll vouch for you. They need to ask me. You were amazing!'

He lifted her hand, pressing his lips against her knuckles. 'You were pretty amazing yourself,' he said. 'Helping with Rachel, and then keeping it all together when you found Brett with his brains blown out. I should never have let you go looking for him.'

'It's how it happened, Nick. If we had to do it all over, we'd do it the same as we did, wouldn't we?'

'Yes, we would. In all my reviewing of the events I can't find anything I would have done differently. Call me an old cynic, but they want someone to blame if the Carmichaels aren't satisfied with the findings and want to take their complaint further. And for whatever reason, they've picked me for the role.'

'What do you mean?'

Nick waited a beat before saying, 'Neville made some snide remarks about my relationship with Rachel Carmichael. Questioned why I went to Brett's funeral. And the Carmichaels seem to know an awful lot about my personal life.'

'Nick, you should have told me! I'll go first thing in the morning and discuss it with Kyle, and then I'll talk to Neville, and whoever else needs to hear my take on the whole episode.'

Nick's hand tensed in hers. 'I think you should wait until they ask you,' he said.

'But it needs to be cleared up. They need to know you only went to his funeral because I didn't want to go on my own.'

'Neville knows that already, Anna. It'd be best if you waited until they asked you. And they will.'

Anna lay beside him, her eye's wide open, seeing nothing. 'All right,' she said. 'If you think that's the way to go.'

'I do. And there are reasons.'

'Reasons you aren't going to share with me?'

'Don't involve yourself in this any more than you have to.'

For several minutes neither of them spoke, lost in their own thoughts. And then he tipped towards her, throwing a large, muscly thigh over hers, effectively pinning her to the bed. 'We've about done with the talking, haven't we?'

Anna opened her mouth to say, no, they hadn't, that she had more questions. But then he pressed his lips against hers and whispered, 'God, I've missed you,' and she swallowed her words of protest. Because she'd missed him even more.

41

Trailing his fingers across the warm, smooth skin of Anna's naked shoulder, Nick smiled. Her eyes were closed. She was lying on her stomach, the sheet draped across her waist.

'Are you going for a swim?'

'Nah,' she said, her lips moving but her eyes firmly shut. 'I've already had my quota of exercise for today.'

So they had. 'Let me take you out to lunch. Today is the closest we get to a day off together.'

'Mmm,' she murmured and one eye opened. 'Okay. Where?'

'Silverton … I'll take you to the Silverton Hotel.'

'I've never been there.'

'What? You've been in Broken Hill how long now, and you've never been to Silverton? To the Mad Max Museum?'

'Bit boring on your own,' she said, both eyes closed again. 'What time is it?'

'Eight-thirty. Beth's gone to work.'

'Couldn't you sleep?' Anna rolled onto her back, tugging the sheet up to cover herself.

'I had some sleep,' he said, levering himself up and around until he was sitting on the edge of the bed, his back to her.

He was tired; he'd missed out on roughly a night's worth of sleep over the past week. On night shift there was a 70 per cent chance you'd fly sometime during the twelve hours shift, and Nick's experience was at least that.

Sleeping in the day wasn't the same. Tonight he could catch up because their rosters reversed, putting Anna in the sleep-deprived cohort.

Beside the bed, his phone buzzed. Reaching for it he grimaced when he saw the caller ID: *Lauren.* She'd been hassling him for days. She could go on hassling him because he wasn't talking to her now. He let it go through to voicemail, dropping the phone onto the pile of clothes he'd stripped off earlier.

'Not important?' came Anna's sleepy voice from behind.

'Nothing that can't be sorted out later.'

Regardless of how he felt about Lauren, buyer interest in their Sydney property had dwindled, and she was adamant they take the offer they'd had, even though the house hadn't yet been to auction.

Nick was torn. As much as he wanted to put that chapter of his life behind him sooner rather than later, he was reluctant to take whatever they could get. The house was old, it did need lots of work; however, it was in a good area and he was convinced it'd bring more at auction.

Nick had invested part of himself in that property, and it'd pain him to have to walk away with minimal money, on top of everything else.

Ideally, what was needed was a quick trip to Sydney so he could make up his own mind about what was or wasn't happening with the property. Lauren could be a bit casual with the facts.

He dropped his head into his hands.

'Nick? What's the matter?'

He lifted his head slowly glancing over his shoulder. Anna was kneeling behind him, clutching the sheet to her chest, not quite covering her breasts. She was watching him intently, that cute worry line pulling her eyebrows together. Her hair was sleep-mussed, her lips rosy red and swollen. She looked like a woman who'd been well and truly loved.

Because she had been. And what was he doing stressing about all that other shit, when she was right there, waiting to be loved some more.

'I'm good,' he said.

'If you're worried about all that stuff at work, I can—'

He shook his head. 'Anna, we've discussed it. Please wait until they ask to interview you—'

'Why?' The worry line between her brows deepened.

'Otherwise, they'll think I put you up to it.'

'No, they won't.'

'Yes, they will. And then they'll wonder why, wonder if you and I are more than work colleagues.'

'I can tell them—'

'Anna,' he growled, cutting her off. 'Please trust me on this.'

With a sharp exhalation she sat back, pouting in a way he found incredibly hot, despite the reason behind it.

'All right, we'll do it your way, this time.'

'Thank you. Now, do you want coffee? Breakfast? Or more sex?'

The pout smoothed into a sultry smile. 'More sex, please,' she said, and he willingly obliged.

Afterwards, they crammed into the shower cubicle together, proud of what they managed in the tiny space. Getting clean was only part of it.

By midday they were travelling to historic Silverton, twenty-five kilometres from Broken Hill, through the arid landscape of the western Barrier Ranges. The road was sealed but narrow and undulating. They spotted wild horses and emus among the mulga scrub and saltbush.

'You know this time next week it'll be Christmas Day,' Anna said, her attention wandering from the scenery whipping past the passenger window of Nick's ute.

'Christmas? Next week? That snuck up quick. Not that it's any big deal for me,' Nick said. 'As you can imagine, Mum's not exactly into Christmas trees, gifts and sumptuous family dinners.'

Ignoring his sarcasm, Anna said, 'We could take Marlene to the pub for Christmas dinner. I'm on a day shift. You go on nights that night.'

'Are you serious?'

Anna angled herself towards him, leaning forward, and he took his eyes off the road for a moment. How could he resist the smooth expanse of tanned leg, the snug fit of her skirt, and the provocative glimpse of cleavage when she leaned forward like that?

'Of course I'm serious. Unless you have other plans.'

'None that I can think of,' he said, refocusing on the bitumen unfolding in front of them at eighty kilometres an hour.

He shifted in the seat, his jeans suddenly uncomfortable. 'As far as I'm concerned, it's just another day.'

'It's Christmas, Nick.'

'Aren't you going south?'

'Yes, but only for three days; I'll be back for work on the twenty-fourth.'

Nick never took any notice of the windup to the festive season. Even as kids, Christmas had been a non-event.

'I dunno, Anna. Mum might have plans.'

'You think?'

'Who knows? She muttered something about my brother coming home. Can't see it myself.'

'Nick, she might have disappointed you as a mother and trust me, I know firsthand what that's like, but I'm sure it'd mean the world to her if you spent some time with her on Christmas Day. And if your brother's here as well—'

Nick clenched his fingers on the steering wheel, slowing down as they entered the township of Silverton, population less than fifty.

His jaw tightened, his lips pressing into a firm line. 'Not going to happen, Anna, so don't go getting your hopes up.'

Would he ever stop being angry with his mother? He couldn't remember a time when he hadn't been angry with her.

He felt the pressure of Anna's hand on his arm, his heart bumping furiously in his chest when, reading his mind she said, 'I know what it's like to be angry at someone forever. It sucks all your energy. And in the end …'

They'd come to the hotel and Nick pulled into the shade, putting the ute into park and leaving the engine ticking over, the air conditioning on. Her hand fell away from his arm, dropping into her lap, her sigh audible.

'I can't imagine you being angry with anyone forever, Anna. You're too pragmatic.'

'Not all the time, Nick.'

'So tell me who you're so angry with.'

'My mother! Who else?'

Nick pushed his sunglasses onto his head, regarding her thoughtfully. 'You know the reasons I'm angry with my mother. Tell me why you're so mad at yours.'

'What child isn't angry with their parents at some time or other. Children do things their parents don't like, and vice versa.'

'That's not a real answer,' he said, wishing she'd take off her sunglasses so he could see what was going on back there. But she made no move to do so and her shoulders took on a new stiffness.

'Well, it's all the answer you're getting,' she said.

'You didn't hold back telling me what I could do to make my mother happy this Christmas. What are you going to do to make your mum happy?' He knew he was niggling at her, but couldn't seem to help himself.

Anna chewed on her bottom lip. She suddenly looked incredibly sad, and he regretted that he'd done that to her. But he wanted to know more about her, what had made her the woman she was; why she was still angry with her mother. It was beginning to frustrate him that everything about her life outside of Broken Hill was a no-go zone, at least to him.

'Let's leave it for now. Please,' she said and unbuckled her seatbelt and climbed out.

His expletive filled the cab. He closed his eyes.

Anna was powering across the road to the pub when he caught up with her. His relief was potent when she didn't stop him from taking her hand, intertwining his fingers with hers.

'Not many people about,' she said, crossing the threshold into the coolness of the hotel.

'Can't say that I blame them. It's too bloody hot,' he said, prepared for now to forget their disagreement. Not to say he'd give up as easily next time.

A square affair, the bar dominated the centre of the historic Silverton Hotel. Memorabilia, some from the hundred or more films and commercials the hotel had featured in, plastered the walls and every other available space.

'I can't believe you've never been here,' Nick said. He leaned against the bar to wait for the barman, and to watch Anna gape at the eclectic display.

There were hats and boots and photos—framed and unframed, some defaced by scrawling signatures. On the mantelpiece a collection of formalin-filled jars housed a grisly collection of spiders, snakes and scorpions. Clichéd sayings handwritten on cards swung from the tiled ceiling on lengths of string.

'This place is crazy,' Anna said, smiling with delight.

'It is. What do you want to drink?'

'Mmm, I could be flying in six hours so make it lemon squash,' she said. 'But you have a beer. I can drive.'

They ate fish and chips served on throwaway plastic plates. Nick had one light beer. When he knocked back Anna's offer to buy him another one, she said, 'You don't want me driving your beloved ute. You trust me in the cockpit of a plane, but you don't want me behind the wheel of your car!'

He didn't deny it. 'It's a man thing,' he said, and her eyes turned heavenwards.

Anna perused everything on all four walls of the hotel bar before Nick prised her away to drive out to Mundi Mundi Plains, where scenes of the movies *Mad Max* and *Priscilla, Queen of the Desert* had been filmed.

'As much as I'd like to, I really need to go home and have a nap,' Anna said when he suggested they stop off at Umberumberka Reservoir. She yawned, her jaw creaking. 'I didn't get much sleep last night, if you remember rightly.'

'Oh, yeah, I remember,' he said.

'And being a Friday night the chances of me flying are higher than average.'

They drove home. The outside temperature had risen to 39 degrees, with not a two- or four-legged creature to be seen. Stark against the blue sky was the silhouette of an eagle, drifting lazily on the thermals.

'Thanks for today,' Anna said, as they whizzed past the eighty kilometre sign on the outskirts of town. 'And I'm sorry for interfering in what's yours and Marlene's business, not mine.'

'Oh, I don't know about that.'

'What do you mean?'

'Thinking about it, I'd say you have earned the right to have an opinion where Mum's concerned. You visit her, feed her junk food and help out in other ways. She rings you more often than she does me. She likes you.' Nick flashed her a sideways smile. 'I like you … A lot. And I value your opinion. And, I promise not to ask any more questions about your mother, or your father.' In the hope you'll tell me when you are good and ready.

They turned into Beth's street. Anna clasped and unclasped her hands where they lay in her lap.

'It's complicated, Nick,' she said. 'My mother and I rarely talk, and when we do, it always gets ugly. It's like we don't know what to say to each other so it's better that we don't say anything. It never has been much different.'

'What, not even when you were a kid?'

'Maybe she tried in the early days. But Teresa agrees that Mum's heart was never in being a mother.'

'What about your dad?'

'He checked out emotionally way back. Divorce was the best thing for them both. Dad found a woman who dotes on him, and Mum lives on the Sunshine Coast, stays single and wishes she was still in her forties.'

'Do you have much to do with your dad?'

Anna shook her head, and Nick knew by the set of her mouth that she'd said all she was going to on the subject of her family.

He flipped his sunglasses onto the dash and turned off the ignition. Across the console their eyes met, and held. Nick reached out and brushed his knuckles across her cheek.

'I'm looking forward to the time you trust me enough to tell me everything,' he said.

She didn't look away. 'I don't expect you to tell me everything.'

'No, but maybe you should,' he said, and reached for the door handle. 'It's what makes relationships work.'

42

Exhilaration rippled through Anna, while at the same time dread lodged like a lead ball in the pit of her stomach. Night landings by a flare path were the hardest. The moon had set and it was like dropping into a black hole.

The airstrip was familiar and the weather favourable—had it not been, she would have given it second thoughts. It was the pilot's call, after all.

When it came, that bump as the landing gear bit into the dirt strip, relief coursed through her. Behind her, the tension lifting in the cabin was tangible. No crew *liked* landing in a black hole, but sometimes it was unavoidable.

It was the early hours of Monday morning, Anna's third and final night shift before days off and her pre-Christmas trip to Adelaide. Contrarily, her first two nights had been quiet: Friday, they'd flown early in the shift, the sun yet to set when they'd taken off, and Saturday night they hadn't flown at all.

On a priority one, there was a doctor as well as the flight nurse on board. Doctor Bryan Jenner was new to Broken Hill RFDS base and came across as a quietly competent medico.

Tommy, the flight nurse, tended to be officious and Anna had never warmed to him. When she'd asked Nick what he thought of Tommy, he'd said, 'He's a pain in the arse, but good at what he does.'

Bryan and Tommy took no time unloading their gear, piling into one of the station vehicles and heading off towards the homestead. After securing the aircraft, Anna followed in another dusty ute beside a taciturn station hand. But then, it was the middle of the night when most people were in bed and fast asleep.

The trip to the homestead took ten minutes, the wait while they stabilised the patient a lot longer. An hour in, Tommy informed her that they needed to move the patient to Adelaide, not Broken Hill as first planned.

Anna phoned in a revised flight plan. They'd be taking off in pre-dawn light and they wouldn't make it back to Broken Hill before the end of their shift.

Finding a comfortable armchair in a quiet corner of the empty sunroom, she tried to power nap. Normally she wouldn't bother, but when she finished work a six-hour drive to Adelaide stretched out in front of her. She had hoped to get away early.

So much for making plans. Acute disappointment came with the realisation she wouldn't get to say a proper goodbye to Nick. Never mind, she'd only be away three days—back in time to have Christmas with him.

It struck her then that she didn't want to go at all. The visit seemed redundant now that Izzy was coming to Broken Hill after Christmas.

As soon as she'd thought it, remorse followed. The idea was to spend some sort of Christmas with her daughter. Nothing had changed there.

The bigger issue was that between now and the thirtieth of December, she had to tell Nick about Izzy.

Guess what, honey? I have a fifteen-year-old daughter and she's coming to stay indefinitely; and no, I haven't told her about you either.

The outing to Silverton had presented another opportunity to own up, and the topic of families had been raised, but yet again she'd shied away from telling him. But, it had been their first real date …

Folding her arms across her tummy she pressed down, trying to ease the knot of apprehension she experienced whenever she thought about what she needed to say to him.

With a thud her phone slid off her lap and hit the floor as she bolted upright in the armchair. A four-letter word froze in her throat. It must've been folding her arms across her abdomen that had prompted her subconscious …

Eyes wide, she did a rapid calculation in her head. Yes, there was no doubt about it—her period was late.

'Anna! We need to get this show on the road, like now!' Tommy bellowed, and she leapt to her feet, scooping the phone up off the floor with trembling fingers.

Compartmentalise, she ordered herself. It was something she was usually good at. Pushing all thoughts of a late period and its ramifications to the back of her mind, she made a quick detour to the bathroom. She was back in the ute alongside the station hand and on the track out to the airstrip minutes later.

Anna heard the front door open, but it was as if her backside was welded to the edge of the bathtub. Reeling with tiredness and disbelief, her fingers gripped the package on her lap. Try as she might she hadn't been able to open it, unable to get past the memory of a scared teenager fumbling with a similar cardboard package.

With the back of her hand she scraped at the tears, sticky on her face.

'Anna,' Nick called. 'Where are you? I was hoping you'd still be here. I haven't got long.'

The sound of his step on the squeaky floorboard outside her bedroom door flicked a switch inside her, galvanising her into action. Three more steps and he'd be at the bathroom door.

She shoved the unopened paper bag from the chemist into the vanity drawer and turned on the handbasin tap, splashing cold water onto her blotchy face.

'I'm so glad I caught you before you left—' he said from the bathroom doorway. Then his gaze locked onto her reflection in the mirror. 'What's up?' he said. 'Have you been crying?'

'Nothing's up,' she said, swiping at the water dripping off her chin.

In the mirror, his eyes narrowed. 'Convince me.' He folded his arms.

She spun around, grabbing her towel, pressing it to her face. 'My period is late,' she said, her voice muffled in the folds of fabric.

'How late?' he said, his arms dropping to his sides, his face a shade paler than it had been.

'Almost two days, but I'm usually as regular as clockwork.'

'Two days,' he repeated. 'That's nothing.'

Anne peeked at him over the towel.

'And we used condoms every time,' he said.

'I know. And I'm sorry.'

'For what? I don't remember either of us forcing the other into anything?'

'No,' she said quietly. 'It could be because of night duty, lack of sleep.' She hugged the towel to her chest. 'Who knows? If nothing happens in a few more days I will do a pregnancy test.'

Anna thoughts skipped to the paper bag in the vanity drawer. The woman at the chemist said that today's pregnancy tests were incredibly sensitive to hormonal changes and would tell you if you were pregnant before you'd even missed a period. Nick was a midwife, he'd know that.

If she'd had the courage to use the test kit she had, she'd know now.

'When were you going to tell me, Anna?'

'There was nothing to tell. It was only this morning I realised I was late. Don't worry, Nick—after me you'll be the next person to know.'

His phone chimed with a text message. With a sigh he rummaged in his pocket for the phone, scanning the screen. 'I've gotta go. There was a hold-up with a patient we're transferring—that's how I managed to duck out—but it's been sorted now.'

He didn't move from the bathroom doorway.

'I came to say goodbye,' he said. 'I waited as long as I could this morning. Then I thought I'd catch you at the base.'

'We were late ... Tommy needed a lift ...' I stopped at the chemist.

Nick's expression softened. 'You look worn out. You have a long drive ahead of you. Why don't you sleep before you go?'

'I need to get on the road,' she said, hanging the towel on the rail. 'I'm later than I wanted to be as it is. I have to drive back the day after tomorrow.'

'Beats me why you're not flying. For that matter, why you're going at all. I'm sure your sister could manage without seeing you for one Christmas.' This was said over his shoulder as he walked towards the front door.

How could she explain that she needed her car? There were Izzy's Christmas presents, surreptitiously stashed in the boot of the

Commodore. And Izzy had gear she wanted brought back to Broken Hill, stuff she couldn't take to the Sunshine Coast but said she couldn't do without during the holidays.

Nick stopped suddenly, turning to face her.

'Why don't we drive down together after Christmas?'

'And when would that be, with the rostering the way it is? We rarely get one day off together.' Anna avoided looking at him. She was horrified by how easily evasions and fabrications rolled off her tongue.

'I could swap some days—' His phone rang. 'What now?' He pressed it to his ear. 'I'm on my way. Ten minutes,' he snapped, to whomever was on the other end.

Shoving the mobile into his pocket he pulled Anna into a fierce hug. 'Drive carefully,' he said, his lips moving against her temple. 'I wish you didn't have to go.'

He drew back, tipped up her chin with a finger. His eyes were grey and stormy. 'And promise me you'll ring the moment you get your period, or not.'

Anna nodded.

'Promise me.'

'Okay, I promise!'

Watching him drive off, Anna clutched her abdomen, blinking back bitter tears. He hadn't said once that he'd be there for her if she was pregnant.

43

'Where's Izzy?'

Anna loaded colourfully wrapped parcels into Teresa's waiting arms. 'I can't wait to see her.'

'She should be back soon. She went into Rundle Mall with Clara to finish Christmas shopping,' Teresa said.

'Oh, that's a shame.' Annoyingly, Anna's vision blurred with tears. She fumbled with the handle of her suitcase. If she had flown she would have been here hours ago, and nowhere near as exhausted …

'Come inside. I'll make you a coffee.'

'Tea, please. I don't think I could stomach another coffee.'

They finished unloading the car and Teresa busied herself making a pot of Lady Grey. 'Have you eaten?'

'Yes, thanks. I had something greasy at Yunta and a meat pie at Riverton, both washed down with copious amounts of coffee.'

'Annalise! No wonder you look like death warmed up, eating that garbage.'

'Oh, gee, thanks. I look like this because I've driven for six hours and haven't slept in over twenty-four, not because I ate a meat pie.'

The tea leaves hissed when Teresa poured on the boiling water. She set down the pot. 'I'm sorry. You do look wrecked. But you must admit, sometimes your food choices—'

Anna glared at her sister, cutting her off mid-sentence. It was an age-old argument.

They drank tea. Teresa caught Anna up on the plans for Christmas: Izzy would fly to the Sunshine Coast on the morning of the twenty-fourth, and Teresa would wing her way to Sydney later that same day.

Anna reached across and squeezed Teresa's hand. 'I hope it all works out with Vanessa,' she said.

Teresa's shoulders lifted in a seemingly careless shrug. 'I am looking forward to seeing her again. But like I said before, I'm nervous, and a bit hesitant about the whole thing.'

'Nothing ventured, nothing gained, or so they say.' Anna picked up the teapot, topping up her cup.

For the umpteenth time that day she did a quick assessment of how she felt, reassuring herself the nausea and fatigue were by-products of shift work, roadhouse food and too much coffee, not an unwanted pregnancy.

Anna had had six uninterrupted hours to ruminate. While it might be unplanned and mightily inconvenient, a pregnancy wasn't entirely unwanted. That's what was freaking her out the most.

'What about you? No tall, dark and handsome men on the horizon?'

Anna hesitated, the cup halfway to her mouth. Teresa pounced on the pause.

'There is someone. I knew it. Come on, tell me all about him. And why you haven't told me before.'

Carefully replacing the cup on its saucer, Anna said, 'His name is Nick Harrison. He's a flight nurse. We're sort of together, but we're keeping it to ourselves.'

Teresa was grinning, nodding vigorously. 'Didn't I tell you you'd meet someone out there? This is fantastic. When do we get to meet him?'

'Teresa, he's only relieving in Broken Hill. He'll probably go back to Sydney when his contract finishes next month. He has a house there. It's probably just a bit of fun.'

Even as she said the words, Anna realised the likely truth in them, as much as Nick had tried to convince her otherwise.

Unconsciously, her hand went to her abdomen. Amazing the clarity 500 kilometres and the familiar face of her sister had brought.

'Oh well, like you said to me, nothing ventured, nothing gained. And you are long overdue for a bit of fun in your life.'

'Yeah, it's been a strange sort of life, living all the way up there, away from everything familiar.' Anna fiddled with her teaspoon, stirred the tea unnecessarily.

'What?' Teresa said, eyeing her sister. 'There's something you're not telling me.'

There was a lot Anna wasn't telling her … Having an affair with a married man, sort of. Thinking she might be pregnant again. Sound familiar?

'Rod Stilwell emailed with a job offer,' Anna said, choosing something safe.

'Really?' Teresa said. 'I bet that was unexpected.'

'It was. A few months ago I might have jumped at it. But now?' She lifted her shoulders, let them fall on a slow exhale. 'When I took the job in Broken Hill I thought it'd be a stepping stone to something similar closer to home. Would you believe I'm beginning to like living there this time? I love the flying. I really feel as if what I do makes a difference.'

'You know if you came back you'd be welcome to live here.'

'Thanks, Teresa, I appreciate that. Someday, I really do want to buy a home of my own.'

'So why are you even considering Rod's job offer?' Teresa frowned.

'Rod assured me there'd be job security this time around. I'd be back with Izzy. She wouldn't have to board. You'd be free to do whatever you decide to do. There's a lot going for it.'

'Don't worry about me! What does your gut tell you?'

Anna snorted. 'That I've eaten too much greasy food and drunk too much bad coffee.'

'Seriously, Anna.'

She yawned, scrubbing her face with her hands. Resting her elbows on the table she said, 'My gut tells me that I love the job I have, I like living in Broken Hill, and I want to see where this thing with Nick goes. And even if it goes nowhere, I'd like to stay with what I'm doing, for the time being.'

'There's your answer. When are you going to tell Izzy about Nick?'

'Soon, given she's coming to stay. I haven't told him about her yet.'

'Why not?' Teresa's voice shot up an octave or two.

'At first there was no need, we were only colleagues, it was none of his business. And then—'

'You kept putting it off, and now it'll come across as something else entirely.'

Anna closed her eyes. 'Something like that. And he's made clear his aversion to parenthood.' She dropped her hands into her lap, opened her eyes to meet her sister's watchful gaze.

'He's from Broken Hill. We were in the same year at high school. He remembered me, and Dad. I have only vague memories of him, but then my focus was elsewhere that year.'

'You need to tell him about Izzy.'

Anna picked up the fine china teacup, disappointed to discover it was empty except for the dregs in the bottom. She studied the tea leaves, gave up when she found no answers there.

'I might not see him for dust once he finds out I'm a single parent.'

'Nothing wrong with being a single parent. Look at me, a divorcee about to try a same-sex relationship. We're a pair, aren't we? Not exactly a brilliant track record when it comes to affairs of the heart, either of us.' Teresa stood up. 'If I didn't have work to finish before the break, I'd open a bottle of wine and we could get drunk.'

'I'd be asleep after the first glass.' And until I'm 100 per cent certain I'm not pregnant, I won't be drinking alcohol.

But sharing that thought would be too much information for her sister. And anyway, if she wasn't pregnant, no-one else ever needed to know except her and Nick.

Teresa carried the tea things to the sink, carefully rinsing the teapot. 'Why don't you go and have a lie-down until Izzy gets home. I thought we'd barbecue for dinner. I bought those chicken sausages you like, the ones with spinach and pine nuts.'

Anna yawned widely, testing with her tongue that she hadn't split the corners of her mouth. 'I will have a quick shower and take a nap. Thanks for the tea, and for everything.'

They hugged briefly, but tightly.

Anna woke to the throb of a V8 engine and the sound of giggling. Rolling out of bed and padding to the window, she peeked through the curtains. From the bedroom she had a clear view down the driveway to where a black ute with a surfboard strapped to the back was idling. Squinting, she could barely make out the driver. She knew it would be Damien.

A giggling Clara tumbled out of the open passenger-side door, followed by Izzy and several shopping bags, and male laughter.

When had her daughter's legs gotten so long, her breasts so well developed? Who was this girl-woman? This stranger?

Anna felt sick. Her head pounded as if it was going to explode. She pressed her face closer to the window.

Clara climbed back in and the passenger door swung shut. Izzy leaned into the open window. More giggling before her daughter stepped back, waved as the ute reversed down the driveway. A toot of the horn, a throaty rumble, and the car and its occupants disappeared.

A light tap and then the bedroom door opened, Teresa stood on the threshold gripping the handle. 'I had no idea, Anna, I swear. She hasn't mentioned Damien since she had her appendix out, and I hadn't seen him until now. His dad's been coming on his own to do the yard and the pool.'

Anna's eyes met Teresa's. Her sister looked distraught.

'It's okay,' Anna said. 'But what do I say to her now? I almost want to pretend I didn't see him.'

'Do that. But don't be angry with her. In my experience anger never works.'

Anna nodded. A door banged, followed by an excited squeal of, 'Mum, you're here!' and footsteps pounding down the passageway.

Teresa stepped back, barely missing being bowled over as Izzy launched herself across the room at her mother.

Anna buried her face in Izzy's strawberry-scented hair, hugging her close.

This was her daughter. Then holding her at arm's length, taking in her youthful, vibrant beauty, Anna couldn't hold back the tears.

'Mum! You're not crying again?'

'I'm so happy to see you,' Anna said and dragged Izzy in for another hug.

'I saw my presents under the tree. Guess what I bought you for Christmas? You. Will. Adore. It.'

'I've no idea, and I'm sure I will love it. How's Clara? And your other friends?' Over her daughter's shoulder Anna locked gazes with Teresa. Teresa shook her head slowly.

'Clara's cool,' Izzy said, disentangling herself from her mother's arms. 'They're all going to the farm until after the new year.'

Anna waited a beat, hoping Izzy would mention Damien, but her daughter kept chattering on about anything and everything except him.

Bemused, Anna listened, tried to keep up, grateful when Teresa cut in saying, 'Why don't we go for a swim before we make salads and fire up the barbecue?'

'Sounds like a plan,' mother and daughter said in unison.

'I'll see you both at the pool in ten,' Teresa said.

Izzy skipped off to change and Anna rummaged in the chest of drawers, looking for her spare pair of bathers.

44

'Did you tell Nick about Izzy?'

When Teresa's ID had flashed on the screen, Anna knew the question would be asked, but not so early in the telephone conversation. Her sister hadn't even said hello.

It was early Christmas morning, Anna was on call and she was sitting in the cool of the back verandah feeling decidedly un-festive.

'Hi Teresa, and a Merry Christmas to you too. In answer to your question, it turned out I didn't get the chance to tell him.'

'How come?'

'When I got back, he'd gone.'

'Gone where?'

'Back to Sydney by all accounts.' Anna could barely believe it herself, except that he wasn't there and she couldn't pretend he was.

'Anna! The total bast—'

'Please don't, Teresa. He said he had no choice, and that he'd be back. Currently, I'm doing a good job of pretending I believe him. How's Vanessa?'

'She's good, but never mind her right now, how are you?'

'Fine. I've talked to Izzy, and to Mum. She was her usual cheerful and supercilious self.'

'I've talked to them too. They were opening their presents. Then they're going to some flashy restaurant for Christmas lunch. And Mum said she'd spoken to you and you were your usual serious and disagreeable self.'

'You don't say. Maybe we get each other more than I thought.'

'It's about expectations,' Teresa said. 'I've learned with Mum not to have any, then every now and then she delivers.'

Maybe that's what Anna should have done: never expect anything from her mother, especially mothering.

When they disconnected, loneliness weighed down on Anna. It was Christmas Day and here she was on her own.

There was no tree, no Christmas dinner, only packing boxes stacked in every available space. Beth had left for work before seven and Nick was hundreds of kilometres away. She willed herself not to think about what he might be doing, or who he might be doing it with.

While she'd been in Adelaide they'd kept in touch with text messages and the occasional phone call. Nick had been on day shift, while she'd been busy with Izzy.

Anna had taken Izzy out for a special lunch. Then she'd helped pack a suitcase for Izzy's trip to her grandmother's, and gear for the stay in Broken Hill.

After the tedious drive home, Anna had scarcely stepped through the door at Beth's late Wednesday night, when Nick had called. From Sydney.

He'd sounded dog-tired and disgruntled, about the same mood as she'd been in.

'It is a long and boring trip on your own,' he'd said.

'I'm still struggling to get my head around why you're there and not here.' In an effort to avoid sounding how she really felt, Anna had come across sounding angry instead. Nick had bitten back.

'I'm not exactly thrilled about being here either, but the effing house has termites. Apparently, a buyer put in an offer but wanted an engineer's report first. That's when they discovered the place is riddled.'

'But how did you get time off work? At Christmas time?'

'Ah,' Nick had said, and the way he said it made Anna's heart skip a beat.

'What happened?'

'Neville had suggested earlier that I might want time off—'

'Earlier? When? Because of Brett Carmichael?'

'Yes, although then there was no reason to take time off.'

'What changed?'

Even across the distance that separated them Anna hadn't missed the sound of Nick swallowing. Her heart rate had ratcheted up a few more beats.

'The weekend before you went to Adelaide, Rachel Carmichael was in town. She rang me, wanted to meet and talk. I said no, blocked her number and reported it to Neville immediately. Then after you'd gone Lauren called in a total panic about the house, and I thought, why not take Neville up on his earlier offer and get out of town until this blows over.'

'Why didn't you tell me?'

'You were on nights. You didn't need to be bogged down with my crap.'

'The way they've treated you doesn't sound very fair to me.'

'Who knows? Hopefully it all makes better sense after I've slept.'

'For what it's worth, I have my interview with Neville tomorrow.'

'Only give them the facts, Anna,' was all Nick had said to that.

They'd said goodbye shortly after, both yawning into the phone. When they'd disconnected Anna realised neither had mentioned her late period.

The pregnancy testing kit remained in its paper bag. Before she'd left for Adelaide, she'd stashed it in the bottom of her wardrobe underneath the shoebox the black sandals were stored in.

Nick had promised to call the following day, Christmas Eve. But Anna went flying and missed his call. Then she had the interview, which turned out to be a repeat of the statement she'd given to the police. Nick's advice to only give the facts had reverberated in her head through the entirety of the interview.

When Neville had slipped in a more personal question about her relationship with Nick, the chief medical officer had cut him off. He'd thanked her for her professionalism, and referred her to the employee assistance program.

Nick hadn't left a message when he'd phoned and she'd stared at her phone for several minutes and then decided against ringing him back.

Finding it hard enough accepting he'd left without telling her, imagining him in Sydney, catching up with his ex-wife, sharing Christmas Eve drinks with old friends, was more than she could bear.

After talking to Teresa, and with nothing better to do on her own, Anna settled at the table on the back verandah with a mug of tea and the fruit mince pies Beth had left for her. She booted up her laptop.

Rod Stilwell had emailed asking if she'd made a decision. He needed to know asap. If she hadn't made up her mind yet, she had until the following Tuesday morning, given Monday was a public holiday, to decide. After that he'd advertise and if she was interested, she'd have to apply along with everyone else.

Anna checked the date on his first email. Wow! That two weeks had flown by. Was she still interested? Would Broken Hill and the RFDS be as attractive without Nick?

The alternative on offer—moving fly-in-fly-out workers, tourists and public servants to the same destinations day in, day out—wasn't overwhelmingly attractive either. The upside of that option was she'd be there for Izzy every morning, night and weekend, and the flying was more straightforward with fewer inherent risks. The downside was boredom, pure and simple.

And what if she was pregnant?

But they *had* used protection every time. Anna Googled condoms: they were 98 per cent effective in preventing pregnancy. How unlucky could she be?

That morning she'd woken with a dull ache in her lower back—a precursor to menstruation, or too many hours behind the wheel of her car?

Tears sprang into her eyes and the mince pie caught in her throat. What if Nick didn't come back? What if this trip to Sydney on the pretext of a termite emergency was his way of opting out?

Anna wasn't a teenager anymore. She knew how difficult it was to bring up a child alone, and there were two more years until Isabelle finished high school. Who knew how long before her daughter would be financially independent. How on earth would Anna manage on her own with another child?

The tea cooled and flies crawled over the pastry crumbs while Anna second-guessed her decisions. From leaving Izzy in Adelaide, to throwing herself at Nick in a moment of vulnerability and need. And then to hoping they might have a future together.

What would she tell her daughter? Here, meet your baby brother/sister. Their father doesn't want them either.

Anna wanted to cry out with the pain and unfairness of it all. But self-recrimination wouldn't undo what was done. She straightened up in the deckchair and threw the crumbs to the ants. Enough time wallowing in self-pity. It was time now to start making decisions.

If her period hadn't arrived after the Christmas break, she'd do the pregnancy test. No matter the result, she'd make a doctor's appointment and trust that she had the courage to do what needed to be done.

Whatever happened, a clear plan of action was essential, and she'd set it in motion before she collected Izzy from the airport in five days' time. No more moping allowed.

She flicked Rod Stilwell an email saying she hadn't made up her mind, and if she decided she was interested she'd take her chances and apply along with everyone else.

Feeling marginally better, Anna rang Marlene and asked her if she wanted to go to Macca's for Christmas lunch.

45

In Sydney less than a week, Nick was already over the noise, the traffic and Lauren's whingeing. Nothing satisfied her. One minute he was working too slow, and the next she was telling him he was working too hard, that he needed to take some time off and come out for drinks with her and their old friends. Not happening. Nick didn't give a toss about the festive season.

Repairing the damage the termites had done was turning into a bigger job than he could have foreseen, and way more expensive. His credit card was maxed. The holiday break wasn't helping—supplies were cheaper at wholesale outlets but he had had to purchase them at local hardware shops because the suppliers were closed. In his desperation to get the job finished and get back to Broken Hill, he was paying top dollar for everything.

The pest controllers had been in and done their bit, and he felt nauseated all over again when he re-read the invoice they'd left. Seven days to pay.

'I don't have any spare money,' Lauren told him when he handed it to her. 'You'll have to pay for everything and we'll settle up when the house sells.'

'What if I don't have any spare cash either?'

She flipped her hair over her shoulder and shoved the invoice back at him. 'You'll have to get rid of that ute of yours, won't you? Or hit up one of your friends for a loan.'

For a split second Nick's vision went red. Lauren looked smug.

'You know what, Lauren?' he said evenly, and her cocky smirk faltered.

'What?'

'Sometimes you're a hard person to like.'

She gave him the finger, said, 'I'm going out,' grabbed her shoulder bag and flounced out the front door.

Nick stood in the doorway of their single-fronted cottage long after she'd gone. His 4WD ute was parked on the kerb.

What seemed like ages ago, Anna had also suggested he sell it to free up some money so he could help find his mother a place to live. He'd refused then too, adamantly, from memory. He couldn't believe he was giving it a second thought now.

He pulled out his phone, swiped through until he hit Anna's number. It rang and rang, finally going to message bank.

'Hi,' he said. 'I wanted to talk. I miss you.' He disconnected, stashed the phone. She'd call back. Or not.

They'd talked most days but he was beginning to sense a distance that wasn't all geographical. It was like she was stealthily withdrawing from the relationship. It didn't matter how many times he told her he'd be back.

And he'd heard nothing from the RFDS. He didn't know what was happening with the Carmichael business, if anything. Perhaps no news was good news.

When he'd called his mother, all she could talk about was how chuffed she was that Anna had taken her to Macca's for Christmas lunch. Grateful for her thoughtfulness, he was now bitterly sorry he hadn't been there with them. He'd laughed at the irony of it. There'd been no mention of his absent brother.

Every time he spoke to Anna he wanted to ask if she had her period. But he hadn't. It had taken him the trip from Broken Hill to Sydney to get his head around the thought of her being pregnant. He still had trouble grasping the notion that she might be carrying their child.

Parenthood was something he'd only thought about other people doing. His own experience had been one of having parents who'd been around, but somehow not there. There was no way he'd want to repeat that. But the longer he contemplated it—imagining a toddler with Anna's glossy curls and quiet self-sufficiency—the more it appealed, and the thought helped pass the mindless hours he was spending ripping out the white ant–infested woodwork and replacing it with new.

That night, Lauren cooked dinner. Even more surprising was that she'd bought him beer, and they sat outside and managed to eat without sniping at each other every minute. Bone-weary after a long day of physical work, Nick was thankful for the small mercies.

'Are you glad to be back in Sydney?' she said, when they'd finished eating, the evening air balmy but tainted with exhaust fumes and other city smells.

He stretched out his legs and took a slow sip of beer. 'As soon as I've finished the house, I'll be heading back to Broken Hill,' he said.

'More fool you.' She reached for the wine, refilling her glass. Nick glanced at the almost empty bottle.

'What happened to us, Nick?' she said wistfully.

'Something did. You must have locked me out for a reason.'

She chuckled, nudging his leg with her bare foot. 'We were always good in bed though, weren't we?'

Nick didn't answer. At one time he would have agreed. Before Anna. Now he knew differently, knew that *great* sex was more about giving than it was about taking, that when feelings ran deep it added another dimension, and it was then about making love, not only having sex.

Lauren rubbed her foot higher, insinuating her toes under the hem of his shorts. He leapt to his feet, beer spilling onto his hand. He flicked it off. 'No way, Lauren,' he said, taking another step away from her, holding his hand up like a shield. 'We are definitely not going there again. Ever.'

'What, not even for old times' sake?

'No,' he said. He might have been on his third beer but his thinking had never been clearer.

'I'm here to fix the house so we can sell it. If we'd spent the money on termite control when we bought the place, like I wanted to, instead of all the crap you wanted, I wouldn't be here now. When the job's done, I'm out of here.'

He braced himself for a mocking comeback, but all she said was, 'Whatever,' and drained her wine glass, looking disappointed when what was left in the bottle didn't quite fill it again.

'That's a whole bottle, Lauren. Reckon you've had about enough to drink, don't you?' The words came with a distinct feeling of déjà vu and Nick shuddered.

'Piss off, why don't you. How much I drink is none of your business anymore. I'll clean up, do the dishes,' she said, her words slurring slightly. 'You, get lost.'

'Whatever,' he said, imitating her.

Nick withdrew to the tiny second bedroom where he'd spread out his swag on the floor. Closing the door he wished, not for the first time, that there was a key for the lock. He jammed a kitchen chair under the handle. He'd been doing that since the first night he'd slept there. He wouldn't put anything past Lauren, and he was taking no risks with himself or his possessions.

Sitting on his swag, propping himself up against the wall, he struggled to fight off a defeating wave of loneliness. Here he was again, sleeping in his swag in a place he didn't want to be.

He rang Anna, almost overcome with relief when she answered on the third ring.

'What are you up to?' he said, his longing to be there with her a tangible thing.

'Not much. It's hot, for a change. Beth's last shift was today and she's out on the town with Carol and the girls. Probably come home drunk, but then again she may not because she has a lot to do before she leaves for Melbourne on the weekend. Albert hasn't a clue what's going on, the poor bugger. He's been sleeping on my bed.'

The husky sound of her voice soothed him like nothing else. He let her talk.

'Christmas break or not, the agent brought someone to look at the house today. I was on reserve and there was nothing happening so I offered to finish cleaning out the shed. Did you know that one of Beth's relatives lived in that shed once upon a time?'

'No, I didn't.'

'It's got a bathroom and everything. Anyway, I made myself scarce when the agent arrived by taking a load of junk to the dump for Beth. She'd left me her ute.'

'And what did you think? Not a bad ride, eh?'

'It did the job.'

'You're a hard woman to impress, Anna. Did you swim this morning?'

'Yep. The usual. Not many people there. It'll be packed again after new year with everyone trying to undo the damage they did over the break. What about you? How are the white ants?'

'The amount the pest controller charged, they'd all want to be dead. I've taken out the damaged doorframes, ordered new windows and whatnot, but building suppliers are closed for the break. It's a pain in the backside because it's slowing me down.'

'So where are you now?'

Nick's grip on the phone tightened; he'd known she'd ask eventually. 'I'm at the house,' he said. 'In the spare bedroom, lying on top of my swag.' He could feel the distance between them widen some more. That's why he hadn't told her where he was staying.

'Anna,' he said gently. 'Please understand. If I could afford a hotel, I would. I wish I didn't need to be here, but me doing the work is the cheapest and most practical solution.'

There was a pause before she said, 'Of course it's the most practical solution,' her tone bland, and then Lauren banged on his bedroom door shouting about the kettle boiling if he wanted a hot drink.

'I'd better let you go,' Anna said, and when Lauren kept pounding on his door, Nick reluctantly said goodbye. 'We'll talk again soon,' he added.

Her lacklustre reply, 'Sure,' landed like a physical blow. They disconnected. He hadn't asked her about her period, and she hadn't volunteered any information. It was as if not talking about it would make it go away. And she'd stopped asking him when he was coming home.

If there were prospective buyers looking at Beth's house, she would have started her search for another place to live. If things had gone the way he'd hoped back in Broken Hill, they'd be accommodation-hunting together.

With a hissed expletive, he chucked the phone onto the floor beside the swag. Lauren would have heard him talking on the phone and purposely interrupted him.

Pushing himself to his feet he grabbed the chair and shoved it away from the door. Then his hand stilled on the handle. What value was there in venting his anger and frustration on her? None at all, and it's what she'd expect—and why she would have baited him by banging on the door in the first place.

After carefully replacing the chair under the handle, he stretched out on the swag's thin foam mattress, reaching for the phone. It pinged with an incoming message. His mood lifted when he saw it was from Anna. Reading it wiped away his smile.

Meant to say, you can stop worrying. I have my period.

'Damn,' he muttered, staring at the screen, reading the message over.

Thumbs hovering over the keypad he racked his brain for a response. Nothing suitable sprang to mind.

'Bugger it,' he said, calling her instead.

She didn't answer. He didn't leave a message. A few minutes later he tried her number again. 'Call me, Anna,' was his terse message this time.

Hands cradling the back of his head he lay down. Scanning the peeling paint and pockmarked plaster of the bedroom walls, Nick tried to ignore the knot forming in his gut.

So focused on sorting out his own crappy problems, he'd handled everything else wrong: leaving without waiting for Anna to get back; dismissing her need to go to Adelaide before Christmas in the first place; not considering her feelings knowing she could be pregnant.

Nick knew that he'd be there for her no matter what. But when she'd needed to hear that from him, he hadn't taken the time to tell her, to reassure her.

Impotent was how he felt now, and he didn't like the feeling.

46

It was nearing sunset after another sizzler. Anna had flown a priority two earlier in the day and spent the afternoon pottering around the base. Now she was back at the airport, the domestic terminal this time, and relieved Izzy's flight from Sydney was on schedule.

'It's not a very big airport,' her daughter said, taking in the Broken Hill terminal while they waited for her luggage.

'No, not after Sydney and the Sunshine Coast, or Adelaide for that matter. But remember, the population of this place is less than 20,000.'

They watched while the luggage-laden trolley was towed across the tarmac.

Anna draped an arm over her daughter's shoulders. 'You look worn out. Did you have a good time with Grandma?'

'I had an awesome time. Tina took me everywhere ... Shopping ... Dreamworld ... Out to this really posh restaurant for Christmas.'

'Tina?'

'She told me to call her Tina,' Izzy said, shrugging off her mother's arm. 'She said she didn't feel old enough to be a grandmother. She said if you hadn't—'

Anna held up her hand. 'Stop right there, Isabelle,' she said, knowing fully what her mother would have said. 'And think about it, she was already a grandmother twice over before you came along.'

'Oh, yeah. Tom and Miranda …' Izzy's nose wrinkled. 'She still wants me to call her Tina, short for Valentina. How cool is her name?'

'It was her mother's name, and she was Italian,' Anna said and hoisted Izzy's suitcase off the baggage trolley. 'That's where our dark hair and brown eyes come from.'

'What about my father? What colour was his hair?'

They were crossing the road to the carpark and Izzy's question sent Anna's stomach into free fall. She stumbled. Izzy's hand shot out to steady her.

'I think I trod on a stone or something, nearly turned by ankle.'

'Sure, Mum,' Izzy said, reaching for the suitcase handle. 'Here, let me take that.' Heart pounding, Anna relinquished it. Izzy hadn't asked anything about her father for a long, long time.

When the suitcase was stowed and they were belted in, without looking at her daughter Anna said, 'Your father's hair was so dark it looked black, and his eyes were blue.' A guileless blue that had completely taken her in.

Izzy twirled a hank of hair around her finger. 'My hair's darker than yours so I could have got my hair colour from him,' she said. She flipped down the sun visor to peer at herself in the tiny mirror.

Anna took a deep swig from the water bottle stashed in the console. To date, fate had been kind; Izzy had only ever shown the mildest curiosity about her father, and had always seemed satisfied with Anna's explanation that it'd been his choice not to be involved in their lives.

'Yes, you could have,' she said, now that her mouth was moist enough to form words. 'His hair was straight like yours. But your eye colour is most likely from my side.'

'Do I look like him in any other way?'

Anna studied her daughter's profile. 'Maybe the shape of your nose is more like his.'

Izzy took one last look in the mirror, flipping the sun visor back into position then angling the air conditioning vent to blow on her face. 'Is it always this hot?' she said.

'This is my first full summer here, and so far it's always hot. And cold in winter.'

Letting the cool air blast onto her face, Izzy rested her head back and closed her eyes. Anna focused on the road, her shoulders tense. Traffic was sparse.

When they were halfway to Beth's place, Izzy said, 'Mum, I know my father chose not to have anything to do with me, but what was he like? Why didn't he want anything to do with us?'

The hurt and bewilderment in her daughter's voice tightened the band that had begun insinuating itself around Anna's chest.

Although she'd been expecting this conversation, Izzy's questions had caught her on the back foot.

'Is now a good time to talk about this? You've travelled all day. It's hot,' Anna stalled, fumbling for the water bottle.

'I know you don't like to talk about him, so I asked Tina what she knew about my dad.'

The water bottle thudded back into the console. 'And what did Tina say?'

'She got kind of funny and said she didn't know anything about him, but I wondered if she didn't want to tell me so she told a little white lie about not knowing.'

'No, Izzy,' she said. 'Your grandma told you the truth. I didn't ever tell my parents who your father was.'

The seatbelt clunked when Izzy jerked forward. 'Really?' she said, twisting towards her mother.

'Really,' Anna repeated, easing her foot off the accelerator. She indicated and turned left. 'Let's go to Macca's,' she said, struggling for equanimity as both her heart and her stomach clawed their way up her throat. 'You can have a drink, something to eat if you want, and I'll tell you what I know about your father.' The little I do know.

She took her eyes off the road for a moment to glance at her daughter. 'Unless of course you're too tired, and want to go straight to Beth's? But she'll be there, and so will her friend Carol.'

'Let's go to Macca's.'

The band around Anna's chest loosened ever so slightly. As much as she didn't want to have this conversation, it was inevitable, and she'd be relieved when it was over.

Rapt, Izzy sucked on her chocolate thickshake and listened while Anna told the story of a naive and lonely seventeen-year-old girl who fell in love with flying, and her first flight instructor. Ending up pregnant and abandoned.

'I thought he was the most incredible person I'd ever met. He was funny, smart, a fantastic teacher, and he seemed to *get* me.' Anna chewed her bottom lip. 'I had no idea he was married until his wife bailed me up. I believed, stupidly, that he'd eventually see the light and marry me. We'd fly off into the sunset, or some such garbage ...'

'Wicked,' was all Izzy could manage.

They each sat in their own silence, oblivious to the feeding frenzy happening around them. Then Izzy slurped the dregs of her thick-shake, the disgusting sound snapping Anna back to the present.

Collecting her scattered thoughts, she saw her daughter's eyes were glistening with tears. Anna reached for her hand, grasping it tightly.

'Izzy, please don't *ever* think I regretted having you. I know it's been hard not having a dad and I'll be eternally sorry about that, but I've tried to love you enough for two people.'

Izzy sniffed and Anna handed her one of their unused paper serviettes. She blew her nose. 'Do you know what happened to him?'

Anna shook her head.

'Do you have a photo? Anything?'

Anna reached for her wallet, searching through the pockets until she found what she was looking for. She handed it to Izzy.

Reverently, Izzy unfolded the newspaper clipping. A postage-stamp-sized headshot of a handsome, lean-faced and dark-haired man, faded with time. It was the only tangible memory Anna had to share.

'Anton Leclerc,' Izzy whispered, running her fingers over his picture. She even pronounced his name correctly.

Neither of them spoke for several minutes. Izzy read and re-read the few lines of copy that ran alongside the photo: a brief article from the Broken Hill newspaper welcoming the new aero-club flight instructor to town.

Anton Leclerc had known Anna for three months. Charming and attentive, he'd groomed her to the point she'd believed they were in love. It had seemed natural to offer him her most precious gift. He'd taken it without conscience or consequence.

A powerful love swelled inside Anna as she watched Isabelle study the picture of her father. Look what Anton had missed out on? He had stolen Anna's innocence, unwittingly giving her a priceless gift in return.

When she looked up from the clipping Izzy's first question was, 'Why didn't you tell Grandma and Grandpa who he was?'

'No good would have come of them knowing. I was a virgin but I knew about sex, Izzy. He didn't force me, but he was more than twice my age and he took advantage of my naivety. He was married and he wasn't going to leave his wife and two sons for me. I think Dad might have suspected who it was, but—'

'But what, Mum?'

With a wad of the remaining paper serviettes Anna started mopping up the condensation that had dripped from their thickshake cups onto the table. She began fussing with their rubbish until Izzy grabbed her wrist stopping her. 'Say what you were going to say, Mum.'

Anna rolled her lips together, searching for the right words.

'Izzy, you have a good relationship with your grandparents, and so you should. They love you, and I don't want to do or say anything that changes the way you feel about them.' She paused, squeezed her eyes shut for a moment. When she opened them again her daughter's dark gaze was locked on her face.

'They wanted you to have a termination, didn't they,' Izzy said matter-of-factly. 'And you wouldn't. Anton probably doesn't know I exist.'

Anna's mouth opened, and then closed. She swallowed hard. The strawberry thickshake had left a sour taste in her mouth.

'I'm not stupid, you know,' Izzy said.

Anna smiled, the smile segued into a laugh, an unexpected burst of mirth that had the family at the table nearby turning to see what was so funny. Izzy joined in.

'On the contrary, you continue to amaze me by how smart you are. I'm not sure how I would have reacted if I were in your situation.'

'I am nearly sixteen.'

'Oh yeah, you're ancient.'

'Seriously Mum, what would you think if I decided I wanted to find him?'

Anna had considered this and wasn't convinced it would ever be a good idea. However—

'When you're old enough I won't be able to stop you. But be prepared because he might not want you to find him. Remember, he doesn't know you exist. I'm sure he expected me to have a termination. And there's always a chance he's not even alive.'

'Yes, but what if he is? What if I contacted him and he wanted to meet me? And I have two half-brothers out there. I could have half-sisters. Who knows? Maybe they'd all want to meet me?'

Anna raised her eyebrows.

'Aren't you a tiny bit curious? Haven't you ever wondered what happened to him?'

'No, not really. At first I was too busy trying to survive to be anything but angry with him. Eventually I had to accept that it had happened, that there was no going back. I have no wish whatsoever to see or hear from him ever again. But like I said, he is your father and I wouldn't stop you if that's what you wanted.'

It was getting dark by now. Cars drove in and out of the carpark, a constant stream of customers queuing at the counters. Izzy yawned and rubbed her eyes.

'Let's go,' Anna said. 'You're about done, and I'm on a day shift tomorrow and we have a patient transfer first thing.'

'Yeah, I am tired. And with all this ...' Izzy handed back the newspaper clipping to her mother.

'No, I kept that for you. We could get it laminated. Take photocopies.'

'Maybe,' Izzy said and folded it up, slipping it in with her phone. 'Thanks for telling me, Mum.'

'It was always my plan,' Anna said, reaching for her bag on the chair alongside.

Then a familiar voice said, 'I thought that was your car out there. Now I don't have to sit on me own,' and Anna froze.

Marlene Harrison gaze swung from Anna to Izzy and back. 'You didn't tell me you had a younger sister,' she said.

'She's not my sister, she's my Mum.'

Marlene's eyes bulged, and Anna wondered if this day would ever end.

47

Marlene Harrison proved to be a godsend. After Beth left for Melbourne, Anna had little choice but to accept Marlene's offer to look out for Izzy during the days when Anna was working. They agreed that afternoons hanging around the pokies wasn't suitable for a teenager, with Marlene promising to keep Izzy away from the hotels.

Anna wasn't comfortable leaving her daughter without any adult supervision when she could be hundreds of kilometres away and difficult to contact.

Marlene was as delighted as Anna was relieved. Izzy had serious reservations.

'She's so old, Mum. Don't you have any younger friends? And she lives in her car and smells like an ashtray.'

'It's how Marlene choses to live. She did have a flat but she didn't pay her rent so they evicted her.'

'If she can't afford a place to live, surely her family could help? And what about an old folks home? She'd qualify.'

'It isn't always that simple, Izzy. Marlene's determined to live the way she wants, and she says she's happy. But that doesn't mean her family agrees and haven't tried to find suitable accommodation for her.'

Izzy looked sceptical. But most of her reservations were forgotten after the first afternoon spent in the older woman's company.

'Marlene's kind of cool,' she told Anna later. 'She showed me where she camps. There's no toilet or anything. I helped her do her washing at the laundrette and then we went to the shopping centre to hang out. She knows heaps of people. We had cake and cappuccino. Can you imagine Tina living in her car?'

No, Anna couldn't imagine her mother living anywhere that didn't have at least four bedrooms and two bathrooms, and ducted air conditioning.

Thoughts of bedrooms and bathrooms brought a familiar surge of anxiety. Because Anna couldn't decide what to do about her job and accommodation, she hadn't done anything. Never before had she found herself in the grip of such inertia.

And then in a flurry of activity, because she needed to do *something* proactive, she'd emailed a job application to Rod Stilwell. The position with the regional airline had been advertised and her application would be considered along with other applicants. If he offered her the job, she could always say no if things worked out here.

The couple who'd looked at Beth's house after Christmas had made an offer and Beth said they were waiting to have the bank approve their loan. All the more reason for Anna to get her act together and find somewhere to live. So why wasn't she?

Most days she was in touch with Nick. They talked or texted. He seemed upbeat, and while he talked about all the things they'd do together when he was back in Broken Hill, there was no mention of when that might be. The only upside of him being away was that Izzy could use his bedroom.

She'd asked if he'd heard from the RFDS. 'Yes,' he'd said. 'The Carmichaels were satisfied with the explanations given. I think it's more about them having time to come to grips with their son's death. Neville asked when I'd be back.'

Anna had held her breath. He was coming back! But then he said, 'I had to tell him the job here was bigger than I'd expected and I was happy to resign from my contract, given there's only a couple of weeks to go anyway.'

'So when are you coming back?'

'When I finish the job, and I'm sorry but I don't know how much longer that'll be.'

They'd disconnected and Anna's disappointment had left her feeling sad and lonely.

As the days stretched into weeks, missing Nick became a dull ache that never went away.

Anna vacillated between wishing he'd come back soon, and convincing herself he wasn't coming back at all and she should get on with her life. She finally admitted to herself that procrastinating in the hope that he would be back wasn't in her or Izzy's best interests. She had always prided herself on her independence.

One evening when they were cleaning up after their meal, Izzy said, 'Mum, how did you meet Marlene? She's old and you don't exactly hang around the places she does.'

Packing the dishwasher, Anna paused and looked at her daughter. 'You know the bed you're sleeping in? That belongs to Nick, Marlene's son. He's a flight nurse, or was.'

Izzy frowned. 'He lives here?'

'Yes, he did for a while. He's in Sydney at present.'

'Is he coming back?'

'He says he is.'

'Can I put his clothes somewhere else until he comes back for them? The wardrobe isn't very big and I can't fit all my things in.'

'Oh.'

'Come and have a look,' Izzy said, and Anna wiped her hands and followed her into the third bedroom.

Izzy opened the door and there, pushed up one end of the narrow wooden wardrobe was a sports jacket, and Nick's suit and his dress shirt and tie: the clothes he'd worn to Brett Carmichael's funeral. Izzy unhooked the coat hangers and handed them to Anna.

Anna stared at Nick's suit remembering the time he'd worn it. And what had happened afterwards. She draped the clothes over her arm, resisting the urge to press her face into the suit fabric. 'I'll put them somewhere else so you have more room.'

'Cool,' Izzy said, and began rearranging her clothes out along the rail.

'I guess when the house sells I'll have to ask him what he wants me to do with these, and the bed,' she said.

Izzy stopped what she was doing and zeroed in on her mother. 'What's the matter? You sound kind of weird.'

'Oh, you know, some things never turn out the way you hoped they would.'

Izzy closed the wardrobe door. 'No, I don't know. Tell me.'

Anna made a face, regretting not keeping her mouth shut and her thoughts to herself. For once she wished her daughter wasn't as perceptive, and persistent.

'Nick and I, we—'

'Was he your boyfriend?'

Boyfriend? There was nothing remotely boyish about Nick.

'Sort of. We became friends through work. He knew Beth from way back and when he needed a place to stay she rented him this room. I thought ...' Ridiculously, Anna could feel her cheeks pinking up.

'Yeah, I know what you mean, Mum. I thought Damien really liked me but he really wanted to hook up with Clara.' Izzy flipped back her hair. 'Men,' she said, sounding so grown-up. 'And you were right, he was too old for me. And he's a bit of a dick, even though he's nearly twenty.'

'But Clara—'

'Oh, she's had older boyfriends before. Her parents are cool with it. And she is already sixteen.'

Anna scratched her head. 'And you and Damien?'

'Just friends,' Izzy said matter-of-factly. Her phone pinged and she pulled it out of her pocket, grinning when she looked at the screen. 'It's Clara.' Obviously no ongoing grudges. When Anna didn't move Izzy guided her out the door. 'Mum, some privacy, please.'

'Privacy, right,' Anna said, but she was talking to bedroom door as it closed with a click.

Carrying Nick's clothes to her room, Anna wondered if he'd left them behind on purpose or he'd simply missed them, pushed in the corner like they had been.

Not giving herself time to speculate on the implications of either scenario, she stashed the clothes in her wardrobe and went back to packing the dishwasher and feeding the cat. Finishing that she went outside and watered the pot plants on the back verandah.

It was strange without Beth. She'd been gone a week now and would be starting work in a few days. Anna missed her, but not as much as she would have if Izzy hadn't been there.

For the first few days Albert had moped around the house, then shifted from Anna's to Izzy's bed at night and now appeared content. For some bizarre reason, even Hercules had calmed down.

Although the house was far from homely, with boxes stacked between the remaining furniture—the pieces Beth wanted sent when she found her own place to live—Anna and Izzy settled into a loose sort of routine.

Beth's friend Carol offered to be Izzy's first call when Anna was on nights, and Anna graciously accepted her offer. She hadn't wanted to impose on Marlene more than she had already.

Underneath it all, Anna was embarrassed to admit that after almost a year in Broken Hill she'd made so few friends, and two of them had left.

Izzy, on the other hand was having no such problems. When she hadn't been gallivanting around with Marlene, she was at the swimming pool or hanging about with Carol's daughter, Belinda, and her friend Olivia—who happened to be Kyle Peterson's daughter.

Two weeks into Izzy's stay Anna reluctantly acknowledged that her daughter had made more friends in that short time than she had in nearly a year. She made a belated New Year's resolution to make more friends.

48

Impatiently, Nick drummed his fingers on the steering wheel. It was six-thirty in the morning and the traffic was already heavy. A haze of smoke from bushfires burning in the mountains shadowed the horizon. He closed the car window and turned on the air conditioning.

The voice on the radio droned on about another scorcher of a day with little relief in sight.

Early morning peak-hour traffic was one of the reasons Nick preferred working night shift. It also meant he could work on the house in the relative cool of the mornings, sleeping away the sweltering late afternoons.

Until now he'd resisted nursing agency work, but no money coming in and lots going out had changed his mind. And he'd still been on their books.

The previous night the agency had called, asking—begging, really—for him to do a day shift at an aged care facility. Aged care work was definitely not in his comfort zone but the agency needed a pair of hands, expert or not; they were so short-staffed they would take anyone.

He took the shift. He was increasingly desperate to get out of Sydney and back to Broken Hill, back to Anna to pick up where they'd left off.

When they'd talked the night before, she'd sounded distracted.

'Is everything okay?' he'd asked.

She hadn't answered for a beat and he remembered clearly the flash of fear he'd felt. And rightly so because then she'd said, 'Nick, what is the point to this?'

'To what?' he'd said, pretending he didn't know what she meant.

'To us, talking on the phone about nothing because we don't have anything to talk about. You're living your life there, I'm living my life here. I'm beginning to feel that what we had together never happened—'

'Stop,' he'd said. 'It happened. You'll have to trust me when I say I'm coming back, Anna. Where I want to be is there with you, but I need to finish at the house first.'

The seconds had ticked by in silence. 'I guess I'm preparing myself in the event that you don't come back.'

'I will be back, so let's not have this conversation again, all right? Now tell me what you're doing tomorrow, and have you seen Mum?'

They'd chatted for another ten minutes and Nick had reluctantly hung up when she'd said she had to go. He could hear a female voice he didn't recognise in the background.

Now, pondering the conversation while he waited for the lights to change, Nick realised he'd been in Sydney for several weeks. He couldn't believe he'd once enjoyed living there.

Peering through the windscreen at the smoke smudging Sydney's skyline, he wished for the clear and endless blue skies of the outback.

He hadn't planned on being away so long, but each day brought another set of challenges and another set of expenses. Nick had learned fast that when you were fixing up an old house, everything cost double what you'd budgeted.

Timeframes ballooned out because a job that on first inspection looked simple and straightforward generally wasn't.

For example, when they'd arrived, two of the new window frames had been the wrong size. Replacements were yet to be delivered. Then he'd put his foot through the floorboards in the front room. They were supposed to be undamaged. He was lucky he hadn't broken his ankle. Replacing the boards and meticulously examining the remaining wooden floors for termite damage had added more days to completion.

The traffic lights changed again and Nick accelerated through the intersection. His stomach rumbled. He hadn't made time for breakfast. He yawned, regretting lying in bed the extra few minutes he could have used to fill his travel mug with coffee.

His GPS told him to turn left in 50 metres and he'd have reached his destination.

Nine hours later Nick was back in the traffic, afternoon peak hour this time and he ached with fatigue. Though he wouldn't admit it voluntarily, today he'd worked physically harder than he had for a long time. A day humping window frames into position and fixing floorboards wasn't as exhausting.

The care staff were effusive in their gratitude for his help with the heavy lifting, and there'd been plenty of it. From the minute he'd introduced himself, taken handover from the night nurses, it'd been a production line of personal care, medication rounds and mealtimes. No sooner had they finished breakfast and cleaned up, than the residents were being propped up and prepped for morning tea, then lunch, with excursions to the bathroom in between.

It was while he'd been helping herd the more able residents into a large common room to attend diversional activities that he'd had a weird sort of epiphany.

Was it any wonder his mother, who still had all her marbles and was relatively able-bodied, was so against living in a residential aged care facility? She'd be like a square peg in a round hole. It hadn't been fair of him to expect her to do so, and for her to be grateful for the opportunity to boot.

Now, stuck in bumper-to-bumper traffic, Nick accepted that having Marlene in a nursing home might make him feel better, but it would be soul-destroying for her. That didn't mean living in her car was a suitable alternative.

When Nick finally manoeuvred into the squeezy parking space outside their house, he noticed the large envelope crammed into the rusty letterbox—his redirected mail had finally caught up with him.

Standing on the verandah he tore open the envelope, shuffling through the stack of letters inside. Opening his credit card statement first, he quickly wished he hadn't.

He swore, flicking through the remaining mail. Predominantly bills. The registration for the ute was due along with the comprehensive insurance. He flinched at the amounts. He'd have to put his name down for more shifts; but then the house repairs would stagnate. He was going backwards here. Any wonder Anna was having doubts about him ever returning.

The house was cool and quiet inside, with no sign of Lauren except for the dirty dishes in the sink. He dropped the pile of mail onto the breakfast bar in the kitchen. Grabbing a beer out of the fridge, he slipped it into a stubby holder and sipped slowly as he wandered through each room.

A film of sawdust and powdered plaster covered the furniture not protected by drop sheets. Power point fittings dangled from raw skirting boards. The new woodwork had been primed and was ready for its coats of paint. The tins of paint were stacked in the laundry.

Standing in the centre of the sitting room he turned through 360 degrees.

The beer was cold but he barely tasted it as he remembered how he'd talked with Lauren about what he'd do with this place ... Extend out the back ... Build a bigger shed ... A spa ... Perhaps even build up, eventually.

He sighed. The reality was he'd been the only one who'd ever talked and in hindsight, apathy had been at work undermining his relationship with Lauren long before the termites had started on the woodwork.

Carrying his beer across to the nearest drop sheet-covered armchair, Nick lowered himself down without a thought to how dirty and dusty it was.

Nick knew it was time to take stock of his situation. He wanted to put the Sydney chapter of his life behind him forever, and after the previous night's conversation with Anna, being there was becoming more untenable by the day. And he couldn't blame anyone but himself for the situation he was in.

It galled him to admit it, but taking leave, packing up and driving to Sydney in those days before Christmas had been impetuous. But he hadn't understood why Anna had been hellbent on going to Adelaide, and the more he'd mulled over Rachel Carmichael's phone call, and Neville Abrahams' earlier insinuations, the more ticked off he'd become.

And it rankled him that he'd resigned before his contract was completed, no matter that it'd already been a fait accompli. His departure was an opportunity for the organisation. If they'd needed someone to blame to make the Carmichaels feel better, he'd made himself the most obvious target.

But he'd had a *cunning* plan. Confident in his own skills as a handyman, and for the cost of the materials only, he'd repair the termite damage and the house would be ready for auction. And he'd be back in Broken Hill before Anna had time to really miss him.

Loud and colourful curses bounced around the sitting room. So much for cunning plans. Lauren had promised to help but hadn't. He was knee-deep in debt. The noise, the traffic, the takeaway food, the sleeping on the floor and living out of a duffel bag—Nick was over it all. The only people that mattered to him were on the other side of the state.

The bottom line was, he did not want to be there any longer. Whatever it took, he'd do it to get out of the place.

Without giving himself time to renege on the decision, Nick dragged out his phone to make the call he should have made weeks ago, mentally crossing his fingers.

49

January would soon be a memory. Driving home after a long, hot, temper-fraying day on a clinic run, Anna almost didn't pull over when her phone rang. But then, thinking of Izzy and slowing, she eased onto the shoulder to take the call. It was Beth.

'The house is sold. Settlement's February the tenth,' Beth said, after she'd assured Anna nothing was amiss. 'And so you don't have to deal with all my furniture and belongings, I've organised for them to go into storage down here. I'm looking for a place of my own.'

'Sold ... Right ... February ten ... Furniture going into storage,' Anna said, rapidly calculating that this gave her less than four weeks with a roof over her head.

Crap!

And with Beth's furniture gone they'd be sitting on the floor and eating off their laps. No television, no washing machine, no dining table, no anything.

Anna owned her bed, a chest of drawers and a canvas deck chair. Home, sweet home.

She pushed trembling fingers through sweaty hair, trying to ignore her pounding pulse and the tightening band of tension.

'You might have to repeat that,' she said, tuning in again when Beth kept talking.

'I said, the furniture removal is next Wednesday. If you can't be there to let them in, tell Carol. She said she can come around.'

'I'll check my roster,' Anna said, staring through the windscreen but not seeing anything. Next Wednesday was six days away.

'You sound a bit hot and bothered.'

'I'm parked on the side of the road and it's forty freaking degrees in the shade, so yeah, you could say that.'

'Oh shit, sorry, and I'm doubly sorry for uprooting you like this, with Izzy there and all.'

'Don't worry about me, and it's not as if you haven't given me any notice,' Anna said, and meant it, but right then she was far from feeling the graciousness the words implied.

'Anyway, for the way I've mucked you about I've refunded your rent for the last couple of weeks and through until settlement. Is Nick back?'

'No, and I'm not sure he's coming back at all. He said yesterday he's doing a few agency nursing shifts.'

'He's probably broke. But he'll be back.'

'Yeah, well, I've been offered a job in Adelaide. Teresa said we can live there. It'd be the answer to my housing and my parenting dilemmas.'

'What? But you love the flying you do there. And I thought you were beginning to enjoy living in Broken Hill. For God's sake, please don't make any rash decisions.'

Sweat trickled into Anna's eyes. 'Thanks for the rent relief and don't worry, Beth, I won't make any rash decisions. Anyway, I need to get moving, the car's starting to overheat.'

They said their goodbyes and Beth promised to keep in close touch.

Izzy was sprawled on the sofa, the overhead fan on high when Anna let herself in.

'Hi, Mum,' she said without glancing up from her phone. 'I've eaten. Macaroni cheese. There's a bowl for you. Zap it for a minute. Aunt Tee wants you to ring her, asap.'

'Okay, thanks. What did you do today?'

Anna hadn't spoken to her sister for ten days. The last time they spoke, Teresa had been full of her fabulous Christmas break.

'Stuff,' Izzy said, and Anna couldn't summon the energy to probe deeper.

'Did you feed the cat?'

'Yep. We're nearly out of cat food.'

'Did you put it on the list?'

'Yep.'

Anna untucked her shirt and started unbuttoning. 'I need a shower. I'll call Teresa later.'

Izzy grunted. Anna shook her head and made for the bathroom. She stripped off and stood under the shower, turning her face into the cool water. It felt heavenly. She shampooed her hair, all the time wondering how her life had been turned upside down in such a short space of time.

Nick Harrison, that's how.

Soaping up, Anna's hand stilled on her flat abdomen. Imagine how much more upside down everything would have been if she'd been pregnant. Again. And with the father absent again.

Smoothing a soapy hand across her skin, she thanked fate and refused to let her thoughts wander to that fantasy place where circumstances were different ... Where she was in a loving and committed relationship and looking forward to the birth of another child.

Anna stepped out of the shower, willing her whimsy back where it belonged—the recesses of her mind. She reached for a towel.

Refreshed of body, if not spirit, Anna zapped the macaroni and cheese and filled a glass with cold water. Beth had left oddments of crockery and utensils for them to use but they were drinking out of old jam jars.

Shoving Izzy's legs off the sofa, Anna dropped down beside her and said, 'Beth rang. Put down your phone and I'll tell you what she had to say.'

Between mouthfuls Anna relayed the conversation to Izzy, leaving out the bit about Nick.

Izzy didn't say anything. Not one word. She picked up her phone again, started texting. Anna nudged her with her elbow. 'Well, aren't you going to say something?'

Izzy threw down the phone. 'What is there to say? You'll find someone else's spare room to camp in, and I'll go back to school.' Scowling, she went back to her phone.

'Isabelle?'

Appetite suddenly deserting her, Anna put the bowl of food on the coffee table, steadily watching her daughter.

'Talk to me, Izzy.'

Izzy's scowl deepened. She jiggled her right knee up and down and Anna resisted the urge to reach out and stop her fidgeting.

When Izzy finally looked up and met her mother's gaze, tears ran down her cheeks.

'Izzy girl, please don't cry,' she said, opening her arms.

'I like it here, Mum. Belinda and Olivia are amazing,' Izzy snuffled against Anna's shoulder. 'And since Beth left it's like we have our own home. At last.' She pushed away, sniffing. 'Why can't I stay here with you? Why do I have to go back to that school?'

'I've applied for my old job back and if I get it I'll be in Adelaide again. Aunt Tee said we could live there. You won't have to board anymore.'

'Yeah, but you don't want your old job back and we'd still be living in someone else's house, not our own. You remember our old flat off Prospect Road?'

Anna nodded. It had been a dump, the rent outrageous. Not forgetting the two flights of stairs and parking on the street.

'It was great. We had all our own stuff, I could go to the fridge when I wanted to, have friends over anytime ...'

The macaroni cheese she'd bolted down sat like a stodgy lump in Anna's stomach. Bloody hell, as a parent she really had dropped the ball.

'Mum, it's not like I'm not grateful. I am. Living with Aunt Tee is okay, but she's kind of bossy and likes everything done her way.'

No surprises there.

'Why can't we stay *here*?'

'Because this house is sold. The people who've bought move in next month.'

'I don't mean this house, I mean here, in Broken Hill. You have an awesome job. We could find a place to rent, get our stuff out of storage. I could go to the same school as Belinda and Olivia. Think of all the money you'd save on private school fees.'

'But what about Clara? Wouldn't you miss her, and all your other friends?'

Izzy sighed, pulling at the fraying threads on the hem of her cutoff shorts. 'Maybe, but Belinda and Olivia are excellent. And anyway, Clara hasn't got much time for me now she's got Damien,' she said, turning up her nose.

'I don't know, Iz—'

'Will you at least think about it, Mum? You're always telling me the best solution is sometimes the simplest one, and how much more simple could it be?'

Anna reached for the unfinished food. Was it that straightforward? Had she been making things more complicated than they were? With Nick gone, who was there to care if she had a teenage daughter? And after all, whose business was it but her own?

The cat flap clunked and Albert announced himself with his trademark yowl. Izzy pushed herself to her feet. 'Come on mate,' she said to Albert, 'I'll go get your food. And Mum, finish your dinner, and don't forget to ring Aunt Tee.'

Anna perched on the edge of the sofa, her thoughts racing.

Later that night, as Anna was tossing and turning in her sweltering room and hopelessly trying not to wonder what Nick was doing, she decided that perhaps the answers were as simple as her daughter had made them sound.

Nick would fade into memory; it'd take time for that to happen, but it would happen. Marlene was still around of course, but Anna liked her regardless of her connection to Nick. And Anna realised that the bad memories she carried about Broken Hill needed to be relegated to the past, where they belonged.

When the following morning Anna woke to a message from Beth saying, *Buyers pulled out at VERY last minute!!! House back on market. Arrrgh! Talk later,* it wasn't surprising then that Anna began thinking about how she could work the turn of events to her advantage.

50

For a heartbeat Nick was eighteen again. Then he closed his eyes, opened them and no, he wasn't eighteen and the girl propping open the screen door wasn't a teenage Anna. What he was was overtired.

The alarm had woken him at five and he'd been on the road by five-thirty. He'd driven from Dubbo that day, the best part of 800 kilometres, stopping only for fuel for the car and for himself.

The girl holding open the screen door was peering at him, a quizzical expression on her face.

'I'm looking for Anna Kelly ... I see her car's in the driveway.' He tipped his head in the general direction, towards where his 'new' old white ute was parked behind Anna's red Commodore.

The girl's eyes narrowed and Nick realised she was younger than he'd first thought. Although she was a lot like Anna, her hair was nearly black and minus Anna's curls. 'Mum isn't here. She flew to Adelaide this morning. For interviews,' the teenager said.

Nick gripped the edge of the open door, his mind struggling to make sense of what the girl had just said. The sound of the road still thrummed in his ears. He shouldn't have driven so far in one day.

'You're Nick, aren't you,' she said, and it was almost an accusation.

'I am. Who's asking?' Maybe he'd misheard the 'mum' bit.

'I'm Izzy … Isabelle Kelly, and Anna Kelly is my mother. Like I said, she isn't here right now.'

He nodded slowly. He hadn't misheard, and with that realisation so many things began falling into place. 'So you're the family crisis, eh?'

'Excuse me,' she said, indignant, sounding like her mother did on occasion.

'What I mean is, you're the reason Anna took off for Adelaide in such a rush way back in November—'

'Appendicectomy,' Izzy said, pointing to her abdomen. 'The surgeon said I would have been a lot sicker if my appendix had burst.'

'—And why she had to go to Adelaide again before Christmas.'

'We had to have our Christmas a couple of days early because Mum had to come back here to work. We went out to lunch.'

'Izzy, love? Who's at the door?'

'Mum?' Nick said, perplexed now, and leaning sideways to see beyond Izzy. What was his mother doing here? This was getting weirder by the minute. He'd only been gone five weeks and it felt like he'd come back and unwittingly stepped into a parallel universe.

'I told Anna you'd be back,' Marlene said, pushing the screen door open as wide as it would go. 'Girl didn't believe me.' She brushed past Izzy and stepped out onto the verandah. 'And I told her she should have filled you in about Izzy weeks ago. But I reckon she'd worked that one out for herself.

'What happened to your flash 4WD?' she said, walking to the edge of the cement, standing with her hands on her hips and scrutinising the weary-looking utility.

Nick struggled to keep his temper in check. He couldn't stop staring at Izzy. Where was her father? Did he live in Adelaide? Had Anna been married to him?

'This car looks like a heap. And it's a *Ford*.'

'I sold the dual cab. I couldn't afford it anymore. And this *heap* got me here in one piece,' he snapped, dragging his gaze from Izzy to his mother. Her expression was filled with compassion.

'Do you want to come in? Have a cool drink?' Izzy said, standing back in invitation. 'Mum's plane gets in after six, in another hour or so.'

And didn't she have some questions to answer when that time came! Nick sucked in a tight breath, letting it out through his nose. None of this was the girl's fault, he mustn't forget that.

'A cool drink would be nice, thanks,' Nick said.

But before he followed Izzy inside he scanned the street, and frowned. 'Speaking of heaps, where's your car, Mum?'

'Bloody engine seized. That robbing bastard of a mechanic says he can put in a new one but not until he sees the cash. It can sit in his backyard until then.'

'You are supposed to check your vehicle's fluids regularly, and get it serviced from time to time.'

'I know that,' Marlene shot back.

Nick's gaze swung from his mother to Anna's car, and back to his mother. 'Please don't tell me you're driving Anna's car.'

Marlene squared her shoulders, drawing herself up to her full 157 centimetres. 'And what's wrong with me driving Anna's car? She says it's the least she can do seeing I'm looking out for Izzy.'

Nick was beginning to believe he *had* stepped into an alternate reality.

He wouldn't let his mother drive his car, but if Anna was comfortable with Marlene driving hers, who was he to contradict.

When he walked into the sitting room his discombobulation was complete. 'Where's the furniture?'

'Furniture removals,' Izzy said. 'Beth thought the house had sold so she put it all in storage in Melbourne for when she finds her own place.'

He stared at Isabelle. 'You know Beth?'

'Of course I do. She's cool.'

'And how long have you known my mother?'

'I met Marlene at Macca's the night I arrived. Is cold water okay? Mum won't let me have Coke or anything like that. But there's beer.'

'Water's good, thanks, and how come everyone but me knows Anna has a teenage daughter, and I was the one—' *Sleeping with her,* he'd almost said.

Marlene snickered. Izzy deadpanned. 'Mum said you were sort of her boyfriend, but it hadn't worked out the way she'd hoped it would.'

'Really?' Nick said, sounding hopeful, even to his own ears.

'By the way,' Izzy threw over her narrow shoulder as she went to the kitchen, 'you left your clothes in my wardrobe. Mum put them in hers so I'd have more room.'

'*Your* wardrobe,' Nick muttered. 'Last time I looked it was *my* wardrobe.'

Marlene was watching from the passage doorway. He threw his hands up. 'At least she didn't throw them out,' he said, 'I can be grateful for that.'

'Nick, the poor girl didn't know what to think when you upped and left like you did.'

'Mum, I had my reasons. Anna and I have spoken nearly every day. I explained, and I thought she understood. And by the way, why didn't you tell me?'

Marlene shifted her feet. 'Not my story to tell. Your girl's fiercely independent, probably has trust issues. You might have to go gently with her.'

Gently! He thought he had been. Nick glared at his mother. 'She's the one who failed to mention she had a kid,' he hissed.

Izzy cleared her throat. Nick swung around to where she stood, holding out a large glass of water. 'Here's your drink,' she said. Judging by her tone, she'd overheard.

'Thanks, Isabelle,' he said, forcing a levity into his voice that he certainly didn't feel. Her cool expression didn't change. Nick could have kicked himself.

'You wouldn't mind making me a cup of tea, would you love?'

'Sure thing, Marlene,' Izzy said, and retreated to the kitchen without a backwards glance.

Nick paced around the empty room, pausing at the window. 'If your car's off the road, where are you staying?' he said.

'In Beth's old room. I bought a foam mattress to put my sleeping bag on. It's good that I'm here when Anna works at night.'

Nick focused on the view outside the sitting room window: the dying lawn, the rusting wire fence, the tenacious weeds growing through the gravel path. His mother was staying with his lover and looking out for her teenage daughter. How long had he been away?

'They needed me, Nick,' Marlene said, her voice quavering with uncertainty.

Turning to her, he said, 'Lucky you were here then, ready to help out.' Her expression brightened. 'But I thought the house had sold? Anna said settlement was early February. Did she not tell me the truth about that either?'

'No! Folks changed their minds at the very last minute. The house is back on the market.'

'Oh.' His travel-fatigued brain was struggling to take everything in. 'Why didn't she tell me she had a teenage daughter? And why is she going for a job interview in Adelaide? I told her I'd be back.'

Her brow furrowing, Marlene studied her son. 'Why don't you go and have a shower, change your clothes? We'll make you something to eat, and then you pick her up from the airport. I'm sure Izzy won't mind.'

He stood for a moment, motionless, considering what he needed to do, as opposed to what he wanted to do.

'Maybe it'd be better if I go someplace else for now, talked to her in a day or two—'

'That's bullshit, and you know it. The sooner it's all out in the open, the sooner you can get on with being together.'

'I dunno what I'll say to her.'

'Don't say anything, just listen.'

'But I'm so angry with her.'

'Guess you're entitled to be mad, and hurt. But Izzy is a great kid, and Anna's a terrific mum. Single parent or not, she's made a better job of it than I ever did. Let her explain first.'

'I'll try,' he said, surprising them both by leaning down to kiss Marlene on the cheek.

It wasn't until later that he realised she hadn't smelled like an ashtray.

Nick would have recognised Anna's purposeful stride anywhere. She walked towards the terminal, overtaking other passengers meandering along. The short, black shift she was wearing was the same dress she'd worn to the funeral. No high heels today.

He knew the moment she saw him: her face lit up and she mouthed his name, but when his expression remained stony, her delight disappeared and apprehension took its place.

He stayed where he was, letting her come to him. A large shoulder bag was her only luggage.

'Nick,' she said. 'This is unexpected.'

'Surprises seem to be the order of the day.' She looked so good. He fisted his hands inside his pockets to stop himself from reaching for her, reminding himself he was angry. She'd lied by omission. What else hadn't she told him?

'You've been to the house,' she said. He didn't answer because it wasn't a question.

'At least let me explain—'

'We'll talk in the car,' he said, cutting her off.

She fell into step beside him. Her expression set. Silently they walked to the carpark. When he stopped alongside his seen-better-days ute, her eyes nearly popped out of her head.

'I downsized,' he said tonelessly, ignoring her unspoken question.

'Oh,' she said, and he knew she'd appreciate the implications. So what if it made her feel worse; for a second he'd felt better.

They climbed in. Anna didn't ask where they were going and Nick didn't have a plan until he turned towards Federation Way and up the hill to the Miners' Memorial.

The parking area was deserted, sunset over an hour away. He parked, opening the windows before turning off the ignition.

Anna pushed open the passenger-side door and a marginally cooler breeze swirled around them. She angled her body towards the open door, folding her arms.

'I thought the girl in the photo on the chest of drawers was your niece. Not for one moment did I think she could be your daughter.'

'You should have asked me.'

'No, Anna, *you* should have *told* me you had a teenage daughter.'

Anna closed her eyes, swallowing hard. 'I'm sorry, Nick. I know I should have told you.'

'Then why didn't you?' he said through gritted teeth.

'Would you have told me about your *wife* if Serena Morris hadn't dropped that little bombshell?'

'Moot point, Anna. You knew all about Lauren before things between us went that next step.'

Her tongue darted out to moisten her lips before she said, 'I didn't think you'd want anything to do with me if you knew I was a single parent.'

He shook his head slowly. 'This isn't just about you being a single parent. I've made no secret of how I feel about you Anna, but you didn't trust me enough to tell me, to let me decide for myself how I felt about it.'

In her lap, Anna's hands shook. Nick gripped the steering so hard his fingernails bit into the palms of his hands. The silence between them hummed.

51

Anna bit down on her bottom lip to stop it from trembling. Knowing Nick was right only made her feel worse. Hauling her shoulder bag onto her lap she rummaged around for her water bottle.

'Do you want some?' she said when she found the bottle, holding it out to him.

He shook his head.

She unscrewed the lid, took a long swallow. 'Why didn't you tell me you'd be back today?'

'I wanted to surprise you,' he said, with a wry twist of his lips.

'You did. When I walked into the terminal and saw you waiting for me …' She sighed. She'd wanted to throw herself into his arms, confess everything and ask him never to leave her ever again. If that's what falling in love felt like, well, she was falling in love with him. 'But you looked angry and I knew straightaway you'd been to the house and met Izzy.'

'I can't understand why you didn't tell me.' He looked genuinely perplexed. 'I wouldn't have judged you.'

'No, I don't think you would have. But at first it was none of your business. We were work colleagues, nothing else. Beth didn't know I had a daughter until Izzy had her appendix out. Then I had no choice but to tell her.'

'But why keep it a secret in the first place? It's nothing to be ashamed of.'

'I was waiting for the right moment, I suppose,' Anna said. 'That's what I kept telling myself. Then there were some right moments and I didn't tell you. '

'And?' he prompted when she fell silent, staring off into space.

'And after hearing you say that parenthood wasn't for you, I got the impression you didn't like kids much, and you definitely didn't want any of your own. When I told you my period was late, I thought you were going to pass out.'

'I was in shock.'

'Do you think I wasn't? And then we didn't even get to talk about it because you weren't here when I got back from Adelaide.'

'We talked on the phone,' he said.

'And what if I had been pregnant, Nick?'

She turned towards him. He shrugged but his attention remained fixed on the view outside.

'You have to understand, I was seventeen when I got pregnant with Izzy. You asked me where I went after we finished school? My parents withdrew their support because I wouldn't have a termination. I was on my own. I had a car, and I had six hundred and fifty-three dollars in the bank. I drove to Adelaide and I lived in that car while I tried to find a job.'

She had his attention now.

'I hardly slept because I was so scared. And I had the worst morning sickness. When I finally admitted that I couldn't do it on my own, I fronted up to my sister's. Teresa's a lot older and she was amazing—her husband, not so much.'

The inside of the car was uncomfortable. Nick opened his door, letting the air flow through. Under any other circumstances she would have asked him if they could go some place cooler. But she needed to get this out, and if she stopped now, she might not want to start again.

'The next years were difficult,' she said. 'After Izzy was born I eventually leased a flat and I worked two, three jobs, and took flying lessons whenever I could afford it. And I studied hard.'

'Now I get why you're so familiar with op shops,' Nick said, with the closest thing to a smile she'd seen since he'd collected her from the airport.

'Yes,' she said. 'Op shops and social security: a single parent's lifelines.'

'What about Isabelle's father? What did he contribute?'

'The sperm, Nick, that's all he's ever contributed.'

'Is he the reason you didn't want anyone to know about your past connection to Broken Hill?'

'Sort of,' she said. 'He was married. He led me to believe he was separated. He wasn't. And he had no intention of leaving his wife. How did I find out? She came by the high school one afternoon and told me. They already had two children.'

Nick closed his eyes, letting his head flop back against the headrest. 'No wonder me being separated bothered you.'

'Then when my period was late and you disappeared, I thought I'd gone and done it all over again. And you staying with your ex-wife kind of did my head in.'

He opened his eyes and turned to her. 'I should have waited until you came back. But I was so pissed off by that whole Carmichael thing ...'

'You should have been up-front with me about all that right from the start. I would have vouched for you. I was there.'

'I know that, but I was trying to protect you and your privacy.'

'I'm sorry, Nick. In hindsight we both made some poor decisions.'

'Didn't we just. So why didn't you tell me about the job interview?'

Anna looked away. 'There was nothing to tell. Initially, I didn't seriously consider the offer. But then Beth left, and the house went on the market, and my sister met someone who lives in Sydney of all places, and Izzy needed somewhere to go for the holidays—you'd gone—and it felt like everything in my life was unravelling.'

'Why didn't you talk to me?'

'Nick, we'd been work colleagues for a couple of months, had only been in a relationship for a matter of weeks before you left. We barely knew each other.'

'You knew how I felt about you and I said I'd be back.'

'You got a job.'

'I needed the money.'

'Sure, but the longer you were away, the more the time we spent together seemed like a dream. I'm sorry, but I had to get on with my life. Izzy was and is my first priority.'

'You should have trusted me, Anna.' Nick closed the driver's side door and started the ute.

Anna stared at him. Hadn't he heard anything she'd said? Worn out and too despondent to argue she followed suit with her door. She felt sweaty and sick.

When they arrived back at Beth's, Nick slipped the car into park but didn't turn off the engine.

'You're not coming in?'

'Nah, probably a bit crowded, with Mum—and Isabelle. I'll camp down at Danny's, or some place,' he said without glancing in her direction.

'Nick—'

'Anna, we're both tired. It's been a lot to take in and process, and I'm not thinking very clearly right now.'

'But we'll see each other soon?'

'We will.'

'All right. I'm glad you're here.'

His lips lifted in a not-quite-there smile. When he drove away, Anna wanted to cry.

52

'Where's Nick?'

Leaning heavily on the scuffed plastic outdoor setting they were using as dining room furniture, Marlene pushed herself to her feet. She tottered around to where Anna stood, face creased with concern. Reaching for Anna's hand she gripped it firmly.

'He said he'd camp at Danny's.'

Marlene clicked her tongue. 'That boy needs a damn good shake. Are you all right, love?'

'No, not really, but I will be. I should have told him about Izzy, Marlene. When we started—' She coughed, cleared her throat. 'When our relationship began.'

The back screen door snapped shut and Izzy strolled in, phone in one hand and Albert close on her heels.

'Mum, you're back. How'd it all go?'

'About how we thought, when we talked about buying this house and staying in Broken Hill,' Anna said. The older woman squeezed her hand before letting go.

'Tea?' Marlene said. Anna nodded.

'Firstly, I talked to Rod Stilwell, apologised for wasting his time and withdrew my application.'

'Awesome,' Izzy said, smiling widely. 'What about the other?'

'The school? The administrator was—'

'A stuck-up old cow?'

'Don't be rude, but she wasn't the friendliest person I've ever met, and there's no way they'll make an exception and waive the fees.'

'So that means I have to go for the first term?' Izzy screwed up her face.

'We discussed this, remember? It's what we expected. I've already paid the fees and board for first term.'

'Oh, bollocks,' Izzy said, her palm hitting the counter top with a resounding crack.

'Bollocks?' Anna repeated, voice rising, her gaze swinging to Marlene.

'Sorry, love,' Marlene said, glowering at a red-faced Izzy.

'Sorry, Mum,' she mumbled, scooping up Albert and sloping off towards her bedroom.

'Don't you want to hear what they said at the bank?'

Izzy paused, hitching her shoulder in a couldn't-care-less shrug. Anna took a fortifying breath. Her rubber band was running out of stretch.

'I'm dying to hear,' Marlene said, filling a mug with boiling water.

'They said they would lend me the money, but first I need to save another ten thousand towards the deposit.'

'Crikey,' Marlene said, frantically jiggling the tea bag. 'Will you be able to do that?'

'Yes, I think so. It's much less than I would have had to save for the next installment of school fees.'

'Shit,' Marlene muttered. 'Bloody expensive school.'

'Maybe we should start a swear jar,' Anna said. 'We'd have the house deposit in no time.'

Izzy smirked; Marlene looked sheepish. 'I'll email Beth tonight. Ask about renting for six months while I save the balance for the deposit. She could take the house off the market and then sell it to me privately, and we'd both save money.'

Izzy hovered in the passage doorway, Albert squirming in her arms before springing to freedom. 'How was Aunt Tee?'

'She was good. She picked me up and ferried me to all the appointments, and took me to this flash place for lunch. She sends her love and said you're welcome to stay on weekends, just like before.'

'Until she sells *her* house.'

'It's not even on the market. The school term is eleven weeks, Izzy. I doubt she'll be doing anything before that.'

'Do you reckon we'll ever get to meet Vanessa?'

'I'm sure we will meet her sometime.'

Izzy frowned. 'Where's Nick?' she said, like his absence had only just registered.

Anna's gaze flicked to Marlene's. 'He's staying with a mate … '

Izzy gave derisive snort. 'Men!' she said, and disappeared to her room.

'Indeed,' Anna acknowledged, summoning the energy to carry her cooling tea to the table and sit down. Marlene plonked herself down opposite her.

'Sorry about the swearing. Promise I'll try harder in front of the girl.'

'It's okay. She knows not to swear.'

'He can be stubborn, but he'll eventually come around.'

'I hope so. It's a lot for him to get his head around. And we were tired.' It had been a huge day for both of them.

'We'll need to get more furniture,' Anna said, contemplating the tacky outdoor setting they'd brought in from the back verandah.

'I can pay rent, love. That'll make it easier for you to save the deposit,' Marlene said, carefully examining the tabletop in front of her. 'That's if you still want me here. Now that Izzy's going back to school—'

'Of course you can stay here. You have a home with Izzy and me for as long as you want it, no matter what happens between Nick and I.'

Marlene's eyes were glassy with gratitude when she raised her head. 'Izzy showed me the shed out back—'

'Oh yeah, I'd forgotten about that space.' Anna grinned at Marlene. 'What a perfect place for you to live!'

'I reckon the girl was thinking about it for herself.'

'No way. Izzy stays in the house.' Resting her elbows on the table, Anna said, 'So, what do you think? We could clean it out, paint it, make sure everything works, get some furniture and voila, you'd have your own private place. You could come and go as you pleased. There's even an air conditioner.'

Marlene scratched her head, her brow wrinkling. 'That's if Beth'll rent you the house.'

'She'd be crazy not to.'

'Well, then I'd be crazy not to take up your offer. Thanks, Anna. You're alright.'

'Okay. If Beth's happy, we'll get on with tidying it up and work out a reasonable rent. That'll be a big help.' They shook hands across the table, Marlene's delight taking over her face.

Anna stood up, stretching. 'I'm about ready to collapse. I have a clinic run tomorrow, so another full day. Sleep tight, Marlene, and thank you. Knowing you're here for Izzy when I'm not takes a load off my mind.'

Half an hour later Anna lay in the dark, eyes wide, the sheet kicked back, the overhead fan doing its best. How weird was life? Everything was coming together: for Izzy with a home at last, and a place for Marlene. And she got to keep the job she loved. Who knew if she'd get to keep the man ...

It was hard to comprehend that Nick was here but not *here*. Smoothing a hand across the empty space beside her, she fought to keep the doubts, and hurt, at bay.

Twenty-four hours later, Anna hadn't heard a word from Nick and she started to worry. Her text messages went unanswered. When she woke early the following morning and there was still nothing, anger flared. Insidious hairline cracks were threatening her resolve to trust him.

He'd said he'd see her soon, and she had to believe he'd meant it. The alternative didn't bear thinking about.

Bouncing out of bed with renewed vigour, Anna showered, dressed and checked her email while shovelling in muesli and washing it down with coffee. Maybe Nick had emailed her.

No, he hadn't. But Beth had replied to her email: she could rent the house for as long as she needed to. Beth was thrilled she'd finally made up her mind to stay in Broken Hill.

Izzy's head popped out from under the sheet to say a sleepy goodbye when Anna tapped on her bedroom door. Marlene's door remained closed.

'We're doing patient transfers to Adelaide so I should be back after lunch,' she said. 'And Beth said we can rent while I save the deposit.'

'Okay,' Izzy mumbled without opening her eyes.

The morning was cloudless, a hint of dew lingering sweetly in the air. It was barely seven but traffic was already building as she drove through the city to the base.

The aircraft was on the tarmac, the flight nurse rushing around collecting equipment. Anna checked the weather, reviewed her take-off data and filed the flight plan before heading out to complete her external and internal pre-flight checks.

When she climbed into the cockpit and folded herself into her seat, she let the familiar calm wash over her. Here she was in control.

With the patients and crew loaded and the cabin secure, she made her taxiing call to air traffic control. Anna lined up on the runway, letting herself sink into the moment, letting everything else fade into the background. It'd all be there when she landed.

'All traffic Broken Hill, ambulance two seven five entering and rolling runway Broken Hill,' she said, and they were away.

53

For the first time ever, Anna wanted to be on the ground rather than thousands of metres up in the air. The patient transfers had been quick and they were ahead of schedule, but the time was dragging.

Somewhere in the airspace between Broken Hill and Adelaide, Anna made up her mind that if Nick wasn't coming to her, she'd go to him. While she hadn't purposely set out to deceive him, the end result had been the same. If they were to have a future together, which was something she was sure she now wanted, Nick deserved a proper apology and a proper introduction to Isabelle.

Danny's place wouldn't be hard to find again, and if he wasn't there, she'd scour Broken Hill until she found him.

From the second she'd made the decision, hyped up on the anticipation of seeing him and telling him how she felt, time seemed to slow down.

Not long now, she thought, when she finally began her approach into Broken Hill.

'Really,' she mouthed, almost in disbelief when, selecting the landing gear to the down position, only two of the three landing lights showed green. The right main wheel light glowed ominously red.

The wheel was either still in the wheel well, in transit, or down but not locked in.

Instantly aborting her approach, Anna notified air services that she had an issue with the landing gear. She advised them she'd fly clear of the aerodrome circuit area to troubleshoot the problem. When operations were normal she'd re-join the circuit.

The flight nurse took the news with a sharp intake of breath. 'Glad we don't have patients on board,' he said.

But the right main-wheel light remained red after she'd carried out the troubleshooting procedure, manually pumping down the landing gear.

'Crap, and double crap,' she muttered, before making direct contact with the Broken Hill base.

Anna couldn't believe her bad luck. Desperate to talk to Nick, to apologise for not telling him about Izzy, and to tell him how much she wanted them all to be together, and she was stuck up here flying around in circles.

And they would be until an engineer and the base safety officer, using binoculars, could confirm if the wheel was in position or not when she made a low-level fly past.

Whatever the engineer saw it'd be a while before they could land. And if the gear wasn't down, they'd be on their way back to Adelaide for an emergency landing.

It might be hours before she could talk to Nick.

Anna gave herself a mental shake. Now was not the time to be distracted. The engineer and safety officer were in position. Crossing her fingers she went around and lined up for the flypast.

Anna was the last crew member to make her way across the tarmac. The engineers, safety officer and chief pilot were clustered around the aircraft, now safely parked on the apron. She'd never seen a flight nurse get the door open so fast.

Mouth dry, her fingers clutching the flight bag shaking, she lengthened her step telling herself her knees weren't the tiniest bit wobbly. Adrenaline still coursed through her bloodstream but she was coming down fast.

After getting the go-ahead from the engineer, that second when the landing gear had hit the tarmac, the flight nurse in the brace position, her own knuckles white on the control, Anna had prayed it'd hang together and she'd get to see Nick again.

The automatic doors closed behind her with a clunk and Anna slid off her sunglasses, blinking, her eyes adjusting to the cool dimness of the emergency room.

Next thing she knew she was enveloped by a pair of arms, and then her whole body was pressed against Nick's familiar strength, her face nestled in the warm curve of his neck.

'I'm sorry,' he said, voice muffled against her hair. 'I shouldn't have left you the way I did, not when I went to Sydney, or when I came back.'

'No, I'm the one who needs to apologise,' she said, her lips moving against his skin. 'I should have told you about Izzy right at the very start. Please forgive me.'

'Of course I forgive you.' His arms tightened around her. 'You gave me such a fright just now.'

'I gave myself a fright. Just when I've decided I can't live without you, and I can't wait to tell you, the landing gear malfunctions—'

'I was waiting for you, but you didn't land. Then they were out there with binoculars and next thing I know there's an ambulance and fire trucks racing towards the runway—'

'—Just as I touched down I had a horrible moment when I thought I might never see you again.' Anna closed her eyes, her arms firmly around Nick's waist.

Someone nearby cleared their throat. Startled, Anna dropped her arms, moving away from Nick.

'They're heading this way,' Tim said, from the doorway of the doctor's room. 'You better skedaddle before they see you.'

'Thanks, mate,' Nick said, as Kyle and the safety officer trudged towards the entrance. This area was for staff only and Nick wasn't staff anymore.

'I'll wait for you out the front,' he whispered, lifting his hand, sweeping his fingers along her cheek. His smile was as intimate as a kiss. The pad of his thumb feathered across her lips, sending tingles to every one of her nerve endings.

'Okay,' she said, tilting her face into his palm. 'But I might be a while. There are reports and all that.'

'I'll be waiting,' he said.

Nick disappeared a second before the automatic doors opened and the men came in on a gust of hot, dry wind.

'Anna, there you are. We'll do those reports now,' Kyle said, sweeping his hair back into place.

An hour and a half later, Anna found Nick in the reception area, playing games on his phone. Her heart leapt at the sight of him. He stood up, wordlessly held out his hand. She linked her fingers with his and they walked out together.

'How'd it go?' he said.

'Much as I expected. Management types are generally middle-aged men, and they're always thrown when a woman deals with an emergency situation as well as a man.'

'They're idiots,' he said, and some of her tension eased.

Nick headed towards the visitor's carpark. She stopped, yanking on his arm. 'My car's in the staff carpark.'

'Mum needed to use it so I drove her out here and said I'd wait for you. You've made a fan there, for life.'

They reached his ute, he stopped and she bumped up against him. He smelled good and he felt good—strong and solid.

'I'm a big fan as well,' he said. 'In case you hadn't noticed.'

His eyes caught hers and held. Anna said quietly, 'Yeah, I noticed, and I wasn't going to let you get away that easily.'

Unlocking the ute he said, 'What made you think I wanted to get away?'

'Oh, maybe the sudden appearance of my teenage daughter? I thought that could be enough to frighten you off.'

'It'd take a lot more than that, Anna,' he said, serious now. 'I needed to sleep, and then get my head around it all.' He opened the passenger-side door and she climbed in, stowing her bag on the floor beside her feet.

Sliding into the driver's seat he turned on the ignition and opened the windows. He turned sideways and said, 'Danny and Brooke weren't home, so after I'd dropped you off I checked into a motel, slept all night and half of the next day.'

'Why didn't you come back to the house instead of going to a motel?'

Sighing deeply he said, 'I was so pissed off, and hurt, that you hadn't told me about Isabelle. Once I'd made up my mind to leave Sydney, I drove nonstop because I couldn't wait to see you. I'd imagined how it'd be when I first saw you again, and it turned out nothing like I'd imagined. It took me until this morning to come to my senses and accept that we'd both had lives before. Honestly, if Serena hadn't blurted out that I was separated, I might not have—'

'You would have told me, Nick. I know that. And if I had the time over, you know I'd do things differently.'

'Not too differently, I hope.'

'You know what I mean,' she said, playfully swatting him on the arm.

'I do.' Catching her wrist, he tugged her closer. 'I love you, Anna, and I'm going to kiss you now. I wanted to the moment you walked across the tarmac and in through those doors.' Lifting his hands he cupped her face, firmly and possessively, his lips gently searching.

Anna's heart skipped, and she put into that single kiss what she couldn't yet put into words.

'That's more how I imagined it'd be when we saw each other again,' Nick said, forehead resting against hers.

He started the engine, and the air conditioner cut in. Cool air swirled into the cabin.

Fastening her seat belt, Anna said, 'Why'd you get rid of the dual cab? It was your pride and joy.'

'I needed cash to pay someone to finish fixing the house so I could get back here.'

'Nick—'

'Everything cost more and took longer than I'd ever imagined. Sydney started to really suck, and I could feel you slipping away from me.'

'I—'

'It was only a car, and in the end being where you were was more important. It was as simple as that.'

'You know you don't only get me, you get Izzy as well? We're a job lot. I'll understand if you have reservations. Teenagers can be tricky. And they're expensive.'

'Mmm, tough decision,' he said, his eyes dancing with amusement. 'But you get Marlene, so I reckon we're even.'

'Mmm, that seems fair,' she said. 'You know she's given up smoking? Said she wasn't being a good role model smoking around Izzy.'

'Huh? My mother and role model, both in the same sentence?'

'People get older, they change, learn from their mistakes. Sometimes all they need is a reason.'

'I'm sure you're right,' he said.

It wasn't long before they were turning into what Anna would always think of as Beth's street.

'When I came here looking for you earlier this morning, Mum said you're buying the place.'

'Yeah, I hope to. It needs work but we like it here, and Izzy needs a proper home.'

'They showed me the shed. Mum's beside herself. I'll help clean it out and paint it, do any maintenance. Until I find a job I'll have time. It's very generous of you, Anna.'

'Shed's sitting there, empty; a purpose-built granny flat. There's room for your brother when he comes to visit.'

'Yeah,' he said, frowning.

'What's the matter?'

He pulled into the empty driveway and glanced her way. 'Five weeks I've been away, and in that time you've bought a house—'

'Almost! There's the deposit to save.'

'Yeah, but it's as good as a done deal. And you've achieved what I couldn't—solved Mum's accommodation problems, and given her the motivation to give up smoking. I'm humbled.'

'Get out of here,' Anna said. She dragged her bag off the floor and onto her lap, reaching for the door handle.

'Seriously, I haven't seen Mum this happy in years.'

'Don't make me sound better than I am, Nick. For a while there my life was going down the toilet. I wanted to howl at the moon, then bury my head under a pillow and hope it all went away.'

'But you didn't.'

'No, I didn't. That's the thing about being a parent, it never stops. When I accepted the job, knowing that I'd be coming here without Izzy, for a while it felt like I was abdicating from the role. And then you came along, and I almost forgot I was a parent first and foremost.'

'Sure, you're a parent, and from what I've seen of Isabelle, you're good at it, but you can also have a life of your own.'

Absent-mindedly smoothing his fingers over the steering wheel, Nick stared through the windscreen while the car idled.

'Are you coming in?' Anna said, experiencing a flutter of apprehension.

'When Mum moves into the shed you'll have a spare bedroom, right?'

A hint of amusement touched her lips. 'What's wrong with my bedroom?'

'Nothing! But there's Isabelle. I didn't want to presume—'

'Izzy goes back to boarding school for a term before she comes to live here, with us.'

The last two words were a question, and they both knew it. Nick turned to her, eyes narrowing. 'Are you proposing to me?' he said.

'Not quite! You probably need to file for a divorce first.'

'Last week in March is less than two months away.'

'But then, who's counting?'

His face relaxed. He turned off the engine and climbed out.

'I wonder where Izzy and Marlene are?'

Nick draped an arm around Anna's shoulders, hugging her close. 'Mum's taken Isabelle to the pictures, and then they're going to Macca's.'

'We have the house to ourselves?'

Nick looked at his watch. 'For another three hours and twenty-two minutes.'

'Then what are we doing standing out here? Let's go and revisit your homecoming, practice until we get it *exactly* how you'd imagined.'

Nick opened the screen door for Anna to slot her key into the lock. She laughed when he swept her off her feet, dipping in for a quick kiss before carrying her across the threshold.

ACKNOWLEDGEMENTS

A heartfelt thank you to Jo Mackay, Laurie Ormond, and the team at Harlequin. Thanks Dianne Blacklock for your editorial insights. And Clementine Edwards, copy editor extraordinaire, it was a treat to work with you again. The biggest thank you to Judy Whitehead, former Royal Flying Doctor Service Director of Nursing and my go-to person. Also, former flight nurse Geri Malone, thanks for sharing your experiences. Not forgetting RFDS flight nurse Tony Carter and his memories of growing up in Broken Hill. And thanks Kerri Rothery, RFDS Primary Health Care Nurse. Your enthusiasm for the job was inspiring. Many thanks to Gillian Haldane, wife of Alice Springs based RFDS pilot Mark Haldane. Gillian was a fabulous go-between. I'd message Gillian the questions, she'd ask Mark and relay the answers back in a language I could understand. It worked extremely well, and thank you Helene Young for introducing me to Gillian. My sincere thanks to Shane Brook, RFDS Senior Base Pilot South East Section; to Clyde Thomson, retired RFDS Chief Pilot; and Steve Davis, Line Pilot RFDS Central Operations. Of course, I take full responsibility for any mistakes or misinterpretations of the information so generously provided. Thank you Tricia Stringer, friend and fellow author, for being there through the highs and lows of the writer's life. A special thank you to my husband and casual research assistant, Ken Bemrose, lover of all things aeronautical. If he had his life over he'd be a pilot. To my sister Sandra Appleyard, thanks for always listening, no matter how much I go on!

And to my readers: I am eternally grateful to you.

While this is a work of fiction, Broken Hill is a real outback city and there is an RFDS base there. Silverton and Yunta are also existing towns. However, all the stations, communities, characters and scenarios are a product of my imagination and not intended to represent any real place, person or situation.

LET'S TALK ABOUT BOOKS!

JOIN THE CONVERSATION

HARLEQUIN AUSTRALIA

@HARLEQUINAUS

@HARLEQUINAUS